PRAISE FOR STINA LINDENBLATT

One More Secret

"Heartfelt, evocative, mesmerizing, and riveting, you absolutely won't want to miss this masterful romantic suspense!"—Book Addict

"I am Addicted to the characters and Jessica's story."—Reading in the Red Room

One More Betrayal

"This is a riveting, poignant, extraordinary romance for the ages, and you won't want to miss it."—Book Addict

"Stina Lindenblatt did a great job of showing PTSD and domestic violence, and not romanticizing it."—Read with Alea

"This book has soo many layers and so many moving parts you are truly entertained."—Reading in the Red Room

"This series is like nothing I have ever read in just how unique the story feels, how intricate the plot is, and just how much depth these characters have and I can't wait for the conclusion coming in One More Truth! 5 stars!"—Janine Reads

One More Truth

"This trilogy is one of my all-time favorite reads, and I highly recommend this unforgettable, masterful, extraordinary romance."— BookAddict

"The conclusion to this incredibly emotional trilogy...was soo worth the wait."—Reading in the Red Room

Other books by Stina Lindenblatt

"Romantic angst powers this fast-paced novel, and readers will return to the series to learn more about the enigmatic side characters whose own stories are waiting to be told."—Publishers Weekly

"A well-written story that kept me entertained from start to finish."—Harlequin Junkie

"This story had me hooked and addicted on page one!"—Reading in the Red Room

"Made me laugh, sigh and cry a lot."—Only. Ever. Books.

"Wow! Talk about getting hooked on a story right away!"—Red Hot Blue Reads

"I loved this book; this is romance at its best, this is that perfect ending we all read romance for, this is an absolutely beautifully told love story."—Guilty Pleasures Book Reviews

"The story is amazing and the suspense is thrilling."—Just One More Chapter

"The author has an amazing and deep connection with her characters. . . . I loved every single page."—Extreme Damage Blog

"TELL ME WHEN is a heartbreaking and emotional story. Be prepared to do nothing else but read once you start this book!"—Fresh Fiction

"Six stars—Stina Lindenblatt has a skill to write heroes with some depth like few can."—Collectors of Book Boyfriends & Girlfriends

"I Need You Tonight is one of those books that you go into thinking one thing and end up getting your mind blown because you were not expecting the emotion that this made you feel. Honestly, this had to have been the best book of the series because of that."—Life of a Crazy Mom

"There are so many, many things that I loved about this story. . . . I hadn't realized I'd been missing and I was craving the Pushing Limits boys until this one came along. And it came with a bang."—Collectors of Book Boyfriends & Girlfriends

"I. LOVED. THIS. BOOK!!!!"—Seeking Book Boyfriend

"I love Stina's writing style. It's very emotive, and flows beautifully. I felt connected to the characters from very early on and cried several times at the pain these characters go through"—Reading Realm Blog

"This was an amazing read, I could not out this down. The author really wrote this one so beautifully. Let me say that

the author's writing bought out so many emotions from me,
I just loved it"—Lustful Literature

"...a truly unique and utterly swoon-worthy romance." —
Mary Dubé at Frolic/USA Today's HEA

ALSO BY STINA LINDENBLATT

CONTEMPORARY ROMANCES

Carson Brothers Series

One More Chance

One More Secret

One More Betrayal

Pushing Limits Series

This One Moment

My Song For You

I Need You Tonight

SPICY ROMANTIC COMEDY NOVELS

By The Bay Series

Decidedly Off Limits

Decidedly with Baby

Decidedly with Love

Decidedly with Mistletoe

Decidedly by Chance

Decidedly with Luck

Decidedly with Wishes

Visit stinalindenblattauthor.com for more books

ONE MORE TRUTH

HIDDEN SECRETS TRILOGY BOOK 3

STINA LINDENBLATT

*To the women whose stories
were the inspiration behind
the Hidden Secrets Trilogy...*

ONE MORE TRUTH

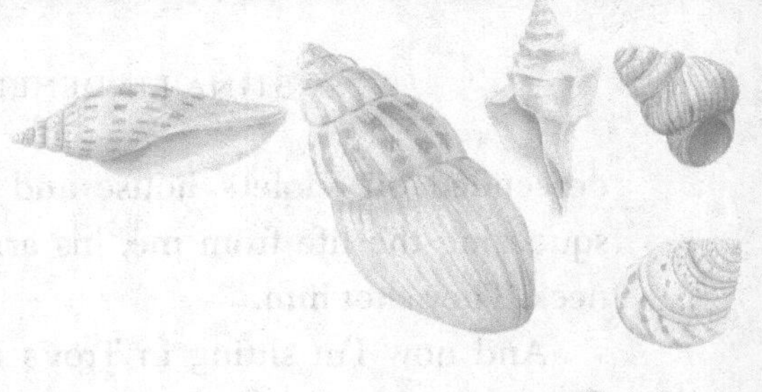

1

JESSICA

August, Present Day
Maple Ridge

The great French dramatist Jean Racine once claimed there are no secrets that time does not reveal. I don't know how true the quote is, but I do know my secret, the most important one I've been trying to hide, is now public knowledge.

I stare dumbfoundedly at the back of the newspaper in Troy's hand. The ramifications of Cora's article about my former life as Savannah Townsend twist in my head like a deadly cyclone, uprooting my emotions, uprooting my life. The article reveals that I'd spent time in Beckley State Correctional Institution, a maximum-security prison for women. It includes a recent photo of me with bottle-blond hair and scars on my face.

An hour ago, I was in Violet Wilson's house, fearing for my life. My hand goes to my sore neck. The FBI had descended on Violet's house and found Officer Dunbar squeezing the life from me, his arm clutched around my neck. They shot him.

And now I'm sitting in Troy's ER room, on the chair next to his bed, waiting for news on his shoulder. He had reinjured it during a fight for *his* life.

Zara and Garrett are with us. Zara's perfectly shaped black eyebrows pinch together, her frown directed at the newspaper.

I push to my feet and move to stand next to Troy. I glare at the article in question, wishing this was just a bad dream. That I'll wake up in a few minutes and none of this is happening. Troy and Garrett won't look as if they've been traipsing through the forest. Troy's face and navy T-shirt aren't smudged with dirt.

A reporter. For the past several weeks...all the questions. I'd thought Olivia's sister had just wanted to get to know me better. Turns out she was preparing to write an exposé. Informing the world I now live in a small, mountainous Oregon town.

Informing everyone in Maple Ridge about my dark past and my shame.

How long will it take before more people in Maple Ridge see the article? How long before they piece together that the woman in the photo is me?

Cora didn't mention that my new name is Jessica Smithson. What she had done was explain that Savannah Townsend, widow of Officer Wayne Townsend, had been released four months ago from the California prison after new blood evidence came to life. Evidence proving I wasn't the one who pulled the trigger that killed my late husband.

The article talks about how I'm slowly piecing my life back together. I've been quoted a few times, each quote taken out of context. Some of my comments originally had to do with the With Hope Festival—a festival Troy's organizing to help individuals in the area who struggle with PTSD and their families. Not once during her time here have I spoken to Cora about my own experience with PTSD.

Not once have I talked to her about my time in prison or about my abusive husband.

Yet here it all is in the article—but with no mention of the festival. It's all about me and my dark past.

Troy stands from the bed, his hand going to the lower curve of my spine.

I inch closer to him, needing to feel the reassuring warmth of his body. "Everyone is going to...know." My whispered voice comes out rough, the words irritating my injured throat and vocal cords. "They're going to know... about my past." They're going to judge me in the worst possible way.

Troy shoves the newspaper at Garrett, who takes it from him. "It's gonna be okay, Jess. No one will think worse of you because of what happened." Empty hope fills Troy's words, trying to mask itself as something better, brighter. But it's human nature to judge, even if the negative thoughts only last a flutter of a heartbeat. People will judge me because of my past. Maybe not my friends, who already know the truth. But there will be plenty of others in Maple Ridge who will.

"Which part of your past are you worried about?" The frown on Zara's face eases, compassion nudging it aside.

"All of it." The truth of my words sits on my chest like a dead weight. "People wondering why...I didn't leave my husband. If it was really all that bad...why not just divorce him? Why put up with his abuse? But that won't be the worst of it. I spent five years. In. A. Maximum. Security. Prison. Not a five-star resort...where you come out refreshed and feeling like a new person." Just the opposite. My throat aches, but I push forward, pressing my case. "My past...that's how people will view me. Their prejudice...will determine how I'm treated."

"Jess, you're supposed to be resting your voice," Troy tells me, his tone gentle but firm. "Doctor's orders." The flicker of understanding in his eyes sides with me. He knows I'm right about everything I just said.

My throat feels like I swallowed coarse-grit sandpaper, but it's not enough to keep me from powering on. "I spent five years with prisoners...you don't necessarily want to...to introduce to your grandmother. People will believe I might have gone in innocent...but they'll think the experience changed me in the worst possible...way. How could they not?" Air enters my lungs in shallow breaths. It scratches my throat, flames taunting the lining, fueled by the panic flooding in.

Troy takes hold of my elbow and guides me to the chair by the bed. My legs give out. I sit, but my breaths still race.

He kneels next to me. "Breathe into your cupped hands, Jess."

I do as he suggests, and after several breaths, my panic eases. I lower my hands to my lap, which is currently in blue scrubs since my regular clothes are covered in blood.

Troy takes my hand and caresses the back of it with his thumb. "You've been living in Maple Ridge for four months and haven't given anyone a reason to believe you're anything other than a decent person."

Garrett shoves his hands into his shorts pockets. "Prison didn't turn you into a bad person, Jess. It didn't turn you into someone to be rejected."

"It made you stronger," Zara adds. "*You* hid Violet and Sophie when Violet escaped her husband. No one else did. Even after Alex Wilson beat you when he suspected you were hiding them, you were still determined to help them."

"Yes, but what about—" I begin but the door to the ER room opens, interrupting my counter argument. I was about to remind them of what happened when Kellan returned to Maple Ridge after a three-year prison sentence. He'd only hacked a computer. He hadn't been incarcerated for murder.

Zara's brother, Dr. Samuel Thompson, enters. His handsome features slide into a semi-reassuring smile, his teeth white against his copper-brown skin.

He walks over to join Troy and me by the bed. "Good news, Troy. You don't need surgery. This time. But that's only because of PT and the work you've done to build up the supporting shoulder muscles. However, there will be a point where the joint has had enough, and even PT won't prevent further injury."

Troy straightens to his feet. "Now that the FBI has arrested Alex Wilson, you don't have to worry about me screwing up my shoulder anymore."

Samuel regards him for a beat, his lips rolled in a flat line. He grunts a small disbelieving noise. "I still think you'd be better off if I put you in a body cast for the next two months." His mouth twists into a teasing smirk. It was the same suggestion he'd made when Troy arrived in the ER.

"I'll pass, thanks," Troy says, his tone wrapped in a sardonic growl. "Does that mean we're free to go?"

"Yes, you're free to go. But remember, the sling stays on for three days." Samuel turns to me. "And you're not to talk much for the next three or four days. Give your throat a chance to recover." He throws me a pointed look that says he knows I've been ignoring the order.

I reluctantly nod and flash him a tiny grin, hiding the

fear anchored in my chest. One of the hospital staff might have recognized me from the article. Maybe even the triage nurse, whose eyes lingered on my facial scars for a beat too long when I arrived. How long will it take before my past identity becomes common knowledge? Especially since the staff has access to my new name.

They have a name to connect to the one from my past.

"Do you want me to stay at your place for the next few days? While you have to wear the sling?" I ask Troy, already knowing the answer—and it has nothing to do with *him* being hurt.

His smile is soft, concern reflecting in his pained eyes. "I do."

I go into the bathroom and change out of the hospital scrubs and into the shorts and pink T-shirt that Zara grabbed from my house.

Troy and I walk out of the room, Zara and Garrett following behind us. We head for the exit. Gazes trail us as we walk through the ER waiting area.

Please let them be looking at Troy and Garrett.

Please tell me no one is paying attention to me.

2

TROY

August, Present Day
Maple Ridge

Garrett drops Jess and me off at my place. My truck was at the warehouse crime scene, but since I can't drive with my arm in the sling, Garrett drove me to Wilson's house after we learned Jess was inside it with Violet and Dunbar. My truck is now sitting in my driveway.

I hold Jess's hand like I did on the drive here as we walk to the front door. *Thank God she's here with me. Thank God the FBI got to her in time.*

I open my front door. A nanosecond later, Butterscotch and Bailey careen into the foyer, their nails clicking on the wood flooring. Jess barely steps through the door before they rush to her side, barking excitedly.

She crouches next to Bailey and hugs the one-year-old golden retriever.

I kneel next to Butterscotch and stroke my dog. "How are you feeling?" I ask Jess. "Does it hurt?" My gaze drops to the bruising around her neck. Her eyes are bloodshot, reminding me how close I came to losing her. *Fuck.*

"I'll be fine. I *am* fine. I'm alive. Thanks to you. If you hadn't told the FBI where to find me..."

"Hell, if it hadn't been for Ethan Philips"—the undercover FBI agent—"none of us would be here right now." I owe him everything for that. For saving my ass. For making sure Jess lived to photograph many more sunsets.

"I guess I owe him a big hug." Her voice comes out teasing and rough, and her mouth twitches into a smile.

"How about we just send our thanks and you hug me instead." I flash her a one-sided grin, which quickly fades away. "Since you don't have to worry anymore about revealing Violet's and Sophie's location, will you go back to therapy now?"

She was struggling before, but after what happened this evening, I imagine it will be even harder for her to get better without Robyn's help. "My company insurance'll cover it. As my employee, you're entitled to that. Just like Lance and everyone else who works for me."

Jess bites her bottom lip in a move I recognize as her thinking through her options.

"You shouldn't have paid for the therapy to begin with, especially once I got the restitution payment." Her voice is a hoarse whisper due to the damage Dunbar caused, but her tone is unbending.

"Is this where I'm supposed to apologize? Because I'm not going to." I rise to my feet. "Yes, I'm sorry I lied to you about the state paying for it. But I'm not sorry I did what I could to get you the help you needed."

She stands, a crooked smile curving her sweet lips. "Do I want you to apologize because you were concerned about me?" She takes a step closer and wraps her arms around my neck. "No. Never." She kisses me, her lips a brief touch I feel over every inch of my body and deep in my soul. "Am I sorry I started seeing Robyn because you thought it would help me?" Another kiss. "Definitely not. You're just lucky you apologized for lying." Her smile wavers, and she reverses a step. "But just so you know, I won't put up with you doing something like that again. I never again want to feel like I'm being manipulated. By you or anyone else."

"I promise I'll talk to you first." I don't want to argue or diminish her reasons for feeling that way. I get it. As much as I want to help her, I don't want to be the asshole who takes away her independence or dictates her life like her husband did.

Her smile returns, and she shakes her head in disbelief. "I can't believe I fell for your lie. Why would I believe for even a second the state of Oregon was paying for it?"

I hook her waist with my good arm and pull her to me. "I love you, Jess. I don't regret paying for your therapy. And I wouldn't have regretted it even if you hadn't found out and paid me back. But like I said, my company insurance'll cover it now. You don't need to pay for it out of your restitution payment. That money is for building your future."

I press my finger to her lips. "You're supposed to be resting your voice." I hate to make her stop talking, but she really does need to let her throat recover. When I first met her back in March, she barely spoke. She has come a long way since then, giving voice to her beliefs and her thoughts. But as much as I love that, her recovery is more important for now.

"What I need is a shower," Jess says against my finger. "I know I had one at the hospital..." A shudder punctuates the end of her sentence. "I just want to make sure I got everything out of my hair."

She doesn't have to say it. I know what she's referring to. Dunbar's blood.

"I can help you. If you want."

"I was counting on that," she whispers.

Jess leads me upstairs to the bathroom and closes the door. And then she just stands there, shaking, as if the past few hours are finally catching up with her. She seems smaller, fragile, as though she's teetering on a narrow ledge, ready to fall.

I put my hand that's free of the sling onto her hip, curling my fingers around her, letting her know I'm here for her.

She blows a slow breath over her parted lips and nods. She tugs her top over her head, revealing her pink bra and the pushed-up mounds of her sweet breasts. Peaked nipples press against the cotton of her bra, silently pleading for me to worship them, to soothe away her worries and her fears.

Her T-shirt drops to the floor.

Jess unfastens my sling, places it on the bathroom counter, and lifts the hem of my T-shirt up my body. I grab the fabric with my good arm and remove the T-shirt. It lands on the floor, somewhere near Jess's top.

I don't make a move. I wait to see what she wants to do next. She's the one in control. I sense she needs that.

She shimmies out of her shorts and watches me one-handedly rid myself of my shorts, socks, and boxer briefs. I'm standing naked and exposed, my cock at half-mast.

I trace along the gentle curve of her shoulder and down the silky length of her arm. My gaze remains locked on hers. Desire and an unnamed emotion shine back at me and send a wave of heat sweeping through my body.

I lower my head and take her mouth in a tender kiss. I want to devour her, to fill her with my love, but something about her expression, the grief and regret, has me holding back. I kiss her lips again, the touch of our mouths brief, then plant a gentle kiss on her forehead.

I turn on the shower. Steam pours into the bathroom from the other side of the glass door.

Jess reaches behind her and unhooks her bra. It drops to the floor, and she slides her panties down her legs, leaving her naked...other than the bruises on her neck and the scars on her body from the years of abuse.

Bruises and scars I wish I could simply kiss away. Kiss away and leave her fully healed both inside and out.

Without waiting for me, she steps into the shower. Water sluices over her body, loving every inch of her skin. Water soaks through her hair, turning the blond strands dark.

My length hardens at the sight in front of me, but as much as my body wants her, as much as *I* want her, I'm not going there.

I join her in the shower and grab the shampoo from the shelf. I pour the liquid into my hand, lather it up, and massage it into her scalp. My shoulder protests at the movement but not enough for me to stop. This—washing Jess's hair—won't make things worse as far as my shoulder is concerned. It's stiff, achy, a little crabby, but the heat of the shower is also helping it.

I continue massaging her scalp, kneading it, circling my fingers through the thick, wet strands. The movement is intimate. I don't ever want it to end. Don't ever want to stop touching her this way. This fully.

Jess moans and lays her head on my good shoulder. I kiss the crook of her neck. "I love you," I whisper on her wet skin, the words not loud enough to be heard over the water raining against the tiles. I repeat it, allowing the whispered words to soak into her body, to be sent to her heart.

I know she's not ready to say the words back to me—maybe she never will be—but I want to make sure she knows that she is loved. Her parents didn't care enough to show her any love. Only her grandparents did that, but they're gone. It's my life mission to never let a day go by without her feeling adored, wanted, cherished.

Jess's body trembles under my fingertips. I wrap her in my arms and kiss her temple. I don't ask her if she's okay or what's wrong. I don't need to. The adrenaline overload from this evening has peaked and has nowhere to go.

Her trembling increases to shaking. I tighten my hold on her, letting her know without words that I'm going nowhere. I'm her rock, her lighthouse—her whatever she needs me to be. I caress her back, drawing light circles on her wet skin.

She rests her forehead on my good shoulder and a sob takes over her body.

"I've got you, Jess," I tell her, my breath fanning the shell of her ear. The words aren't whispered. They're clear and true, a sonnet, a song. I gently rock her, my hand still drawing circles on her lower spine.

She lifts her chin, and her beautiful brown eyes—rich with flakes of gold—lock with mine. "Make love to me. Here. Now. Help me forget..." A slight desperation marks her tone.

I glance around the large shower. My eyebrows are raised when I return my gaze to hers. "In the shower?" My voice is deep and husky. I enjoy shower sex as much as the next man. There's something sinfully carnal about it. But making love in here with an injured shoulder is going to be more challenging.

She nods. The look in her eyes reaches in where my heart beats wild and strong for her, and I know there is no denying her. There isn't anything I wouldn't do for this woman. No mountain I wouldn't climb. No creature I wouldn't fight to protect her.

"Okay," I whisper against the side of her head, my voice gravelly, rough.

I kiss her temple, the shell of her ear, her neck, the curve of her sweet-smelling shoulder. One arm keeps her close. The other hand slides down her spine.

Her body is still bruised from the day Wilson confronted her about his missing wife and child. I lower to my knees and kiss each black-and-blue stain on her body, doing what I can to help her forget or at least lessen her burden.

Water rains on my body, hot and sensual, but that won't last forever. And as much as I want to taste every part of Jess, we don't have long before we'll be facing a cold shower.

I seek the sweet bundle of nerves between her legs and flick my tongue against it, kiss it, suck on it.

Jess's head falls back on the tiles. "Oooooh, Trooooy."

Smiling, I push to my feet and kiss her deeply, completely. Our tongues tangle and glide, explore and seduce. I turn her so the curve of her spine faces me. My hand reaches in front of her and finds the sweet bundle of nerves again. I nudge her legs wider with my knee, and my fingers circle her mound.

A needy moan escapes her once more.

I plant a light kiss between her shoulder blades and lightly flick the tip of my tongue along her skin, tasting her sweetness.

Then I take my time, stroking her, worshiping her, bringing her to the brink. My mouth whispers my love on her skin, painting invisible tattoos with my breath.

I take her hand and place it on the tiles. She bends at the hips, and I trail small kisses along her back, wishing I could take longer. Knowing once I take her to bed, we'll have all night for me to show her how much I love her.

I position the tip of my length at her entrance and inch in, groaning at how the heat of her body stretches around me, hugs me. I plunge in the rest of the way. My hand continues tracing circles on the most sensitive part of her, teasing sweet gasps from her.

I rotate my hips, my movements slow and deliberate, as I thrust fully inside her again and again. Her breaths come in short and ragged gasps, a harmonious symphony to the deep bass of my groans.

Her heat tightens around me, and a cry tumbles from her, the sound echoing off the tile walls. "Oh, God. Oh, God. Oh, God. Oh. God. *Trooooy.*"

My hips shift gears and move deeper, faster, harder, thrusting with a new desperate rhythm. Her inner muscles pulse along my length, pulling me farther in, squeezing until I lose the final threads of control.

I release inside her, my cry a guttural plea for her to never give up on us.

It's an unspoken prayer she'll forever let me love her.

Because there's no other place I would rather be than by her side.

3

JESSICA

August, Present Day
Maple Ridge

I dial Violet's phone number. Again. It's been three days since her husband was arrested, and I haven't been able to talk to her. She hasn't answered my calls or responded to my texts.

I'm clicked through to her voicemail. I don't bother to leave a message. She hasn't replied to the half dozen others I've left her, checking to make sure she and Sophie are all right.

Bailey and Butterscotch are snoozing on the large dog bed near Troy's patio door. Early afternoon sunlight streams through the living room windows and bathes the two golden dogs in a warm glow.

I stand from the couch and walk to the window that overlooks the neighborhood street. Two doors down, three girls around six years old are playing hopscotch on the sidewalk. Four boys bike past the house, reminding me that my bike and Bailey's trailer are in my garage. At home.

Troy is at work, mostly overseeing various projects and catching up on paperwork. His shoulder is all but back to normal, and as of this morning, my voice is too. But he wants me to take a few extra days to recover before returning to the office. Great. Except I'm already bored.

Part of me longs to be outside. To enjoy the beautiful sunny day. The other part wants to hide, afraid someone will recognize me from Cora's article.

"No, I'm not going to do that. I'm not going to hide," I say, giving myself a half-hearted pep talk. The dogs need walking. I need to get out.

I put on my usual makeup: a light brush of eyeshadow, mascara, foundation, and lip gloss. But the foundation isn't heavy enough to camouflage the scars. I don't think there's a foundation thick enough to create miracles and turn scars, like the one by my mouth, invisible.

I tie my hair in a low ponytail and grab the Minnesota Wild baseball cap from the hall closet. I doubt Troy will mind if I borrow it. I pop it onto my head and slip on my sunglasses.

The hat and glasses do nothing to hide the scars on my face, especially the thick one stretching diagonally from the corner of my mouth to my jaw. The scar was noticeable in the photo the newspaper ran.

"Who wants to go for a walk?" I ask the two sleeping dogs.

They scramble to their feet. I don't bother with Bailey's *Service Dog in Training* vest. It's her playtime.

They practically drag me down the street to the park where Violet admitted to me her husband was abusive. My thigh muscles ache from where Wilson kicked me. The pain isn't enough to deter me from the walk, but it is enough to leave me with a slight limp.

The park is busy with families enjoying the warm summer day, kicking a soccer ball around, playing Frisbee, chasing each other. Laughing. Shrieking.

Violet and Sophie aren't sitting on the bench like they were the last time I saw them here. I take a wide detour to the off-leash area, ducking my head so the red scar by my mouth isn't a beacon for the curious.

I let the dogs loose and toss their tennis balls for them to chase. My side is sore from where Wilson funneled his anger at me because he suspected I was hiding his wife and daughter. He didn't fracture my ribs—thank God—but they were still healing from my car accident a month ago, which is why they still hurt.

Between being wrongfully incarcerated, the car crash, and Wilson and Dunbar, I think by now I'm due for some better luck. Surely my guardian angel can finally put in a good word for me.

The tennis balls only travel two yards, thanks to my weak underarm throw, but the dogs don't seem to care. They chase after them and drop them by my feet for me to throw again. While I play with the dogs, I keep my eyes open for Violet and Sophie.

"I'm gonna drop you off at your daddy's house," I tell Butterscotch once we've finished playing. "Bailey and I will be back in a few hours, but I need to check Violet's house to see if she's home." The distance to her house is too far for Butterscotch's short legs.

Bailey and I drop him off and walk to Violet's house. I keep my head down. Between that and the hat and the sunglasses, the ugly scar near my mouth shouldn't be too noticeable.

The afternoon sun heats my bare skin, the temperature

cooler here than in San Diego. I breathe deeply in the fresh air, the kind I've grown to love since moving to Maple Ridge. This, the mountainous small town, is my life now.

If only my daughter were with me.

I look up as I reach Violet's street. The outside of her two-story house hasn't changed since the last time I saw it, the curtains still drawn.

I walk up the path leading to the front door. With each step, the muscles in my body knot tighter and tighter. The sequence of events from that night unfolds in my memory. Violet screaming. Me rushing in to help her. Dunbar's arm crushing my throat. The FBI barging through the front door and shooting the cop gone bad.

The memory of that night sends my heart stumbling. It recovers, but only to pound frantically faster. I ring the doorbell and listen for any signs that someone's home. Nothing. I try again. *Where are you, Violet?*

"You lookin' for Chief Wilson or Mrs. Wilson?" a female voice asks behind me.

I whirl around. A woman in her late sixties or early seventies is standing a few feet from me. Her eyes are narrowed to a squint as if she can't quite make out my face. Pink tints the ends of her shoulder-length white hair.

The knots in my muscles ease a fraction. If I'm lucky, she can't see the scars on my face clearly. "Mrs. Wilson. Violet. She's a friend of mine, but I haven't heard from her in a few days. I want to make sure she's okay. Has she been here since the FBI arrested her husband?"

"Nope. Not that I've seen." The woman shakes her head. "Can't say I blame her. All those damn reporters camping out here—I'd have stayed away too."

"Reporters?" I glance about as if expecting them to ooze from cracks in the sidewalk. Of course there would be reporters. It's not every day the chief of police in a small idyllic town is arrested for trafficking assault weapons.

Maybe that was the real reason Troy had wanted to keep me at home—at *his* home. He knew about the reporters. He'd been trying to protect me. I'd been so focused on how I haven't seen or heard from Violet since Tuesday, news of the events of that night hitting the media hadn't occurred to me. Ironically.

"They were camped out until yesterday," the woman says, "askin' all their nosy questions. With Mrs. Wilson gone and the questions all asked, I guess there was no point in stickin' around."

Thank God for that. "So, there are no more reporters in town?" *None who stayed because they caught wind I'm living here?*

"That's right. The lot of them have left."

"And you have no idea where she went?"

"Her and that adorable little girl of hers haven't been back. Maybe she went to visit family." The woman continues to squint at me, but I can't tell if she's attempting to put a name to my blurry face. "Once she returns, do you want me to tell her you were lookin' for her?"

"No, that's okay. I'm sure I'll talk to her before then." If she ever answers the phone or replies to my texts.

The woman ambles away and crosses the street.

Since there's nothing more I can do here, Bailey and I head home to get my bike and trailer. Maybe Noah knows something about where she went. I need to know she's all right. Need to let her know if she needs anything, I'm here for her.

Bailey and I walk up the driveway to the rear of the house, enter the garden through the wooden gate, and unlock the back door. I disengage the security alarm.

The newly renovated kitchen looks like it did when

Troy and I were here on Wednesday, picking up my things for my stay at his house. The kitchen is tidy and clean—nothing forgotten on the counter. The fresh lemony smell from when I cleaned the sink faintly lingers in the air.

I trace over the light-gray marbling that runs through the white-granite island countertop and grin at the beautiful open space. The white walls, tiles, and cabinets make the place appear bigger, but my favorite part is the creamy-blue feature cabinet doors—so different than the original, outdated ones.

I remove a glass from the cupboard, fill it with water from the tap, and greedily gulp the contents. The cold water is a soothing kiss to my still tender throat.

I fill Bailey's dish with fresh water as she pads across the wooden flooring to where she left her favorite toys in the living room. She grabs her fire hydrant in her mouth and shakes it. *Squeeeeaaaak.*

"We can bring it with us if you want," I tell her, even though she already brought several of her toys to Troy's house.

Squeeeeaaaak.

"I take it that's a yes." I go over and pet her. "I'm going upstairs to grab a few more things. Come." My gaze darts to the front door where Chief Wilson barged his way in just days ago, and my heart shudders. I draw a shaky breath.

Desperate to avoid a flashback, I knead the muscles in my upper arm. I don't think I'll have a flashback, but I can't be certain. My mind is still a land mine because of the complex PTSD.

Once I'm satisfied I'll be fine for now, I head upstairs to my bedroom. Bailey trots alongside me.

The room hasn't changed since I moved into the house four months ago. The floral wallpaper still clings to the walls. It's peeling and faded, but it's obvious the white paper, with delicate yellow flowers, was once pretty.

I open the bottom dresser drawer and remove one of Angelique's journals. I just have two more left to read and transcribe and then I can give them, along with the medal and heart pendant, to Anne Carstairs. Troy will be away this weekend for a Wilderness Warriors excursion. I might as well come here while he's gone, do some gardening, and read the journal.

I return it to the drawer and grab clothes for the next few days. I put them in my backpack, and Bailey and I go downstairs.

I check the time on my phone. "We gotta get going. It's Game Night, and it's Troy's turn to host it."

Which means two things.

I'll be joining Troy and our friends for Game Night for only the second time. The first was when I discovered Avery's boyfriend, Noah, is a cop. I was so nervous around him, I was on the verge of having a panic attack the entire time. After that, I always found an excuse as to why I couldn't join them just so I could avoid him.

But after all the therapy I've done and the things Avery has shared about Noah, I know he's nothing like my late husband. He's not a cop I need to fear.

The other thing it means is that I need to make snacks. I told Troy I'd cater tonight, so I'd better get started on that.

Bailey and I go outside, and I retrieve the bike and trailer from the garage. I'm helping Bailey—who's carrying her toy hydrant in her mouth—into the trailer when I'm hit with a weird feeling someone is watching me.

I glance over my shoulder toward the street. A man in his late forties with a German shepherd by his side is standing at the end of my driveway. He's one of my neighbors from a few doors down. Usually, he waves at everyone when they walk past his house while he's mowing his lawn. He doesn't wave at me this time. He slowly nods as if silently answering his own question, a frown wrinkling his brow, and walks on.

I close my eyes against the growing fear churning inside me.

Please tell me he didn't recognize me from Cora's article.

Please tell me he has no idea about my past.

4

ANGELIQUE

October 1943
France

"We know you are in there, Angelique D'Aboville! Or should I call you Carmen?" The Gestapo agent's words through the closed farmhouse door aren't in French. They're in English.

Oh, God.

They know.

My heart doesn't just pound hard and fast in my chest. It hammers against my ribs, desperate to escape.

The Gestapo have figured out the widowed daughter living with Jacques Gauthier is an English spy.

But how? How do they know? Most people either know me as Angelique or Carmen, but very few people know I am English.

I glance at Jacques sitting at the kitchen table. Only a

few moments ago I was busy cleaning the stove, the late morning sunlight a pale strip across the wooden floor.

Jacques knows I am English, but surely he didn't say anything about it to anyone. He has rarely left the vineyard since his son, Yvon, was captured by the Germans. And the number of non-German visitors who drop by diminished once Johann moved into the farmhouse.

The look of shock in Jacques's eyes confirms I am correct. He's not the one who turned me in. But who did? No one else from the area knows I am English, other than Désirée. Not even the members of the parachute reception parties know the truth. They all believe my instructions come from someone else in the network who is linked to London and Baker Street. I am only the worker bee.

Jacques's weathered face is pale, his eyes wild. Are the Gestapo planning to take him too, or is it just me they are after?

ThinkThinkThink.

I glance around the hallway, up the wooden staircase across from me, and then my gaze slides towards the doorways on either side of the hallway, leading to the kitchen and the drawing room. "Go to the drawing room," I whisper to him in French. "Pretend you're reading one of your winery journals."

Doubt stares back at me in his worried eyes. He's right. That won't make a difference, but it's better if he does not attempt to hide should they search the house. They'll find him, and hiding will only make things worse for him.

Jacques walks to the drawing room, and I take a deep breath. Perhaps I can talk our way out of the situation.

The knocking on the door becomes more insistent. The heavy banging vibrates through the house, settles in my chest, rattles my bones.

"*Mon Dieu,*" I say loud enough to be heard on the other

side of the door. "I am coming." The words are in French, the only language I plan to speak for the entire conversation with the Gestapo.

I open the door. "Sorry. I was upstairs. I didn't hear you. What can I do for you?" I take a moment to study the man in the grey Gestapo uniform. He appears to be in his late thirties and is sharp-eyed. The cold blue depths of his eyes reveals the lack of a soul.

"You're under arrest, Madame D'Aboville. Or whatever your legal name is." Like a moment ago, he speaks solely in English.

"Excuse me. I don't understand what you are saying. Do you speak French?"

Another man dressed in the Gestapo uniform approaches the door from the second of the two black cars parked on the gravel driveway. He's stockier than the other agent and close enough to hear me. "Do you speak French?" I ask him in the tone of a tourist inquiring if the person she's talking to speaks her native tongue.

The curl of his mouth is as soulless as the agent standing before me. "Yes, Madame D'Aboville, I do." His words are heavy with the guttural German accent, but it's clear he can speak some French.

"Good. Can you please translate for me?" I shift my gaze to the taller agent and pray I can convince them I am not an English spy. I will be as good as dead if I cannot do that. "Is he asking for my *carte d'identité*?"

I fight the urge to place my hand on my stomach, to protect my unborn child from our harsh reality. I don't wish to alert these men to my pregnant status. They will not go any easier on me if they know the truth. If anything, things will be worse for my baby and me if they find out.

"Yes, let us see your *carte d'identité*," the stocky Gestapo agent replies.

"It's in my handbag on the hall table." I make a move to turn to reach for it, but the stocky agent pushes past me and snatches up the bag.

"You're under arrest, Frau D'Aboville, for treason." The words are spoken by the taller agent, and this time they are spoken in French.

"I don't know what you are talking about?" I rush to say, my voice infused with soft-spoken innocence. "I haven't done anything traitorous."

He grabs my arm, roughly yanks it behind me, and snaps on the handcuffs. He does the same with my other arm. *Fight. Fight for your life because you're about to lose it.*

The more rational part of my brain warns me I won't survive if I attempt to fight my way to freedom. I'll be shot before I step out the door. If I can convince them I am not who they think I am, I'll be safe. They have no proof that I am indeed Carmen.

He shoves me out of the farmhouse and towards the first black car. He opens the rear passenger door and pushes me into the vehicle. I duck and narrowly miss hitting my head on the frame.

I sit on the hard seat, the cold black surface biting my legs through my dress. I swivel around as much as possible to look over my shoulder at the house. The movement is awkward and uncomfortable with my hands cuffed behind me.

One of the Gestapo agents—with a small scar on his chin—slides in next to me.

Two others lead Jacques from his house, and my insides clench. *OhGodOhGodOhGod*, what are they going to do to him? All they have to do is find proof I am not his daughter, and they will kill him for aiding an English agent.

Tears slide down my face. "Please don't hurt my papa," I whisper, my voice strained. "He did nothing wrong."

I don't turn to face the front. I stare at the car with Jacques in it, repeating the words until my voice is hoarse. Silently willing them to let him go. I'll never forgive myself if something should happen to him.

"Face forward," the Gestapo agent sitting next to me says in French. His tone is harsh, his unspoken warning clear in each syllable. Ignoring him won't help me. He'll roughen me up if it suits him.

I do as I am told. The agent who accused me of treason is sitting in the driver's seat. The stocky agent sits next to him.

How could they have figured out I am an English spy? The question keeps pounding in my head like a drum and forms into a headache. Was it Johann? It couldn't have been. Not after all we have shared...

But the more time that passes, the more doubt lurks in the recesses of my mind. If not him, then who?

There's simply no one else—no one else who knows.

How could he do this to me?

I'd been a fool to trust him? He must have informed on me. I'd thought he was different. I'd thought he was nothing like the Nazis, that he had a heart.

I was wrong. So very wrong.

A sharp pain slices through my heart at how he betrayed me.

My thoughts shift to Oskar, Margrit, and Sonja, and the pain in my heart lessens a tiny amount. Sonja's brave smile squeezes my insides like a precious hug. Oskar's words fill me with warmth: *"Johann is a good man. He is not like the rest of them."*

How would Johann have even known that Carmen is my code name? I was careful and would know if someone had broken into my hiding spots in the farmhouse. My security measures have never been disturbed. And if he had gained access to them, there was nothing in them to link me to the name.

No, it could not have been Johann who told the Gestapo. At most, he would have guessed I was a member of the maquis or the local resistance.

Was the traitor someone from within those organizations?

But how would they know the name Angelique D'Aboville, the name I use as my cover? They would only know my code name.

Except...that isn't completely true. Some people, the people I thought I could trust, know both, but they don't know I work directly for the SOE. They believed I was recruited into the *Cashmere* network like they were. They have no idea I am English.

The only exception is Allaire. He too is English. But why would he betray the SOE and our mission? Or was it his wife, Élise? She is French, not English. But that means she betrayed her husband, the man who I know she deeply loves.

Or...or was it Pierre? The SS tortured him before they hung him in the village square. In a moment of weakness, when he hoped the truth would be enough to save him, he might have told them his suspicions that I am English.

It's feasible, but I don't believe that is what happened. Not unless they found another way to torture him. They might have given him a choice: tell them the truth or be forced to watch them torture someone he loved. That would be enough to make most people crumple.

But his capture occurred three months ago. Surely they would not have waited so long to arrest me. None of it makes sense.

In the end, it doesn't matter who betrayed me. The Gestapo knows the truth, and I will pay dearly for it.

The car I'm in pulls away from the farmhouse. The autumn colours of the vineyards stretch in all directions outside the car windows. It's the middle of harvest season, and Jacques is behind schedule because of the lack of workers to help him. A heavy percentage of the wine will be taken by the Germans without compensation, leaving only a tiny fraction for the French.

It's the same with much of the food produced in France. The Germans take it all and leave only a few scraps for the French citizens. Yet so many farmers who live here are doing nothing to fight back. They're hiding in the shadows, hoping the Germans will go away.

And there I was, fighting for our survival—and look where it's gotten me now.

"Where are you taking me?" I ask no one in particular, my voice lacking its usual bravado. Bravado could get me killed—or worse.

"How long do you think it will take Captain Krüger to break her?" the agent in the front passenger seat says in German.

The other two men in the car laugh and voice their opinions. Neither has high expectations I will last long.

"The last man he interrogated squealed like a pig in less than five minutes," the agent next to me replies. His clothes reek of stale cigarette smoke.

I work hard to keep the growing fear off my face. The less they know about my language abilities, the better. If they realise I understood everything I overheard at the grand ball for von der Osten, I'll never survive the torture they'll inflict to extract more information.

We pass a woman with a slight limp, as if her feet are blistered, walking in the ditch on the side of the road. Her clothes are dingy and threadbare, and I imagine the soles of her shoes are worn to the point of having holes in them.

"Too bad she's in the ditch," the agent who is driving says. "I bet I could knock her a far distance if I hit her."

The other two monsters laugh.

The woman's hair is long and blond like my sister's, and I let my thoughts drift to Hazel and what she's doing right now, instead of thinking about how I might never see her again.

It must be nearly nine o'clock in England. And it's Monday. So, unless things have changed since the last time I saw her, she will be at work. I close my eyes and see her at her typewriter, typing whatever report her boss asked of her. Hazel isn't the one with a sense of adventure. She isn't the one who loves exploring new places. She loves her routine. But she also loves hanging out with the women in her sewing club on Monday afternoons. And she loves to volunteer at the library on Fridays. Has her routine changed due to the war?

The car drives through Dijon, down the wide streets flanked by tall stone buildings with arched windows and decorative wrought-iron railings. We keep travelling until we arrive at what was once an elegant hotel. I suspect it is no longer used for that purpose, its purpose now far more ominous.

The car pulls in front of the building, and the driver climbs out. He opens the door and roughly drags my trembling body from the car. I land on my shaky feet, my knees almost buckling under me. And as the driver tugs me towards the doors, the afternoon sun slants its golden rays across the street.

My stomach lurches.

Is this the last time I will ever see sunlight?

5

JESSICA

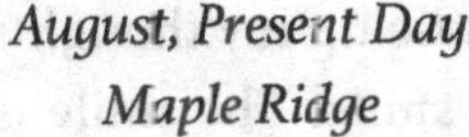

August, Present Day
Maple Ridge

I slice a red pepper, slowly, methodically. Bailey and Butterscotch are peering up at me from near my feet and flashing me hopeful expressions. A not-so-subtle hint they want a snack.

The garage door clicks open. The two dogs race into the hallway leading to the laundry room, barking excitedly. Troy's home.

I grin at their enthusiasm.

Then I imagine a little girl and boy racing to the hallway and their cries of "Daddy!"

An emotion I can't label clutches at my heart. Joy? Peace? Surprise? Grief? Grief for the life I once dreamed of —the life I almost had until it twisted into something ugly and feared.

I'm not sure after everything I've been through I can

risk having another child. Anything could happen to them. They could get cancer. They could be in a car accident. They could wind up with a rare genetic disease I didn't know I was a carrier of. I wasn't worried about any of these things while pregnant with Amelia. I was just filled with hope and love for my unborn child.

Tears blur my vision at how much I miss my daughter. I place my hands on the counter, steadying myself.

Troy walks into the kitchen, the two dogs trailing him. "Hey." He smiles at me, his love for me unmistakable in the curve of his lips and the warm glow in his eyes.

Guilt slithers in and wraps around my stomach. He deserves so much more than me and the mess that currently defines who I am.

But for now, I bottle up my thoughts, toss them into the ocean of regret, and smile. The smile is fueled by so many emotions, except the one I know Troy is waiting for me to feel for him: love.

And knowing that increases the guilt another two notches.

"How was work?" I ask. The domesticity of the question doesn't skip my notice, what with me standing in his kitchen, the food I've prepared for tonight sitting on the counters.

Troy pulls me into his arms. "Good. Busy. I missed you." He gives me a chaste kiss.

"You missed me because you had to answer your own phone calls?" I grin and tease him with a kiss of my own. "It's a good thing I'm returning to work Monday."

"Are you sure about that? Maybe it wouldn't hurt to have another week off? So your throat is a hundred-percent better."

I somehow manage not to roll my eyes. "It's already better. It's had three days to get better. And it has the weekend to recover too." I put my hands on his shoulders. "I promise, I'm fine. I need to go back to work. I need to be doing something other than sitting around."

His lips smooth into a line; his brow furrows. It's his thinking expression. His I-don't-exactly-agree-with-you face. "You have been doing something. You've been writing the articles about the PTSD survivors you interviewed and their families. That's extremely important for the festival."

I lean my hip against the counter. The coolness of the granite seeps through the cotton of my sundress. "I know. And that's been great. I've loved writing them. But you hired me when your previous assistant quit and you needed someone to replace her. You can't do everything, Troy. You're already stretched thin with your regular work responsibilities, Wilderness Warriors, volunteering, and organizing the festival. You can't do all of that and my job too."

He grunts, and I have a feeling he believes the opposite. He thinks he's Superman—invincible. But his injured shoulder proves he isn't. It's just as well he can't help me with my renovations right now; otherwise, he'd push his body to the brink.

"If you're not careful," I warn, "you'll be the one having a mental health crisis. I'm just trying to avoid that." I kiss him again. "I care about you, Troy. A lot." I give him another kiss—one that is less sweet than the other kisses but no more demanding.

Troy groans, and his lips gently coax me to let him in. Not that I need much coaxing. I deepen the kiss, my hands shifting from his shoulders to cup his face.

I vaguely hear the clicking of nails across the floor as the dogs give up on us and return to the living room. Troy and I keep kissing. Part of my brain nudges me to ask him what's driving him to overextend himself, but the rest of my brain is enjoying the kiss too much to formulate the question.

"I saw your bike in the garage. Did Simone drive you to your house?" He strokes his thumb across my kiss-swollen lips.

"No, Bailey and I walked there. I wanted my bike for while you're away this weekend."

"I could have picked it up after work."

I shrug, the movement a quick jerk. "I know, but I wanted the exercise. And I wanted to see if Violet had come home yet."

"Any luck?"

I shake my head and move my hip away from the kitchen counter.

"Maybe ask Noah when he comes over." Troy's eyes search my face. "Are you still okay with him joining us tonight?"

I nod. "Avery and I talked about my fear of cops. She understood and told me I have nothing to worry about with Noah. She's never fully trusted cops, but she trusts him." Her distrust of them isn't as strong as mine, but her words did give me some comfort when it comes to her boyfriend. And after my conversation with her when Violet was hiding in my house—the conversation about Avery's father being an abusive husband—Avery's words mean a lot to me.

Troy's gaze searches my face once again, the furrow back on his brow. "Okay." He doesn't seem entirely convinced. The mist of doubt colors his tone.

"I can always step outside for a few minutes to catch my breath if it becomes too much." I reach up and attempt to smooth away Troy's frown. I don't think I've met anyone who worries about me as much as he does. And that surprisingly turns my insides gooey.

I press my mouth to his.

The kiss isn't meant to be a quick peck on the lips—nor does Troy take it as one. He welcomes my tongue into the depths of his mouth, and with my blood simmering, our conversation is swiftly forgotten.

Troy and I eventually come up for air, and he glances at the microwave clock. "Looks like we have time for a shower before everyone gets here. You in?" He flashes me a smile that turns my simmering blood to a full-out boil.

"I'm in," I say, my still-slightly-rough voice now husky and low.

I'M PUTTING THE FOOD ON THE COFFEE TABLE WHEN AVERY and Noah arrive, their voices coming from the foyer.

Zara puts a plate of samosas next to the baked cheese dip. "How're you doing?" she asks me. Her gaze cuts to the foyer, and I know what she's really getting at.

"I'll be fine. He's not my late husband, and he's not the cop who tried to strangle me or the one who assaulted me."

Avery and Noah enter the living room. Avery comes over and hugs me.

Noah and Troy join our little group. Troy takes my hand, his grip warm and supportive. "Noah wants to talk to you for a moment."

My breath stutters in my chest and my muscles go twitchy. "Okay?" I hadn't meant for it to come out as a question.

"Troy can come too." Noah says. "This also involves him."

I nod, my curiosity overcoming my nervousness of

being around Noah. *Baby steps.* I'll eventually get there with him; it will just take time.

We go into the kitchen. Zara and Avery stay in the living room, though I'm sure they can overhear our conversation, if they really want to, from where they are sitting. The open concept design doesn't give much privacy.

"Troy told me Cole Dunbar made a false police report about what happened Sunday night. It wasn't a break and enter that caused your injuries." Noah's tone is warm and friendly, but the name causes my stomach to twist and churn.

"That's right," I reply.

"Troy also said the former chief of police assaulted you." Noah's voice doesn't suggest he thinks I'm lying. He believes me.

"That's right. He figured out Violet and Sophie were hiding in my house and confronted me." I'd done a crappy job hiding evidence they were there. He'd found an empty box of toddler diapers in my recycle bin. "When I wouldn't tell him where they were, he started punching and kicking me. He had Officer Dunbar fill in the police report and told me nothing would come of it."

"I took her to the hospital to see Dr. Samuel Thompson," Troy says, still holding my hand. "Samuel documented the injuries in case we need it for evidence later on."

"That was smart thinking," Noah replies. "Jess, I think you should go to the station and request to refile the report."

The thought of stepping into the police station sends my heart pounding. My grip on Troy's hand tightens. "Won't I be charged for falsifying a police report?"

"Not when you were coerced by the former chief of police and a former police officer. And not when both have been charged with multiple counts related to the trafficking of assault rifles. Were there any witnesses who saw what happened or could collaborate your story?"

My grip slackens a tiny amount, but I keep holding Troy's hand like it's a lifeline. "Violet Wilson. She told her husband she wouldn't leave him if he stopped hurting me. At that point, she was too scared to tell anyone what really happened. And now...and now, I can't get a hold of her. It's like she's vanished."

Noah glances at Avery and Zara on the couch, talking. "The FBI put her in witness protection. I don't know much more beyond that."

So, in the end, Violet's in the same situation she would've been in if we had succeeded with the plan to get her and Sophie out of Oregon. She's starting her life over again—pretty much like me. But this way she won't be charged with kidnapping her daughter.

It also means I've lost a friend. A friend who partially understands what I've been through.

The doorbell rings. Zara looks over at us. Troy nods, and she heads for the foyer.

"I won't be able to contact her, will I?" I ask Noah, suspecting I already know the answer.

"Unfortunately, no." He leans back on the island. The dark-gray granite counter gleams in the overhead lighting. "I'm sorry for everything that happened to you, Jess. And for how the justice system failed you so many times. I can understand why being around cops makes you uneasy."

My mouth curves into a wry smile. "You noticed that, huh?"

"It was hard to miss. But hey, if you ever need to talk to someone in the police department, let me know. If I can't help you directly, I'll still be there to help you one way or another."

"Thanks," I say softly, relieved to have an officer on my side for once. I don't remember the last time that happened. If it has ever happened.

Kellan, Garrett, and Emily enter the living room. Jasper rushes in after them, signaling that Simone and Lucas are also here.

"I should probably let the dogs out so they have more room to play." Troy glances at the two large energetic dogs and his small Cavapoo.

I laugh, the sound low in my throat. "Good idea. There's too much puppy energy to contain in the living room. It's nice out. Maybe we should play charades outside." The sky is cloud free, the warm breeze light.

"Sounds like a solid plan." Troy pulls me to him and kisses me on the brow. "You good?" he murmurs against the shell of my ear, his voice a sexy rumble that sends a wave of tingling skipping across my skin.

I swallow a moan. "I am. Now."

He goes to the fridge to grab the beer and drinks. I collect the plates from the coffee table. Everyone helps to take the food outside and places it on the short table on the patio.

Troy sits on the sectional and pulls me onto his lap, making more room for everyone else.

I give Bailey the signal to play with her friends. She doesn't need to be by my side while I'm hanging out with these people. They're my safe zone. The people I trust.

It's the world beyond the fence I have little faith in, especially now that the photo Cora took of me is in the public domain.

And there's nothing I can do about it.

TROY

August, Present Day
Maple Ridge

I lie on my bed, exhausted. Happily sated. Fighting to regain my breath after I made mind-melting love to Jess. My brothers and our friends left less than an hour ago after she and I beat everyone at charades.

Jess rests her head on my chest, and I trace lazy patterns on the small of her back. "Tell me about your daughter." The request rolls quietly from between my lips.

Until five days ago, I had no idea Jess had a daughter. A daughter she gave away her rights to so Amelia could grow up in a stable home with loving parents.

Amelia was two years old when Jess was charged with first-degree murder over five years ago. She won't remember Jess. She won't recognize the woman I just made love to as her biological mother.

My heart clenches at the pain Jess struggles with daily

because she misses her daughter. The pain responsible for her risking everything to get Violet and Sophie away from Wilson. She didn't want mother and daughter to be separated and have to face the same heartache as her.

Jess doesn't reply at first, as if collecting her thoughts. Or maybe her daughter is an invisible line I crossed, and Jess is annoyed.

She draws in a long slow breath, her breasts pressing against me with the rise of her chest. "She's the best thing that's ever happened to me. She was my reason for getting up each morning, the sunlight on the darkest days. Whenever it was just the two of us, she would be all smiles and giggles." The equivalent of an easy grin sneaks into Jess's tone. "She loved playing on the sand and jumping in the water when the small waves rushed up the beach. And she loved shells. We would go to the beach and hunt for them whenever we could."

"What else did she like?"

"Bunnies and dogs and cats. Any animals, really. She had a floppy puppy that she took everywhere with her." Jess laughs, the soft vibrations traveling through my body. "The poor thing would get so dirty, but it was impossible to wash it. I couldn't get her to part with it long enough. I managed to find an identical puppy one day while we were shopping. Amelia had fallen asleep in the stroller and didn't notice me buying it. It was in better shape than the original because it hadn't been crazily loved at that point, but Amelia didn't notice. Whenever it was laundry day, I would switch the two puppies and wash the dirty one. The trick worked like a charm."

I laugh, still stroking the curve of Jess's spine. "You're very resourceful."

She grins at me, her beautiful brown eyes sparkling

with love for her daughter. "You have to be when you're a mother."

"You miss her." It's not a question. I already know the answer.

"Every day." Heartbreak splinters her voice, twists my insides into knots. I love Jess and miss her when she's not with me. I might have only known her for four months, but I already can't imagine a life without her in it. But what Jess is going through...I hope I never have to experience that level of loss with a child.

I tuck her hair behind her ear, tracing my fingertips along the curve of her cheekbone. "Do you regret giving her up for adoption?"

"Yes and no. I didn't want her growing up resenting me every day of her life, believing the worst about me. If I had served the full sentence, she would've been twenty-seven by the time I was released. I doubted she'd want anything to do with me by then." Jess lightly caresses my chest. "Knowing that made it slightly easier to let Craig and Grace adopt her. They're good people. They aren't anything like my husband and Lincoln—Craig's youngest brother.

"But at the time of my sentencing, I had no idea I would only serve five years. It's just as well I hadn't known. I was a mess when I was released from prison, as you know." She gives me a sad smile. "I'm still a mess, trying to figure out who I am. Amelia needs a mother who has it all together."

"You're not a mess, Jess. You're doing well, all things considered." I tighten my good arm around her, wishing I knew how to steal away her pain and doubt and insecurity. "You mentioned you want to convert Lizzie's old bedroom into a room for Amelia?"

Her smile is wider this time, but her eyes are no less sad. "I did say that. It's a silly dream. I was hoping Craig and Grace would eventually let Amelia visit me. But why would they?" Jess rests her hand above my heart. "Why would they risk their daughter's well-being with someone like me? Someone who's spent five years in a maximum-security prison?"

"Have you talked to them since you moved to Maple Ridge?"

"Yes." Jess looks away from me to the darkness outside my bedroom window. "They were the ones who set things in motion for me to come here. They and Anne Carstairs share a mutual friend. When Grace told their friend I needed a place to stay for a few months to heal, the friend talked to Anne. She didn't tell Anne all the details about my past, but she told her enough, and Anne offered to let me stay in Iris's house."

Jess shifts to rest her head on the pillow, her gaze moving to the ceiling. "I phoned Grace a few weeks ago, asking for a chance to be in Amelia's life again. Not as her mother, mind you." Jess's words are so pained and soft, I'm almost afraid to find out what happened. I have a feeling I already know. "I thought given what she and Craig had done to help me start over...I took that as a good sign."

"What happened?"

"She told me it wasn't a good idea. It was too soon." Jess's voice cracks. "I'd just gotten out of Beckley. She and Craig needed more time. I needed more time to...to get my life together."

"How much time?" My voice comes out harsher than I expected, and it's directed at the woman who has Jess's bruised heart in her hands.

"Grace didn't say. She had to go help Amelia find her missing sandal. But ever since I told Robyn what happened, I've been working at getting my life on a better footing." Jess shrugs, her shoulder brushing mine. "I mean, other than the part about me hiding Violet and Sophie in my house. Anyway, I'm almost ready to ask Grace if I'm together enough for her to let me see Amelia. I'm going to ask her soon."

I kiss the top of Jess's head, wishing I could protect her from the world that has let her down in so many ways. "You obviously love Amelia, and it sounds like you were a great mom. Would you like to have more kids one day?" I've asked her the same question previously, but that was before I found out she had been a mother prior to her life taking a hard turn. I'm curious if her answer has changed.

"I don't know. It hurts not having Amelia in my life. I'm not sure I could survive losing any more children. Loving someone is the best feeling in the world. Losing them isn't."

I close my eyes against the truth of her answer and the underlying message clawing at my heart. She's scared of love.

She once loved her husband, and that didn't end well. She loved her mother, but her mother didn't love her enough to stick around. She loved her grandmother, but her grandmother died. She loves Amelia, but the sacrifices she made for the little girl have crushed Jess. Crushed her and left her dealing with the loss of the one person she loves the most.

I open my eyes. "I love you and I'm not going anywhere," I say softly. *Not willingly, anyway.*

But maybe that's the point to what she's been telling me. I love her, but she's not planning to give me her heart. She's not interested in taking that risk. In the end, I could lose her like she's lost people she's loved.

My chest tightens, a vise whose handle has been turned one too many times. If she doesn't want to have kids, doesn't want to let me in, what kind of a relationship can we have? I have no words, no suggestions to make things better. For me. For Jess.

Jess flips onto her elbows. A smile curls onto her face, so full and sweet, but the sadness in her eyes guts me.

She cups my face in her hand. I turn my head and kiss her palm.

She doesn't say anything, doesn't dispute what her eyes are telling me. That she's not sure she can ever give her heart away again. And I don't push the topic.

I once fought the enemy in Afghanistan. Faced life and death situations there. But right now, Jess is the strong one. I'm the coward. A coward because I'm afraid of rocking the boat of what we have between us.

Afraid of tipping it over and losing everything.

Of losing Jess.

7

JESSICA

August, Present Day
Maple Ridge

"You've been busy," Robyn says late Saturday morning. We're sitting in her office, and I've just explained everything that has happened since I saw her three weeks ago.

"You could say that," I reply. "I'm just happy it's over and Violet is free of her husband. She no longer has to live each day in fear." As long as justice gets it right, and he ends up doing time. A very long time.

"How about you?"

I shift on the couch and focus for a second on the tall ficus in the corner of the room. I haven't figured out yet if it's real or fake. I'm almost tempted to walk over and check. "What about me?"

"Do you still live each day in fear?" Robyn's gaze is all knowing, and I inwardly wince. Not much has changed, even after I was released from prison. My body is programmed to expect the worst and constantly hovers in fight-and-flight mode.

The one thing that has changed is, I can now hang out with Noah during Game Night and not have a panic attack.

"I guess so. There was an article in *USA Times* the other day that pointed out I now live under a different name in a small Oregon town. It had a recent photo of me. People will soon figure out I'm Savannah Townsend." And changing my hair color once more won't prevent that—not when the scars on my face are difficult to hide.

"And you're concerned?" Robyn's tone is smooth and gently coaxing.

"Yes." I explain what it will mean if people learn where I spent the past five years—how they'll ostracize me. How I'll be isolated again. "I'm trying to start over and work on my mental health, like you suggested. That'll be hard to do if people have an issue with my past. Which will happen."

"You need to work on your mental well-being and focus on yourself so you can regain the sense of power stripped from you over the years. Part of that lost sense of power came from the trauma bond that developed during your marriage."

"Trauma bond?"

"It's an emotional attachment an individual has with their abuser. You mentioned before that your husband could be kind and loving, and he was especially that way at the beginning of your relationship. He showered you with affection."

I nod.

"It was during those periods of kindness that you developed the bond with him. It's only natural. It happens for most people. But then there were the moments later when he made you feel devalued, worthless, or was violent with you." She leans back in her chair. "A trauma bond is the repeated cycle of the abuse, devaluation, and positive reinforcement. The positive reinforcement comes from those periods when your husband was kind and loving. The periods of positive reinforcement overshadowed the fear of him being abusive again."

A breath of silence falls over us, allowing me a moment to digest everything Robyn's telling me. When I look back to that time in my life, everything she said makes sense. I did focus too much on the good days and excused his behavior. I had truly believed he loved me and wouldn't be mean or hit me again.

I had lied to myself so many times...until I couldn't lie anymore.

"Women don't ask to be in an abusive relationship," Robyn continues, "but our bodies can end up working against us. Dopamine, which is a hormone, plays a role in addiction. It also has a similar role in trauma bonding. Abuse causes an increase in your stress hormones, such as cortisol. After the abuse, during that period of calm when your husband would be kind and loving, dopamine was released. Dopamine creates feelings of pleasure, and that helps strengthen your connection to the abuser."

"And that's why it's so hard for a woman who's in an abusive relationship to leave," I venture.

Robyn nods. "That's one of the reasons. In addition to dopamine, the hormone oxytocin is also released. That's another hormone that gives you the sense of feeling good, and it can help ease fear. And this further strengthens the abuser's connection to the woman."

"So, we become addicted to the abuser?"

"That's right."

"Damn." That explains so much. "Is that why so many women keep returning to their abusers?"

"Yes. That, and the imbalance of power the men exert on them. The woman feels like he controls her to the point where she doesn't know how to resist or break free. She feels incomplete or lost without her abusive partner. That's why if a woman leaves an abuser, she needs professional help to end the cycle. Otherwise, she's more likely to return to him."

"But in my case, I was forced to go cold turkey." My husband's death and my prison sentence made it impossible for me to return to him. That helped break my cycle of abuse.

Only for me to fall into a different pattern of abuse in prison.

"Yes, you were forced to go cold turkey. But that doesn't mean, as you know, you could easily shed the impact his abuse had on you. So that brings us back to your mental well-being. How is that going?" Robyn's eyebrows lift a small amount.

"I'm trying. But knowing that at any moment someone might figure out my identity makes it difficult to focus on my mental well-being."

"It's possible nothing bad will happen if your former identity is exposed, Jessica. It's possible you've mentally built the problem up to something bigger than it needs to be. We won't know for certain until the moment happens— if it happens. Have you found anything yet that will help you feel more grounded? Something that will give you a sense of purpose?"

I shake my head, wishing I had something better to report on that front. "I tried wedding photography, but it didn't really do as much for me as I'd hoped. I enjoyed it, but it's not something I would do on a regular basis." I feel the same about photojournalism. It's not the same shooting it with the iPhone. I can get the equipment I need, thanks to the restitution payment, but I haven't gotten around to buying it. Something tells me the sense of purpose I'm searching for isn't a career as a photographer or photo-journalist.

"Don't give up yet on figuring out what that special something is you feel passionate about," Robyn says. "It might take time, but the outcome will be worth it for your long-term mental health."

"Okay."

"Are you familiar with Maslow's Hierarchy of Needs?"

I nod, slightly surprised at the question. "It's been a while, though, since I've studied it." During my freshman year psychology course.

"As you might remember, there are five basic groups. Before you can reach the higher levels of esteem, recognition, and self-actualization, you have to make sure your physiological, safety, and security needs are met first."

That does sound familiar. The middle level is love and belonging. If I don't feel safe, it's hard to feel worthy of love. That rings true for my marriage. Only my physiological needs had been met. For the most part. The rest had felt a million miles from being obtainable.

Robyn leans forward an inch in her chair. "How have you ensured your physical and security needs are met?"

The physical needs in Maslow's hierarchy include sex, but I'm not about to admit to having a healthy sex life with Troy. There are some things Robyn doesn't need to know—especially since she went to school with the man. "Troy had the security system installed in my house last month. And Troy makes me feel safe."

The corner of her mouth twitches. "How does he make you feel safe?"

I smile, the curve of my lips generous, and heat touches my cheeks. "Well, he's a retired Marine who works out."

The result of his working out—the image of the hard, well-defined planes of his body—pops into my head, and the heat in my cheeks turns up a few degrees. "Who wouldn't feel safe with him around?" Other than anyone who would try to hurt his friends and family.

Robyn chuckles, amusement sparkling in her green eyes. "I'll give you that." Her amusement fades and her expression turns serious. "So, you can talk to Troy in the event that anyone has an issue with your past and you don't feel safe. What about the police?"

I squirm on the couch. "They don't make me feel safe. I haven't had a great track record with them. Even in Maple Ridge."

"Alex Wilson and Cole Dunbar were bad cops. I personally know a few members of the police force, and they're good people."

My gaze flicks briefly to the ficus in the corner. "I only know one Maple Ridge cop I think I can trust." Noah.

"Would you call them if you felt your safety was at risk?"

Maybe. Possibly. "I don't know."

She slowly nods, her expression revealing nothing about what she thinks of my answer. "What about military? Do you trust someone in military uniform?"

"I trust Troy and his brothers. They were all Marines." It's taken me time to get to that point, but they've done so much for me since I moved to Maple Ridge. Troy has done so much for me.

"Anyone else?"

"You mean other than you?" I nod at Robyn in her green Army uniform.

"Do you trust me?" The question is asked straightforwardly, like she's asking if I drink coffee.

"I'm talking to you about things most people don't know

about, so I must." It took me a while to even admit them to Troy.

"Have you had any negative experience with any member of the armed forces?"

"No. Only cops."

"So, that's something we can further explore after I return from my vacation, starting with when Alex Wilson assaulted you in your own home. The goal will be to help you learn to trust members of the police force."

"Okay." Except I can't see that happening anytime soon. Not after everything I've been through. It's going to take time. And lots of baby steps.

I DIG UP A STRAY DANDELION FROM THE FLOWERBED AND TOSS it into the bucket next to me. The hot afternoon sun kisses the backs of my bare arms, and small birds in the trees serenade me. I should be weeding the front yard, but the idea of being in plain view of my neighbors has my stomach twisting in tight knots.

You're being silly. No one has probably realized it was you in the newspaper. You're getting worked up over nothing. Five years in prison has made you paranoid.

Bailey and Butterscotch chase each other on the grass.

"Hello?" a woman's voice says, startling me.

I turn to the wooden gate separating the backyard from the driveway. The hedge on either side of the gate is my height, but the gate is shorter—reaching my waist—and reveals Anne Carstairs on the other side of it. Her chinlength blond hair ruffles around her face in the light breeze. She's wearing tailored shorts and a short-sleeved top in the same lavender as the blossoms in the flowerbed near the gate.

I push to a stand, beaming at the woman who is partly responsible for my life becoming better. "Hi, Anne!" I walk to the gate and open it.

She looks at the two dogs who are now watching her with great interest, heads cocked to the side. "Who do we have here?" She steps through the gate as Bailey and Butterscotch bound the short distance to us.

Bailey leans against my leg, and I stroke her. "This is my dog, Bailey. I'm training her to be my psychiatric support dog." Shame heats my face at admitting that much to Anne, even though she knew I needed a place to stay while I was recovering from a traumatic event. She just didn't know the details. "And that is Butterscotch. Troy Carson's dog."

She crouches and strokes Butterscotch, who happily laps up the attention. "You hired Troy for the renovations? Good choice. And you're now his dog sitter?"

I can't help the grin that spreads across my face. "More like his girlfriend. We're still working on the renovations, but he injured his shoulder during a search and rescue last month." The same shoulder that has been hurt two other times since then. "So the renovations have been temporarily put on pause. Would you like to see what we've done so far?"

"I'd love that. The outside looks great." She glances up. "You had the roof redone."

"I did. I hired a roofing company Troy recommended so he and I could focus on the inside of the house." Troy and Lance helped me with additional repairs on the outside, and we'd repainted the wooden siding a light blue-gray. On top of that, the shutters have been replaced and the front and back doors painted a medium blue-gray.

We go inside through the back door. "How was the trip to the UK and Europe?" I ask.

"It was wonderful. We went to the usual tourist spots, of course. But we also spent a lot of time exploring small towns that tourists tend not to bother with."

"Did you go to France?" An intense craving to show her Iris's journals buzzes under my skin. I just have to wait a little longer. Wait until I've finished transcribing them so Anne can easily read her great-aunt's words.

"Yes. We visited Bordeaux and various vineyards in the area. And Paris, naturally." Anne's gaze travels over the kitchen, with the predominantly white and creamy-blue colors. "Wow. I don't even recognize the room." She skims her fingertips over the white-granite island countertop. "It's gorgeous."

"Thank you. What about Burgundy?" The region where Jacques Gauthier's vineyard and farmhouse were located. "Did you go there?"

"Unfortunately, not. We probably needed a month just for France if we wanted to visit all the wine regions. Maybe that will have to be Dan's and my next trip."

The craving buzzes again under my skin. I'm barely able to keep from bouncing on my toes with all the pent-up excited energy crackling in me.

I show Anne around the parts of downstairs where the renovations have been completed, which is just the kitchen, the living room, and the hallway so far. The downstairs washroom and the laundry room still need work done on them. We didn't have a chance to start them before we were injured. "Troy and I are still working on downstairs," I explain. "We haven't done any renovations upstairs yet."

"Well, so far it looks incredible," Anne says, her smile bright.

"Once we've finished the major renovations, I'll paint

some of Iris's old furniture to fit in with the aesthetic." I run my hand over the sturdy wooden bookshelf that would look gorgeous in a whitewash.

"Auntie Iris would be impressed with what you've done. It's so pretty and cozy. It's perfect. She would have loved it."

I try to appreciate the living room through the eyes of the woman who had been an SOE agent and risked her life in occupied France. "I would love to learn more about Iris." I bite the inside of my mouth to keep from blurting about Iris's journals, the medal, and the pendant I found in the secret room. A tendril of guilt curls in my stomach at the secret I'm still keeping from Anne.

Not much longer...then you can really surprise her.

"I can tell you she would be happy you're the one who bought her house. Not because of what you've done here, but because of what you've been through. As Savannah." The name is spoken softly without any recriminations or regrets.

But that doesn't stop the sharp lungful of air that drags into my chest.

Anne's kind eyes search my face, but it's not enough to blunt the unease and shame swelling in me.

"I had no idea you were Savannah Townsend until recently," she says, her voice the gentle caress of a mother consoling a frightened child. "I knew you had been through a lot based on what little Florence told me. I could tell the day I first met you that whatever happened to you had pretty much crushed you. But I never imagined it would be something as bad as not only surviving an abusive husband but also the prison system."

Butterscotch sits next to Anne's feet. She crouches and strokes him. "One of my friends was raped when she was in her early twenties. The guy had been the college's football hero, and the administrators did what they could to bury the truth, not wanting it to become a scandal. They paid her off to keep her quiet. She wasn't the same after that. She fell into drugs to cope with the pain. She lost her job and her home. She felt like she had nowhere to turn. In the end, it was the drugs that did her in. She saw them as her safe haven." The corners of Anne's mouth are weighed down with sadness.

A chill skittles over my skin at the story. "I'm so sorry for your loss, Anne."

"Me too. That's why I offered Auntie Iris's house for you to stay in. I didn't know what had happened to you, but I wanted to make sure you had a safe place to stay while you healed."

I look at the wood flooring by my feet, hiding the tears that blur my vision—tears for Anne's friend and for Anne's generosity for what she has done for me. "And now that you know the truth about my past, you don't have second thoughts about selling the house to me? Knowing I was once an inmate in a maximum-security prison?"

"Not at all. If anyone belongs in this house, it's you, Jess. Or do you prefer Savannah?"

My eyes meet Anne's, and the kindness reflected in them knocks a small amount of the burden of truth from my shoulders. "I haven't been Savannah in a long time." Not even while I was in Beckley. "I don't feel like her anymore. I'm Jess now." I just have to figure out who the heck Jess is. "What else can you tell me about Iris? I would love to hear more stories about her."

"You should visit me in Ash Falls some time, and then I can show you old photos of her. Family photos—including pictures of my grandmother and grandfather. That would be Iris's sister. And I can tell you all kinds of stories about my great-aunt."

"I would love that. Thank you." I would love to learn

more about the woman who risked her life to make a difference in the war. Maybe I'll be able to finish transcribing the journals by then to give to Anne.

Anne walks to the bookshelf and picks up the framed photo of Troy and me that Simone took at the Sunshine Festival in June. Troy and I are smiling at each other, having just kissed, and we look like we're in our own little world.

"You two really are a cute couple. And it's obvious he cares a lot for you." Anne returns the photo to the shelf.

I don't respond, crossing my fingers she doesn't ask me about my feelings for Troy. They're still a knot of emotions, and I'm not sure how to unravel them.

Angelique was brave, fighting for what she believed in.

I'm nowhere near as brave when it comes to my heart. And Troy.

8

ANGELIQUE

October 1943
France

The two armed guards outside the glass hotel door watch me with a mix of interest and disdain.

I glance over my shoulder to see if the vehicle Jacques was in is behind us. "Please, tell me where my papa is. He's sick. He needs medical assistance." Their manhandling of him might make his cough worse.

"He'll be here soon enough," is the only answer I get. The Gestapo agent pushes me forwards.

I stumble, my legs refusing to cooperate. My arms and shoulders ache from my hands being secured behind me for what feels like forever.

The other two Gestapo agents lead me into the building and escort me to the front desk. The man behind it could easily be a hotel employee if not for his Army uniform.

Bile rises in my throat. This man looks nothing like Johann, but that doesn't dull the reminder that I'm pregnant. Pregnant with a baby whose father is the enemy.

"We have Angelique D'Aboville," the stocky agent says in German to the soldier. "Captain Krüger is expecting us."

The man nods at them, and I am taken into the awaiting elevator. We ride it to the top floor, where I am escorted down the hallway and into a suite designed for French aristocrats.

Under different circumstances, I would appreciate the crystal chandelier and the intricate gold patterns on the walls. Under different circumstances, I would enjoy the lush red carpet and the exquisite paintings. Under different circumstances, I would dream of holidaying in a place like this.

A heavy, ornate desk is situated in the middle of the room with two wooden chairs in front of it. The faint metallic scent of blood and fear looms in the air like a phantom.

The stocky agent drags me to one of the chairs and pushes me into it. I lose my balance and fall onto the cushioned seat. The hem of my skirt flutters up, revealing the bandage wrapped around my calf—the bandage concealing the gunshot wound I got during the mission five days ago to destroy the train tunnel.

I subtly move my feet under the chair, attempting to keep the injury out of plain sight. I don't need to give them any evidence to support their claims that I am English. And a bullet wound on my calf will only raise questions I don't wish to answer.

The handcuff is removed from one wrist and fastened to the arm of the chair.

"What is that from?" The question is spoken in French. The stocky agent points at the bandaged leg.

"A crow spooked me while I was working in my papa's vineyard," I reply, "and my leg brushed on something sharp."

He kneels and unties the knot of the bandage. His actions aren't gentle, and the friction of fabric against my wound tears at the scab. I don't so much as flinch.

The bandage is ripped from my skin, taking parts of the scab with it. A searing pain shoots through my calf, and my muscles tense. Blood trickles down my leg and pools in the heel of my worn-out shoe.

The door behind me clicks open and shut. The two Gestapo agents stand to attention and salute. "*Heil* Hitler!"

A terse male voice responds in kind.

I take the moment to scan the room, searching for something to aid my escape. But given that I'm handcuffed to the chair, my options are practically nonexistent.

"I hear you found Angelique D'Aboville," the new addition to the group says in German. His tone is crisp, the temperature of frost.

"That's right, sir."

"That's good. I was hoping you would succeed in tracking her down." The man belonging to the voice moves in front of me and continues to his desk. He pulls out the chair behind it but doesn't sit. Captain Krüger, I assume. The man's height stretches well above where I am seated, his shoulders broad and threatening. Another time and place and he might have been considered distinguished. "Did she cause you any trouble?"

The stocky Gestapo agent's posture becomes less rigid. "No, but she insists on speaking in French and pretends not to understand English."

"Is that so?" Captain Krüger's eyes roam over my features. "She is most certainly the woman they call Carmen. Did she have her *carte d'identité* on her?"

The stocky agent hands him the papers he found in my handbag. There's nothing incriminating in the bag, other than the secret pocket, which is currently empty.

Captain Krüger inspects the papers and gives a small nod. "She is indeed the whore who has been feeding secrets to the other side." He puts the papers on his desk, moves around it to stand in front of me, and speaks directly to me in English, "Madame D'Aboville, would you like something to drink before we have our little conversation? Perhaps some tea?"

I look from man to man, as if hoping one of them will translate his words. "What did he say?" I ask the stocky agent who does speak French.

He doesn't answer.

"Perhaps we need to convince you to speak in your native tongue, Angelique." A small smile curves on Captain Krüger's face and sends a chill racing along my spine. "Or do you prefer Carmen?"

I don't say anything and work at keeping all emotion, other than confusion, from my expression.

"That's what I thought." He pulls his hand back and slaps me hard across the face.

My ears ring. My lip stings. A metallic taste assaults my tongue. But I still fight to keep all emotions from my expression, including pain. I don't even fake confusion this time.

"Alright, Angelique. Should we try this again? Who forged your papers?"

Once more, I look at the stocky agent for a translation. And once more, I am slapped in the face. Blood trickles down my chin and drips onto my dark-green skirt.

"Who forged your papers?"

This time I don't bother to look at the stocky agent. I sit motionless, waiting for the next blow to come. It doesn't matter who forged the papers. The person lives in England. The Gestapo is unable to touch him. But that's not what this is about. Captain Krüger wants me to confess I am an English spy. Once I give him that information, there will be no stopping him.

When the third hit to my face still doesn't loosen my tongue, the stocky agent tells him about my wounded leg.

Captain Krüger kneels and lifts the hem of my skirt high enough to expose the wound. "That looks like it could be the result of a bullet. Who was firing at you, Angelique?"

Silence.

"It's certainly a nasty wound. You wouldn't want it to get infected, now would you?"

I turn to him. "I'm sorry. I don't understand you. I only speak and understand French." I release a long, exasperated sigh, as if growing bored of repeating myself, and begin to inwardly shut down.

My mind drifts to the last night I was with Johann. To his whispered words of love. To his tender and passionate kisses. To the promise we would be a family one day. To the feel of him inside me.

If this is the room where I'll breathe my last breath, these are the last memories I want to have. I want to die remembering the love I feel for him, the love he feels for me. Because when I reach down to my soul, to my very being, I know it's true. He might have been born to the side of the enemy, but he's not one of them. I believe that—like Oskar does.

And if I am wrong, it won't matter. I won't live long enough to learn the truth.

But the one thing I do know is, I won't betray my country. I won't betray the people I love. I won't give this monster what he wants.

He digs his fingers into the wound, doing what he can

to draw a confession from me. A sharp pain tears through my calf, and I cushion my soul in a bubble, restraining myself from telling him what he wants to hear.

The brief torture ends, and I know I haven't given him what he wants. The only words I uttered were in French.

My skin is damp with perspiration and my heart is hammering hard. I don't have to look at the gunshot wound to know the damage is severe. If I am able to walk out of here on my own two feet, it will be a major accomplishment.

I send a silent message to the baby in my womb to stay safe, to not give up. Until the final beat of my heart has played out, there is always a chance. The moment I surrender to my fate, it will spell the end for both of us.

Right now, I need a reason to live beyond seeing Johann again. The life growing inside me is that reason.

"You can play the simple country whore all you want, Carmen, but I know the truth. And do you want to know how I know the truth?" This time Krüger's words are spoken in French, and a chill passes through my body.

He nods at something or someone behind me, and the door clicks open.

Heavy footsteps approach from behind me. I fight the urge to turn my head to see to whom they belong.

A man steps into my periphery, but I don't dare to look at him.

"Hello, Carmen. It's nice to see you again." The words are spoken in English with a true aristocratic English accent instead of the guttural German accent of Captain Krüger.

I turn my head. My heart slams into my ribs. My pulse pounds a funeral march in my ears. Because as much as I want to deny my identity, the man standing next to me knows the truth.

Christian. The SOE agent Allaire introduced me to over five months ago in Paris.

He's a double agent? A traitor to king and country?

Bloody hell and fuck twice over. This is not good. Not good at all.

9

———

TROY

August, Present Day
Maple Ridge

Six retired Navy SEALs in their late thirties, my brothers, and I are sitting around the campfire, our five tents erected a few feet away. Our talking and laughter are the only sounds in the night air heard above the crackling flames.

Allan pops open a beer can and takes a swig from it. "You guys are lucky to live close to all this." He gestures with his can to the towering pines skirting the area. "It's a huge improvement over San Diego."

"But you have the ocean," Tim points out. "And beaches."

"Plus, San Diego doesn't get buried under dumps of snow," Kevin, who's from New York State, adds.

"Does get pretty cold in Manhattan," Allan says, tipping

his can as if to acknowledge Kevin's point. "But you sure do have a lot of fancy restaurants."

The men's conversation shifts to a story about their last deployment together. My thoughts drift to Jess—and how we've been dating for the past month, but we haven't gone on a date. The kind of date that involves dinner. In a restaurant.

"I heard the other day that Savannah Townsend is living in Oregon." Eric's tone is casual, as if he's discussing his favorite beer, and his words yank me from my thoughts.

Allan makes a scoffing noise that sets off warning sirens in my gut. "I still can't believe she got let off. She was the mastermind of Wayne Townsend's murder."

Kevin's forehead creases into a frown. "Savannah Townsend?" He slides a puzzled glance between Eric and Allan.

"The cop killer?" The lilt at the end of Allan's reply isn't so much a question about whether she killed a cop as it is inquiring what rock Kevin has been living under. "She got her lover to murder her husband. She was originally convicted for killing Wayne and was sentenced to twenty-five years. A technicality got her out of the slammer after she only served five years."

The technicality being she was wrongfully convicted of the crime.

I tighten my grasp on my beer bottle and open my mouth to defend Jess to this asshole. My gaze falls on Kellan. He slowly shakes his head, his eyes never leaving mine.

Message received.

Me going land mine on Allan won't change the SEAL's mind. If anything, it will just draw their attention to which Oregon town Jess lives in.

"What happened to her lover?" Kevin asks.

"Don't know," Eric responds. "She's probably with him."

"No doubt killed him too," Allan pipes in. "Or she's plotting to do that as we speak."

Kellan glowers at his beer. Lucas and Garrett look like they don't know what to say or do.

Fuck that.

"From what I heard about the case," I note, keeping my anger to a low simmer, "Savannah's husband was an abusive asshole. I'm not saying he deserved to be killed." *He totally deserved what happened to him after what he put Jess through.* "But if the cops hadn't arrived at her house when they did, she would have died from a drug overdose." I keep my opinion out of my tone. I'm just impartially relaying the facts. "She hadn't knowingly taken those drugs. Someone gave them to her." That part was on the news a few months ago, after a blood splatter expert had raised new questions about the legitimacy of the previous testimony.

Allan snorts, shaking his head like I'm the one who's the idiot. "That's what she wanted the media to believe. It was a great excuse. Except I'm sure she hadn't taken enough to end her life. She wouldn't have actually died."

He's wrong. She would have. An anonymous phone call alerted 9-1-1 that they had heard shots from the house. That fed into the conspiracy theory her lover had been the caller. To this day, no one knows where the call came from, other than it was probably sent from a burner phone.

"Did the news say where she's living in Oregon?" Kevin's question is directed at Eric and Allan. The other three SEALs sit there quietly, apparently having no opinion on the topic. Or maybe they do, but they're not willing to voice it. Two of them watch the campfire.

Unable to listen to this bullshit any longer, I stand from the log I was sitting on and walk past the tents.

I turn on my phone flashlight and do my best not to

look like I'm storming off because of what Eric and Allan said. I just need a moment to collect myself, to focus on the woman I love and nothing else.

I head deeper into the forest. The crackle and pop of the campfire becomes a faint noise in the background as if playing an accompaniment to the night sounds—the occasional rustle of dead leaves on the ground and the steady chirping of insects. The men's voices carry but not loud enough for me to make out what they're saying.

I enter a clearing overlooking the valley and park my ass on a boulder. Above me, billions of stars sparkle in the dark sky. Jess's and my conversation from a few weeks ago about The Great Cock constellation slips into my thoughts, and my lips twitch into a smile. "Are you watching the stars, Jess, and thinking about it too?" The murmured words mingle with the cool night air.

The news about Savannah Townsend living in a small mountainous town in Oregon was in Tuesday's newspaper, but other than Zara, no one has said anything about it to Jess or me. She's an introvert and hasn't spoken to a lot of people since moving to Maple Ridge, but she has been seen in enough places to be recognized from the photo. Yoga class. The Veterans Center. The grocery store. Theresa's wedding. The library. Or even walking along Main Street.

All it takes is a few people to tell their friends or coworkers they've seen her, and for those people to tell someone else. And before long, too many people will know where she's living.

If people respect her privacy and don't judge her like Jess fears will happen, her location being revealed is no big deal. But that won't be the case. There will be people, like the idiots at the campfire, who will judge her and twist the truth to fit their narrative. I have no idea what to do about that.

For the first time since I've been away on a Warriors trip, I don't want to be here. I want to be with the woman I love.

I have no idea how long I've been staring at the stars when I hear the crunch of hiking boots stepping on the undergrowth. My stalker isn't trying to be stealthy.

I glance over my shoulder. A flashlight—probably from a phone—moves toward me, the beam focused on the ground.

"You're losing your touch if you actually want to be left alone," Garrett says, humor lightly warping his otherwise neutral tone. "You were too easy to track."

"That, or you really are part wolf like I suspected when we were kids," I deadpan.

Garrett chuckles, the sound barely heard over the steady chirp of night insects. He sits on the boulder next to mine. "How're you doing?" The humor in his tone has flatlined.

"It's not me you have to worry about." I turn my attention to the valley and pine trees in the bright glow of the almost full moon.

"I'm worried about both you and Jess. I'm not so worried about those two jerks. Or at least I don't think you're gonna throw them off the mountain."

I rub my hand down my face. "Believe me, it is tempting. None of what they were saying surprises me. It's not news that some people think Jess was guilty of her husband's murder. Like it's not news that some people think the moon landing was faked or believe thousands of other conspiracy theories. I just don't know what to do about it."

"I'm not sure there is anything you can do. Jess has been through a lot, but despite all of that, she's still standing.

She's still strong. She's probably stronger than any woman I know."

"You don't have to tell me that. But even steel has its breaking point."

A heavy silence falls between us, the night sounds filling in our gap in the conversation. "Is she starting up therapy again?" Garrett asks after a long moment.

"She had an appointment this morning with Robyn." Thank Christ for that. "Hopefully it will help Jess cope with the current situation."

"There's also a chance what those guys said doesn't echo the sentiments of anyone in town. And if it does, they'll keep their opinions to themselves."

I smirk. "You really believe that?"

Garrett huffs out a hard breath. "Maybe it's just wishful thinking. But until we know if that's the case, it won't do us much good dwelling on it. That won't solve the problem."

"I just like being prepared." It's what we did in the Marines. It's what I do with my job. I anticipate problems I might have to deal with and have a contingency plan.

"I know you do. But sometimes it's too easy to get caught up in the maybes and forget to live in the here and now. Remember, you and Jess aren't in this alone. She has friends who believe in her and who will stand by her, no matter what."

I nod and go back to staring at the stars.

"Have you told her you love her?"

I'm quiet for a moment, half ready to brush off the question and not answer it. I'm not particularly interested in laying out my emotions raw. But this is Garrett, my brother. I might not always agree with his opinions, but I do trust him. "Yes. But she's not there yet. Or maybe she'll never be there."

"What happens if she never gets there?"

I flash him a one-sided grin he probably can't see even in the moonlight. "Luckily you're not a romance writer."

"Hey, I have a romance storyline threading through my series." He might not say it, but the implied *dumbass* is there in his tone.

I bark out a laugh, head flung back. "That's your idea of a romance storyline? You killed off the love interest in the last book."

"You know that because you read the book or because Zara told you?" From the way he says it, I can tell Zara gave him heck for killing off the woman.

I inwardly roll my eyes. "You know I read all your books. Wouldn't miss 'em. I'd say I'm your biggest fan, but that would be Zara." She always buys his latest releases in hardback and gets him to sign them.

We sit quietly for a few minutes. All I can think about is what Jess could be facing if more people in town discover her secret. The campfire continues to crackle and pop in the background. The men's laughter isn't so loud now, but the low murmur of their conversations remains a constant.

"You ready to join everyone, or do you need more time?" Garrett asks. "Everyone's gotta be wondering about your digestive system. You've been gone a long time."

"Let them believe anything they want. I just need a few more minutes."

"I could send Lucas to give you advice on your love life if you want. He knows what he's doing." The smirk Garrett flashes me is enough to coax a chuckle from me.

"Ha! I don't know about that. He almost messed things up with Simone."

"True. But compared to you, me, and Kellan, he's the smart one with figuring out this love stuff." Garrett screws up his nose as if he's caught wind of bear shit on his boots.

"What about you? You've been in love before. You don't have any advice for me?"

"My advice is don't bother, but you're already too gone for that." He laughs, a low rumble deep in his chest, but there's also something off about it.

"Are you ever planning to tell me what happened between you and Kenda?" Garrett and Kenda—Garrett's girlfriend from college and one of Zara's close friends back then—had practically been engaged, which is why I could never figure out what went wrong between them.

"There's nothing to say. Her career goals didn't involve living in Maple Ridge. She was planning to make a big difference with her journalism degree. And she couldn't do that in Maple Ridge."

"You could've gone with her."

"I could have. But I was headed for the Marines, and she wanted to be free to disappear for long periods while doing investigative journalism. She didn't want to be stuck in Maple Ridge, and she didn't want to worry about someone impatiently waiting for her to return home." He shrugs like it's no big deal.

Except I know it was a big deal at the time.

I can't see Jess leaving Maple Ridge since it's her home now, the place where she's rebuilding her life. But the risk is still there that she could bail if the thing she fears most comes true—if people target her because of her past.

Does that mean my heart's still at risk of losing the woman who's important to me?

10

JESSICA

August, Present Day
Maple Ridge

The rumble of Troy's garage door opening can be heard from where I'm sitting in the living room, transcribing Iris's journal. He's early. He and his brothers were supposed to drive the retired SEALs to the airport in Eugene after their weekend excursion.

I close the journal and return it to my book bag on the floor. I was going to start making dinner soon, anyway.

I walk over to the kitchen and pick up a carrot from the counter as Troy strolls into the room, his hair damp and smelling of the pine shampoo they have at the Warriors cabins. It's one of my favorite smells. It reminds me of him.

"Hey," I say, smiling at Troy. "I wasn't expecting you for another two hours."

His arms go around my waist, and he pulls me to him. "My brothers took the men to the airport." He takes the

72

carrot from my hand and puts it on the counter behind me. "You and I are going on a date."

"A date?"

"Yes. A date. It's when a man takes a woman he's interested in out to dinner. We've officially been a couple for over a month now, but we haven't been on a single date. That changes tonight. I'm taking you to dinner."

My smile slips a little, and I focus on the sexy-as-hell stubble on his face. "You don't need to take me to dinner. I'm perfectly happy having dinner with you here." Where I'm safe from questioning eyes.

"I know you are. But I wanna take you on a real date. And afterward, I'll walk you to the front door of this house like I would if this were our first date—which it is. And then if it's okay with you, I'll kiss you like this." He presses his mouth lightly to mine. My lips tingle, and I release a dreamy, heartfelt sigh.

"What if I want more than a sweet kiss?" I whisper, my breath skimming over his lips.

"For our first date?" His mouth presses into a serious line that twitches at the corners. "First date is just the kiss. That's the proper dating etiquette."

A giggle bubbles inside me. "What if I want to do this?" I press my mouth to his and encourage his lips to part. My tongue dips into his mouth and strokes across *his* tongue.

His lips curve against mine, and a soft laugh vibrates low in his throat and spreads throughout my body. "I'm sure we can bend the dating etiquette rules just a little."

"Only a little?"

"Sweetheart, I'd like to bend you over the counter and do wicked things to you." His voice is a low growl that ignites the nerve endings between my legs. If he keeps this up, I'll explode into a million stars before we get to go on a date.

A tiny whimper escapes me, and I press my body into his. His length hardens in his shorts, and I trace the tip of my tongue along his lower lip, enjoying this game.

Troy's hand goes to my ass. "Like that, huh?"

"Uh-huh." I can barely talk or think or...

Troy's other hand cups my face, and his mouth moves to my neck. He plants soft kisses along my skin, and I melt at his touch. Another whimper breaks free.

Troy takes a step back, a cocky grin on his face. "You're very good at distracting a man."

"Is that what I'm doing? Distracting you so you don't take me out on a date?" I lean into him.

"Nope. You're distracting me so I forget the proper dating etiquette."

"From the 1950s." I bite my lip, holding back my comment about how Iris hadn't worried about dating etiquette with Johann. But why would she when she had no idea if she would survive the war? Why wait for tomorrow when it might never come?

"My mother taught me to be a gentleman." Amusement shines in Troy's warm brown eyes.

"I'm sure your mom will be proud that she did a good job instilling those lessons." Smiling broadly, I widen the gap between us. "So, where will this date take place?"

"La Brezza Ristorante."

"I've never been there before." It's one of the fancier restaurants in town, but not over-the-top, suits-and-tie fancier.

"We have a reservation for six-thirty."

Surprise widens my eyes, kickstarts the fast beating of my heart. "You've already got a reservation?" *God, am I ready to be out in public like that so soon after the newspaper article?*

"Yup, booked it once I returned to town."

I nod because I don't know how to respond. I can't

remember the last time I went on a date. "How was the trip this weekend?"

"It was good."

Something about the way he says the three words has me raising my eyebrows. On the surface, there's nothing sinister about them. It's that subtle, barely noticeable pause before the "good" that says the opposite.

"What...what happened?"

"Nothing exciting. It was mostly a reunion for these men. They all retired from the military ten years ago. Needed a break from their desk jobs. They met up in Portland for the week."

"So, nothing bad happened?"

Troy's brow pulls into a frown. "No. Were you expecting something bad to have happened?"

I shake my head. I must be imagining things. I'm paranoid after everything that's happened to me, and I'm reading too much into his reactions.

Troy pulls open the door to the restaurant, and his warm gaze locks on me like I'm a grand prize he's won. The love in his eyes sets off a flutter of butterfly wings in my stomach.

I'm wearing the gorgeous floral sundress Anne gave me when I bought Iris's house. Troy has on pants and a button-up shirt. And *damn*. Troy in jeans and a T-shirt is good-looking, but that's nothing compared to dressed-up Troy. He's hotter than hot.

The way the young hostess is batting her eyelashes at him tells me I'm not the only one who thinks that. I'm not sure she even notices he's holding my hand.

That's fine with me. As long as she's paying attention to him, it means she's not seeing me. Or my scar. Or noting how much I resemble the woman in the newspaper—assuming she reads the one Cora's article was in.

I duck my head. I have a little more makeup on than normal, but it's not enough to hide the scar by my mouth.

"We have a reservation for two under Troy Carson," he tells her.

"Yes, this way, please." She grabs the menus and leads us to a table in the middle of the room, to a location that puts me on display. My muscles tense, and my hand tightens around Troy's.

"Could we sit somewhere a little more private?" He nods to several empty tables near the exposed brick wall.

"Of course." She takes us to a table for two tucked in the corner. Troy pulls a seat out for me that has my back facing the restaurant patrons, and the tension in my body lessens.

"Thank you." I smile at him and sit, relieved he understood the problem without me having to voice it out loud.

He takes the seat opposite mine, and the hostess recites the specials. I don't dare look at her, keeping my head tucked down.

She leaves, and Troy wraps his fingers around my hand resting on the table. My skin is no longer dry and calloused like it was when I was released from prison. Even my fingernails are in better shape. They're longer now, prettier, with a light gloss to them.

Troy's hands are warm and strong. They're perfect for holding, for making me feel safe, for giving me orgasms. He strokes my hand with his thumb, setting off the delicious tingles that happen whenever he does that.

"Did this restaurant exist when you were a kid?" I turn my head to check out the place. The restaurant has a quaint charm to it that reminds me of pictures I've seen of outdoor courtyards in Italy and the Mediterranean.

"Yes and no. There was a restaurant here, but the owners sold it about fifteen years ago. Everything about it changed when the new owners took over. For the better. It wasn't so trendy when I was growing up. It was more like a diner."

Wow. I never would have guessed. "Have there been a lot of changes to the town since you were a kid?"

"It's grown since then, but not enough to lose the small-town charm that has the tourists coming here. Some of the buildings on and near Main Street have seen updates over the years, but it's pretty much the same." His thumb continues to stroke my hand. I'm close to purring at his touch.

We gaze into each other's eyes. The warmth of the chocolate-brown flakes in his eyes has me mesmerized. I could easily get lost in them for all eternity.

"Would you like anything to drink?" a woman asks us, startling me. I didn't notice her approach our table. She's in her early twenties, her black hair styled in sleek waves like a 1950s Hollywood starlet.

She smiles at Troy, all warmth and sparkling eyes.

The same warmth is then directed my way. Her gaze drops to the scar by my mouth. Her expression doesn't change, but her smile now seems almost frozen in place. Her eyes lack any hint of recognition.

We pick up the menus and I hurriedly read the options. Rich and delicious aromas tease the air and remind me I'm hungry. Everything looks so good and smells amazing, making it harder to choose what to order.

We order wine and our food. She gathers our menus, her smile unchanging, and leaves.

Troy takes my hand again. His thumb strokes the side of

my wrist, soothing away my unease from the waitress's reaction to my scar.

It doesn't mean anything. She's not the first person to be distracted by it. She's probably...she's probably wondering why someone as hot as Troy is with someone scarred like me.

Or maybe she saw your photo in the newspaper.

"What was your childhood like living with your grand-parents?" Troy asks, clearly oblivious to the waitress's reaction...or maybe he's trying to distract me from it.

I decide to lean into it. "The best. I swear Granny was a flower child in the sixties, and she kept that part of her alive after my grandfather died."

"Were you close to them both?"

"I was. But after my grandfather died, Granny and I grew even closer." I smile, the curve of my mouth wistful and wide. "My grandfather was great. He would walk into the kitchen while Granny was cooking dinner and get her to dance with him to whatever was playing on the radio. But he was a terrible dancer, which only made it that much sweeter."

I laugh at the memory—one of many I had tucked away when my life hadn't been a reflection of theirs. It feels great to have the memories again—a benefit of therapy.

I wipe at a stray tear, the result of laughing and the bittersweet pain of losing him. Of losing them both.

Troy squeezes my hand, and I smile at him, thanking him without words for bringing back the memory.

"Do you miss San Diego?" he asks.

"Sometimes. I loved it there when I was growing up. I loved taking Amelia to the beach and searching for shells with her. Just like Granny used to do with me. At least Amelia didn't have to give it up when she moved to Seattle. When Craig and Grace visited me in Beckley"—my voice drops so low on the last word, I'm not sure Troy even hears it—"to ask me if they could adopt my daughter, I made them promise to keep taking her to the beach and look for seashells with her." This time the pitch of my voice is normal, but the words come out rough, like wet sand between bare toes.

I blink away the tears and brighten my smile. We're on a date. A first date. Men tend not to like their dates crying on a first date. Or on any date.

We spend the rest of our meal talking about beaches and Troy's family and our lives growing up.

"You're lucky having such a close family," I tell him.

"I am. We weren't always close. There were times when our fighting drove Mom nuts. When you have four kids, there's always someone who's mad at someone else. But we were there for each other when it counted the most."

"Do you want a big family like that?" The question slips out before I realize I've said it. I hold my breath.

Troy's eyes, warm like melted chocolate, hold on to mine. "I would love to have kids one day. And I would love to have more than one. It was crazy in the house with so many of us—especially when my brothers and I hit our teens—but it was a good kind of crazy."

He doesn't look away. And I suddenly wish I could yank back my question.

11

JESSICA

August, Present Day
Maple Ridge

After dinner, Troy drives us to the beach where we first met. He leaves his suit jacket in the truck and rolls up his shirt sleeves, exposing his tanned, muscular forearms. He removes a blanket from the back seat and takes my hand. "I thought we could watch the sunset."

"I would love that. I happen to love watching sunsets," I add, as if it is our first date and he doesn't yet know that about me.

The grin he flashes me almost has my panties incinerating. "I thought you might."

We walk to the sand and slip off our shoes. We continue, barefoot, our fingers linked, and find a quiet spot on the sand away from another couple sitting on the beach. The tension that thickened the air between us in the restaurant has dissipated. It's still there lurking in the recesses of my mind—*How can I be with Troy if I can't give him what he wants?*—but under the brilliant orange-and-pink sky, with the water lapping at the shore and this handsome man by my side, it's all too easy to forget.

Troy lays out the blanket. A lightweight cardigan covers my arms since the evening mountain temperature has dropped over the past hour, but it's not low enough to chill my bare legs.

I sit on the blanket. Troy lowers himself next to me and pulls me to him. I rest my head on his shoulder and inhale the clean mountain scent that's all Troy.

The sun is low in the sky, casting the world in a beautiful golden warmth. The lake ripples in the light breeze, disturbing the sun's glow reflecting off it. It's so peaceful.

I glance at Troy. His expression, full of longing and love, is breathtaking in this light. I wish I had a camera so I could capture the moment, but all I have is my phone camera, and it's not enough for what I have in mind.

He lowers his head to mine, and our lips touch. My pulse throbs a quick-step in my veins, and I release a nearly breathless gasp.

My lips part, letting him in. My tongue craves to dance with his, to explore his mouth. To taste him. I cup his face in my hand. His stubble tickles my palm, so sensual, so hot.

The kiss deepens, and I whimper and moan. I don't push him for more, even though more is what I want.

His hands remain chaste, his left arm pressing into my back and keeping me from melting into the blanket. His other hand rests on my face.

His hands might not be touching me like my body aches to be touched, but his tongue is another story. It flicks the roof of my mouth, thrusts and swirls, and I sink deeper into the kiss.

The breeze picks up, fluttering my skirt against my legs, as if to remind us we're here for the sunset. Troy and I separate, his arm still pressed to my back, and we turn to the low sun. The sky is bright with a mix of oranges and mauves and purples showing off cotton-puff clouds.

Troy's finger taps my arm, the movement both rhythmic and offbeat.

It takes me a few seconds to figure it out. "You're doing Morse code? On my arm?" I'm used to decoding the dots and dashes when we write our secret messages to each other. We haven't done Morse code like this before.

He taps the sequence of dots and dashes again. "I... love...you. But how about I simplify it to this...?" He taps another version that spells out three letters: ILU.

I smile at him and go back to watching the sunset in silence, my body tucked into his. This—us being here together, the sunset—feels so right and so good.

Troy keeps softly tapping the letters like a whispered endearment, and I release a content sigh.

Best. Date. Ever.

TROY PARKS ON HIS DRIVEWAY, WHICH IS STRANGE SINCE HE usually parks in the garage. He gets out of his truck, walks to the passenger door, and helps me down. He links his fingers with mine, and we slowly walk along the path to his front door, as neither of us wants the evening to end.

Troy turns to me, humor and heat and love shining in his eyes. "I had a great time."

A full smile stretches across my lips, ripe with amusement and rich with longing. "I did too. That has to be the best first date I've ever been on."

"I hope that means there'll be a second date." His voice is deep and oh-so husky.

A soft laugh tickles my throat, masking how turned-on I am from the way he's looking at me. "Yes, there'll be a second date. If you want there to be one."

"Definitely." He leans down and kisses my cheek, the press of his lips tender and brief.

Troy pulls away and unlocks the front door. "Well, good night, Jess." He turns and starts to leave.

I grab his arm. "Um, where are you going?"

"Home."

I glance up at the house. Yep, it's Troy's house. For a heartbeat, I thought we'd been sucked into the *Twilight Zone*.

Troy jogs to his truck, climbs in, and turns over the engine. The garage door lifts open, and I laugh.

Butterscotch is waiting by the front door when I go into the house. "Your daddy is coming in through the garage door," I tell him.

Butterscotch turns his head in that direction and scurries toward the laundry room. I follow him, albeit at a slower pace, and let Bailey out of the extra crate I keep here. I hug her, relief washing through me that I didn't need her with me this evening.

The hum of the garage door closing comes from the other side of the wall. Butterscotch stares at the door leading into the garage. It opens, and Troy steps into the laundry room. The dogs bark their welcomes.

"They're asking how your date went." Laughter rings in my tone, and I push to my feet.

"It was great. My date said she was game for a second one." He steps closer to me, my favorite grin on his face. "I'd say that's a good sign. Wouldn't you?"

I can't keep the big dopey smile from my expression. "A

very good sign. Did you kiss her good night?"

"I might have. But I wouldn't have minded if she'd let me kiss her again."

I shorten the distance between us. "Really? How many times did you kiss her?"

"Just the once. On the cheek." His grin remains in place, his eyes glinting with challenge.

My eyes widen in feigned surprise. "On the cheek? How do you know she doesn't just want to be friends? Sounds pretty platonic to me."

Troy leans forward and traces his lips along the curve of my jaw. "I promise what I feel for her is far from platonic." His low growl of a voice vibrates through my body, teasing me, seducing me. I let loose a small whimper.

I turn my head a tiny bit, but that's all it takes.

Our mouths reunite, leaving no question as to how un-platonic our relationship is, the kiss even hotter than the one we shared at the lake.

And all thoughts of how incompatible our wants are, how he needs more than I could ever give him, leave my mind—for now.

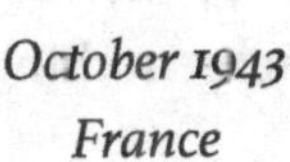

ANGELIQUE

October 1943
France

Christian, the tall, hazel-eyed SOE agent standing before the chair I am handcuffed to, appears to be quite pleased with himself.

He looks as if he belongs in the elegant hotel room. His clothes are clean and well tended to. Not a single bruise mars his near-perfect features. He is not a man who was tortured to reveal his secrets. Quite the opposite.

"When was it that we last met?" Christian asks in English. He smiles at me as though we are old acquaintances, but there's something poisonous about the curve of his lips. "Right, I believe it was back in April. Oh, and before I forget, Allaire and Élise send their regards."

Oh, God. Poor sweet Élise, my friend. She fell in love with Allaire, an English spy, the leader of the *Cashmere* network, and helped him because she wanted to save her country. For her, it was about love and duty. Two things Christian knows nothing about.

I glare at the man with the accent of an English aristocrat. Prior to the war, members of the upper class sided with the Nazis both in general principal and with their anti-Semitic views. The group of aristocrats tried to convince the British parliament to make peace with Hitler. They didn't see the vile monster for what he is. They viewed him as a saviour, much like the Germans and Austrians still do.

I don't doubt the lure of money and power were also instrumental to Christian's actions. Money and power have divided France. Collaborators have willingly turned on friends and neighbours for money and prestige. Christian might be English, but he is nothing more than a traitor to both countries.

He continues staring, a patient smile on his face.

I glare at him with all the loathing that simmers beneath the surface.

The scowl on Krüger's face is not that of a patient man. "She refuses to talk." The words are spoken in English.

Christian walks leisurely to the window and peers out. "Carmen, things will go much easier for you if you cooperate." He pivots to face me. "Is it all right if I call you Carmen? It suits you better than Angelique. That name suggests you are an angel, and we both know you are anything but that."

He strides back to the desk and picks up the large stone paperweight. He examines it for a moment and returns it to the desk. "The Gestapo has arrested all the agents in the *Cashmere* network. Thanks to one of the agents who landed in France a few months ago, I secured the SOE's list of all the agents, their aliases, code names, and where they were sent to work. The fool had it on his person when he came to France. Baker Street is slipping in its standards lately with their new recruits."

Christian shakes his head as if that really is a shame. "Although given the life expectancy of an agent landing in France, at this point they can only recruit simpletons. No one else is ridiculous enough to agree to do the job.

"I can't say I was too disappointed by the turn of events. But the list only contained the names of the agents in the *Cashmere* network, and you and I both know there are many more networks in France. You've been working with a satellite network as well as with several rebel groups." He leans against the desk behind him and bends forwards, violating my personal space. "We want from you the names of everyone involved." His foul breath assaults my face, his low voice confiding and cruel.

I stare at him, grappling at everything he's telling me. He really believes I am the coward that *he* is? That I would sell out those who are fighting against Hitler?

"We also want the locations of the safe houses," Krüger adds, his voice sharp and curt.

He knows? He knows my original role in the region? I was supposed to locate safe houses close to the parachute drop sites and landing zones. He would only know that if the list also contained the agents' roles in France. But what Krüger and Christian don't seem to realise is, my role in France changed once Johann moved into the farmhouse. Thank God they don't know I've been harbouring escapees as well.

I remain silent, the tension in the air growing tauter with each passing second.

A muscle in Christian's jaw twitches, signalling his patience is a fine wire about to snap. He steps up to my chair, his lean body looming over me. "You're a pretty woman. I bet it is useful in getting what you want." He tenderly traces the rough pad of his thumb along my jaw and presses it into my split lip.

A sharp pain radiates from the wound, and I wince, remembering a moment too late not to give him the satisfaction of knowing he's hurting me.

He smears the blood along my lower lip. "So pretty indeed," he coos and lets his gaze drop to my breasts.

My stomach turns violent at the hunger in his eyes. I jerk my arms up to cover myself. The handcuff binding my wrist to the chair brings the movement up short.

Christian reverses a step. "You can undo her handcuffs." He turns to the desk and picks up something. His body blocks whatever is in his hand.

The clanging of keys comes from behind me. The stocky Gestapo agent approaches my chair, and with a click, my other wrist is freed. I rub it, attempting to ease the discomfort.

"Will you tell me what I want to know?" Christian asks, his voice low as if sharing a secret, his tone pleasant like we're old friends.

I don't respond, my chin lifted in a stubborn tilt.

He grabs my wrist and yanks me to my feet. His other hand is kept behind his back. "I hope you don't mind a little blood on your desk, Captain Krüger."

Christian jerks me to the desk and puts my right hand flat on the cool dark wood. I attempt to pull my hand away. He's not an imposing man, but he is stronger than I am.

Another set of hands holds on to my arms from behind, pinning me in place. Christian lifts his hand, revealing the stone paperweight in it.

I slip into my memory of Johann, but not fast enough. The paperweight slams down hard on my hand, and a blinding pain roars up my arm. I cry out.

When the Gestapo agent hurt the wound on my leg, I

had been able to disappear into my mind and minimise the pain I felt. This time, I am not so lucky. My body is drained of all energy, weary from pain, and I'm unable to mentally separate myself from the world. The persistent thrumming in my head, the hurt of Christian's betrayal, might have something to do with that too.

"The names and the locations, Carmen," Christian barks, the feigned pleasantry leached from his tone.

Forty-eight hours. That's how long my SOE instructors told me to hold out before saying anything if captured. Hopefully in that time, word would get out to the network that the agent had been arrested. Plans could be changed, keeping all those involved safe, preventing the Germans from converging on a mission. Allowing individuals to escape the region and avoid being caught.

Forty-eight hours. That's how long I need to endure the torture in silence.

As best as I can estimate, it's been only three hours.

I shake my head, no longer keeping up the pretence that I don't speak English.

He lifts the paperweight and brings it down again and again and again, crushing delicate bones in my hand. The faint crunch of my bones and the pain in my hand has me close to vomiting on the desk. Nausea twists and churns in my belly.

"I won't repeat it," Christian says. "The names and locations. Now."

I shake my head once more.

Forty to fifty more hours. I just have to survive that long.

He lifts the paperweight, but instead of hitting my hand, he strikes my temple. Hard.

And I spiral into a world of darkness.

13

JESSICA

August, Present Day
Maple Ridge

Tuesday after work, I bike to the grocery store with Bailey in the trailer. Gray clouds hunker in the distance with the promise of an evening storm.

We enter the store.

I grab an empty basket, and we head for the produce section, with me constantly reinforcing Bailey's positive behavior with treats. I select several ripe peaches and put them in my basket.

As I glance up, I catch a short, gray-haired woman staring at me from the other side of the display. A deep chasm forms between her eyes. She doesn't say anything. She just looks at me as if Medusa has strolled through the store and turned her to stone, hatred frozen in her expression.

An uneasy feeling settles in my bones and sets up residence in my stomach. I open my mouth to say something. What? I don't know.

She turns and walks away, glaring at me over her shoulder one last time.

She disappears around the corner—and I get a sinking sensation it's not Bailey, who's wearing her *Service Dog in Training* vest, the woman has issues with.

She knows. I don't know who the hell she is, but the reverse isn't true. She has read Cora's article, has memorized my picture as if it were an FBI Most Wanted poster.

I hurry through the store, not wanting to risk someone else recognizing me, and collect everything I need for tonight's dinner.

I walk to the haircare aisle and stop in front of the boxes of hair color. My roots will need touching up soon, but maybe instead of blond, I should select a different color. Something that will make me look less like Savannah or Jess. Something that won't draw attention—so no pink or purple or blue.

The clatter of a shopping cart from the end of the aisle jerks my attention that way. A woman pushes her cart toward me, a dark-haired toddler sitting in the seat. The back of the little girl's head resembles Amelia's at that age. My heart clenches to the size of a walnut, the ache something fierce.

Gotta get out of here.

Gotta get out of here.

Gotta get out of here.

The hair color can wait for another time.

I hurry out of the aisle and join the line for self-checkout, my head kept down to hide the scars on my face.

I PEDAL UP THE DRIVEWAY TO MY HOUSE AND DISMOUNT AT the backyard gate. Now that I'm home—my safe place—the tension in my muscles, the panic vibrating under my skin, eases.

I lift the trailer cover and let Bailey out. She intently sniffs the ground under the hedge.

"What is it, Bailey? A rabbit?" I open the gate and let her into the garden. "I'm just putting the bike away. I'll be right back."

She knows the routine by now, but repeating it to myself helps me. Makes me feel like I have a little more control over my life.

I wheel the bike and trailer to the garage and unlock the side door.

Troy's truck turns onto the driveway. I wave at him and push my bike and trailer into the garage. I come out carrying the grocery bags and find him standing by his truck door.

"I wasn't expecting you yet," I say, walking to him. He's three hours early.

"I know." He smiles at me but stays beside the truck. "I'm taking Nova and Butterscotch to the lake. Do you and Bailey want to come with us?"

"Okay. Let me just put these groceries in the house first and get changed. I'll be quick."

"Go ahead."

Bailey follows me into the house and sits patiently by my side while I put away the food that needs to be refrigerated. The rest can wait on the kitchen counter until we get back. I go upstairs and swiftly change into shorts and a T-shirt.

Bailey and I step out of the house. She's no longer wearing her training vest. She gets to be a regular dog for now.

Troy is still by his truck, the rear passenger door open, and he's talking to Nova. She's buckled in her car seat and holding a stuffed bunny that looks like it's been hugged one too many times.

"Hi!" She lifts her bunny for me to see. She's adorable and reminds me so much of Amelia at that age, I have to swallow past the tightening in my throat.

But the little girl means the world to Troy. I can't let my pain at missing Amelia ruin things for them. And it might do me some good to spend time with them together. "Hi, Nova. Is it okay if Bailey and I join you, Uncle Troy, and Butterscotch?"

"Hi!" she replies, which I interpret to mean yes. Maybe?

I bring Bailey to the other side of the truck and help her into the front. I climb in and sit so that she's between my legs, the typical location for service dogs when riding with their owner—unless the owner is driving. I give her a treat.

We pull into the beach parking lot ten minutes later to find it half-full. Troy and I click the leashes onto the dogs' collars. I carry the net bag holding an assortment of colorful beach-friendly toys to an open stretch of sand. He carries Nova.

The wind hasn't picked up yet beyond creating gentle waves on the lake, but the temperature has dropped a few degrees, making me glad I wore my cardigan.

Troy crouches to Nova's level. "You want to build the sandcastle there?"

Nova nods. She grabs a small plastic shovel and digs it into the sand. She flicks the shovel up, flinging clumps of sand into the air.

Butterscotch and Bailey get to work, digging in their own patches of sand. They, too, send it flying.

Chuckling at their zealous digging, I slip off my sneakers and socks and put them to the side. Troy does the same with his and helps Nova remove her cute little pink shoes.

Troy takes one bucket and fills it with water. He carefully pours it on the sand where we're working, making sure it's wet. He goes back to get some more water.

Nova scoops up a shovel full of wet sand. She walks the two feet to one of the buckets and dumps the sand into it. She repeats the cycle. Dig, toddle, dump.

I take one of the other buckets and fill it with sand like I used to do with Amelia. Instead of sadness taking root in me like I thought it would, joy slips in as I work.

"Should we make the sandcastle big enough for Butterscotch to live in?" I ask Nova. My smile is as big as the feeling of freedom that courses through my body.

She vigorously nods.

I don't relive my memories of building sandcastles with my daughter. This—building castles with Nova—is different. Instead of the briny ocean scent on the breeze, the air is rich with the soothing pine scent of the forest. The water isn't rushing up the beach as the tide advances. Seagulls aren't squawking overhead. Here, several ducks quack and bob on the water not far from us.

Troy returns with another bucket of water. His wicked grin is the only warning I get. He splashes the contents at me. Several cold droplets hit me in the face. I giggle-shriek and scramble away from him.

"Hey, you're not playing fair," I protest, the wide curve of my lips saying otherwise.

Nova jumps to her feet and giggles at my reactions. Troy flicks water at her, and she giggles louder.

Nova and I share an impish glance, and we both, by some unspoken agreement, lunge at him. He retreats a few feet into the water, his eyes alight with mischief.

We chase after him, still laughing. Nova attempts to splash him, but her water droplets don't go far enough.

"Watch and learn, Nova," I say and send a large wave at Troy. Water splashes his legs, abs, and chest. Droplets sparkle in the sun and travel down his hard body. *Lucky droplets.*

"That's the best you can do?" Troy taunts, his sexy grin turning me heated.

The dogs bark excitedly at our game, unable to join us because their leashes are attached to the spike in the sand. I'm sure if given a chance, they'd be in the water, splashing us.

Troy lunges toward Nova, scoops her up, and tosses her in the sky. Her squeaked giggles have me laughing even harder.

He lowers her to the sand. We call a truce and return to our sandcastle in progress. Nova crouches next to the hole that Butterscotch has been digging and starts digging there.

I'm about to help her, but Troy pulls me into his arms. One second, I'm smiling at him, grateful he invited me along. The next, his mouth is on mine, and he's reminding me how good we are together. My arms loop around his neck.

Troy deepens the kiss, but it only lasts a brief moment. He pulls away. The heat in his eyes tells me he would keep kissing me but that's not why we are here. We're here to spend time with Nova.

Grinning, we get back to building the sandcastle, talking to Nova and laughing with her as we work.

I pull my phone from my pocket. The lighting is perfect for the kinds of photos I want to take, with the sun shining behind Nova, haloing her head. Nova's expression as she works on the sandcastle with Troy is too cute not to take pictures of her.

I take a dozen photos of them together and of them separately, none with them looking at the camera. "Hey, you two," I say to gain their attention. They turn my way, and I take several more photos of them together, but this time with them smiling at the camera.

"What an adorable family," a female voice gushes not far from us.

I glance up from the phone. A couple in their sixties is walking toward us. They're holding hands, their gazes on us, and they're smiling.

Heat flushes my cheeks. I pretend I didn't hear them, lower to my knees, and pat the sand on the side of the castle. Troy doesn't seem to hear her as he doesn't say a word or react to her comment. Troy, Nova, and I aren't a family—mother and father and child. But I know someone who would like Troy to be part of her family with Nova.

It was obvious when I interviewed Olivia last month for the PTSD articles that she cares for Troy as more than just a close friend. Does she even know I'm here with Troy and her daughter?

I go back to working on the sandcastle, but my mind keeps returning to how cute Troy and Nova are together. She's not his daughter, but he clearly loves her like one. He really is great with kids. I saw that in the spring while he was playing street hockey with the kids in Simone and Lucas's neighborhood.

Troy is meant to be a father, and he wants to be one eventually.

He has frequently told me he loves me, and I don't doubt it. But maybe he's meant to have children with someone else. Maybe in time he'll realize that too.

He should be with a woman who isn't afraid to give him kids. Who isn't afraid of possibly losing someone she loves.

A woman who has lost someone she loves and has come out the other side stronger. Like Olivia has.

14

TROY

August, Present Day
Maple Ridge

I park my truck in Jess's driveway. Nova is passed out in her car seat after the fun we had at the beach. The wind has picked up with the storm rapidly approaching.

"You gonna be okay?" I ask Jess.

She smiles, a teasing spark in her eyes visible in the dim light of the cab. "It's just a storm. I think I can weather it."

She leans over the console and kisses me. I make the most of it and capture her mouth, not letting her get away with only a quick peck on my cheek or my lips.

I'm not even halfway satisfied when we pull apart. I could keep on kissing her. And I will once I've dropped Nova off at her home.

Jess glances behind me at the sleeping little girl. "You two are adorable together. She loves you." Jess's voice

98

catches, and she smiles. It's not one of her full smiles, but it's breathtaking all the same.

"I love her too. She's a sweet kid. It kills me that she doesn't remember her father." I took that from Nova when I couldn't help him. I should have pressed harder for Colt to get help, should have pushed for him to see that real men can go to therapy.

Jess threads her fingers with mine. "That's not your fault, Troy. What you can do is make sure she continues to feel loved. And when she's older, you can tell her all about her father." Jess gently squeezes my fingers, a slight tremor in her touch. "I bet you've got tons of funny stories about your time growing up together."

I nod. Do I ever. "I'm sure if Colton were alive, he wouldn't want Nova to hear many of them. They're funny as fuck. Hell, Olivia probably wouldn't want her to hear them since Olivia was involved in many of the escapades. There's a reason the three of us earned the nickname The Three Musketeers."

"Those...those are the best kind of stories. Especially when she's older. They'll help keep his memory alive. That, and continuing what you're doing. Spend a lot of time with her." Jess releases my hand. "You should probably get her back to her mom."

"I'll be right over after I drop her off." I kiss Jess, taking a little longer than I should, knowing I'll have a hard time leaving if I don't go now.

Jess pulls away, gives me a quick smile, and climbs out of the truck. She and Bailey walk along the pathway to the front door. Jess unlocks it, and they go into the house. The porch light flashes on and off, Jess's signal that she has reactivated the security alarm.

I reverse out of the driveway and drive to Olivia's house. Thickening storm clouds darken the sky. I arrive to find the living room light on, a glowing strip peeking between closed curtains. I parallel park on the street and let Butterscotch out of the truck.

"Hey, little princess," I say to Nova. Her eyes remain shut. "We're home." She looks so sweet and peaceful. I hate to wake her up.

I unbuckle her seat belt and slide her arm through the harness. Nova blinks her eyes open. "Hey, sleepyhead."

She was holding her stuffed bunny when I put her in the car seat. Now, it's half dangling off the seat. I hand it to her.

She grabs her bunny in one hand and stretches her arms to me. I scoop her up, and her arms automatically go around my neck in a hug, her bunny dangling down my back.

Nova rests her cheek on my shoulder. She smells sweet, like fruit and the mountains rolled up in a pint-sized package. I kiss the top of her head, her warm body held snuggly against my chest.

Butterscotch and I make our way along the path to the front door. I open it and step inside. "We're back," I call out.

Rock music comes from the kitchen, too loud for Olivia to hear me.

"Should we see if we can make your mommy jump?" It was something I used to enjoy doing when Olivia, Colton, and I were kids. I only had to walk into the room Olivia was in, say something while she was preoccupied, and she would shriek.

Nova shifts in my arms, her head moving from my shoulder, and she looks toward the kitchen. "Yes!" She giggles, but not loud enough for her mom to hear her.

"How was quilting club, Aramis?" I ask, walking into the kitchen.

Olivia is standing at the sink. A startled scream escapes her, and she practically jumps to the ceiling.

She whirls around and clutches her wet hand to her chest, leaving a damp print on her T-shirt. "Fire truck you, Athos." She laughs and grins at her daughter. "Hey, sweetheart. How was the beach?"

"Fun!" Nova exclaims, her squealed voice filling the room. Her arms go up as if she's showing us just how much fun she had.

Olivia grabs a tea towel and dries her hands as she closes the distance between us. "Did you have fun with Uncle Troy?"

"Yes!"

"I bet you're covered with sand." Olivia pokes her in the tummy, and we're rewarded with a giggle. "Should we give you a bath before dinner?"

"Yes!"

"You want Uncle Troy to help?" Olivia asks.

"Yes!" Nova points to Butterscotch. "And doggy!"

Olivia kisses her daughter on the forehead. "I hope you're not expecting him to join you in the bathtub. How 'bout he watches from the sidelines?"

I doubt Butterscotch would complain about joining Nova in the bath, but the room would be a disaster by the time those two were finished.

We head to the bathroom. While Olivia fills the tub with water, I send Jess a quick text.

> Me: I'm helping to give Nova a bath
> first and then I'll be over.

"So how was quilting club?" I inquire again since Olivia never answered the question earlier.

"It was good. But since it's summer, only a few people

were there. We discussed possible themes for this year's charity Christmas quilts."

"What charity are you supporting this time?"

"We haven't decided yet. The final decision will be made in the fall, once all the members are back from their vacations."

"Well, you know my mom will be bidding on yours." I lower Nova to the floor.

"That's because your mom's super sweet. Or a super-competitive bidder."

"Mom happens to love your quilts." I check the water temperature and dump several of Nova's bath toys into the tub.

Olivia removes Nova's clothes. "I swear you've got a beach-full of sand in your hair. It's a good thing its hair-washing night." She lifts her up and lowers her into the tub.

Nova sits and splashes the water, sending it everywhere. Warm droplets soak through my T-shirt.

I sit on the closed toilet seat since there's not a lot of room in here. Olivia suds up Nova's hair, making funny shapes with it, even though Nova can't see them. We laugh at them. She giggles and splashes.

Butterscotch props his paws on the rim of the tub and barks. That only makes Nova giggle harder and makes it more difficult for Olivia to wash her squirming daughter.

I chuckle, the deep sound echoing off the bathroom tiles. Being with Olivia and Nova like this helps dull the pain I often feel at the loss of my best friend. It's like he's here in the room, smiling at us, much like he would've been smiling at Olivia and Nova if he were alive and helping Olivia clean their daughter.

I take one of her colorful rubber fish and push it through the water like a boat while making goofy noises. Nova laughs so hard, she almost slips under the water.

My chest aches at how much I enjoy moments like this—with a little kid around. Moments I might never have with Jess.

Once Nova is clean and rinsed off, Olivia dries her and dresses her in her pj's.

"You want to join us for dinner?" Olivia asks me as I carry Nova downstairs. A loud noise crackles the air outside as lightning splits open the sky. Nova covers her ears. Butterscotch whimpers.

"Sorry, I can't. Jess is expecting me."

Olivia winces, and her lips press into a flat line for a fraction of a second. "You really want to go out in that?" She jerks her head toward the front door. "It sounds pretty bad out there."

The wind is howling something fierce, and I don't have to check out the window to know the rain is coming down in diagonal sheets. Butterscotch won't be too impressed if he has to go outside.

But I also have no intention of standing up my girlfriend because of a little rain.

"I'll be fine." I have Jess's warm body to look forward to. And her kisses will definitely heat me up.

I kiss Nova on the top of her head. "Bye, little princess. I had fun at the beach. Be good for your mommy, and I'll see you soon." I wave at her.

She waves back, flashing me her toothy grin. "Bye-bye, Troy."

I crouch and hoist Butterscotch into my arms. "Don't worry," I tell him. "You'll be okay. I'll dry you once we get to Jess's." He peers at me with remorseful round eyes, no doubt telling me he wouldn't be getting wet if I'd left him at her house when we dropped her and Bailey off.

Usually, rain doesn't bother him. It's the combination of

rain with thunder and lightning and high winds he has a problem with.

"Let me get him a towel so he doesn't have to get too wet." Olivia rushes off to the laundry room before I have a chance to tell her not to worry about it, her daughter in her arms.

Butterscotch flashes me a look that implores, *At least she gets it.*

Olivia and Nova return with Nova's Eeyore hooded towel. I put it on Butterscotch, the hood covering his head. He barks as if to say, "Thank you," and the action makes it appear as if Eeyore nods.

Nova bursts out giggling.

"You look adorable, Butterscotch," Olivia says. "Eeyore always was my favorite Winnie-the-Pooh character." She puts her hand on my arm. "Call me or text me once you get to her place, so I know you got there safely." She seems so uncertain, worried, her eyes wide, which doesn't make sense. I've driven in storms plenty of times. Colton had too, and he never got into an accident.

I kiss her on the cheek. "Don't worry, Aramis. I'll be fine. But if it makes you feel better, I'll text you."

"It would."

As predicted, the rain is coming down diagonally and the mountain air has chilled several degrees since we arrived. Lightning streaks across the dark sky, beautiful and potentially deadly. I head for my truck. Thunder booms overhead, and Butterscotch lets out a frightened bark.

"It's okay, little buddy," I tell him. "We're almost there." I keep my arms tight around him to make sure the towel doesn't whip off him in the wind and to reassure him he's safe.

The rain is hitting so hard, I'm not sure the towel will be much use. I jog to the truck.

I'm drenched by the time I get there. I open the front passenger door and put Butterscotch on the seat, the towel still covering him. I close the door and jog to the driver's side, the force of the wind fighting against me.

I get into the truck. Butterscotch is free of the towel and appearing mighty smug. He's dry and I'm not.

But the joke's on him, because I'm going home to the best woman in the world—even if maybe there's a possibility we'll never have what I just shared with Nova.

15

JESSICA

August, Present Day
Maple Ridge

I hit Send on the email to Theresa with the link to her wedding photos. I finished editing the last of them a few minutes ago, the entire time itching to put the photos aside and resume reading Angelique's journals.

From my book bag on the kitchen table, I pull out the journal I'm currently transcribing. Excitement vibrates through my body. Excitement to return to her story. Excitement to find out the answers to so many questions.

My doorbell rings, the noise barely heard over the intense wind and my house creaking in protest at the storm. Rain hammers my windows, and for the tenth time since the storm started, I'm thankful I'm cozy in my secure little house and not outside.

Thunder booms overhead. Bailey barks, pressing her

106

warm body against me, either because she's scared or thinks I am.

"So much for finding out what happened to Angelique next," I say to no one in particular, the excitement waning to a slight disappointment. But given the storm outside, the doorbell can only mean one thing. It's probably not Delores. It's Troy.

A different kind of excitement sparks to life, and my heart does a fluttering little happy dance.

I stuff the journal back into the bag. Looks like I won't be able to give Anne the transcription when I visit her tomorrow as I had hoped. I still need a little longer. But soon. Soon I'll find out how Angelique escaped the war.

Bailey walks alongside me to the front door.

I open it. Troy's standing on the stoop, his wet T-shirt molding quite spectacularly to his chest and ab muscles, outlining their ridges and valleys. Water drips from his hair and down his face. In his arms is a bundle covered in a towel that resembles…

"Is that Eeyore?" I point to the blue-gray towel with the Winnie-the-Pooh character's head for the hood. Amelia had one like it, but hers was Pooh. An ache grips my heart, squeezes the air from my lungs.

I don't even know what happened to her towel. Lincoln probably threw it out—along with anything else that linked her to my past. My husband had willed the house and all its contents to him. He'd left me nothing. And I hadn't been in the position to protest the will from prison.

Troy steps inside my house, and I shut the door. Bailey barks at the bundle in Troy's arms. The bundle barks a reply.

I lift the hood, revealing the cute golden cavapoo. "Love the new jacket, Butterscotch." Compared to Troy, he's relatively dry. The rain had only started to soak through the towel in a few places.

Troy puts Butterscotch on the floor and pulls me to him. Water seeps through my shorts and T-shirt where we're pressed together and plasters them to my skin. His clothes might be cold and wet, but the heat of his body causes mine to sizzle.

"We should probably get you out of these wet clothes. I wouldn't want you to get a chill." I take half a step back and scoot the hem of his T-shirt up his defined abs.

He grins wickedly at me, and I know without a doubt, dinner is going to be delayed.

He pulls the fabric over his head.

"Maybe we should go to my bedroom so I can warm you up." The pitch of my voice drops.

"Good plan." He takes my hand. "Sorry I'm so late," he says on the way upstairs. "Nova was covered in sand, and I stayed to help give her a bath."

Something cold twists inside me. I shove it aside. He stayed to help Olivia give her daughter a bath, but I'm the one he's with now.

A sweet domestic image of a family flashes in my mind. A mother and a father and a child. The loving family I never really had with my late husband. The family Troy wants to have one day.

A family I'm not sure I can give him.

I push that all aside. Troy is here with me now, and I plan to make the most of it.

We go into my bedroom and kiss in the way that wasn't possible at the lake. Our tongues glide and dance and taste. I slip my hand past the waistband of his shorts. His length is hard and ready for me, the skin warm and velvety.

I run my hand along it. Troy moans into my mouth. I swallow the delightful sound. I'm the one he'll be making love to. That much I do know. I have no doubt that for now he loves me. Like I...

I push the rest of that thought from my mind and help him rid us of our clothes. We climb onto the bed.

He lightly strokes my body, sending need quivering through me. I stroke the ridges and valleys of his chest, playing with the splattering of dark hair there.

We don't rush things. Our kisses and touches and moans are the orchestra, the emotional music scoring a movie. He plays my body like a well-tuned violin. Tears cloud my vision from the beauty of it.

His fingers trail down the front of my body, *down, down, down*. I watch them slip between us, slip between my bent legs. His gaze drops to his hand.

His fingers slide across the building wetness, spreading it over my mound and parted lips. He lowers his head to my breast, and his tongue toys with my nipple. Heat and blood and everythingness rush to my core, and I'm sent soaring skyward to the heavens and the stars.

"Oh, Goooooooood," I cry out. *Oh, God Almighty.*

It takes a second or two to gather my senses, and I smile, the movement languid and easy. "I want to ride you," I murmur, Troy's breath kissing my lips. "Long and slow." I tenderly press my mouth to his, a seductive dance, an unspoken promise.

A lazy smile full of heat curves across Troy's face, and he sits up, pillows propped behind him. I position myself so his swollen tip is pressed against my entrance and slide down him, taking him all in.

I move my hips in slow, deliberate circles, my eyes locked on Troy's. This moment—the achingly sweet communication between us without words—takes me further into uncharted territory.

And that...that thrills me and scares me.

Troy rests his hand on my bare hip and softly taps out ILU. We're on our sides, facing each other on the bed. "I forgot to tell you I have search-and-rescue training tomorrow night after PT with Lucas. So I'll be late coming here."

"That's okay. I'm meeting with Anne Carstairs tomorrow after work."

"She's coming to Maple Ridge?"

"No, I'm taking the bus to Ash Falls. I want to learn more about her great-aunt, and I'm curious what Anne remembers of her." I'm interested to find out more about the woman who had a secret life during the war. Even if that means I have to take the bus there at the risk of people recognizing me due to Cora's damn article.

I'm really hoping, though, I blend in—just another person on a bus, heading into town.

"How come you want to learn more about Iris?" Troy's finger stops tapping on my hip, and a series of emotions flicker on his face. They land mostly on surprised and confused, a small divot forming between his eyebrows. Then his lips sink into a sexy one-sided smile. "You planning on turning this place into a museum?"

I laugh. "Hardly. I'm just curious about her, especially after all the work I did clearing out her place and going through all those magazines."

"Did you find her diaries about all her long-lost loves? Men no one else knew about?" Troy chuckles, not realizing how close he is to the truth. I have to bite my lip to keep from blurting everything I know so far.

"Definitely no diaries about long-lost loves." Only the one...and I don't know what happened to Johann after the

Gestapo captured Angelique. Hell, I don't even know yet how she escaped them. I can't get back to the journals soon enough to keep reading and find out. "I'm just curious about her. If not for this house and Anne, I don't know where I would be." And that's the truth.

"You can use my truck. Garrett can give me a ride to the training. He'll be there too."

"You trust me to drive it after what happened last time?" I quirk the corner of my mouth, trying to infuse a little humor to soften the reality of those words.

Troy's thumb caresses my hip. "That accident could've happened to anyone. Maybe if the road hadn't been slick from the rain, you could've stopped and not gone through the guardrail."

"In that case, maybe I should take the bus. Then I won't have to worry about another Bambi jumping in front of me."

Troy's brow creases into a frown. "Or you can postpone seeing Anne until I can drive you to Ash Falls."

I run my fingers through his hair, attempting to erase his frown. "I can't rely on you to drive me everywhere, Troy. You're not my chauffeur. And I've waited so long to finally regain my independence."

He nods, still looking no happier than he did before. "What time's the bus scheduled to leave for Ash Falls?"

"I'm taking the four-oh-five bus after work and returning home on the nine thirty-one." Which will see me in Maple Ridge around eleven, and then I'll need to bike home. That's the only return bus scheduled after five.

"I guess you can't take Bailey with you."

"That's right." The unease I feel when she's not with me turns my skin itchy. "She's not a certified PSD, so she can't come on the bus." It's not enough she's training to be one.

Troy's thumb strokes along the curve of my hip and

down to my outer thigh. "Take my truck, Jess. I'd rather you take it than be without Bailey. You'll be tense the entire time she isn't with you."

I hate that he's right. I'll be constantly glancing over my shoulder, checking if the boogie man is watching me. That much hasn't changed since I moved to Maple Ridge. I'm still a work in progress. Bailey helps to ease some of that tension. Stroking her eases some of that tension.

"You borrowing my truck doesn't make you any less independent, Jess." Troy leans in and kisses my forehead. The tip of my nose. "And maybe I like the idea you'll be here when I return from the training session." His mouth brushes mine. "Otherwise, I'll have to wait until Thursday to see you. And then I'm away for the weekend again."

I laugh a soft rumble deep in my throat. "Are you going to pine for me if you don't see me tomorrow night?"

His eyes flash a devilish gleam, and he has me flat on my back, his hot body pressed against mine. "I'm absolutely going to pine for you. So much so that I'll get in trouble with the trainer, because I'm not paying attention to what she's saying."

I grin. "Well, then. I wouldn't want you to get into trouble."

But despite my amusement, the tightly wound fear that I'm making a mistake borrowing Troy's truck doesn't loosen.

Not because I'm worried I'll drive it off the road like I did with his old one.

It's a gut reaction—an unease in my bones—I can't explain.

16

ANGELIQUE

October 1943
France

Hazel laughs and straightens the yellow picnic blanket on the grass. It's been in our family for as long as I can remember. The edges are frayed, and we've had to patch up holes in it on more than one occasion. Around us, the hum of bees fills the air.

Giggles float from the other side of the hill, and two little girls with light-blond plaits skip into view. Both are wearing daisy crowns perched precariously on their heads.

The hum of the bees grows louder, more insistent.

Hazel's laughter is cut short, and she looks up at the sky. "Girls, get down," she screams and jumps to her feet.

She races to them as my eyes are drawn to the Luftwaffe planes flying towards us.

An icy wave sweeps through me, and I shiver uncontrollably. I attempt to stand, but my legs won't cooperate.

The peace from a moment ago is shattered by the loud drone of engines, the rat-ta-ta-ta of machine guns, the girls' screams, the panicked symphony of my heartbeat.

Bullets hit the ground. Dirt and grass and clover explode into the air. I reach out to the girls, but there is nothing I can do. Hazel and our daughters slump to the ground as if they are nothing more than discarded dolls.

I scream. And scream and scream. And shiver. Why am I so cold?

My nightmare fades, and I slowly become aware of the ache consuming my body. My head throbs. My hand throbs. Everything inside me throbs.

One eyelid flutters open. The other eyelid can barely move more than a fraction of an inch. I'm met by darkness and the smell of mould.

I'm not on the floor. That much I can tell. But the fabric under me isn't much better. It's rough and scratchy and doesn't smell of warmth. It smells of danger and death and hopelessness.

I cautiously push to sit with the hand that doesn't feel as if a tank drove over it. A rush of dizziness assaults me, and nausea tries to force me to lie down again.

My non-injured hand goes to my belly and the child growing there. My body might be aching, but I haven't lost my baby. Not yet, anyway. I take the lack of stickiness between my legs as a good sign.

A relieved breath escapes me, even though there is nothing to be relieved about. I didn't give Christian and Krüger the information they want, which means they won't give up trying to get it from me.

I cannot see my hand, but I can tell it's broken and swollen and bloodied. I cradle it to my body and lean back against the wall.

I blink away the forming tears. They won't do me any

good. They won't heal the wound. They won't take me away from here. They're just a waste of energy.

Sounds begin to seep into my awareness: the distant crying, perhaps from one prisoner; the groaning of another; the scurrying of tiny claws on stone. The latter noise is closer than I would like. I swiftly lift my feet onto the filthy mattress.

Faint light from the half moon spills through the barred windows, and my eyes slowly adjust to the darkness. Except there is nothing to see other than the bed and the metal door opposite the window.

Exhaustion ebbs and flows through me. I fight to keep my good eye open, but it proves to be too much. I succumb to the battle, my eyelids falling shut.

I JOLT AWAKE FROM A NEW NIGHTMARE. OR PERHAPS IT'S THE same one that has been repeating in my head from the moment I arrived. I don't know how long I've been sleeping, but the lazy fingers of dawn have since visited. A light wash of blue stretches beyond the barred window.

My head and body hurt, and I cannot bend my fingers of the injured hand due to the swelling and excruciating pain. My mouth is drought dry, and overwhelming nausea still keeps me company.

German male voices approach from the other side of the door. I cannot make out what they are saying. Something about taking the prisoner to Avenue Foch for interrogation, and that he has papers authorizing the move.

My cell door opens, and two soldiers enter. One is taller and broader in his chest and shoulders. The other is long and lanky. My vision is blurry. I cannot make out their faces.

"Can she walk?" the taller soldier asks. Recognition stirs at the sound of his voice, but the pounding in my head makes it difficult to figure out why.

"She wasn't able to when they brought her in yesterday." The other soldier sounds bored. "Do you have handcuffs for her?"

"From the looks of it, she doesn't need them. She barely looks like she can walk, never mind run."

The shorter soldier makes an amused sound. "French women are only good horizontal, anyway."

The taller, broad-shouldered soldier doesn't respond.

My vision slowly clears a little more. The shorter soldier approaches the bed, grabs the wrist of my damaged hand, and drags me to my feet. A vicious pain shoots through my hand and wounded leg. My vision flashes white and a half gasp, half shriek escapes me.

Forty-eight hours. That is all I have to last for, without saying a word, to keep everyone safe.

I have no idea how long I was passed out for. Have no idea how many hours I have left before I reach that number.

"She cannot leave here without handcuffs." The shorter soldier's breath is as foul as his disposition. His hand remains tightly clasped around my injured wrist, and I bite back a whimper.

The taller soldier produces the required handcuffs and steps into my line of vision. I gasp.

Johann's indifferent gaze flicks to me. The man I love is gone. In his place, is the enemy.

It's not him. I've seen Johann pretend to be something he isn't in front of other officers. It's how he has survived in the military for as long as he has. This level of indifference...it's not Johann. He loves me. I know he does. I've seen how he looks at me. That was not pretend.

Hope. That's all I have left. Hope that I am right. Hope that Johann is here to save me, to save his child.

Because without hope, I have nothing left to keep my heart beating. Nothing left to ensure my baby and I make it through the war.

"Hands behind you," Johann says to me in French, his voice crisp, harsh. There's nothing in his tone that reminds me of the man I love.

It's not really him. It's not my Johann.

The shorter soldier yanks my hands into position before I can brace myself for the pain, and I am unable to stop the whimper in time.

A wave of nausea hits me hard, but the soldier's hands on my wrists prevent me from doubling over.

He releases his grip, and Johann places the cold metal around my wrists. His calloused finger subtly caresses the skin on the inside of one wrist in a way that couldn't be accidental. The movement is so tender, it summons a flash of longing and memories of other times he touched me that way.

The moment ends as abruptly as it started, and the cuffs click shut. I flinch but don't dare to look at Johann, to see the cruelty in his eyes I have witnessed so many times in the enemy.

It's not really him. It's not my Johann.

The shorter soldier shoves me towards the cell door. I stumble. Johann grabs my arm, preventing me from sprawling onto the concrete floor, and allows me to get my footing.

He nudges me forwards, his hand on my shoulder. The action puts him between me and the other soldier.

They escort me out of the cell and down the corridor.

We walk through a maze of other corridors until we come to the prison entrance. Johann shows the soldiers on duty the papers that release me into his custody. I am to be delivered to a senior officer in Avenue Foch, Paris.

Not a single word is exchanged between us.

He dismisses the shorter soldier and hope spreads through my chest. My last car ride required three escorts. I had two when I was taken to the hotel suite where I was interrogated. Now I have only one. I do not believe it's because Johann does not see me as much of an escape risk. If there was another soldier waiting at the vehicle Johann came in, wouldn't he have come inside the prison to help retrieve me?

I want to ask him what is going on, but now is not the time to voice the question out loud. I hug tightly onto my hope like it's a warm blanket on a blustery autumn day.

Johann walks me to a black car that resembles one I have seen visit Jacques's vineyard on several occasions. I want to ask about Jacques, but I am also not ready to hear the truth. For just a few more minutes, I want to believe the man I consider to be my father is alive and back at the vineyard, harvesting grapes.

Johann opens the rear door of the car. "Get in." His tone is cool and brisk, a tone that is unfamiliar coming from him.

It's not really him. It's not my Johann.

Three soldiers march past but do not spare us a glance. The slap of their boots against the pavement has my body stiffening.

I half expect Johann to assist me into the car with a rough shove, to keep up the pretence, but he just waits for me to obey his command.

Nausea hits me hard again, sending my body reeling. I

double over, retching, but nothing comes up. No relief is provided. My body hurts more than before.

Be strong, I silently pray to my baby. *I'll do whatever I can to protect you.*

Johann braces my shoulder with one hand. The other hand rubs soothing circles between my shoulders. "Are you all right?" he asks in French.

The concern in his voice tucks in memories of the man who hid his Jewish friends from persecution. The man who talked lovingly about his father and his mother and his sister. The man who was broken after his best friend was executed for desertion.

I nod and straighten, breathing slowly through my nose.

I climb into the car and resist the urge to curl into a ball on the back seat. I'm tired. So very tired. The lack of desire to lie on the dirty prison bed and the nightmares prevented me from getting much sleep.

My cuffed wrists and injured hand make it impossible to get comfortable. I shift, resting my left shoulder on the seat.

Johann shuts the door and starts the engine. The silence in the vehicle is thick. It suffocates. Squeezes the air from my lungs. I lean the non-injured side of my head on the seat, my tender temple still throbbing.

I close my eyes and pretend I'm somewhere else. Someplace warm where there is no war. Perhaps a sunlit meadow covered with a blanket of bluebells.

The car stops. "I'm transporting the prisoner to Paris for interrogation," Johann explains in German. There's a rustle of paper.

Paris. Has everyone in the *Cashmere* network been taken to Avenue Foch to be interrogated? How long has the

Gestapo been in possession of the list Christian mentioned —assuming he was telling the truth about it?

How long have they been watching me?

The car moves forwards. "As soon as it is safe to stop," Johann says in English after a minute. "I will undo the handcuffs."

"Okay," I whisper, speaking in my native tongue for the first time in his presence.

The scenery soon changes from the once beautiful brick buildings of Dijon, now a stark reminder of the German infestation, to the soothing autumn colours of the countryside. There are no Nazi flags flapping in the wind. No Wehrmacht or SS or Milice inciting fear in the people on the streets.

If not for the scars in the ground caused by the bombings and machine guns, it would be so easy to forget about the war and the horrors of the occupation.

Eventually, Johann turns down a country road, a sentry of tall trees and bramble standing on either side of it. He drives a little farther and then stops. He kills the engine and gets out of the car. We're in the middle of nowhere, surrounded by little more than farms and open space.

17

JESSICA

August, Present Day
Maple Ridge

"This is my English grandmother, Hazel." From the wicker chair next to mine on the patio, Anne points at one of the pretty women in the black-and-white photo she's holding. The woman's in her late twenties with wavy shoulder-length blond hair. She's smiling at the camera, the curve of her lips carefree and wide.

"And this is my grandfather, Charles." Anne's finger slides to the man between the two women. He appears to be the same age as Hazel. His dark hair is short and slicked back. He's good-looking. I'll give him that even if he did cheat on Iris, his fiancée.

Anne points to the other woman in the photo. "And this is Auntie Iris."

She resembles a slightly younger version of her sister.

121

Same wavy bond hair. Same eyes. Same dimple. Same smile—except Iris has a more impish look to her expression.

I stare at the woman whom I've never met but admire so much. I guess in a way I have met her—within the pages of her journals. She appears as strong and beautiful as I've imagined her to be.

I want to reach out and touch her image as if she's the real flesh-and-blood woman standing before me, to say thank you for giving me the strength and idea to help Violet hide from her husband. I rein in the urge, eager to learn more about Iris. The Iris Anne knew and loved.

I'd be surprised if Anne didn't somehow feel the excitement humming through me at getting to talk to her about her great-aunt. "When was the photo taken?"

A butterfly flutters over to the nearby flowerbed. Bailey scrambles to her feet, the butterfly snaring her attention.

"Lie down, Bailey," I instruct her. She follows my command, and I reward her with a treat.

Anne flips the photo over. "August, 1939." Just prior to the start of World War II.

"Were Iris and Charles engaged then?" I ask and cringe at my mistake. As far as Anne knows, I shouldn't know that.

"You mean Hazel and Charles. No, from what Auntie Iris told me, they got engaged during the war and married a few months later. But the three of them had been friends for five or six years before that. It wasn't love at first sight. My grandparents' love for each other grew over time."

I wince on the inside at the version of the truth Anne had been told. She never knew about the heartache her great-aunt had suffered through after discovering her fiancé and sister in bed together.

Would Iris want the truth to come out now? She'd had

decades to tell Lizzie and Anne about what happened, but she chose to keep it a secret.

No, that's not true. She wrote it in the journals. Had Iris planned to give her niece the journals, only for her niece to die in the car accident before that could happen?

I pick up my glass of strawberry lemonade from the table. "What else did your great-aunt tell you about your grandparents?"

"They loved each other very much. And they fell in love with my mother the moment they saw her. They thought she was the best thing to happen during the war. The only good thing to happen."

"What else?"

"Other than that, Auntie Iris didn't talk much about my grandfather, other than saying he was a good man. I don't think she really got over losing him as a friend. She talked more about my grandmother. She would tell me all kinds of stories about when they were kids. My grandmother loved folklore and was positive fairies and other mythological creatures existed."

That fits with what I read in Angelique's journals. Johann's sister had believed in them too at one point.

"You mentioned Iris was fluent in French and German, and your great-grandfather had been an English diplomat in both Paris and Vienna. Did Iris ever visit France and Austria during the war or afterward?"

"Not that I know of. Definitely not during the war. I doubt she could have entered either country since she was a British citizen at the time. The Nazis would never have allowed it. She would've been killed. And after the war?" Anne shakes her head, her gaze directed skyward.

Not much longer before I'm finished transcribing the journals. Not much longer before I can share the truth about her great-aunt with her.

I know Anne will be even more proud of her great-aunt, at what Iris accomplished during the war, than Anne already is about the woman she did know. *God, I can't wait for her to find out the truth.*

"I don't think she ever mentioned going back to France or Austria," Anne ventures. "She might have and didn't think to tell me. And I didn't think to ask. She and my mother moved to the U.S. in 1949 or 1950."

Anne picks up a framed photo from the table and passes it to me as the gate to her backyard clicks open. The three women in the colored photo are all smiling. I recognize Anne. She looks to be in her early twenties. The older woman was in her seventies, and the woman in the middle could be in her forties. It's obvious the women were related.

"This is my mother." Anne points to the woman in the middle. She's blond like Anne, Iris, and Hazel.

"Hi, Catherine," Anne calls out cheerily, shifting my attention from the photo in my hand.

A tall blond woman Anne's age walks up the wooden porch steps. She has on yoga pants and a tank top that's snug on her curvy frame. "Hi, Anne." The pitch of her voice is high and has the singsong quality of a chickadee. "I'm sorry. I didn't realize you have a guest." She smiles, flashing her bleached-white teeth at us.

Anne rests her hand on my forearm. "Yes, this is Jessica." She turns to me. "Catherine is my neighbor."

"And her dear, *dear* friend." Catherine laughs, the girlish sound matching her chickadee voice. She gives me a once-over, and her gaze lands on my face. Her eyes widen a minuscule amount.

She quickly recovers her composure before Anne can catch her reaction and takes a seat next to her. "What are y'all talking about?"

"My great-aunt Iris," Anne says, apparently at ease with

her friend joining our conversation. "Jess bought her house a few months ago."

"So, you're the one." Catherine's tone switches from friendly to something a little chillier, but maybe I'm just imagining that. Her eyes seem to be locked on the scar by my mouth. I squirm on the seat as if I'm sitting under a microscope, waiting for her to dissect my past. The wicker creaks under me, loud enough to give away my discomfort at her scrutiny.

Anne looks fondly at the framed photo in my hand. "Iris was smart. Clever. Generous. Brave. And she was very much hands-on. She loved to do things herself, even when her right hand caused her trouble at times. Even more so when it became arthritic."

"Her hand?" *Oh no. The hand Christian hit with the paperweight?* I take a sip of the lemonade, growing more and more curious about the woman she remembers—and more and more disquieted by her neighbor.

"It was caught in some machinery during the war, and her hand was badly injured."

Machinery? More like the result of an English traitor who sold what little there was of his soul to the devil. Christian's greed and ambition cost a lot of people their lives. And it sounds as though he might have caused Iris to have only limited use of her hand.

The next hour is spent with Anne telling me all kinds of stories about her great-aunt. The great-aunt she knew growing up. Not the one who lived in occupied France for part of the war, and who helped to bring down the Germans and liberate the country.

The person Anne knew is obviously the same one who lives in the pages of the journals. Iris's spirit and courageous and caring soul never changed, even after everything she had survived through during the war.

I don't look at Catherine at all while Anne talks, and Catherine fortunately doesn't interrupt her. I'm vaguely aware of her pouring herself a glass of strawberry lemonade at one point, but other than that, I pretend she isn't sitting on the porch with us.

I get lost in Anne's fascinating stories about a woman I feel like I've gotten to know almost better than I know Anne. "And she never married here in the States or had any children?"

"No," Anne says, and my heart breaks for Iris. "She didn't have time to date when they first moved to the States, and after the loss of her sister, Hazel, my mother became the most important person in Auntie Iris's life. She didn't want to risk falling for a man who couldn't love her niece the way she did. I think as courageous as Auntie Iris was, she was afraid of loving someone who wasn't Lizzie—other than me later on. She had lost her sister and brother-in-law. I think she was afraid to risk her heart to anyone else and have it crushed when she lost them too."

That I can relate to only too well. Iris had been pregnant when the Gestapo captured her. The conditions of the war would have been enough for anyone to lose their baby. She was in love with her unborn child. Had that loss scarred her in the way losing Amelia has made me scared of giving my heart to yet another person?

My heart aches for Iris, and if she were alive, I would hug her. Hug her and thank her for all the sacrifices she made, especially during the war. I can only begin to imagine how much it changed her...like my past has changed me.

Anne's phone rings on the coffee table. She checks the screen and stands. "Sorry, I have to get this." She answers the phone and walks into the house—leaving me with Catherine.

"So, Jessica..." Catherine draws out both words. They roll unpleasantly from her tongue. If I didn't know better, I'd say she bit into an underripe lemon doused with paint thinner. "My husband is a retired cop." She glances briefly toward Anne's house.

I nod, having no idea what she expects by way of an answer. Congratulations? Good for you? I'm sorry?

"He's a good man. Hard working. Put his life on the line so many times to protect our community from scumbags." Her eyebrow rises on the last word.

She knows. She knows who I am...or was.

I have no idea where she's going with this. Okay, I do know. She's clearly on the Savannah-Townsend-killed-her-husband side of the fence, but I don't get what point she's trying to make.

I open my mouth to defend myself, but nothing comes out. Mostly because I know it won't make a difference. It won't change her mind.

"We used to have a little boy," she goes on, her voice turning into cracked ice. "He was the sweetest thing. But then one day a stray bullet struck him down. He died in my arms." I almost stop breathing at the last part. If there's one thing I can relate to, it's losing a child.

Not once does her voice soften while she's telling me that. If anything, it grows harder. Colder.

I close my eyes for a beat, searching for my own voice, her pain a screwdriver turning in my chest. "I'm sorry for your loss."

She releases a noise that's somewhere between a snort and a huff. "I'm sure you are. Your type generally is, aren't they?"

"My type?" The words barely make it past my suddenly parched mouth.

"My son died when an ex-convict decided money was

more important than my son's life." She stands abruptly. "Does Anne know who you are, Savannah?"

I slowly nod. *God, please tell me my being here won't end up hurting Anne.*

The door to the house opens, and Anne steps out. "Sorry about that."

The coldness on Catherine's face washes away, and she smiles at Anne as if she and I didn't just have that conversation. "I need to get back home. It was nice meeting you, Jess." Catherine's voice is, once more, that of a perky chickadee.

I nod again, the movement robotic this time. "You too." I stretch a smile on my face, which I hope doesn't look anywhere near as awkward as it feels.

Anne seems to buy it. She says goodbye to her friend and resumes telling me all kinds of stories about Iris.

I shove my hands under my thighs so she doesn't see they're shaking. It takes me a few minutes, but I eventually push my conversation with Catherine aside and focus on what Anne says, laughing along with her. I decide not to tell her about Catherine. It's best not to make a big deal out of it—but I won't visit Anne again here and risk making things difficult for her.

It's getting dark by the time I drive home, my thoughts full from everything Anne told me. I focus on that and only that. There's so much Anne doesn't know yet about her great-aunt. So many things involving Iris the world has no idea about.

Things the world should know.

There are books published about some of the more well-known female SOE and OSS agents: Virginia Hall, Nancy Wake, Odette Sansom, Andrée Borrel, Lise de Baissac, Yvonne Rudellat, and so many others. But so far, I haven't seen Iris's contribution to the war mentioned.

The journalist in me—the one responsible for the World War II research I've done to date—wonders if I could write a nonfiction book about Angelique's time in France. But that would require me traveling to London and France and possibly even Austria and Germany to locate as much documentation as possible. Some of it might even need to be translated to English. I can't rely on only the journals to write Iris's story.

It would require me leaving my safe haven of Maple Ridge. I'm not ready for that yet. Maybe I won't ever be.

And the idea of writing a nonfiction book sounds daunting, especially if it's based on history.

But maybe I don't have to write a nonfiction book to acknowledge the sacrifices Iris made for her country and king. When I first moved to Maple Ridge, I told Delores I was writing a thriller. The next thing I knew, the lie took root, and several people now think I'm actually writing one—including Simone, Zara, and Emily.

I told them the thriller was on pause while I did the renovations. The excuse was so I didn't have to write said thriller.

But why not write a novel? A historical novel based on what's in the journals? Some of the World War II historical novels I've read were based on real-life people.

For the first time in months, an idea I've had makes sense. I could really see this for me—I can feel it. The fulfillment I'd gain from writing the story.

Is this the purpose I've been seeking?

My blood thrums with the same excitement as earlier. Excitement that I now have a new purpose—which hopefully will get me further than wedding photography. Excitement and a *need* to do this. A need to show the world just how amazing Iris Bromfield was. To give her the recognition she so rightly deserved.

And then I can give Anne not only the journals and their transcriptions—I can give her the novel manuscript. She would have final say if I could query the book to agents...assuming it was worthy of that. It's one thing to write an article about PTSD and the impact it has on the individual and their family; it's another to write a novel.

I don't even know where to start.

But I know someone who does. Garrett.

I can't tell him what I'm writing though. I can't tell Troy or anyone else either. The subject of my novel will need to remain a secret until after I've shown it to Anne—and that's only if she lets me show it to anyone else.

I'm going to do this. I'm really going to do it.

You can't write a novel. You can't do anything right.

The words slithering through my thoughts are in my dead husband's voice.

You're not smart enough to write a novel. It takes a skill you don't have.

"You're wrong," I tell myself. Or him. "I can do this. It won't be easy, but I am a good writer. I have awards stating as much."

I push the self-doubt aside. The desire to write the story tingles on my tongue, pulsates through my veins. I'm smart. I can learn to write a novel. With the right guidance and resources, I know I can do this. It won't be easy, but I can't improve if I don't at least try.

I check the time on the truck dashboard. Troy and his brothers won't be home yet from their training. I'll have to wait until tomorrow to talk to Garrett.

My phone rings. I accept the call.

"Hey, how're things going?" Troy's voice comes through the truck's speaker. A car drives past me, heading toward Ash Falls.

"Good. I'm almost in Maple Ridge."

"Any trouble?" Worry colors his voice, noticeable even over the phone. Unlike the day of the accident, the road to Ash Falls isn't empty of traffic. Nor is there a steep slope on either side of it. If a deer does dart onto the road, the outcome won't be like last time. I won't be stranded overnight in a storm.

"No. Things are good."

"Okay. I'll see you soon." The worry in his voice diminishes to a fine wisp but doesn't entirely go away.

My mouth widens into a smile. "I'll be waiting for you."

"In your sexy purple bra and panties?"

I choke out a chuckle. "You'll just have to wait and see."

18

TROY

August, Present Day
Maple Ridge

"Hey, Boss," Lance calls out, his voice muffled by the shrill noise from the electric screwdriver as one of the men on my crew fastens a new cabinet to the wall behind me. I look up from the iPad in my hands as Lance comes into the kitchen from the hallway. "There's a cop at the front door. Says he wants to talk to you for a second."

"Did he say what he wants to talk to me about?"

"Nope. Just said it wasn't an emergency. He's outside."

"Thanks." I walk to the front door and open it.

The officer is standing on the path, his back to the house. The door clicks shut behind me, and the cop turns.

Noah. The last person I was expecting to see.

I inwardly roll my eyes at Lance. He knew damn well it

was Noah. I'm sure they even chatted for a few minutes before Lance came to get me.

Noah smiles and gives me a chin-nod greeting. "Hey, Troy. Hope I'm not interrupting anything."

"Not at all. What's up? Is there a problem?" I can't think of anything. But for all I know, a neighbor called in a complaint because they felt my crew was making too much noise.

I walk down the steps to join him on the path. His cruiser is parked in front of the neighbor's house.

"I was in the neighborhood on a call and noticed your truck on the street. I've been meaning to talk to you about Jess and the renovations you two were doing on her house."

Not where I thought this conversation was headed. "Sure. What about them?"

"How are they going?"

"Not great. I haven't been able to work on them while my shoulder's healing." Guilt kicks me in the ass over that. My damn shoulder has put Jess's renovations well behind schedule. "Why? What's up?"

Jess has all the necessary building permits. There's no reason for a cop to worry himself about the renovations.

"Avery and I have been talking, and we were wondering what we can do to help Jess with her house. So she doesn't have to wait too long to finish it. After everything she's been through, we want to do this for her." Noah rocks back on his heels, and his expression shifts, the corners of his mouth tilting down. "Avery told me how hard it was for her mother in the beginning after leaving her abusive husband."

"That would be great. Thanks. I'll talk to my brothers and see what I can coordinate with them. I'm sure they'd be happy to help too." Every little bit we can get done will hopefully move Jess closer to her goal of seeing her daughter again—if I can convince both Jess and her sister-in-law that Jess is a worthy mother figure, even if she's no longer legally Amelia's mother. Convince them Jess deserves the love kids willingly share.

I check over my shoulder to make sure none of my crew has stepped out of the house we're working on. I don't want anyone to overhear what I have to talk to Noah about. "Can I ask you something?"

"Sure, what?"

"After Jess moved to Maple Ridge, she saw what people were saying online about Savannah Townsend. There're a lot of theories about who killed her husband, and plenty of people still believe she was responsible." I glance down the sidewalk to where an older man is walking his dog.

I drop the volume of my voice so only Noah can hear me. "Do you think there's anyone at the station who might have an issue with Jess if word got out she was Savannah?"

"You mean, would anyone at the station think she's a cop killer?" His gaze drops to the flowering bush at the base of the steps for a beat and returns to mine. "There's probably one guy I can think of. But so far, he hasn't made any public statements accusing Savannah of killing a cop. Or at least no comments I know of. But he has been known to spout off a conspiracy theory or two since I joined the force."

"Can you tell me his name?"

Noah narrows his eyes. "What are you planning to do if I tell you?" Suspicion sharpens his tone enough for me to know what he's thinking.

I raise my hands. "Nothing. I'm not gonna push him like I did with Wilson. Lesson learned. But I'd rather have a heads-up in case people discover Savannah Townsend is living in Maple Ridge." I don't need to remind Noah what will happen once the town's grapevine catches wind of the news. It won't take long before his colleagues will also hear about it.

"If I think he's going to be a problem, then I'll warn you and Jess. But until then, I have to assume he won't do or say anything—illegal or otherwise. After what happened with Wilson and Dunbar, the police department is under scrutiny."

"Okay. You might be right. Let me know if you hear anything. Jess doesn't need to be blindsided. And I'll get back to you about the renovations once I've talked to my brothers."

"Just promise me you won't do anything foolish, Troy."

"I won't."

Noah shakes his head, but I can tell he's a step away from rolling his eyes. He knows full well I haven't promised him shit. "I won't" could mean anything—including me doing the opposite of what he asked.

19

———

JESSICA

August, Present Day
Maple Ridge

The day after my visit with Anne, I leave the office for lunch and go for a bike ride. Soon, I'm on the outskirts of town...and before I know it, I arrive at Garrett's house.

I didn't intend to come here, but ever since last night, when I decided to write a novel, I haven't been able to think of much else.

"Sit," I instruct Bailey. She parks her butt on Garrett's front stoop, and I reward her with a treat. The metal loop on the back of her *Service Dog in Training* vest, where the leash is attached, glints in the sunlight.

The house is nothing like I would expect for a multiple *New York Times* bestselling author. It's smaller than I imagined, but the bungalow is also larger than my home and more spread out.

136

And secluded...but that's mostly due to the size of his property. There's a considerable amount of space between his house and the neighbor's. The tall hedges and trees, the shrubbery and blossoming rock gardens, the brick path leading to the backyard, all of it fills the sizable front yard and adds to the secluded ambience.

I have no idea if Garrett is home. I'm hoping he is. I biked all this way and he doesn't exactly live close to the main part of Maple Ridge. As it is, I won't have much time before Bailey and I have to return to work.

I probably should have phoned first.

I press Garrett's doorbell and wait for him to answer, but there's no sound from inside.

I really should have phoned first.

Troy and Zara have mentioned that Garrett is a morning person. He gets up at five thirty so he can get in a heavy word count before lunch. If that's true, he's been writing for over five hours.

The front door is flung open, and a series of emotions flickers in Garrett's expression, ending with a smile that unfurls across his face. "Hey, Jess. Bailey." He looks behind me. "What are you doing here? Where's Troy?"

"At a worksite. I'm on my lunch break and wanted to talk to you about what books you recommend for writing a novel." I figure that shouldn't take too long.

I could have waited a few more days to ask him, but I'm dying to start work on the novel.

"You biked here?" The widening of Garrett's eyes tells me he recognizes that wasn't easy for me, especially in the growing heat of the day. But if this were San Diego, it would be a helluva lot hotter than this. Of course, the terrain would have been flatter, so there's always that.

"I did."

He opens the door wider. "C'mon in. Does Troy know you're here?"

"No. Not that it's a secret," I rush out, even though in a way it is. I told Troy last night—while we were lying in bed, happily sated after several orgasms—that I had decided to resume writing my novel. He was supportive of the idea, which came as no surprise. But what I'm planning to write is a secret—even from Garrett.

He leads me through his house—that screams bachelor with its masculine interior—and onto the back porch.

"Wow, you did all of this?" I wave my hand at the lush garden. There's not much by the way of a lawn. Brick pathways meander around various flowerbeds, bushes, and trees. The place makes me think of the enchanted woods in a fairy tale.

"Yup. This garden has gotten me through many a rough time while writing."

God, if my garden looked like this, I would never leave it.

An image flickers in my head of Amelia playing hide-and-seek here and giggling while trying to stay hidden from me.

I push the image away. First things first. I still need to convince Grace and Craig to let me be part of her life once again.

"Have a seat." Garrett points to the small wrought-iron table and chairs on his patio. A laptop sits on the glass tabletop. "I'll be right back."

He closes the laptop and takes it into the house. When he returns, he's carrying a tray with drinks and two bowls of *kuku paka* and rice.

I grin, biting on my lip to keep from laughing. "You bought your lunch from Picnic and Treats?" I recognize the delicious food and the equally delicious smell.

"Yup. I haven't convinced Zara yet to make some for me on a regular basis to stash in the freezer. Apparently, our friendship only goes so far." He lifts his shoulders in a *What-can-you-do?* shrug.

I snort a laugh, which then shifts to a giggle.

Garrett hands me a bowl and a large glass of water. "I'll give you a ride to work after lunch. Troy can pick up your bike and trailer once he's finished at the worksite."

I gulp some of the much-needed water. "You don't have to do that." I don't want to be a bother; he has work to do.

Garrett sits on the other seat. "Don't worry about it, Jess. I'm happy to give you and Bailey a ride. So, you're back to writing your thriller? How's the plotting going?"

"Um, good. Except...I haven't actually started to write or plot anything. I only said I was writing a thriller because it seemed like a good explanation for why I moved to Maple Ridge when Delores asked me."

"And now you're writing one for real?"

"Yeah." Close enough. Both the historical novels and Garrett's political thrillers I've read have several things in common—the main one being the page-turning suspense. And both require research. Lots and lots of glorious research. Some of which I began with my sudden interest in World War II nonfiction books.

"Which thriller subgenre are you looking at writing?"

"I'm not sure what ones there are. I guess that's the first thing I'll need to do...read more in the subgenre I plan to write in." I've been mostly reading historical fiction since I was released from Beckley, so I'm doing well with that requirement.

"Well, with subgenres, you have psychological, legal, and medical thrillers." Garrett lists a bunch more. "And there's romantic thrillers and romantic suspense."

I dig my fork into the rice. "What's the difference

between a romantic thriller and romantic suspense?" I ask, genuinely curious.

"In romantic suspense, the danger or intrigue involves the protagonist or other central characters. With romantic thrillers, the danger or intrigue deals with something on a larger scope. Like stopping a serial killer who marries unsuspecting women and kills them."

I huff out a laugh. "That sounds romantic. How do you even know that?"

"Writer conferences. And I know a few authors in those subgenres."

If Garrett had mentioned these two subgenres five months ago, I would have laughed him off. Romance of any sort was not in my future. But Troy has changed that. And given that I'm writing about Iris's time in occupied France, I need to get past my previous hang-up over reading romances. What Johann did for Iris has to be one of the most romantic things I've ever heard of. Talk about a grand gesture.

I mentally add *Read a few forbidden romances* to my to-do list. Can't get more forbidden than what happened between Angelique and Johann. "What other subgenres are there?"

"Spy thrillers, which can also fall under the category of romantic thrillers. And there are also historical thrillers. Like *Titanic*."

That gets my attention. What happened between Rose and Jack was definitely a wrong-side-of-the-tracks forbidden romance. "I might write historical. I'll have to think about it. I have no interest in writing a romantic thriller, but there will be a romantic subplot." I pop a forkful of chicken in my mouth and chew on it. "Do you usually write outside?" I ask, referring to his laptop being on the patio table when I arrived.

"It depends. When it's nice out, I'll write outside, but

not necessarily here. I've been known to hike to one of my favorite spots and write there for a few hours."

Oh, that sounds nice. Between Troy overextending himself with the festival, the Warriors weekends, and his day job, he hasn't been able to take me hiking for the past few months. But if I were to try what Garrett does, by the time I made it to the top of the mountain, I'd be too tired to write. Plus, my healing ribs might be a little bitchy if I tried hiking right now.

"What about in public places like Picnic and Treats? I know some authors enjoy hanging out in coffee shops to write."

Garrett picks up his water. "The only time I've done that was when I was there to people-watch for character ideas and mannerisms. I don't do that now because people tend to recognize me and want to talk about whatever book I'm writing."

"Or give you feedback on one of your novels," I say, remembering what he told me when I first met him.

"Exactly. Nothing is more satisfying to a political thriller author than having someone come up and complain there're not enough steamy scenes in your books." Garrett rolls his eyes, and I laugh.

"Yes, I can imagine that would be annoying," I reply, still chuckling. "Your books aren't exactly known for the steamy parts." Understatement of the year.

After we finish eating lunch, Garrett takes me into his office, which overlooks the backyard. The room makes me think of a gentlemen's club from the turn of last century. The walls are hunter green and covered with dark-wood bookshelves with a few antique globes scattered throughout.

"This place looks like something from an old movie." I

run my fingers along the leather wingback chair near the window.

"Zara loves to make fun of it being my man cave. I don't usually let women in."

I flash him a grin. "I'm honored to be an exception to the rule." I walk to the bookshelves. He has hardback copies of his books, but there are also plenty of hardback editions from other authors whose names I vaguely recognize.

On one shelf is a framed photo of Garrett, Zara, and another woman, whose skin is a shade darker than Zara's copper-brown skin. The photo looks like it was taken over ten years ago, and all three of them are smiling at the camera. Zara's hair is pulled up with a scarf. The other woman's hair is a medium length Afro. She's gorgeous.

"Who's that?" I point to the photo.

"You mean Kenda? She was my college girlfriend and one of Zara's close friends."

"Does she live in Maple Ridge?"

"No. I don't actually know where she is now. I haven't heard from her in a few years. She has a journalism degree and had planned to make her mark on the world with it. And to travel."

"Is that why you broke up?" Zara has never mentioned her.

I'm assuming they broke up. Maybe she died. *Crap.* Hopefully I didn't just pour vinegar on an old wound.

"Partly. She had ambitions that didn't involve settling down any time soon. And I was going into the Marines. So it made sense to end things." He begins pulling books from a different shelf. I get the feeling there's more to the story, but I don't push for additional details. It's not my place to ask. Besides, I'm writing about Angelique and Johann's love life, not Garrett's.

"With your journalism background, your prose and ability to do research is already strong." He slips another book off the shelf. "But as you'll soon find out, writing a novel is very different from writing an article for a newspaper."

Two more books are extracted and added to the growing pile in Garrett's arms. With each book he pulls out, more panic sets in.

Will this be like what happened with the wedding photography? Something that sounded like a good idea at the time but in the end didn't put me any closer to figuring out who I am than when I was released from Beckley?

It didn't put me any closer to getting Amelia back in my life.

And it didn't put me any closer to untangling my feelings for Troy.

20

ANGELIQUE

October 1943
France

Fear presses in on me from all sides even though Johann is with me, and I consider the low stone wall that separates the road from the copse of trees and the open farmland. Are we truly safe here? Or are the Nazis close by? Maybe word has already gotten out that I've escaped and the Gestapo is trying to hunt me down.

The car door clicks open behind me, and the handcuffs fall open, freeing my wrists. I could almost cry out in partial relief, but the intense throbbing of my right hand strangles that possibility.

I twist to face Johann and rest my hands on my lap. Now that we're in daylight, I can see the mangled mess of what was once my right hand. My knuckles are bruised and swollen, two of my fingers are badly twisted, and the bone sticks out of my index finger. On top of that, a thick red

144

band encircles my wrists where the handcuffs dug into my skin.

Johann curses in German as he gently inspects the damage.

My gaze flicks from his long fingers that are inspecting the ugly wound to his equally ugly uniform. A shudder rolls through me, so intense my hand jerks from his.

"I need to get you to a doctor," he tells me, switching to French. He inspects my damaged lip and temple.

I open my mouth to utter something but change my mind. Afraid if I do talk, this dream will end, and I'll be dragged into another real life nightmare. One where I am at Avenue Foch.

He brushes his thumb over the part of my mouth that isn't split open. The last time I witnessed this level of pain and guilt in Johann's eyes was when he was telling me about what happened to his sister. "Is the..." His words tumble out on a croaked whisper. "The baby?"

"I think it's fine," I say through a dry mouth, my words barely audible.

He closes his eyes and rests his brow on mine. "Thank God." He moves his head away, his expression still pained. "I'm so sorry I wasn't there to protect you. I didn't know."

"H-how did...how did you...find me?" The shudder gripping my body is getting worse.

He reaches over my lap, removes the blanket folded next to me, and gently wraps it around my shoulders. The blanket helps a little but it's not enough. "I returned to the farmhouse and found Jacques muttering that the Gestapo had come for you."

He's alive. Jacques is alive and he's home. I close my eyes in relief.

I reopen them to find Johann staring at me like I'm a buried treasure he thought he would never see again.

"It took me awhile to find out where you were taken, and then to get the required signature forged on the necessary documents to get you out."

"How did you get the forged signature?"

"I cannot tell you. I didn't even know if it would work. The guards were sloppy and didn't check the authenticity of the papers." Johann straightens and kisses my brow. "I need to get you to a doctor so he can reset your hand before it's too late. Can you trust me? I know it's not an easy thing I'm asking of you."

I nod, even though he's right. Trust is hard to come by in my line of work, even more so when you discover one of your own has turned traitor. But I do trust Johann. I trust him with my life.

He cups the less injured side of my face with his hand and brushes his thumb along my cheek. "I love you, Angelique. Though I am guessing that is not your real name." He presses his finger to my lips. "Don't tell me what it is. Not yet."

He lowers his finger, and I nod. It's bad enough the Gestapo knows my code name and alias. I don't need them knowing my real name. If British and American agents are in France, I wouldn't be surprised if their German counterparts are in England. If they were to learn our real names and locate our families, the outcome would be devastating.

"Thank you for finding me," I whisper, barely getting the words out. My mouth is dry, my throat sore. He took a great risk searching for me and getting me out of the prison. I cannot thank him enough for what he did.

"I love you and I love our baby." Johann rests his hand on my flat belly. "I have already lost my father, and I might have lost my mother and sister. I have no intention of losing you too."

My insides squeeze in a good way, his words adding

kindling to the fire of hope burning in me. Hope that burns even brighter with him by my side.

"I love you as well." I hadn't expected to ever get to say that to him again. "I love you so much."

He helps me lie down on the car seat and covers me with the blanket. I manage to make myself somewhat comfortable. Johann starts the engine. The vibration hums through my body.

Exhaustion engulfs me, and I succumb to my fatigue.

"Angelique." Johann's soothing voice intrudes on my nightmare, the name tenderly spoken against my ear. Warm fingers stroke my cheek.

I slowly open my eyes. The blanket no longer covers me, and the sky is a deeper blue.

I push up to sit using my good hand. The excruciating pain in my wounded hand and wrist intensifies, aggravated by the movement. I struggle to catch my breath. "Where are we?"

"There's someone here who can help you."

I scan the area outside the car. The place reminds me of Jacques's vineyard, only instead of vines growing, an orchard stretches in all directions. The nearest neighbour's house isn't visible from here.

I don't recognise the location. I don't think Johann brought me back to the village. That would be too dangerous.

The brick house in front of us hasn't been bombed, but a crater is visible a short distance away in the orchard. It doesn't look recent. The summer grass has found a way to poke through the damaged ground.

Johann guides me to the house, his arm supporting me around my waist.

I hold my injured hand against my body. I'm still woozy from the morning sickness and from being struck in the temple, but it's an improvement compared to in the prison cell.

Johann doesn't rush me. He speaks soothing words about the birds in the trees. I know it's to distract me. I don't remember him being that fascinated by the birds in Jacques's vineyard.

The front door opens, revealing a man, his hair light grey, his face heavily lined. He could be in his early sixties. It's difficult to tell. The war has rapidly aged us all.

He stares at Johann, eyes rounded with fear. "What are you doing here?" There's a quiet desperation to his tone, his French dialect speaking of a high level of education. His eyes shift to me, and deep groves furrow his brow. "What happened to you?"

Johann doesn't say anything until we draw closer to the man. "Gestapo tortured her. I was hoping you could help her, Dr. Hubert." He has the same affection in his tone as he does when he talks about his sister.

The crease between the doctor's eyes deepens. "Why was the Gestapo torturing you?"

I draw in a long breath, questioning the wisdom of what I'm about to tell him, but at the same time, knowing I don't have much choice. Not if I am hoping to gain his trust. "I am part of the movement to free France and end the war."

Surprise crosses his face, widening his eyes even more. I've openly admitted this in front of a German soldier. A captain of the Wehrmacht, no less. He may be familiar with Johann, but he clearly doesn't know everything about the man I love.

Dr. Hubert waves us into the house, his gaze searching

the area. Once we're inside, he closes the door. "You will need to remove that vehicle," he tells Johann. "I won't have anyone believing that I am collaborating with the enemy. And I do not want to get into trouble should German soldiers come around."

"I will. I just want to ensure Angelique is all right first."

"Fine, hide the car in the barn for now. You can do that while I examine her hand."

Johann looks at me, his concerned eyes questioning me, one eyebrow lifted.

"I'll be fine." I don't want that despised car to draw attention to the house any more than the doctor does.

A woman appears in the hallway, drying her hands on a tea towel. A floral apron is tied at her waist, and her dark-grey hair is secured in a tidy chignon.

Her eyes land on Johann in his Wehrmacht uniform, and her expression twists into that of disgust. It doesn't improve when her eyes shift to me. "We don't want your sort here." The words are directed at my face. In her view, I'm a horizontal collaborator. That much is clear.

"Rosita!" Dr. Hubert says in a gentle chiding voice. "Johann was the man I told you about who saved my life. I owe him this one time."

"I am not a collaborator." My voice is soft, my energy waning. The throbbing pain in my hand is quickly sapping me of my strength. "I'm English and I work with the maquis. There was a double agent in my network. He told the Gestapo where to find me." A shudder passes through me at the memory of Christian's betrayal and what followed after my arrest. I have no idea how much of this Johann had already gleaned before he saved me, but there is no point keeping it from him now.

"I'm going to examine her hand and see what I can do to help her while Johann hides his car in the barn." Dr.

Hubert's tone is firm, but I cannot tell if the words are meant for her or Johann or them both.

Johann plants a tender kiss on my brow. "I won't be long."

The front door closes behind him, and Rosita ushers me into the kitchen, though with obvious reluctance. I would be the same if our places were reversed. She is taking a risk in opening her home to me, even if it is only for a short time.

"Sit." She points to a chair at the wooden table. The cabinets and furniture are a collection of sage and dark wood, the walls pale yellow. So beautifully different from the hell I was in a few hours ago.

She goes to the sink and fills a kettle. "Is he really a German soldier? Or is he with the maquis and that uniform is to throw the Nazis off? He doesn't speak with that horrible guttural accent."

"His grandparents are from Switzerland. He's from Austria." I don't answer her question about him being a German soldier. I have no idea what to say. Once the Gestapo discovers I'm missing, they will investigate how I escaped.

He risked everything for me.

Johann didn't desert the Army with his friend Dieter. He was afraid it would put his mother and sister at greater risk than they already are. Yet, that's exactly what he did for me. Surely, he doesn't intend to return to his unit as though nothing has happened.

Dr. Hubert enters the kitchen with a medical bag and puts it on the table. He washes his hands and sits on the chair next to mine. Then he takes my hand and examines it, carefully moving my fingers.

Pain stabs through my hand, and my body tenses. I

squeeze my eyes shut, doing my best not to whimper and yank my arm away.

"Is it true England plans to attack the Germans soon?" Rosita asks, and I have a feeling the question is to distract me from what her husband is doing.

"Eventually. But I don't know when. None of us...will know until closer to the date." They're running out of time if Parliament plans to do it before winter hits.

The kettle whistles on the stove. Rosita gets up and moves it to the side.

Johann strides into the kitchen. Gone is his uniform. In its place are clothes that belonged to Yvon, Jacques's son. Rosita nods at him, the earlier disgust in her expression faded.

"As best as I can tell, you have some broken bones and damaged ligaments," Dr. Hubert explains to me. "I'll need to reset them, but it will be very painful while I do that. I would give you an alcoholic drink to help numb the sensation, but we don't have any. And there's no guarantee the bones will set properly. A hospital would do a better job than what I can do here."

"I can't go to a hospital. Not at the risk of being caught again."

"I agree. It's too dangerous. But I want you to know the risks if I reset your bones. You may never have full use of your hand again."

"I understand." What will that mean once my baby is born? Will I be able to hold my precious child?

I don't voice my fears. Without Dr. Hubert's medical aid, it's guaranteed I wouldn't be able to hold my baby. I owe him everything for what he's doing for me. For the risk he is taking in helping a fugitive.

Johann puts his hand on my shoulder, the gesture

gentle and intimate. "She's pregnant. Will that be a problem?"

That earns Johann a raised eyebrow from Dr. Hubert. "Yours, I assume?"

Johann nods.

Rosita tuts. "What is it with French and apparently English women bedding the enemy? French men are the best lovers. German men..." She makes a sound of disgust.

Despite the levity of the situation, Johann huffs a laugh. "Well, it is a good thing I have French blood in my veins from my great-grandparents."

"How is it you're even allowed to be in the German Army?" she asks. "Hitler doesn't have a favourable view of the French. Our country is good enough to steal from and our women good enough to bed, but any child born to a French woman by a German soldier is looked down upon. They aren't pure blood."

"Somehow, that part was overlooked. They were more concerned about my sister being deaf than they were about my family's bloodline."

Rosita's expression shifts, and the corners of her mouth tilt down. She must have heard of what the Germans and Austrians were doing to adults and children who were physically or mentally disabled or deaf.

Dr. Hubert lowers my hand to the table. "The pregnancy won't be a problem for resetting Angelique's hand. But it will come with risks. It just depends on God's will and the will of your baby."

"I understand." I silently pray to a God I'm not sure I believe in that my baby will be all right.

And that Johann, our child, and I will survive this war.

"I will check your baby's health after I set your hand," Dr. Hubert says, his eyes kind and nonjudgmental.

21

JESSICA

August, Present Day
Maple Ridge

"Which book do you think I should start with?" I ask Bailey. The stack of craft books Garrett loaned me is sitting on my coffee table, taunting me with how much I don't know about writing fiction. "Or do you think I'm crazy for believing I can write a novel?"

Bailey cocks her head to the side.

"You're right. I should probably start with the book on story structure and plotting." Yes, I'm using Angelique's journals to write the story, but maybe the events shouldn't be told in a linear fashion. Structure will help me hit all the right notes for what to include and what to leave out—I hope.

Bailey barks.

"Good point. I need more hours in the day to read all

these books." And to finish reading and transcribing the journals.

I'm definitely crazy to think I can do this. But crazy or not, it's something I want to try, even if Anne's the only one who sees the story.

The doorbell rings as I'm finishing the second chapter of the story structure book. Bailey's head perks up from her snoozing spot on the floor by my feet. Must be Troy. He's due here about now—hopefully with my bike and trailer, which I left at Garrett's.

My body buzzes in anticipation at what the doorbell means. Troy and his golden kisses. I push to my feet from the couch, excitement zipping through me since I plan to tell him about the books Garrett loaned me—the reason I was at his brother's house.

I follow Bailey to the front door. She parks her butt on the wood flooring and looks expectantly at me.

I open the door, ready to fling myself into Troy's arms. But he's not here alone. His brothers are behind him, as are Lance, Simone, Zara, Emily, Avery, and Noah.

It's Thursday, so they aren't here for Game Night.

"Hi?" My gaze lands on each of them in turn, waiting for someone to tell me what's going on. They're smiling, so they're not here to deliver bad news.

Noah steps forward. My heart rate jacks up, but not enough to signal a fight-or-flight panic attack that could still come from him being a cop. A definite improvement at least.

"Your renovations are stalled because of Troy's shoulder and your ribs." Noah's eyes sparkle with warmth. "We're here to help get your plans for the house back on track."

Avery moves up next to him. "Unless you've got someone else hidden inside."

I laugh. I can't help it. "No, only Bailey and I live here

now." My gaze falls on Lance. I've never hung out with him —with or without Troy. I usually just see him at work, when he likes to tease me.

"They had to bring someone who knows what they're doing." He winks at me, and I grin at the only other person in the group who does renovations for a living.

"Ah, that makes sense." I open the door wider to let everyone in. Bailey greets each of them in turn. Butterscotch joins her, and Bailey's tail wags at supersonic speed.

Troy enters last. The kiss he gives me is long and deep and turns my blood to a simmer.

I smile against his mouth. "Thank you."

"Noah gets all the credit for this. He asked me if he and Avery could help with the renovations."

"We know you're starting your life over, and having the safe haven you've been dreaming about is part of that," Noah says from the hallway, clearly having heard the kiss and what Troy said to me.

Troy kisses my brow and smiles at me. "And maybe once we've finished the renovations, your brother-in-law and his wife will be open to the idea of Amelia being in your life."

Oh, God. That's my dream. A dream I'm getting closer to achieving. I turn to the group. "Thank you. There aren't enough words to tell you how grateful I am."

Silly tears prick my eyes. After what happened with Anne's neighbor yesterday, I needed this. I needed to be reminded that once more people piece together the truth about my past, not everyone will despise me. I have friends who believe in me—like Granny did.

"Do I get to see it?" I ask Troy three hours later and peer up the stairs to Amelia's bedroom. Everyone left a few minutes ago. Troy, Noah, and Kellan were working on the second floor the entire time, while the girls and I were downstairs, painting the walls and floor moldings. Lucas and Garrett were busy with the laundry room under the guidance of Lance, who was tearing out the cabinetry in the washroom next to where they were.

"You can see the bathroom, but you'll have to wait to see the guest bedroom." Troy kisses the end of my nose.

"Why?"

The smile that spreads across his face is one of my favorites—amused and incredibly sexy. "You're like a kid who's been told they have to wait until bedtime to open their birthday presents."

I fake a horrified gasp and clutch at my chest. "What kind of monster would make a kid wait that long? And can you blame me?" I drop my hand away and push my lips into a pout. Troy chuckles.

"No. Especially when I know how important that room is to you." Troy's eyes cloud, the teasing glow robbed from them. The moment vanishes as quickly as it came.

"What's wrong?" I ask, surprised at the sudden change in him.

"There's nothing wrong."

"Are you sure?" Did he find the secret room? But so what if he did? Sure, I haven't told him about what I found there, but I don't think me hiding something from him would cause Troy to react like this. The journals, medal, and pendant aren't a big secret like I was keeping before—a secret about me. They're Iris's secret.

He shakes his head. "It's nothing."

"Really? Then telling me shouldn't be a big deal. What

has you so frowny?" The corners of my mouth twitch up a tiny amount.

"I'm not frowny."

I run my thumb over the grooves in his forehead. "Could have fooled me. Just tell me." My arms encircle his waist. He's beginning to make me nervous.

His chest swells with a lengthened breath. A soft sigh blows over his parted lips. "What if your brother-in-law refuses to let you see Amelia? Even after everything you're doing? The house. The job. Therapy. Great friends. A boyfriend who loves you." The optimism in his voice from earlier—when he suggested Craig and Grace might now be more open to the idea of Amelia being in my life—has fizzled. In its place is worry and doubt.

My head droops forward. I don't want to think of that possibility but know it's looming in the shadows, ready to strike me down.

I don't know what I'll do if they never let me see her. Just thinking about it has new fissures spreading through my heart, large chunks of it threatening to fall off.

Troy lifts my chin with his finger. "I'm sorry, Jess. I don't want you to let go of your goal of having her in your life again, but I'm also worried about what will happen if they keep refusing you."

I don't have an answer for him, especially not the one he'll want to hear. Surely at some point they'll realize I'm not a threat to be feared. Realize I'm not going to destroy what they have with my daughter—no matter how much it hurts me not being her mother.

"Jess?"

"I don't know what I'll do...mainly because there's nothing I can do. There is no legal path I can take to undo the choice I made. No time machine I can use to prevent myself from signing away my rights."

Would it have made a difference if I'd known I would be released well before my sentence was supposed to end? I was an inmate for five years before the cops realized their mistake. Before the DA realized I'd been wronged. Even if I hadn't signed the papers that gave away my rights to Amelia, how would she have felt once I was set free?

I'm a stranger to her. She wouldn't see me as her mother.

I would be the woman who disrupted her happy life.

The tears I kept in check earlier now slick my cheeks. I swipe at them. Maybe Amelia would be better off if I stay away, if I pretend she never existed, if I let my heart be ripped in two.

Troy takes my hand and leads me into the living room. The room has changed so much since I moved into the house. Now, it's like a modern-day fairy-tale cottage, warm and airy and cozy.

He walks to the cabinet with the record player built inside it, pulls out an old Billie Holiday vinyl, and puts it on the turnstile. "I'll Be Seeing You" plays through the speaker, the sound slightly tinny.

Troy puts one hand on my waist. His other hand takes my hand. He leads me around the living room, twirling and dipping me in time to the old-time ballad. I laugh, unable to believe just how sweet and amazing and perfect he is. Perfect like Grandpa was for Granny.

His smile is the same one my grandfather always had for Granny whenever they danced together in the kitchen, the love they felt for each other undeniable.

Something in my heart stirs, an emotion I've been in denial of for a while now. An emotion that fills me with warmth, that sets my heart rapidly beating, that makes me feel like I'm soaring among the stars when I'm with him.

I'm in love with Troy.

I'm in love with the man who knows how to make me smile. The man who has done so much to help bring the smile back to my face.

But as much as my heart wants to share that with Troy and everyone who'll listen, my brain knows better.

I might be in love with Troy, but I'm not ready to admit it to him or anyone. Yet.

I need time. Need time to get used to it.

Need time after everything I've been through.

Need time while I still try to find myself.

22

JESSICA

August, Present Day
Maple Ridge

Friday afternoon, I'm sitting in the reception area of Troy's sparsely decorated but very masculine company office, filling in the order form for the screws and nails Troy requested. Bailey snores softly by my feet. The flowers in the vase Troy left on the coffee table Wednesday morning are still fresh and beautiful and remind me that he loves me.

God, how different my life would have been if Anne hadn't offered her great-aunt's house for me to stay in while I recovered from my past. For one, I wouldn't have a boyfriend—a sweet and loving boyfriend.

The phone rings, and I answer it, my smile directed at the flowers.

"Carson Construction. How may I help you?" My

fingers are poised over the keyboard, ready to type a message for Troy if needed.

No one responds, but the deep even breaths of the other person come loud and clear through the phone line.

"Hello?" My voice is a little louder this time in case they haven't realized I've answered the phone.

Still nothing but breathing.

"Can I help you?" Impatience weaves through my tone but is held in check with the need to be polite. It might not be a crank call.

Again, I'm only met by deep even breaths. Whatever. I hang up. It's probably some bored teens who randomly dialed this number.

I complete the hardware order, power off the computer, and head out for the day. "I just have to get a few things from the grocery store first," I tell Bailey as we walk to the front entrance of the building where my bike and trailer are locked up. "And then we can go home."

At the store, I decide to play a game. I'm writing about Angelique's time in occupied France; maybe I should try getting into her headspace and catalog people's appearances like she did. It can't hurt.

A woman walks toward me, carrying a basket. She's about thirty-five, my height, and very curvy. Her wavy hair is a brassy blond, but based on her dark roots, it's not her natural shade. Her eyes are large, chocolate brown, and pretty. Her nose has a small bump on the bridge.

She walks past me before I can catalog anything else unique about her.

I head for the produce section and quickly select a couple of ripe peaches. I put them in my basket and look up. Olivia is inspecting the lettuce display while Nova is sitting in the seat of their shopping cart and cuddling her bunny.

A pang of longing hits me hard in the chest. I used to love taking Amelia grocery shopping and turning the trip into a scavenger hunt. I would cut out pictures of things we needed to buy, like bananas and grapes, and Amelia would help me find them.

I push the memory aside and walk to the lettuce display. "Hi, Olivia. Hi, Nova!" My heart squeezes at seeing the sweet little girl. Squeezes in both a happy and painful way. God, she reminds me so much of Amelia at that age.

Olivia's gaze makes contact with mine, and her eyes widen. It only lasts a nanosecond, but it's long enough for me to notice. "Uh. Hi."

"Hi!" Nova says, a big grin on her cute face. She peers down at Bailey by my side with her *Service Dog in Training* vest on. "Hi, doggy!"

Olivia scans the produce section, her gaze failing to find mine again.

An uncomfortable sensation squirms in my stomach. "How's it going?" Uncertainty and worry twist my tone into something strained and high-pitched.

Olivia clears her throat, her attention on her daughter. "Fine." She's even twitcher than I used to be around Noah —before I realized he really is a good guy. "I should go now. It's...it's almost Nova's nap time."

At 5:00 p.m.?

Olivia hurries away, not giving me a second glance.

Weird. Does her behavior have something to do with Troy—and how she likes him as more than a friend?

I swallow at the other possibility. The scarier one. *Cora.* Cora is Olivia's sister. She's the one who wrote the article that mentioned I'm living under an assumed name in a small mountainous town in Oregon. She would have told Olivia about my old identity.

I haven't seen Cora since the article was published.

Thank God for that. I don't need her writing another article about me. An article that could destroy everything I've worked hard to rebuild.

My eyes make contact with a pair of narrowed ones belonging to a man I don't recognize. I quickly catalog his features—continuing my earlier game. Except this time it feels less like a game. Short black hair with the peppering of graying strands. Thin lips, well-shaped nose. Tanned skin that gives him a rugged appearance. Jeans and a faded navy-blue T-shirt.

In a way, he reminds me of Lincoln, my late husband's younger brother.

I drop my gaze like an ostrich burying its head in the ground, hoping no one will notice it. I hurry around the store, collecting the rest of the items I came for, and pay for them.

I quickly load the groceries into the basket on the front of my bike and pedal home, feeling more exposed than when the article hit the newspaper twelve days ago.

Stop it. I'm letting my past traumas play tricks with my mind. That's all. That man probably wasn't looking at me. And Olivia's in love with Troy, which is why she was acting weird. I'm overanalyzing things and coming to the wrong conclusion because of my fear and paranoia.

Robyn would agree I've got to stop doing that. I'll never get better if I let the mind games win. And that means I'll never get to see Amelia again.

THE FOLLOWING MORNING, TROY'S WARM BODY STIRS NEXT TO me in my bed and pulls me from my dream.

He kisses my shoulder. "I wish I didn't have to leave

yet," he murmurs on my skin. His hand slips under the covers and rests on my stomach, his palm flat, his fingers spread out. "But Garrett and Kellan will kill me if I'm late because I'm making love to my girlfriend."

I laugh softly, the sleepy sound tickling deep in my chest. "Lucas won't kill you?"

"I'm sure he's still in bed making love to Simone. So let him face Garrett and Kellan's ire instead of me this time."

My laugh comes out louder than before and takes the form of a giggle. "Were they really that mad last Saturday when you were a few minutes late?" The early morning sex that made him tardy was definitely worth it from where I'd stood.

Troy's finger taps a rhythmic pattern on my bare hip. The Morse code for ILU. *Tap-tap. Tap-taaap-tap-tap. Tap-tap-taaap.* "Of course. Can't say I blame them, though. I'd be grumpy too if I didn't have a beautiful woman in my bed to wake up to." He kisses me on the lips, not giving me a chance to remind him that I'm not in his bed every night.

It's a quick kiss because we both know we can't stop once things get heated. And then he'll be extremely late.

"I'll see you tomorrow evening. I love you." He climbs out of bed. His hot naked body moves around the room as he gathers up his clothes, giving me a great view of his sexy ass.

"You're drooling." Amusement lilts his tone, his back still to me.

Laughing, I hurl my pillow at him. It bounces off his hard muscles and flops to the floor.

Troy grabs it and tosses it at me, catching an eyeful of my breasts. Something for him to remember while he and his brothers and their guests are being one with the wilderness. I give a teasing little shimmy to really give him something to remember.

"You're killing me, Jess," he groans and walks out of the room.

The sound of water showering against the tub comes from the bathroom. I glance at my phone. And now I'm the one groaning. It's six in the morning. On a Saturday. Since I have no real plans until this afternoon, I drift back to sleep.

Unfortunately, Bailey and Butterscotch aren't big advocates for sleeping in. Butterscotch scrambles into my bedroom a short time later and barks.

"Okay," I grumble while contemplating the odds of getting away with putting my head under the pillow and ignoring him. "I'm getting up."

I drag myself out of bed and go into the bathroom. Stuck on the mirror is a Morse-code message that wasn't there last night.

It takes me a minute to decode it: *Can't wait to have you in my arms again. Love you. T.*

I get ready, take the message to my bedroom, and slip it into the large floral box where I keep all of Troy's Morse-coded messages. I fire off a text to him.

> Me: I can't wait to be in YOUR arms again

Once Bailey, Butterscotch, and I return home from our walk, I head into the backyard and gather a bouquet of flowers from my garden. I fetch a vase from under the kitchen sink, fill it with water, and place the vase with the wildflowers on the small, round patio table outside.

Then I spend the next hour weeding the flowerbeds. As I work, I mentally plan out what I'd like to do to the garden over the next year or so. Like add more flowering bushes. Maybe hydrangeas.

I push to my feet and brush my dirty hands on my

jeans. At Amelia's age, I pretended a family of fairies lived in the tree in Granny's backyard.

The tree in my backyard has a trunk that's perfect for those tiny doors and windows available online that turn a tree trunk into a fairy home. I bet Amelia would love that like I would've loved it when I was a little girl.

I pick up my phone from the table and look at her three photos. The only photos I have of her. It's been six and a half weeks since I called Grace to ask if I can see Amelia again. Maybe she's changed her mind. She didn't say how long they needed to get used to the idea of me being in Amelia's life. Before, I'd hesitated because the house wasn't done, but it's eighty percent there now—so close.

Plus, to begin with, I could visit her in Seattle. If that makes Grace feel more comfortable. And...and Amelia's birthday is a week from tomorrow. I could send her a present if they're okay with that.

I open up my contacts on my phone and stare at Grace's number for several rapid heartbeats. I draw in a long shaky breath and tap on Call.

I release my breath, praying Grace answers. Praying she gives me the response I'm hoping for.

"Hello?" a little girl replies on the other end of the line, her voice sweet and singsong. Amelia.

I love you and I miss you. A small sob falls from between my lips, and I cover my mouth with my hand. *Pull yourself together. You won't be able to talk to Grace if you're a blubbering mess.*

"Hello?" Amelia repeats, her tone more curious this time, her voice less singsong.

"Hi, can I speak to your mother?" I ask in a super friendly voice. Tears sting my eyes. I don't want her to stop talking, but I also don't want to give Grace a reason to refuse my request to see my daughter. I don't want to come off as problematic.

"Mommy!" Amelia yells.

"Indoor voice, Lia," Grace gently reprimands.

I shut my eyes at the name she uses for my daughter instead of the one I chose. The one that honored my grandmother's middle name. I hate that I had no say over that.

I tighten my grip on my phone, fighting the urge to hurl it into the bush. *Pretend. Pretend they're using the name I gave her when she was a precious newborn in my arms.*

"Hello?" Grace's voice comes clearly through the line, a patient lilt to it.

"Hi," I squeak through my tightening throat. The *thump-thump-thumping* of my heart echoes in my ears. "It's Jessica Smithson."

Please remember the name without me having to say Savannah Townsend out loud.

"Hello, Jessica." The words come out flat and lifeless and leery. "How can I help you?"

The question feels loaded, daunting, and I swallow my frustration at the situation I didn't ask to be in. I made a mistake in allowing the wrong man into my life, and in the end, I lost everything. Sure, Amelia wouldn't exist if not for that man, but I also wouldn't know the sharp pain of loss like I do.

"I'm calling for the same reason I did last time." I keep my voice friendly and cheerful. No point giving her a reason to end this conversation prematurely. "I'm not asking to be her mother again. I just want to be in her life. To get to see her grow up." The friendly tone warbles, and an on-the-verge-of-crying tremor slips in.

My daughter's beautiful voice replays in my head. She sounded so happy. That's all I've ever wanted for her.

"And...and I would love to have a more recent photo of her." *Please tell me that's not asking too much.*

My garden turns blurry, and I close my eyes against the tears.

A strained silence stretches endlessly on the phone. Even the birds in my backyard seem empty of song. I open my mouth to utter something, to beg, to plead, but the words disintegrate in my dry throat.

"Craig is away for a few days. I'll talk to him once he gets back and see what he thinks." Her voice is barely more than a scratched whisper.

Please let him be less resistant to the idea than his wife. "Thank you." The words aren't whispered, but they are rough like a steel-wool pad, leaving my throat shredded and sore.

Grace doesn't say anything else. She simply ends the call.

Bailey abandons her game of playing chase with Butterscotch and comes over to my chair. I slide off it, and my knees land on the cobblestones. I wrap my arms around Bailey, close my eyes, and silently sob against her warm body until I'm utterly depleted inside.

I'm being dragged under the surface, and the more I kick to try to break free, the less energy I'll have to suck in a breath.

What do you see? Robyn's words from one of our sessions float into my thoughts.

I open my eyes. "I see Bailey sitting next to me, the green grass, pink flowers in the garden. I see the blue sky and the rainbow the sun's creating through the vase onto the glass tabletop."

What do you hear?

"I hear a lawnmower, birds chirping, a vehicle driving past. I hear kids giggling and a neighborhood dog barking."

What do you feel?

"I feel Bailey's hair running through my fingers, the movement of her chest as she breathes, the warm surface of the cobblestones under my knees. I feel the soft cotton of my T-shirt." I run my hand over two cobblestones and the long blades of grass poking between them. "I feel the velvety grass."

I repeat the five-four-three-two-one exercise four more times, repeating one less item for each question with each round. By the time I'm finished, I can breathe easier again.

"Thank you," I whisper to Bailey and plant my butt back on the chair.

But more than anything, I wish Troy was here to hold me and to kiss away my pain.

An hour later, my phone pings with a text from Grace. There are no words, no answer to my request. It's simply a photo of a young girl with golden-brown hair and eyes like my own.

I draw in a sharp, hopeful breath.

The picture looks to be fairly recent. Amelia is playing with a black Lab in what appears to be a backyard. She's not looking at the camera. She's paying attention to the dog. But the smile on her face, the laughter in her eyes... they're priceless.

My little girl is more than happy—she's living her best life.

And that realization brings a new round of tears to *my* eyes, my chest two sizes too small.

So many emotions...so many emotions whirl and clash inside me, but I can't help the grin that tugs on my damp cheeks.

23

JESSICA

August, Present Day
Maple Ridge

Early morning sunshine stretches across the bed and the two snoring golden bodies next to me.

I push aside all thoughts of yesterday's conversation with Grace and get up with a bounce to my spirit. Today, I want to focus on the steps I need to take to write the novel for Anne. Based on what I've gleaned so far from the journals, I have a good sense of the characters and the story. I was up late last night transcribing the final journal. The ink is so faded, the writing shaky, I need to take a break from it. Working on the novel is the perfect change of pace.

Bailey's head pokes up, and she adjusts her body to a sitting position.

"You ready for breakfast and a walk?" I ask.

Those magic words are all it takes to wake Butterscotch. The two dogs jump down from the bed. Butterscotch heads out of my bedroom. Bailey waits for me, flashing me her adorable puppy eyes that plead for me to move faster.

I laugh. "Okay, I'm coming." I pull on my jeans and a long sleeved T-shirt. Even though it's mid-August, the mornings in the area are cooler than I'd like for wearing shorts at this time of day.

I head to the bathroom and catch my reflection in the mirror. Half circles still darken the skin beneath my eyes, but the nightmares aren't as frequent now, the shadows not as deep.

I go to the toilet, wash up, brush my hair and my teeth, and head downstairs. I tie the laces on my sneakers and clip the dogs' leashes onto their collars. "Just a quick walk. We can go on a longer one after breakfast."

I disengage the alarm system and open the door. Two words, scrawled in bright-red paint, scream out against the door's gray-blue color. COP KILLER.

Sucking in a sharp breath, I stare at the words that weren't on the door last night when I walked the dogs. I tentatively touch the last letter. My fingertip comes away free of wet paint. *Dammit.*

Loud, angry voices jerk my attention from the vandalized door to a small group of people standing on the sidewalk in front of my house. Troy painted the door a medium shade, but the color isn't dark enough to obscure the words. It's obvious the people glaring at me have also seen them.

I hurriedly shut the door.

Oh, God, there's no doubting it. I've been outed. I don't know who pulled the trigger that sent the dominos falling after they realized Cora's article was about me, but it's clear I can't escape the truth and the lies.

"I'll have to take you two into the backyard to do your business," I tell Bailey and Butterscotch. "Hopefully those people don't stay out there long." Surely, they've got better things to do.

We go into the garden, which is somewhat secluded from the street. If there was ever a time to be thankful for the tall hedges skirting my garden, now would be it. But they don't completely hide me. Pockets of bare branches from years of neglect leave me exposed. Vulnerable.

I have no idea what to do about the front door. I don't have enough paint left to cover the lie.

Fuckers. Fuckers. Fuckers. I pace to the rhythm of the words repeating in my head.

My phone rings on the patio table, the round glass top glinting in the sunlight.

I check who's calling. Zara. Relief rushes through me. She knows about my past life. She knows *me* and doesn't buy into the lies and misinformation surrounding Savannah. "Hi, Zara." My voice comes out raw and at a loss.

"How's it going?" There's a hesitancy in her words. Does she know about the vandalism?

"Not great." The speed of my pacing picks up. "Someone wrote 'cop killer' in red paint on my front door."

A string of muttered curses comes from Zara's end, which under any other circumstance would be funny. "I'm so sorry, Jess. I'm at Treats because one of my employees called in sick. I overheard a group of customers discussing that you're Savannah Townsend, and how you spent five years in a maximum-security prison."

Wonderful. "What happened? With the discussion." Do I want to know?

Zara doesn't answer right away, and I get the feeling she'd rather not tell me. Guess that's my answer right there.

"What did they say?" I push, dreading her next words but unable to let it go.

"It resulted in a heated conversation."

"About what?" I close my eyes.

"Whether you really are innocent." Zara's normally smooth and smoky voice is reduced to a gravelly whisper.

"And? What was the verdict?"

A loaded silence stretches between us. And with each passing second, growing powerlessness, resentment, and dismay press down on my lungs.

"What was the verdict?" I repeat.

I see Bailey and Butterscotch and grass...

"They decided it didn't matter if you're innocent. They said the last thing Maple Ridge wants is someone who was incarcerated with dangerous offenders. You'll be no better than the...real murderers." Sorrow colors the tone of Zara's final words. I barely hear them due to the pounding in my head.

I see...

An ant climbs from a short blade of grass onto a cobblestone.

I see the future I've been working toward squished like a stepped-on ant.

I hear...I hear a commotion out front. I hear the angry yells telling me I'm not welcome.

"What's that noise?"

"The villagers with their pitchforks," I reply dryly, a quiver to my voice. "I'm about to find out how Dracula felt when the villagers wanted to get rid of him." They succeeded in killing him. "I guess I need to do a better job at keeping my head than he did."

Zara snorts a humorless laugh. "Have you called the cops?"

I lower myself onto the cobblestones, all my hopes and dreams sinking with me. "I can't. What if they believe I was guilty of my husband's death?" What if they don't give a damn about the vandalism? Or about my safety?

Robyn asked me at my session over a week ago what makes me feel safe. I told her Troy.

But that only works if he's here. He's not due back until tonight.

"Phone Noah," Zara says. "He'll know what to do."

"I can't. He and Avery left this morning for San Francisco." They'll be gone for five days.

"You can still call him."

"He's driving, and I won't dump this on him while they're away on their romantic getaway." After what he did to help me renovate my house, I refuse to interrupt their much-earned vacation.

"I'll be over as soon as I'm done with my shift here. I'll call Simone in the meanwhile so you're not alone." Zara ends the call before I can respond.

I push to my feet, feeling no better than I did prior to her call. I take the dogs inside and feed them. "Maybe Simone can walk you two if she comes over," I tell them as they gobble their food.

I leave the kitchen while they're eating and track down the white paint I've been using on the floor molding. It's better than leaving the words on my door, even if the paint doesn't match the new door color.

I grab the can and a paintbrush and fill a bucket with hot soapy water. I locate an old scrub brush under the sink and step onto the front stoop, leaving the safety of my home.

I shut the door to keep the dogs from getting out.

The crowd hasn't dissipated in the short time since I woke up. Just the opposite. It's grown to over a dozen people. A few of them are holding signs proclaiming, *Convicts Not Welcome!* and *Go Back Where You Belong!* and *Make Our Streets Safe Again!*

"Protect our children! Protect our children!" the crowd

chants, their voices carrying loud and clear.

"Move away, Savannah, or we'll make your life miserable!" one woman shouts.

Ignoring them as best as I can, I scrub, scrub, scrub at the paint. I scrub until my hands cramp. Scrub until I'm not sure if I'll ever be able to straighten my fingers again. Not once does the chanting stop.

Tears wet my face, but I refuse to let anyone see I'm crying. Refuse to give them the satisfaction of seeing what their mean words do to me.

Nothing ever changes when it comes to the mean words. First it was my late husband who used them, who crushed my self-esteem, my self-worth. Then the inmates and the guards. And now this. It's just one endless circle of oppression, and I don't know how to get off.

I dry the door with a wad of paper towels. They come away pink, leaving the red paint no less vibrant than before.

I open the can of white paint. The contents are almost empty. Troy had planned to get more next Friday.

I brush over the two words, but there's only enough paint for one thin layer. The white paint doesn't hide the words. If anything, it highlights them.

Damn. What do I do now?

Does it really matter? Everyone will soon know the truth even if it isn't on the door anymore. The news is spreading like wildfire, and I don't have a clue how to douse it.

I gather up the supplies and go inside the house, shutting the door behind me.

The chanting switches from "Protect our children" to "Convicts not welcome." And now someone with a megaphone has joined the group.

I step away from the door and keep moving in reverse, my mind in a daze. My back hits a wall, and I sink to the floor. I cover my ears with my hands and sing Amelia's lullaby.

Hush-a-bye baby, my sweet little one.
Fall asleep, my love,
And dream of the stars and the sun.
Unicorn wishes and rainbow dreams,
Fairy-tale princesses and butterfly wings.
Hush-a-bye baby, my sweet little one.
I will protect you while you slumber on.

I imagine Amelia as a baby safe in my arms, and I keep singing the lyrics over and over until my throat is hoarse and my body is numb.

No, don't give them that satisfaction. I'm not the person they think I am.

I stand, fetch my laptop from my bedroom, and go to the kitchen table. I hadn't gotten around to opening the living room curtains this morning, and now I'm grateful for that. They give me some privacy against the people on the sidewalk.

I get to work, losing myself in the plotting of Angelique's story.

The doorbell rings, and my heart startles into my throat. I check the time on my phone. I've been working for thirty minutes. I was so focused on the plot and the story, I'd blocked out the chanting. But now it's back, the voices louder than before.

My phone pings with a text.

Simone: Jess, I'm outside your door.

Me: I'll be right there.

I hurry to the front door, open it while keeping out of view, and let Simone and Jasper into the house. The chanting grows more fevered.

I shut the door with the goal of blocking the noise out. Too bad that was wishful thinking.

"Convicts not welcome! Convicts not welcome! Convicts not welcome!"

Bailey and Butterscotch greet their friend. Simone hugs me tight. It feels so good after the morning I've had, I'm afraid to let her go. I'm afraid if I do, I'll lose her too.

We go into the living room.

"I can't believe all those people out there," Simone says. "What the hell is their problem? You were innocent of your late husband's murder."

"Not everyone believes that. I don't even think that's what their major concern is."

"Doesn't matter what it is. They're wrong." Simone flashes me a sad smile.

"Unfortunately, they don't seem to realize that."

Bailey barks, reminding me I haven't been able to walk her and Butterscotch. "Do you think you could take the dogs for a walk?" I ask Simone. "I'm afraid of what will happen if I go out there."

"I can do that." She splits a glance between the front door and me. "Have you called the cops?"

I shake my head and fold my arms across my chest, trying to keep my pieces together at the thought of calling them.

"You really should."

"And what will they do? Yes, someone vandalized my front door, but do you think any of those people will tell the cops who did it?" My voice comes out sounding defeated. Fed up. Frustrated. "Do you really think the cops will do anything about the people out there chanting and waving signs at me? They're not breaking any laws."

Simone releases a long, agreeing sigh. "I wish the guys

were back from their trip. They'd know what to do." Unfortunately, there's no cell reception where they are.

A grin curves my lips, despite the gravity of my situation. "They only have to stand outside and flex their muscles. That might be enough to chase some of those people away."

She laughs. "You might be right about that. All right," she says to the three dogs. "You ready to go for a walk?"

They bark and rush to the door.

"Text me if things get unruly." Simone tilts her head toward the closed curtains.

My stomach twists just thinking about what's waiting for her outside. Sure, we're not talking the zombie apocalypse, but those people might end up being just as dangerous. "Be careful out there. That mob might take offense to you helping me."

Lucas will never forgive me if something should happen to his wife.

"I'm not too worried about them. They won't do anything to hurt me. I've got three guard dogs."

"I hardly think two large energetic puppies count as guard dogs."

Simone chuckles. "You clearly haven't been jumped on by an overly eager Jasper. He doesn't realize his own strength sometimes."

They leave, and I peer through the narrow gap in the curtains, making sure they get past the crowd without being harassed. A few people yell at her. She scowls at them but doesn't respond.

Simone and the dogs walk away from the growing crowd. I remain at the window, watching for her return.

A police cruiser pulls up in front of the house. The officer climbs out but doesn't appear to be in a rush to do anything. He takes his time to assess the situation on the sidewalk.

I recognize him. He's the same officer who came to the door when Violet went missing, and he questioned me about her disappearance. Troy knows him. Roy or Royce or something like that. The man is in his mid-thirties. Works out. Light-brown hair. Nothing particularly noteworthy about him. No scars or visible tattoos peeking from under the short sleeves of his uniform.

He walks up to the protesters, his long stride slow and easy, and I can tell I'll get no support from him.

Some of the protesters smile and nod at him like they know him. Which they probably do.

I'm the stranger, the one to be judged and scorned.

A few faces I do recognize in the crowd, but it's not because I've spoken with my neighbors. I've only seen them walking on the sidewalk or on their front lawn. Except for with Delores, I've mostly kept to myself, too afraid that someone on the street would recognize me.

Guess the joke is on me.

The officer chats with the protesters for a few minutes. No one appears offended by what he has to say. Nor do they disband, taking their hateful signs with them.

Once he's finished catching up with everyone, or whatever he's doing out there, he casually strolls up the path to my house. He draws closer, his hand going to the butt of the gun in his holster. The officer has already labeled me. I'm the trouble-maker. The dangerous offender. The risk to everyone's safety.

He disappears from my view, which means he's on my front stoop. The doorbell rings.

I want to pretend I didn't hear it, stay sheltered in my home. But at the same time, I don't want to be a prisoner in it.

My breath shaky and my limbs trembling, I go to the foyer, disengage the alarm, and open the door.

"I received a report of vandalism." The cop's tone is stiff and unfriendly. I can guarantee it's not the same one he used a few moments ago with the crowd.

"You did?"

"Yes, Zara Thompson called it in." He takes in the red letters on the door. "Do you have any idea who wrote that?"

"No. I was sleeping when it happened."

"I don't suppose you have any surveillance cameras for the door?" He looks up at the wall under the roof overhang.

"No, only an alarm to let me know if someone tries to break in."

"That's too bad." His voice lacks any hint of disappointment. It's neutral at best. His gaze falls to the door again. "Did you attempt to paint over the words or did someone else do that?"

"I did it." I hold the doorknob tighter, hiding the tremor in my hand. I don't want to give away that he scares me and give him an advantage.

He blows a hard breath over pursed lips. "Unfortunately, there's nothing we can do about it. If there was evidence that could lead to an arrest, it was destroyed when you painted the door. Next time, don't touch the crime scene until after an officer tells you it's okay to disturb the area."

Next time? God, please tell me there won't be a next time.

"What about those people?" I point to the protesters.

"What about them?"

I stare at him, dumbfounded. Does he need me to spell things out? "Aren't they disrupting the peace? Or at the very least, harassing me?" I already know his answer, but maybe he'll surprise me.

"As long as they stay off your property and don't break any laws, there's not much I can do about them."

"So what? I have to put up with them yelling at me and making me feel unsafe?" Now that the officer is at my front door, the yelled threats have ceased. People are still chanting but at a more respectful volume.

I'm not deluding myself into believing it will stay that way after he leaves the street.

"I'm sure they'll grow bored soon, and things will go back to normal in no time." He nods at me and heads to his cruiser. He doesn't bother to stop and reprimand the crowd.

And I'm left wishing Troy was coming home soon instead of later tonight.

24

ANGELIQUE

October 1943
France

Dr. Hubert moves a kitchen chair to face mine. "Johann, sit here. You are to hold on to Angelique and do whatever it takes to keep her from moving her arm. Rosita will do her best to keep it pinned down, but the calmer you keep Angelique, the easier everyone's job will be."

What Dr. Hubert doesn't say, I read in his eyes. Their actions combined might make the doctor's job easier, but my pain will not be any easier to bear.

Johann sits on the chair. He cups my face with his hands and kisses me. It's long and deep and passionate, and for a moment I forget the throbbing in my hand.

He pulls away too soon. "I love you." His voice is rough and raw, smooth and embracing. It gives me a strength I wouldn't otherwise be able to find in myself.

182

"Remember that. I love you and will do whatever I can to protect you."

"I know," I whisper. And I do. "I love you too." I turn to Dr. Hubert. "I'm ready."

I bury my face in Johann's chest. His shirt smells like him—reminding me of the man who is strong, brave, and kind. I breathe in the scent, allowing it to ground me.

Johann holds me tightly to him, his arms embracing me. Rosita attempts to use her body weight, which is featherlight due to the declining war rations, to pin my arm to the table.

Dr. Hubert cleans the wound, and a sharp sting torments me. I release a hissed breath.

Next, he begins to reset the bones. An excruciating, white-hot searing pain explodes in my hand. A pain worse than when Christian crushed it.

I whimper and scream into Johann's chest. He holds me tighter, his muscles taut against my body. With each scream I muffle into his chest, his muscles grow more tense.

"You're so brave and beautiful," he murmurs in my ear. "So very brave."

I don't withdraw into another time and place like I did while being tortured. I let the real Johann be my strength, the full moon that gives rise to hope.

I wobble in and out of consciousness as the doctor works, the pain greater than my brain can endure.

"I'm almost finished," Dr. Hubert says after what feels like several lifetimes. Johann's shirt is wet against my cheek from all my tears and the sweat that dampens my brow and upper lip.

Another bite of hot pain shoots up my arm. I'm wavering on the wall again, close to crashing on the side of oblivion. Despite what Johann is saying, I'm not sure I will last much longer.

Dr. Hubert positions my hand on a board and ties it into place. Johann releases me, and my arm is secured across my chest with a sling.

Rosita puts her hand on my other arm, the touch gentle and comforting. "You need to rest now. Do you have somewhere to stay?"

I shake my head. "It's not safe for me to return to where I was living."

If the Gestapo has destroyed the *Cashmere* network like Christian claimed, I have no way to contact Baker Street and alert them to what has happened. And all my money and the gold compact Major Buckmaster gave me are hidden in the farmhouse. I have nothing except the clothes I was arrested in.

"You can stay here while you recover," Rosita says. "Your injured hand will need to be exercised several times a day while it's healing so you do not lose full function of it. I can help you with the exercises. I used to be a nurse."

"Are you sure? I don't want to be a bother."

"You can stay in our guest room," Dr. Hubert offers. "There is no reason for the Gestapo to search for you here. And if they do come, we have somewhere safe where you can hide. They won't be able to find you." He turns to Johann. "But you will need to get rid of that car and the uniform." He eyes Johann speculatively. "Or are you planning to return to the German Army?"

"No. Even if I wanted to, I'll be executed once they piece together that I was responsible for Angelique's disappearance. And even if they don't figure it out, my troop could be sent to the Eastern front soon."

"Yes, but if it weren't for those things, would you return to the German Army?" Rosita presses, leaning towards him, concern and urgency in her tone.

"No. My home was Austria, but that changed once

Hitler came into power. I am not interested in fighting for him." Johann smiles at me, his love for me shining bright in his eyes. "I have someone else I want to fight for." He rests his hand on my lower belly, and the heat of his palm spreads throughout me. "Two someones I want to fight for."

"What about your mother and sister?" I ask, my voice hushed. They are the reason he joined the Army. Has he given up hope they're still alive? Like Dieter had?

"I hope they escaped from Austria and ended up far away from Hitler's reach. I hope one day, once the war is over, I will be reunited with them. And I hope one day my mother gets to meet her first grandchild and my wife." Johann's warm and generous smile is almost enough to make me temporarily forget the war and everything else we're facing.

"But I also know I was a fool in believing that by joining the Army," Johann adds, his smile fading, "I was somehow protecting them." Sadness dulls the hope in his eyes.

My heart splinters for him. Splinters at everything this war has cost him. "I hope I'll get to meet your mother and sister one day soon." *I hope they're alive.* I try to give him a reassuring smile. A smile no doubt dented from the pain hammering my wrist and my hand.

He brushes his thumbs under my eyes, catching the tears from my pain, and turns to Rosita. "I'll stay with Angelique until she falls asleep. Then I'll take the car as far away as possible so the Gestapo and Milice don't find it anywhere near here. And I'll destroy all evidence linking us to it."

Rosita nods her approval. "When was the last time you ate?" she asks me.

"I'm not sure I can keep anything down right now." And I'm not hungry, the pain and morning sickness hindering my appetite.

She looks to Johann for whatever answer I didn't give her.

"She hasn't eaten since breakfast yesterday. Before I left the house. I doubt she was given anything after she was arrested." He doesn't need me to confirm that he is correct.

"You should really eat, Angelique. For the baby's sake. Even if it is just a small amount for now. You need to keep up your strength." Rosita gets up, goes to the larder and the sink, and returns with a glass of water and a small piece of bread. "It is probably for the best if you do only have small amounts to begin with. Until we're certain you can tolerate food."

"Once we've got you settled in the guest room," Dr. Hubert informs me, "I'll check on your baby."

Rosita puts the plate and glass in front of me. I take a hesitant sip of water and a tiny bite of the bread. When it appears that I can keep them down, I slowly drink half the water and eat several small mouthfuls. The queasiness strikes again, forcing me to stop.

Rosita leads Johann and me to a spare bedroom. She leaves and returns with a water jug and a clean nightgown. "I assume since you got her in the motherly way," she says to Johann, keeping her expression free of what she thinks about that, "you are able to help her undress and put the nightgown on?"

One side of his mouth tilts up. "I should be capable of that." His smile softens to that of gratitude. "Thank you, Rosita, for everything you and your husband are doing for us."

"You are welcome. But please don't make us regret it." She nods and leaves the room.

Johann helps me out of my soiled clothes, taking his time. The splint makes things challenging, but he undresses me without hurting me too much.

He takes the washcloth, dips it in the water, and bathes me. The way he tenderly caresses my body distracts me enough so the pain in my hand isn't quite as intense. He lightly kisses my body as he works, further trying to distract me from everything going on. Distract me from the knowledge he will be leaving soon.

He then helps me into the nightgown and into bed.

Dr. Hubert enters the room and has me lie on my back. He covers my lower body with the thin blanket and pushes the nightgown high enough to expose my belly.

He takes a few moments to examine my flat tummy with his hands, asking me questions to gauge how far along I am in my pregnancy. "As far as I can tell, things are progressing well. You and the baby just need to rest now." He smiles kindly at me.

"Thank you," I say, returning his smile, mine filled with gratitude. He nods at Johann and leaves us alone in the room.

I lie on my side, my hand supported by pillows. Johann strips off his clothes and climbs under the bedcovers with me. His hot body cradles me from behind and his warm hand rests on my belly.

Despite the pain in my hand, exhaustion tries to pull me under its spell once more. I fight the urge to close my eyes and give in to it. As soon as I fall asleep, Johann will leave, and I don't know when I will see him again.

"Will you come back once you're rid of the car?" I ask. *Please come back. Please come back safe.*

"I will. As soon as I can. If it weren't for that, I would not leave you. But Dr. Hubert is right. I cannot stay here, even if the car is hidden in the barn. It's too risky. It needs to be dealt with first." He kisses my shoulder, but something about his voice warns me he's not telling me everything.

"You're not coming back right away. Are you?" The two words linger in the air like smoke after a bomb explosion.

For a heartbeat it feels as though he's going to brush off my concerns, and I glance over my shoulder.

He slowly shakes his head. "I want to fight to make sure the world is a better place for our child to grow up. This, the world Hitler is working towards, I cannot let that happen. If there is some way I can help your side, I will."

"And if you can't?" I swallow the emotions that threaten to choke me.

"Then I'll come back to you sooner." He brushes a kiss on my lips, branding them with a promise. A promise I pray he can keep.

"Where will you take it? The car?" My voice crackles with building tears.

"As far away as what's left in the petrol tank will allow. South and away from any areas heavy with patrols. The farther away the better."

"What if someone catches you?" I don't say it out loud, but I have a feeling he knows what I mean. By now the Gestapo will be wondering who helped me escape. I don't know how well Johann covered his tracks—if there is a record at the prison that he was the man who claimed to be moving me to Avenue Foch.

If the Gestapo figure out it was Johann, they will be looking for him, the Austrian traitor among them.

His life will be in as much danger as mine is.

"No matter what happens, Angelique, I will fight my way back to you. I will find you." He kisses the shell of my ear. "But you need to promise me something."

"What's that?"

"If I'm not back by the time you are well enough to travel and you find a way to return to England, you need to go." His hand cups my belly. "For our baby's sake. Promise me that."

"I promise." I don't have the strength to argue otherwise. "But please come back to me. I'll be lost without you."

He kisses my shoulder again. The touch of his soft lips forever marks me as his. "I promise I'll come back." He's quiet for a long moment, and I already miss his deep, resonating voice. "Do you really have a sister?" he asks.

"Yes. I do. Everything I told you about her is true. What I didn't tell you is that she is married to an RAF pilot and is hoping to one day have lots of babies. If she has her way, our baby will have lots of cousins to visit." I leave things hanging about which country we'll end up in once the war is over. First, we have to survive it.

"The people who helped Oskar and his family escape the country. Can you contact them? Will they be able to help you return home?"

I shake my head wearily. "It's not safe for me to try to communicate with my contact. It will only put her in danger. She was the one who made the arrangements to help them." And this is assuming the Gestapo hasn't captured her.

"Do you know anyone who can contact England to get you back home?" His thumb caresses my belly, his voice a hoarse whisper.

"No. Not if what the agent who double-crossed my network said is true. I only knew two or three members at most, and it's impossible for me to contact them now, even if they haven't been arrested."

If the Gestapo got their hands on a wireless-radio crystal and the operator's key codes, Baker Street might have no idea the network has been corrupted.

If we're lucky, Baker Street will recognise that the operator's signature doesn't match their normal one. Each operator signature is as unique as their fingerprints. If someone is masquerading as a wireless operator from the network, Baker Street could figure it out. But if it doesn't…if for some reason they ignore the irregularities, thinking it's just the operator's mistake…

I don't want to think of the repercussions. For now, I'm stranded in an occupied country, pregnant, and the Gestapo is searching for me. They are relentless hunters, and things won't go any easier if they find out I'm pregnant.

That will only make the game of taunting their prey more enticing.

25

___

JESSICA

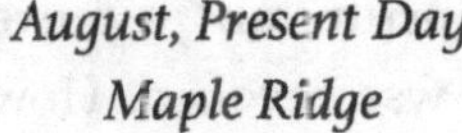

August, Present Day
Maple Ridge

My front doorbell rings. Simone, Zara, and I are sitting at the kitchen table, playing a game of Go Fish. The protesters' chants outside my living room window seem to have gotten louder in the past few minutes.

Inwardly groaning at the noise, I push to my feet.

Zara's dark eyebrows pull together into a worried frown. "I can get it."

"That's okay. I doubt it's one of the protesters." I hope it isn't someone getting ready to hurl something at me. Except if they did, that would be considered an act of trespassing and assault, which might result in the Maple Ridge police actually doing something about the protesters.

Bailey walks with me to the front door.

I peer through the peephole. Cora is standing on the

front stoop, wearing a short-sleeved peach dress. Her blond hair is gleaming and straight, hitting just below her shoulders. And in her hand...is a microphone.

She's not alone. A TV cameraman stands to the side, his lens pointing at her face. She nods at him, says something I can't hear through the closed door, and plasters a smile on her face. There's nothing genuine about it.

I deliberate for a moment what to do, but the anger that once lay dormant when I was too scared to face my husband unfurls from its slumber and stretches its talons. I open the door, not bothering to fix a smile on my face.

"Hi, Savannah." Cora's smile grows wider like we're old friends. There's not an ounce of remorse in her expression for what she did to me. "You were released from Beckley State Correctional Institution just over five months ago after your sentence was revoked. How does it feel to be declared wrongfully accused after spending five years in prison?"

Is she. Fucking. Kidding. Me?

"Why the hell do you think I have anything to say to you? Is that why you sold me out?" I nod at the man with the camera. "So you'd get a job promotion? You don't care who you hurt in the meantime. You're a selfish, self-absorbed monster who would sell your niece to the devil himself if it meant getting what you want. No wonder your ex-husband cheated on you," I say, unable to keep the hurt and anger from spewing into my next words. "He wanted to be with a woman who had more morals and integrity than you."

All right, not my finest retort, but there aren't enough words in the English language to relay how I feel right now.

I look beyond her shoulder, and my stomach plummets down a hundred-foot drop. Cora isn't the only reporter here. She's just the first one to make it to my front door.

Multiple vans belonging to various media outlets—national and local—are parked on the street or are pulling into whatever space they can find.

Reporters and camera people scramble from the vans in their haste not to miss anything I have to say. They hurry up the sidewalk to join Cora, a wake of starved vultures.

And I'm about to become their next meal.

I slam the door in Cora's face.

Oh, God. What do I do now?

The protesters were bad enough, but now the reporters have tracked me down.

Shit. Shit. Shit.

I turn around. Simone and Zara are standing in the entrance to the living room, their eyes wide, mouths slack. I have no idea if they're shocked because reporters are hounding me or because of what I said to Cora.

I wanted to say a helluva lot more, but not while the cameraman was recording my every word. Luckily for Cora, I wasn't holding the open can of white paint I was using earlier. I would have thrown the contents in her face. Zero regret.

I walk into the living room and begin pacing.

I haven't let myself get angry in a long time. Part of that had to do with fear. If I'd gotten angry with my husband, I would have felt the sharp sting of his punishment for talking back. He had torn me down bit by bit over time before I realized what was going on...and then it was too late. All the fight I'd once had prior to meeting him had burned away.

There was nothing left of me once I was locked away in prison. I'd feared even my own shadow.

What now? Those reporters and protesters will destroy everything I've worked hard for since I was released. They have the power to destroy my present and my future.

What did I do to deserve this? Which karma god did I piss off?

I grab a cushion from the couch, walk past Simone and Zara, and enter the laundry room. I shut the door, sink to the floor, lift the cushion to my face, and scream and scream and scream into it.

26

TROY

August, Present Day
Maple Ridge

My phone rings from the van console between Garrett and me. The men behind us are laughing at what one of them just said. Garrett is driving, so I check my phone to see who's calling. *Zara.*

I'd let it go to voicemail since the men in the back should be my focus for now, but for some reason unease stirs in my gut. I answer the phone. "Hey, Zar, what's up?"

"What's your ETA?" There's an urgency to her tone that has me sitting straighter.

"We're about ten minutes from the cabins. What's up?" Cautious curiosity rides my tone. I don't want to draw questions from the men behind me, but I do want to know why Zara's calling.

"Do you think you can come to Jess's house first?"

195

Simone's strained voice comes through Zara's phone. The sound of it hollows out my stomach and fear for my girl claws at my skin. "Her identity is now public knowledge. And protesters and reporters are camped out in front of the house."

Fuck.

I glance at Garrett. He can't hear what Simone is saying. I don't have the phone on speaker.

Frowning, he mouths, *What's going on?*

"I'll be over as soon as we get to the cabins," I tell Simone and Zara. "Can I talk to Jess?" I want to hear her voice. I need to know she's all right.

"She's kinda busy right now." Zara's tone is no less urgent than it was before.

Now I'm the one who's frowning. "Busy doing what?"

"Just get here as soon as you can."

I tighten my grip on my phone, my eyes locked on the road ahead of us. "How's. She. Doing?" My voice is low and rigid.

"Just. Get. Here." Zara ends the call.

Fuck. Fuck. Fuck. What the hell is going on?

I text Jess.

> Me: Zara just told me about the reporters and everything else. I'll be there soon. How are you doing?

No dots pop up to indicate Jess is typing a reply.

"What's up?" Garrett asks.

"Everyone has figured out who Jess is," I say, the volume of my voice still low, keeping the conversation between us. "Protesters and reporters are outside her house."

"Fuuuuuck," Garrett mutters under his breath. "Don't worry about sticking around once we get to the cabins. Lucas, Kellan, and I will deal with everything."

"Thanks." A small growl of frustration vibrates in my chest, too quiet to be heard by the passengers behind us. They're currently talking loudly among themselves. "We knew Savannah's whereabouts would eventually come out. But protesters?"

"How many are we talking about?"

"No idea. But even if it starts with only a few people, it won't take long before the numbers grow." Protests tend to draw supporters of the cause as well as counter-protesters. The more vocal the protest, the more media coverage it gets, and the larger the numbers grow.

The cycle is broken when something new and shiny grabs the media's attention away. But how long can Jess's mental health survive if that doesn't happen quickly? She's seeing Robyn again, but the protesters and reporters could send her recovery into a spiral.

"I'm surprised it took this long before her old identity became known," Garrett says, his eyes on the road. "The article came out almost two weeks ago. And I can't imagine Cora kept the info from Olivia."

"Olivia wouldn't have said anything to anyone. She has no reason to. If anything, she would have told me what was going on."

"But she knew about the article."

"I don't think she did," I tell him. "Like I said, she would have told me. Olivia and I don't keep secrets from each other."

Garrett snort-laughs. "I'm sure you've kept plenty of secrets from each other. I'm your brother, and I didn't know any of that shit Jess has gone through until recently."

"It wasn't my secret to tell you or anyone."

An eerie silence, like that during the eye of a hurricane, fills the van. A moment ago, the retired Navy SEALs behind us were chatting away. Now, it's as if all eyes and ears are turned in Garrett's and my direction.

I inwardly groan. Just hearing the word "secret" is enough to grab anyone's attention. Human curiosity trumps all.

I don't want to explain to the men what's going on with Jess, so I turn up the volume of Garrett's playlist.

We arrive at the Warriors property, and Garrett parks in front of the building where we store the equipment. "I'll get Kellan and Lucas up to speed," he says as I reach for the passenger door.

"Thanks." I bail from the van and sprint to my truck. I click the fob to unlock the door and haul ass into the driver's seat. Then I'm racing out of here, my tires stirring up dust on the gravel driveway.

After what feels like far too long, I turn onto Jess's street. The sidewalk outside of her house is crowded with two groups of people. One group holds up signs and is yelling at the house. Reporters make up the other group, their vans littering the street.

These are the same reporters I saw in town over a week ago reporting on the mass arrests linked to the trafficking of assault weapons. At the time, the reporters hadn't realized the person they'd been reporting on for the past few months, ever since Savannah Townsend had been released from prison, was living here.

But now they know, and like rats after a piece of cheese, they're scrambling to be the first ones to scoop the big story.

"Fuck!" The word is muttered out loud, but it screams in my head in repeat.

I recognize several of the protesters. One is a mother who, from what I remember hearing, is the president of the high school PTA. Skye Backlund. She's vocal about causes she believes in, which would be great if rallying against my girlfriend living in Maple Ridge wasn't one of her new causes. Skye's talking to a reporter but is making sure her sign, *Protect Our Children*, is visible in front of her.

Jess has done nothing to make anyone believe she's a threat to their children. If places were reversed, would they have done what she did—give away the rights to the daughter she loved to ensure the little girl was safe and happy?

I can't park on Jess's driveway. The crowd is blocking it, either as part of their strategy to terrorize her or by accident. I drive past her house and steer past the people spilling onto the road from the sidewalk. This protest isn't just about the people who live in the neighborhood. It has clearly gained support from those who live in other areas of town.

I finally find an empty spot around the corner from Jess's street and swerve my truck into it. I slam the door shut and run to her house. The sheer number of protesters on the road makes it more difficult to get there. I'm forced to waste time ducking and darting past them.

Damn the fucking protesters.

Damn their fucking ignorance.

A reporter steps in my way and shoves a microphone in my face. I don't hear what he asks me. I clench my hands, fighting the urge to grab him and hurl him to the side. It won't help Jess if I'm convicted for assaulting a reporter. It will only make things worse for her.

And the last thing I need is for the reporters to latch on to who I am and my role in organizing the With Hope festival. It could destroy all the hard work the festival committee members and I have been doing to make it a success.

I need to be smarter than I was when I pushed Wilson

at the Fourth of July celebrations because he was staring at Jess. Too much is at stake if I step out of line...for Jess and for those who struggle with PTSD and their families.

I cut past the reporter and sprint up the path to Jess's house.

I reach her front door. COP KILLER glares at me in red paint and turns my blood lava-hot. The offending words have been covered with white paint, but they are still highly visible.

Fuck-damn-fuck. Simone and Zara failed to mention this.

The words on Jess's door, the lies about her, and the ignorance are the last things she needs. She's already dealing with enough with the complex PTSD and starting her life over, as well as hoping to see her daughter.

If I find out who did write...

I don't complete the thought and try to calm my roiling blood. Jess doesn't need to see me ready to rip off somebody's head. She needs me to be there for her.

I ring the doorbell. The distant barking from three dogs welcomes me from the other side of the closed door. "Jess, it's Troy."

The barking grows louder and closer until the dogs are right behind the door.

The front door clicks open, but the gap between it and the doorjamb doesn't widen. "Jasper, Bailey, Butterscotch, sit!" Simone commands, her pitch higher and shakier than normal. The gap widens, and her worried expression meets mine.

I slip past the doorway, keeping the gap as narrow as possible to prevent the reporters from seeing inside the house. They have violated Jess's privacy. No need to hand over anything more to them. I shut the door behind me.

"Where is she?" I ask as Zara walks toward us.

"She's in the laundry room." The usual glow in Zara's brown eyes has dimmed. "She went in there 'cause she needed a moment and hasn't come out since."

I walk to the laundry room, my long legs making short work of the distance. I knock on the closed door. "Jess, I'm coming in."

She doesn't answer, but a soft thumping can be heard from the other side of the wall.

I turn the doorknob and cautiously push the door open. The laundry room is small, only large enough for the washer and dryer, Bailey's crate, and the cabinets Lucas and Garrett recently installed with the sink.

Jess is on the floor, her legs stretched in front of her, and she's gently bouncing the back of her head on the cabinet door. Tears have forged wet trails down her cheeks, but she's not crying now. She looks lost, she looks pissed, she looks devastated. Her gaze is locked on the opposite wall above the washer and dryer, her eyes narrowed.

I shut the door behind me and lower my ass next to her on the cold tile floor.

She continues bouncing her head against the cabinet. *Thump-thump-thump.* The movement keeps pace with my heartbeat. A light-blue cushion that's usually on the living room couch is on the floor beside her.

I slip my hand between her head and the cabinet. "I like your head the way it is. Preferably without any brain damage."

She slides me a glance that seems more resigned than angry. "They're still out there, aren't they?"

"The reporters and protesters?" I nod that they haven't gone anywhere. "How long have they been there?"

"The protesters—since this morning. But there weren't anywhere near as many when I got up. Simone had to walk the dogs. I didn't dare go near all those people."

I let loose a stream of mental curses, keeping what I'm thinking from my face. Those assholes. They stole Jess's sense of security—the thing she's been fighting to reclaim.

I thread my fingers with hers, her hand on her lap.

"The news must have got out on social media," Jess says, her voice soft, defeated. "People kept coming during the day to join the protesters. And then the reporters showed up."

"Have you talked to anyone? The reporters or the protesters?"

"Not really. Cora had the nerve to ring the doorbell. I called her selfish and self-absorbed. Nova doesn't deserve that woman in her life." She sniffs. "I might have also said it was no wonder her ex cheated on her."

I laugh, the abrupt noise erupting from deep in my chest.

A wry smile slips onto Jess's lips, and she shrugs. "Not my finest comeback, I'll admit."

"Wish I'd been here for that." My serious side slips into place once more. "Please don't talk to the media again. We don't want them to twist your words out of context." Which they'll do if they need her comments to fit the rhetoric they're spinning.

"I'm not all that interested in talking to anyone. Especially not the media. I just want them to leave me alone. And the protesters too."

I also want that. I want them all to go away and for them to realize how wrong they are about Jess. "Any idea who painted those words on your front door?"

"None. They were there when I got up this morning. I tried to paint over them. After I tried to scrub them off."

I cringe at what that means. If there'd been any trace evidence, she destroyed it when she attempted to get rid of the words. "Have you reported the vandalism to the cops?"

"Zara did...but I'd already corrupted the evidence by then." Her lips compress into a stubborn line, irritation flaring in her eyes. "Don't worry. The officer told me off for that apparent lapse in judgment."

Christ, nothing like making the victim feel like they're the one who committed the crime. Jess doesn't trust cops as it is. That careless response will only add another brick to the wall of distrust she has built against the police department. "I take it they didn't do anything about the crowd in front of your house?"

"The officer told me there was nothing he could do about it. Not unless they violate the law."

I release a tight breath. After everything Jess has gone through, she deserves to live her life in peace. She doesn't deserve this clusterfuck. "I've got some white paint at home I can use on the front door for the time being. Will you at least stay at my house until this all blows over?"

"I think you already know the answer." She huffs out a dry laugh. "This is my home, Troy. I don't want to give them the satisfaction of chasing me away from it."

I roll my eyes, a tiny smile twitching at the corners of my mouth. "Why do you have to be so stubborn?"

Jess turns her head to me. "Granny always said my stubbornness would get me far in life." She grins, but there's a sadness in her eyes that no amount of smiling can remove. "What she didn't realize was that it would be the one trait that would keep me alive."

Except that's not true. Jess had finally given up on life when she thought she'd never see her daughter again. I tighten my hold on her hand. I came close to losing the woman I love the day she was literally stabbed in the back. Came close to her never being in my life.

"If it makes you feel better, you can stay with me tonight." The smile on Jess's face is brighter this time. Then it fades. "Aren't you supposed to be with the Warriors group until later this evening? I know I haven't been in here all that long. It can't be that late already."

"My brothers can handle it." I would do the same for them if our places were reversed.

"No, you should go back. I'll be fine until you finish there. I'll probably just shoo Zara and Simone away so I can read the books Garrett loaned me."

"I'm still so glad you're attempting new things to try to find what you're passionate about," I say and press a gentle kiss on her forehead. "But either way, I can't leave you here while those assholes are in front of your house."

Jess sits a little straighter. "Yes, you can, and you will, Troy Carson."

My mouth tugs into a wide grin at her indignant tone.

"I mean it, Troy." The flare in her eyes matches her tone.

"Christ, I love it when you're this stubborn." I brush my mouth against hers. "I love you, Jess. Love you and every infuriatingly stubborn bone in your body."

She smiles, her expression bright and so goddamn gorgeous. "Glad to hear that."

Her reaction, her words...they send my heart rate into double time and my gut tightens in a good way. I can't imagine life without her now that she's part of it. And maybe one day...one day she'll feel the same way about me.

I rise to my feet, hold my hand out to her, and pull her up. "Call me if you need anything. I won't be too late."

27

JESSICA

August, Present Day
Maple Ridge

Bailey and I step out the back door of my house, a floppy straw hat on my head. The early Monday morning sunlight greets us, painting long shadows across the garden.

At some point during the evening, the reporters and protesters called it a night. But a bunch of them have reappeared since daybreak. They're quiet now, but as soon as they see me that will no doubt end.

I lock the door and head for the gate with Troy, Butterscotch, and Bailey walking alongside me. Troy opens the gate. The hinges squeak, alerting the reporters and protesters to our escape.

I hurry to the passenger side of the truck with Troy as my shadow, and open the rear door to let Butterscotch in.

"Protect our children! Convicts not welcome!"

And here we go again.

I shut the door, and Bailey and I climb into the front passenger seat. She settles between my legs.

I place the straw hat on my lap and fasten my seat belt.

"Protect our children! Convicts not welcome!"

"I take it they didn't lose their voices last night. Well, that's disappointing," I grumble. "Don't any of them work?" I yawn, unable to chase away the exhaustion due to last night's nightmares.

Troy turns over the engine. "I recognize a few stay-at-home moms. They probably dumped the kids at the grandparents' bright and early so they could be a menace on your street."

I snort a half laugh, but I don't dare to glance out the window to see how many young mothers we're talking about.

"You wanna come to the beach again with me and Nova today?" he asks.

My heart aches with longing, but I scoff. "Not the best idea. Reporters might follow me."

"Well, if you change your mind..." He lets the rest of the sentence hang, but maybe I could join them. Would it be so bad if I saw her? After all, the reporters aren't following us. And if I felt she was in danger, I'd leave.

Maybe some time spent building sandcastles with a kid again is just what I need. I had so much fun hanging out with the two of them last week.

The more I think about the idea, excitement whooshes inside me on a rush of adrenaline.

"Actually, yes," I tell him, a wide smile tugging on my mouth. "I'd love to join you two."

I open the photo app on my phone and go to the folder with various pictures I've recently edited. My *feel-good* photos. Flowers shimmering with raindrops. Butterflies sunning on blossoms. A magical forest. A shirtless Troy smiling at me like I'm something special. His warm smile even now sends my heart fluttering.

I flip to the photo Grace sent me three days ago of Amelia playing with her dog. I touch her grinning face, my heart soaring. She's so beautiful. So happy.

A *thud* next to my head startles me, and I make a noise that's part gasp, part shriek. The dogs bark.

The truck jerks to a stop. "What the fuck!" Troy says, his tight tone filling the cab.

Yolk and egg white and bits of smashed shell slip down the passenger window like debris caught in a mudslide.

Several women are standing near the truck with what could be smug expressions. It's hard to tell for sure through the slimy mess covering the window.

Troy is out the truck and storming to my side before I realize what's happening.

The small group of men and women standing on the driveway take a collective step back, their smirks dropping away.

I lift my phone and record the scene in front of me and the potential suspects for the egging. Maybe it was the same person who wrote COP KILLER on my front door.

Troy painted over the words last night, completely obscuring them with several layers of white paint that he had at his house. But the damage has been done. Everyone on the street now knows my true identity. It doesn't matter how many coats of paint cover the door—he can't erase the lie from everyone's mind. He can't erase the prejudices the lie will cause.

"Who threw the egg?" Troy demands.

"What the hell are you doing hangin' out with that dangerous ex-con?" an older men yells at Troy. His arms are heavily tattooed and his hair is shaved short. "I expected better from you."

"And I expected better from you, Mr. Whitman. We both fought in wars to protect civilians who were being stripped of their rights. And yet here you are, not extending the same courtesy to a woman who was wrongfully accused of a crime and stripped of *her* rights."

"Doesn't make a difference if she were innocent or not. She wasn't stayin' in a day spa. She wasn't makin' macramé hangers in some fancy-ass rehab center. She was hangin' out with the worst of the worst."

"She's lived on this street for the past five months. Has she given anyone a reason to believe she's a dangerous offender? No, she hasn't. Just the opposite."

Troy's words mean the world to me, but it's clear from everyone's frowns I was the only one moved by them. These people are like the jury who found me guilty of a crime I didn't do—unable to see beyond what they and the prosecutor believe to be the facts.

"Give her time. Her true colors *will* shine through, and you'll realize how wrong you were, Troy." The man doesn't walk away. He stands his ground like I imagine he did when he fought in whatever war he'd served in.

I want to scream like I longed to do so many times while I was married and while I was in prison, but that won't make a difference. Other than Troy, no one will hear my voice. No one will listen to what I have to say.

No one moves, and there's nothing Troy can do to make them go away. If he uses force to get them to leave me alone, he'll be the one facing assault charges.

As long as they toe the right side of the law, there's nothing he and I can do.

He can report the egging, but that won't do anything since we don't know who threw the eggs. And the police will hardly give a damn about it. It's not exactly their top priority.

After the rough start to my day—and the delay with getting to work—the rest of the morning passes without incident. Troy is scheduled to spend the entire day at a job site on the outskirts of town, so it's quiet in the office.

A text pings on my phone from him.

> Troy: How are things going?

He's been texting me every thirty minutes. It's amazing he's getting any work done.

> Me: Quiet.

> Troy: Good. Let me know if you need anything.

> Me: Will do.

I send him another text.

> Me: Looking forward to spending time with you and Nova later.

I scroll through the previous messages. I could send him a dirty text to spice things up a little, but do I want to risk Lance or someone else seeing it? Definitely not. I've got enough going on without adding *mortified every time I see Lance* to the list.

I pull up the photo on my phone again that Grace sent me on Saturday of Amelia. My little girl turns eight on Sunday. I haven't heard from Craig or Grace since I called Grace—other than when she texted the picture—

but maybe they'll be okay if I send Amelia a birthday present.

Or I can give it to her when I see her.

An image slips into my thoughts of Amelia smiling at the gift like she's smiling in the photo Grace sent me. The pure delight on her face lightens my heart, brings a grin to *my* face.

I get back to work, but the image in my head sticks around for the next hour. I'm not sure what to get her—but I want to get her something to celebrate her birthday. It will be the first time in over five years I've been able to buy her a present.

I grab my lunch and purse from the bottom desk drawer. "There's somewhere I need to go," I tell Bailey, "before we go to the park for lunch." I pull on the floppy straw hat to conceal my identity as much as possible and lock the door to the reception area on our way out.

The weather is warm with only a few clouds speckling the sky overhead. Storm clouds are gathering on the horizon, but since Troy is driving us home, I won't have to worry about getting soaked.

Praying no one realizes who I am—my hands trembling at the possibility—I walk to Main Street with Bailey by my side. No one seems to give me a second glance. Or at the very least they don't say anything that I overhear.

We stop outside Little Wonders, the children's store where I applied for a job shortly after moving to Maple Ridge. I haven't been inside it since. There hasn't been a need to until now.

I don't know if they're okay with Bailey entering the store with only a *Service Dog in Training* vest, so I tie her leash to the nearby empty bike rack. "I won't be long."

The woman who interviewed me is busy with a

customer at the till. They don't look my way. I'm good with that.

I walk up and down the aisles, checking the different gift possibilities, and end up in the craft section. I have no idea what eight-year-old Amelia would like for her birthday, but the craft kits feel like a safe bet. I loved doing crafts with Granny at that age.

Female voices approach on the other side of the shelves where I'm standing.

"If Savannah was really abused like she claimed during the trial," the slightly high, nasally voice says, "then why didn't she leave her husband? I can tell you if Frank laid a hand on me, I would walk out and not give him another chance."

"No kidding," the other woman responds, her voice smooth like whipped cream—minus the sugar. "Who doesn't have a husband who gets angry from time to time. But if it gets bad, you just leave. You don't stick around 'cause he said he's sorry."

"Do you think she killed her husband?"

"It's hard to know for sure. Stewart believes she had an accomplice. I don't think she was that smart. It was dumb luck if you ask me."

Nasally Voice scoffs. "She probably got some nice insurance money from it."

"I read California paid her a million dollars." A bitter tone curdles the second woman's voice.

A million? I frown. Is that what the article said or what she remembers the amount to be, her memory inflating the real value fourfold?

Nasally Voice responds, but I don't catch what she says, the words too soft to be heard from where I'm standing.

"Guess that's how she could afford to buy that old house

and renovate it." The other woman doesn't even bother to keep the volume of her voice low. "I can't believe Anne Carstairs didn't know Savannah or Jessica or whatever she goes by had just been released from prison. What kind of person rents out their house without doing a criminal check on the applicant?"

"She was probably just happy to have someone rent the run-down old place."

I dig my fingernails into my palms to keep from responding. If not for Anne's kindness and generosity, I wouldn't have had a place to stay after I was released from prison. I wouldn't have had a safe haven while I figured out the next part of my life.

And in trying to repay Anne for her kindness, I've become indebted to her and her great-aunt again. Transcribing the journals for Anne has given me hope.

Be strong.

The Jessica who first moved to Maple Ridge would have slunk out the store door and never returned. But I'm not that woman anymore. If Angelique could survive against the SOE agent who became a Nazi collaborator, I can survive the ill-informed Maple Ridge residents.

I select a craft kit from the shelf. It's for growing a small fairy garden and is perfect for Amelia's age. I bet if Johann's sister, Anja, had been a kid today, she would have loved it.

The women's voices move away, and it sounds like they're returning to the till.

I head that way, carrying the kit, and remove my hat. I'm not looking to hide my identity for what I'm about to do.

"Hi." I put the box on the counter so they know I'm a paying customer. "I heard what you were saying about abused women." My voice comes out annoyingly cracked, the volume barely louder than a whisper. I try to clear my throat, but my rapidly thumping heart is wedged in there. "How you think they can easily walk away from their abusive husbands or boyfriends like I can walk out of this store."

Be brave.

My palms grow clammy, and I release a quick breath. "With some men, it might be possible to leave them. But with many others, the abuse starts out slow, hardly recognizable at first as abuse. It's not until later, when all the pieces of the puzzle slot together, that the woman understands she's been in an abusive relationship all this time but didn't realize it."

The two women stare at me, their cheeks pinking. I make the most of their mute state and power on, determined to get in my say before they come to their senses. Before they argue their misguided beliefs about abused women that society commonly clings to.

"Some men might realize they have an issue and are willing to get counseling. They love their wife and don't want to lose their family," I continue. "But many are more like my late husband. The man doesn't love his wife. His wife is a possession, and he'll do anything to keep from losing her. Even if it means killing her. He'll stalk her and track her down if she does try to go."

A memory creeps in of flashing red-and-blue lights from a cruiser parked behind my car. Amelia was asleep in her car seat, unaware of my attempt to escape her father. "There is no one-size-fits-all with abusive partners. Nor is there a one-size-fits-all with leaving them. And even if the woman escapes him, she's left with a shitload of emotional scars the world doesn't see."

Be a voice.

I try to swallow the pain that scalds my throat with each word. "The woman has to start her life over and figure out who she is because the abuser stole her self-esteem, her self-worth, her identity. He left her always questioning herself. Blaming herself. Doubting herself. And if she has children, she has to do all of that while facing the challenges of being a single mother."

I push the kit closer to the woman behind the counter, the fire in me burning brighter, hotter. "Survivors of abuse don't deserve to be misjudged. They don't deserve the common belief they can just walk away if they are being abused. They don't deserve being condemned for falling for the wrong man, a man who is skilled at manipulation. Survivors of abuse want compassion and understanding. They don't deserve the blame society puts on them for the situation they found themselves in."

Damn, it felt good to get all of that off my chest. To spew out the lava of words I've held back for too long.

The women stare at me, their faces flushed. But their stunned silence only lasts a fraction of a heartbeat. The woman behind the counter narrows her eyes, her gaze falling to the scar by my mouth. "That might be so…" She snatches up the garden kit and puts it under the counter. "But I don't sell to dangerous offenders."

My stomach tightens, and a winter freeze smothers my fire and fight. "I'm not a dangerous offender." The strength behind my voice stumbles and falters. "I've never physically hurt anyone, and I have no intention of starting."

The redness of the woman's face deepens, and her jaw muscle jumps. "That's what you say, but it doesn't mean anything. Now, leave unless you want me to call the police."

"But I haven't done anything wrong. I just want to buy a birthday present for my…" I shove down the rest of the words before I reveal too much.

"I don't care who you want to buy a present for. You'll have to get it somewhere else." The woman glares at me with such cold intensity, I shudder.

The other woman's eyes are no warmer.

The fire and voice I found a moment ago, that spoke of the injustices abused women deal with, fail to reignite. I nod and walk out the door, my body shaking.

I untie Bailey's leash and head for the park. After what happened in the store, my appetite has bailed, so I just walk around the park, keeping a distance from everyone.

My phone pings with a text.

Troy: How are things?

Me: They're good.

I ignore his follow-up texts, defeat and frustration crushing me.

The skin on the back of my neck prickles, like someone is watching me. I glance at my surroundings, my muscles taut. No one seems to be paying attention to me, and the media hasn't tracked me here.

But even so, I can't shake the feeling I'm being stalked.

I've suddenly become the prey.

28

TROY

August, Present Day
Maple Ridge

I sit on the grass with my crew for lunch, the five of us appreciating that the weather isn't cold or wet. Butterscotch flops down next to me.

The houses in this neighborhood are newer—two decades old—and larger than most in Maple Ridge. Other than a few middle-aged individuals walking their dogs, the street is quiet. The opposite to Jess's this morning.

"I heard there were protesters outside of Jess's house yesterday." Lance purses his lips and a frown creases between his eyebrows. All hint of the man who loves to mock and tease is gone.

"That's right. The idiots were harassing her. And someone vandalized her front door. She hasn't done anything wrong, and yet it feels like she's in the middle of a witch trial."

Lance grunts. "No one ever survived those unscathed."

"I'm not sure anyone survived those period. Innocent or not, you were burned at the stake." The protesters haven't tried to burn her, but how far will they take things if they're trying to force her to leave Maple Ridge?

A red Honda Civic pulls in front of Lance's truck. A minute later, Nova comes bounding toward us.

I push to my feet and scoop her up. She giggles. The sweet sound of it is the best part of my day so far, other than when I made love to Jess this morning. I tickle Nova's side, and she giggles and squirms.

Olivia walks over to us, a blanket under one arm. Her other hand carries a picnic basket.

A lovesick sigh comes from one of my crew, but I don't turn to see which one.

"So, when are you and I gonna make sandcastles again?" I ask Nova. "Or do you wanna see if we can find any teddy bears having a picnic this afternoon?"

Nova bounces in my arms, her small hands on my chest. "Teddy bear! Teddy bear!"

"Hey, Nova." Lance waves at her, a goofy grin on his face. She waves back, her smile just as goofy.

"Are you gonna be Goldilocks?" I tickle her side again.

Giggling, Nova rapidly shakes her head.

"Oh, that's right. You don't like porridge." I lower her to the ground, and she toddles over to where Butterscotch is snoozing.

"Hey, Aramis. Wasn't expecting to see you until later— when I pick up Nova." I hug Olivia and give her a friendly kiss on her cheek.

Lance squints up at us, the sun in his eyes. "Do I get a kiss on the cheek?"

"Man. Didn't realize you felt that way about me." I start

to lower to my knees, knowing full well he doesn't mean me.

An abrupt laugh erupts from him. "Not you, dumb-ass." He looks up at Olivia, the grin back on his face. "You."

She rolls her eyes as I straighten, and she gives him a quick peck on the cheek. He smirks at her, but I swear he's blushing under his tan.

"Can I talk to you for a minute?" Her question is directed at me.

"Of course. What's on your mind?"

"I meant in private."

"Sure. Let's go inside." I turn to Lance. "You okay with Nova for a few minutes?"

The owner of the house we're renovating doesn't have any kids...just lots of breakable items they probably wouldn't appreciate Nova's fingerprints on.

"No problem, Boss." He gives me a swift salute, then offers his palm for a high five from Nova. She smacks him one and grabs a dandelion from the grass. She hands it to him, seeming much more interested in him than her mother was a moment ago.

Olivia usually laughs when the guy we've known since elementary school calls me boss. She doesn't so much as crack a smile this time. "Be good for Uncle Lance, sweetheart," she says to her daughter.

"We'll be fine." Lance exchanges a quick glance with me. Uncertainty wars in his expression, but I don't think it has anything to do with Olivia leaving Nova with him.

I take Olivia into the house. We go into the partially renovated kitchen and stop next to the cabinet doors stacked on the newly installed green tile floor. "So, what's up?"

She scans the room, checking it out, before returning

her attention to me. "I heard you brought Jess with you last Tuesday when you and Nova went to the beach."

I shrug, not getting why she wanted to talk to me about that in private. "That's right. We built a large sandcastle."

Olivia folds her arms across her chest. "That was supposed to be your quality time with Nova. Not time spent with your girlfriend at my daughter's expense." Her tone isn't annoyed, but it is venturing close to that territory.

"I didn't think you'd have a problem with it. Jess likes kids, and she's great with Nova."

Olivia chews on her bottom lip the way she does when she's stressed about something. Colton used to say it made her look sexy. I'm not as easily distracted by it as he was.

An uneasy feeling pokes at my gut. "Spit it out. What aren't you saying?"

"I don't feel comfortable with my daughter being around your girlfriend." The snappish tone to Olivia's voice is one I haven't been on the receiving end of for a long time. The unease poking at my gut switches to the sharp press of a knife blade.

I frown. "What are you talking about? You've met Jess. You didn't have any problems with her when she was interviewing you for the article. Why the change of attitude?"

Olivia and Cora have always been close as sisters. If Cora thought Savannah was a risk to Nova, Cora would have said something when she'd first suspected Savannah was Jess—wouldn't she?

"God, Troy. When were you going to tell me that your girlfriend"—Olivia practically spits out the word—"spent the past seven years in a maximum-security prison?"

"It was five." My voice is low and thick with warning. Not that it makes a difference if it was seven or five years. Either number will be bad in Olivia's eyes. "What does that have to do with anything? If you know about that, then you know Jess wasn't the one who murdered her *abusive* husband."

"Doesn't matter. She still spent the last five years in that prison, fighting to stay alive. Fighting, Troy!" Olivia stabs me in the chest with her finger, punctuating each word.

I have no idea what she's talking about, but I suspect whatever it is, is based on lies and half-truths.

"Jess was a victim of a system that was supposed to protect her," I say. "But instead of protecting her, it did nothing but fail her. You want to know how she ended up with PTSD? That's how. She was abused by her husband and she was abused by inmates. Why? Because she never fought back. You know what would've happened if she had fought back in prison?"

"No. What?" The pitch of Olivia's voice jumps an octave, and her volume explodes another notch.

"If the system decided Jess was the instigator, her sentence might have been lengthened. So, she *never*. Fought. Back." I pound my fist on the countertop to emphasize my words.

"I'm sorry, Troy, but I can't let you spend time with Nova if you keep hanging out with that woman. Colton wouldn't want you to be with his daughter, either, under those circumstances. It's my job to protect her since he isn't here to do that."

Fuck. "Colton would never feel that way. He would've seen the good in Jess you're refusing to see."

"Well, I guess we'll never know which of us is right. Because he's not here." Olivia's voice splinters, but her volume doesn't waiver.

"You're being unreasonable, Olivia."

"I'm watching out for my daughter's safety, Troy. Your girlfriend was responsible for Sophie Wilson's kidnapping. Who's to say she won't kidnap Nova?"

"For Christ's sake. Jess didn't kidnap Sophie. She was helping protect Violet and Sophie from Chief Wilson. He was abusing Violet, and she tried to escape with Sophie. What did you expect Jess to do? She knew what it was like for Violet. She knew how difficult it was for Violet to get away and start over when she was married to someone like Chief Wilson."

The air between us remains charged, each of us staring the other person down. The electrical current arcs and flares and sparks. Then the air molecules shift unexpectedly, the movement subtle. A surrender of wills. A stepping down.

"I'm glad Violet and Jess no longer have to deal with their abusive husbands," Olivia says, her tone softening a tiny degree. "I really am. But that doesn't change where Jess was staying before she moved to Maple Ridge. I can't risk my daughter's safety. I thought you of all people would understand."

"Nova's safety is important to me too." I can't believe Olivia's acting as if it isn't.

"If that's true, you'll understand why I'm doing this. You have to make a choice, Troy. You can spend time with Nova or Jess, but you can't be with both at the same time. If you want to spend time with Nova, Jess can't be with you. And that's final." The harshness in her voice is gone, replaced with a plea for me to understand. It's clear I won't win this battle.

Shit. I promised Colton I would be there for both of his girls. I can't go against my promise just because Olivia is being stubborn and can't see reason. And I can't do that to Nova. For now, I'm the only father my goddaughter knows. I can't turn my back on her, especially after I failed her father and mother.

"Okay." I release a heavy breath. "I won't include Jess

when I spend time with Nova." A calm I don't feel levels out my tone, masks the clash of emotions inside me. "It will just be Nova and me and no one else. But I'm asking you not to jump on the bandwagon of believing the worst about Jess like your sister. Jess has done nothing wrong. Think how you would feel if your places were reversed, and you lost everything due to the actions of someone else."

Except...Olivia did lose everything due to the actions of someone else. If the driver of the transport truck had stopped at the stop sign on the highway like he was supposed to, the bus carrying the hockey players wouldn't have collided with the truck. Colton wouldn't have been a first responder at the accident site, and he would still be alive.

"Jess didn't lose everything. She has a house and a job and a boyfriend." An unnamed emotion swims in Olivia's eyes, but I'm too pissed at the situation to figure out what it is.

Olivia walks out of the kitchen. I turn to the counter and clutch the edge of it, my head bowed, my back to the doorway.

Jess doesn't want anyone to know about Amelia, but if Olivia knows the truth, realizes how big a sacrifice Jess made for her little girl's happiness, maybe Olivia will then see Jess the same way I do.

Maybe then she'll give Jess a chance and stand by her side like my brothers and our friends do.

"She lost everything that was important to her," I say quietly, but not too quiet that Olivia can't hear me. "She lost her freedom...and she lost her daughter."

The front door clicks open, but it doesn't close right away. I wait for Olivia to ask me what daughter, but I'm met with silence.

I close my eyes, inwardly cursing myself for revealing the secret. A secret that wasn't mine to share. I had taken a gamble it would change Olivia's mind about Jess. Hopefully it's not too late—that the silence means she's thinking about it.

The front door clicks shut, and I know without a doubt Olivia has made her decision and my final words didn't sway her.

Dammit. Dammit to hell.

Now I'll have to tell Jess she can't spend this afternoon with Nova and me. Tell her even though Jess had been excited to hang out with us at the beach again.

And I have to pray to God Olivia doesn't tell her goddamn nosy sister the truth about Amelia.

29

ANGELIQUE

December 1943
France

I wrap the shawl tighter around my shoulders and stare at the light snow on the driveway that hasn't seen a vehicle in two months. Not since the day Johann drove away. The cold wind is nothing compared to the chill that pumps through me at not knowing what happened to him or where he might be.

Is he still safe?

Is he still alive?

Surely I would know in the depths of my soul if something had happened to him.

Movement in my rounded belly has me glancing down, and I cup my hand on the spot where I felt it. The deep-rooted ache in the bones of my damaged hand flares. I wince and do my best to ignore the pain that never goes away.

"I miss your papa too, *ma petite*," I say in French. I miss Johann's smile. I miss the way he makes me feel even though we're surrounded by nothing but ugliness and despair. I miss his kind heart and I miss his stories about his family and his friends and his childhood.

I stroke my thumb against the spot where our baby poked me. Dr. Hubert has assured me my pregnancy is advancing as well as can be expected given the conditions. The lack of food we're all facing is impacting our baby's growth. I've decided the baby is a girl. But if my mother's intuition proves me wrong, I'll love a little boy just as much.

All I can hope for is that she is healthy and isn't deaf. It's not that I will love her any less if she is like her aunt. It's her safety I'm worried about if Hitler isn't stopped.

"I am not sure if your papa is coming back," I whisper. His absence gnaws at my soul. But it doesn't feel as though that part of me has been cleaved away as it would be if he were dead. Hope dimly flickers that he is alive.

That, and the hope one day soon my sister and I will be reunited. In the spare moments when I'm not doing the painful rehabilitation exercises for my hand, when I'm not helping around the house, when I'm not listening to the BBC French news, I let my thoughts drift to returning home to her.

What if we could let the past be in the past?

What if she could embrace her niece and be the doting aunty, the woman who loved chasing fairies as a little girl?

What if she found out who fathered my baby and hated her for it?

It doesn't matter who fathered my baby, because Hazel will never learn the truth.

The Official Secrets Act I signed before coming to France prohibits me from saying anything about my time here. She will never hear how my baby's father saved me from the Gestapo. Or that Johann was a Wehrmacht soldier until he deserted the Army.

Hope for Johann's return has me reluctant to leave for England. But hope isn't the only emotion twisting restlessly inside me. Frustration stirs alongside it. Frustration that I'm here and not doing my part to help end the war. Frustration that I'm a burden to Dr. Hubert and Rosita. Frustration that my being here could possibly put them at risk. Frustration that one of Baker Street's agents betrayed us, and I haven't been able to warn London.

The rounder my belly gets, the more challenging travelling will be. And it could start snowing soon. If I'm forced to make a run for it, I could end up leaving tracks in the snow. Then it will be easier for the Nazis to hunt me. I could go to Poitiers. One of the agents I came to France with was headed there. I could continue the fight while I am still able—before I get too big to be of much help.

Johann left to fight with the Allies. I need to do my part too. I've waited long enough for his return. I need to do the job I was trained to do. For the sake of my baby.

For the sake of ending the war and being in Johann's arms that much sooner.

"It's time," I tell no one in particular.

I go back inside, mentally preparing for what I must soon do. "One of the agents I trained with went to Poitiers," I tell Dr. Hubert and Rosita that night at supper. "It's time I go there. And maybe then I can get a message to London."

Rosita puts her cutlery on her plate with more force than is called for. It clatters loudly in the otherwise quiet dining room. "Nonsense. It's dangerous. You're with child. You should wait until Johann returns."

"We don't know when that will be. I don't even know yet if London knows what happened to me or the other agents. They need to be told." I would hope they already know—

that they have figured something went wrong because of errors in a radio communicator's messages. But there is still a chance they don't know the truth yet. My consciousness has not let me ignore that reality, the niggling fear growing stronger every day.

Dr. Hubert and Rosita know a little about what I was doing prior to my arrest. They pieced a lot of it together from listening to the nightly BBC news with me.

"Do you think the person you trained with is still alive?" Dr. Hubert asks.

"I can only hope she is." I don't have a clue where Lise might be, but she's the only person I know in France who might be able to help me and who wasn't linked to the *Cashmere* network.

"When do you plan to leave?"

"Tomorrow morning."

"But you don't have your *carte d'identité*," Rosita says.

"That doesn't matter. They will be on the lookout for someone with her name and who bears her resemblance." Dr. Hubert covers my good hand with his.

"I know how to change my appearance so I'm not easily recognized."

"Good. That will help. Wait a few days, and I'll see what I can do. I have a connection who might be able to get you new papers. I haven't said anything until now because I thought you would stay until Johann's return."

"Alright," I agree, "but only three days. And then I will need to leave." For their sake as much as for mine. The longer I stay with them, the more dangerous it is for the pair. I cannot risk that after everything they've done for me.

Dr. Hubert pushes to his feet. "I have something for you." He leaves the room and comes back carrying an envelope. "Johann asked me to give this to you if you left prior to his return."

I take the envelope from Dr. Hubert. "Angelique" is written on the front in Johann's handwriting. I would recognise it anywhere.

I trace over my name as if that's all it will take to make Johann appear in front of me. His smile flashes in my thoughts, and I push down the heartache that deepens every day, even when I try so hard to ignore it.

"Thank you," I tell Dr. Hubert. "I'll read it after I wash the dishes."

"Why don't you go and read it now," Rosita says. "It's not as though there are many dishes. I can clean them myself."

I fix a smile on my face, masking the nerves that churn in my belly. "Thank you."

I go upstairs to the guest room, light the candle on the bedside table, and sit on the bed. My fingers trembling, I carefully open the envelope and remove the single sheet of paper.

I can do this.

I can be brave.

I can be strong.

I read the letter, my eyes misting with tears.

Dear Angelique.

You are asleep now, and I'm watching your slow rhythmic breaths. You have gone through so much in the past two days, but you're still beautiful and strong.

I wish I didn't have to leave you. If I could stay, I would. The desire to see and hold you again are what will keep me going during this war.

I promised you before you fell asleep that

I will return for you. I have every intention of following through with my promise. But like I told you, I also want to make a difference in this war if I can. I want to continue what you set out to do. I want to make the world a better place for our child to grow up in.

I'm going to ask Dr. Hubert to give you this letter if you should leave prior to my return. If I haven't returned, it's because of one of several reasons. I pray neither side chooses to end my life because my alliances have changed and the rebels don't believe me. I pray if I am not by your side, it's because the rebels believe I can be of some use to them.

Eventually, this war will end. Remember what I told you about Maple Ridge, Oregon. One day soon, when the world is less chaotic, I hope to experience the beauty there my friend told me about. And I hope to be able to share it with you and our baby.

I love you, Angelique. Never stop believing that.

Until we meet again,

Johann

30

JESSICA

August, Present Day
Maple Ridge

I return to the office. No one seems to be following me, but I can't shake the feeling I'm being stalked.

It's just your imagination.

Or possibly the complex PTSD working overtime—combined with the reporters and protesters constantly tormenting me when I'm at home.

I push the thought aside and focus on my work. Excitement wraps around me like a soft blanket on a rainy day. Not excitement at the task at hand, but at how in a few hours I'll be spending time with Troy and Nova.

Playing with them. Getting to know the little girl who's an important part of Troy's life.

Getting to know the little girl who reminds me so much of Amelia at that age.

I know she isn't my daughter, but spending time with

230

Nova feels a tiny bit like I'm getting back some of the time I lost with my little girl.

And after what happened earlier at Little Wonders, hanging out with an adorable two-year-old will make my day better. Brighter.

I just hope the media or judgment surrounding me don't follow me to the beach and keep me from spending the afternoon with Troy and Nova. I'll leave if it comes to that—but I really hope it doesn't.

Troy walks into the office a few minutes early for our late afternoon excursion with Nova. The curve of his smile is not quite fully formed, his eyes missing their usual sparkle. Even his shoulders don't seem to have the strength to be strong and proud. They're slumped, deflated, caved in.

It's a good thing I'm joining him and Nova. I'm not sure he'll survive an energetic toddler without me. He has put too many demands on himself, and it's still another six weeks until the festival is off his to-do list. Six weeks until he has one less thing weighing him down.

I walk to him and loop my arms around his shoulders. "Hi." I smile at him, and my mouth finds his, taking whatever he'll give me. Giving him so much in return. My tongue strokes his, and I greedily consume him.

He slips his arms around my waist. The tension in his muscles loosens, but it doesn't fully disappear. With everything he's got on his plate, it doesn't surprise me.

I pull away ever so slightly, our bodies still pressed together. "You ready to pick up Nova now?"

Troy's eyes cloud for a fraction of a second with an emotion I can't read. It sends my heart stumbling.

"What's wrong?" I ask.

He closes his eyes, and his body goes tense again. He releases a hard breath.

Oh, this can't be good.

"Olivia came to the worksite earlier. She..." He opens his eyes, and I can see in them what he's trying to say, but he doesn't have the heart to eviscerate me with the words. He knows I was excited to spend the afternoon with him and Nova.

I step away, and Troy's arms fall to his side. "She doesn't want me to hang out with you and her daughter," I fill in for him, my voice a rough whisper. *Because of the protesters and because of my past and because she might be in love with you.*

I attempt to fix my lips into an understanding smile. It's wobbly at best. "That's okay. I'm not family. You, Olivia, and Nova are family. And given everything..." The rest of my words stick in my throat, their taste bitter and rusty and foul.

Even if the world wasn't imploding around me, thanks to her sister's article, Olivia wouldn't want me to spend time with Nova and Troy. She has feelings for him that go beyond friendship. Troy has become Colton's replacement in so many ways, and that includes being Nova's father.

"I've got lots to do this evening," I tell him. "This way I can get an early start on it all." The novel about Angelique won't write itself.

Troy studies my face, and I do what I can to make my smile look genuine. "Are you sure?" he asks, my smile apparently not convincing enough.

I nod. "Absolutely. The time you spend with Nova is important. It will ensure she grows up strong and brave— like her father would want her to be." Like I'm trying to be. Like Angelique was.

My words to Troy sound pretty convincing even to my ears. They don't come off as if I'm heartbroken by the turn of events. I hope. It's not Troy's fault Olivia doesn't want me spending time with him and her daughter. It's not Olivia's fault either.

"She might be only two now, but the years will go by quickly," I remind him. "Enjoy the time with her while you can. Once she's a teen, she probably won't want to spend so much time with her...her godfather."

Troy grabs my hips and pulls me to him. "I hate leaving you alone with everything going on."

"It's probably better I'm not with you two. I don't want to risk the protesters catching wind of where I am and scaring Nova."

"I hate that it's come to this." He blows a ragged breath, the exhaustion on his face deepening the lines around his eyes and mouth. "I shouldn't have to choose between you two. I should be able to hang out with both of you at the same time."

Olivia is making him choose between Nova and me?

Of course she is. She loves Troy. I'm just the woman who's standing in her way of getting what she's dreaming of —Troy as her husband and Nova's father.

Can't say I blame her. What woman wouldn't want Troy as her husband and the father of her children?

Other than me. But I'm not a good example. I'm bruised. Dented. Broken. I had my chance at a happily ever after and it ended up being anything but that. I lost everything important to me. I don't have it in me to go through that again. I don't have it in me to risk losing another child.

"Have fun with Nova, and I'll be waiting for you once you've finished making her day." I kiss him lightly on the lips. "Okay?"

"Alright. That doesn't mean I like this. Once things die down with the protesters and reporters, I'll talk to Olivia and get her to change her mind."

I nod, unable to voice the truth—that her mind will never change.

THE PROTESTERS AND REPORTERS ARE BLOCKING MY DRIVEWAY when Troy pulls up to it. He honks and advances forward. Some of the protesters scatter to the side. The rest of them hold up their signs and continue chanting. "Protect our children! Convicts not welcome!"

Troy advances another few inches. "Christ, what's their fucking problem?"

"They're hoping I'll just give up and move away."

"They can hope all they want. That's not gonna happen. Not unless you're planning to move in with me." There's a smile in his tone that isn't mirrored in his expression. He scowls at the people outside the truck.

The volume of the chanting increases, but most of the protesters do step aside, allowing Troy to get through.

He pulls up the driveway and parks closer to the rear of my house. Troy, Bailey, and I get out of the truck. Troy opens the back door for Butterscotch to jump down.

Reporters shout questions at me. I can barely make out what they're asking. The clash of questions yelled at the same time and the chanting creates one big noise, making it easier for me to ignore them.

We hurry past the wooden gate. The chanting pursues us into the garden, the distance and hedge barely dulling the volume.

"I need some sort of magical dome over my garden, then I can enjoy sitting outside without having to hear the protesters." I unlock the door and open it.

The dogs rush past us and go into the house. I follow

them, toe off my sandals by the door, and enter the code for the security system.

"I'll be back in a few hours." Troy lifts his phone, finger poised above the screen. "I'll call one of my brothers to come over and keep an eye on things while I'm gone."

"Don't worry about it. I'll be fine. Will the protesters be annoying? Absolutely. But I bet I'm not the only one who's fed up with them. If they irritate my neighbors, someone's bound to complain to the police." *Please, someone, file a complaint.* As long as they're not the ones doing the protesting, of course.

"And you think that will make a difference?" Troy's tone says he believes the opposite.

"They're the definition of disturbing the peace." That's got to count for something. The cops might not do anything to help me, but they can't ignore my neighbors' complaints. I'm the one who's been branded a cop killer and a dangerous offender—not the other residents on my street.

"I'm gonna call Kellan."

I touch Troy's arm, his well-developed biceps firm beneath my fingertips. "No, you're not. He's probably busy with work. And I'm going to use the time while you're gone to figure out the historical novel I plan to write."

"You can still do that with him here." Troy folds his arms, and I let my hand drop to my side, barely refraining from rolling my eyes at his protectiveness. It can be sweet at times. Other times it's damn frustrating. He's not trying to control me. That I do know. It's just part of who he is. He protects those he loves. He protects those who need protecting.

"No, I can't. He'll be too much of a distraction." I lightly press my lips to Troy's mouth, the touch brief. "You should go now. Nova's waiting." I don't need to give Olivia another reason not to like me or to make things difficult for Troy.

"Okay. I'll be back in a few hours. Text me if you need anything."

"I will." The lie slips awkwardly from between my lips, but I don't think Troy notices. I have no intention of taking him away from his time with Nova. The little girl is missing out on having a father due to the cruelty of PTSD. I won't be responsible for taking away the main father figure who's now in her life.

I put my palm on Troy's chest and give him a nudge outside. "Go. Nova's waiting for you."

He and Butterscotch leave, and I go upstairs to my bedroom. Bailey walks alongside me. I retrieve Angelique's journal from the bottom dresser drawer and return downstairs.

The living room is dark, the curtains closed. I spent five years existing without much privacy. I'm not giving up what little I have now by letting the protesters and reporters see into my living room.

I get comfy on the couch and disappear into Angelique's world. The chanting outside the window becomes a ghost of a noise as I focus on her words. Words I attempt to decipher. Words that have become the casualty of shaky handwriting and faded ink.

But now I know why her handwriting is so difficult to read, why she struggled with arthritis and the use of her right hand. An SOE agent who was supposed to be on her side, who was supposed to help France and Britain win the war, became a double agent.

And for what reason? Greed? The lust for power? A disregard for human life? These could be the same reasons Violet's husband joined forces with the criminal organization involved in trafficking assault weapons.

If my late husband were alive, would he have fallen down the same destructive path? He and Chief Wilson had a lot in common. They were abusive, manipulative, and controlling. Maybe those same traits are required for being a *bad* cop. If I can profile these sorts of people, it might help me write strong villains in Iris's story.

I glance at the pile of writing craft books on the coffee table. On the other hand, I should probably try penning the first chapter to see how it goes. It might turn out that I hate writing fiction or I'm awful at it.

I put the journal aside, close my eyes for a moment to visualize the scene, and begin typing.

I've been working away at the first chapter for an hour when my phone rings on the table. I lean over and pick it up. Craig? My heart thuds to a standstill and my mouth turns drought dry.

"Hi, Craig." The greeting comes out crackly and squeaked. I clear my throat. "How are you doing?" I try to infuse an upbeat, happy tone to my words, as if there isn't a large group of protesters outside the window, chanting, "Protect our children. Convicts not welcome."

"I'm good, Savannah." Craig sounds anything but good. He sounds like a doctor who's about to tell a patient they've only got a few hours left to live. My heart sinks. Even a defibrillator won't get it beating again.

"Jessica," I correct and curve my mouth into a smile, hoping it's enough to hide my frustration from him. "I don't go by my old name anymore. New start and all."

"Right. Jessica. Grace told me you called the other day about seeing Lia."

I bite my lip to keep from blurting that my daughter's name is Amelia. "That's right. She's yours and Grace's daughter..." Just saying the words out loud feels like razor blades slicing my throat from the inside. Each word stings my heart and my soul. I put my hand over my heart, as if that's all it takes to keep me in one piece. "But...but I would love to see her again. To be part of her life—even if it won't be in the same way it was before. I have a steady job. And my house has a room that's perfect for children." *Don't cry. Whatever you do, don't cry. Don't give him any reason to doubt I have it all together.*

I keep repeating the words in my head, waiting for him to say the ones I've been dying to hear since I was released from prison.

"I know you miss her." Craig's tone softens. "You love her, and you were a good mother to her. That much was clear to Grace and me. While you were her mom, you raised her to be a wonderful little girl."

There's no missing the huge "but" looming over the words. I bite my lower lip. Hard.

Don't say it. Don't say it. Please don't say it, I silently plead to him. *Please don't say the words that will forever break my heart.*

"But I don't think you being in her life will be possible," he continues, barely skipping a beat. "I know you've been trying to start your life over again, Sav—Jessica, but...but you were Wayne's wife. Wayne. Lincoln. Both of my brothers are part of my past. The reasons I'm estranged from my family. I can't...I can't deal with that part of my life again."

"But Amelia is part of my late husband"—I still can't say his name out loud—"and you had no issues with accepting her into your life despite that." Desperation leaks into my voice, roughing up the calm I'm trying to infuse into it.

"Because she was an innocent child. An innocent child who needed a home and loving parents. I look at her and I don't see my brothers or the bullying I dealt with growing up in that house. I just see a sweet and generous little girl. She's my light. But you...you're a reminder of the darkest time of my life. I'm sorry, Jessica, but my decision is final."

He does sound sorry, but that doesn't make me feel better. His words slice deep into my soul, spill the hope I'd been harboring since I was released from prison. It drips to the floor, spreads into a puddle, evaporates.

And I'm left shredded and spent.

I'm hollow.

I swipe at the tears soaking my cheeks. "I understand," I say, attempting a smile. I don't want him to know how much his words are destroying me. It won't sway Grace's and his decision. "But maybe if you give it a little time. Give me a chance. You won't feel that way. Once you get to know—"

"I don't know, Jessica. I don't see that happening. It's just too much." There's a finality to his words, a door slamming shut in my face.

A hiccupped sob escapes me, and the hand holding the phone shakes. "Okay." Disappointment and pain leak into the word, cracking my insides to pieces. "I'll let you go now. Thank you...thank you for calling me."

I end the call and put the phone on the coffee table next to my World War II research books.

My hand hovers over the phone, then with a strangled cry, I sweep my hand across the surface of the table, knocking everything off. The journal. The books. My phone. Only my laptop is spared from the grief gutting me.

I want to punch something, to scream, to cry. But I don't want to risk anyone outside hearing me and having that reported on the evening news. It will only feed into their lies, as well as their fear and distrust of me.

I pick up Angelique's journal, clutch it to my chest, and walk upstairs on trembling legs.

I open the door to the room that was to be Amelia's. I don't even register the work Troy and his brothers have done on it and head for the closet. I pull open the door to the secret room and crawl inside. The blankets and pillows I'd given Violet and Sophie are still here, forming a makeshift bed.

I curl into a fetal position on the blankets and scream and scream and scream into a pillow. I scream until my lungs are burning. Scream until I have nothing left in me to give.

A whimper comes from the doorway, and a warm hairy body lies next to me. Bailey whimpers again.

"Everything I've done has been for nothing," I say through the flood of tears. My voice is hoarse like it was after Dunbar strangled me and my throat is equally sore. "I've lost my daughter forever."

Another sob wracks my body, and I let myself get pulled under, the overwhelming grief making it difficult to catch my breath.

31

TROY

August, Present Day
Maple Ridge

I kick the kid-sized soccer ball toward the makeshift goal—two twigs stuck in the field—and pretend to run after it.

Nova giggles and goes chasing it too. Butterscotch pulls on the leash I'm holding, also wanting to go after the ball as it rolls over the grass.

Nova kicks at it, but her motor skills haven't quite got things figured out yet, and her foot misses by an inch. She bursts out giggling again, and an infectious grin spreads across her face.

I nudge the ball with my foot, sending it a few feet. Nova tries once more to kick it, this time with more success. The ball rolls farther than my faked kick sent it.

"Whoo-hoo, Nova!" I cheer with the enthusiasm of someone watching their favorite team win the World Cup.

I scoop her up and swing her high. She giggles and attempts to yell, "Hoo hoo!"

I lower her to the ground and check my phone. Jess hasn't texted, but I'm not sure she would even if she needed me. While she might have pulled down most of the barrier between us, a few fragments remain, like a castle that's partially standing after centuries of neglect and bad storms.

Shit, what I would give to bring in a wrecking ball and permanently knock down those walls.

Nova yawns. I check the time on my phone. "Okay, princess. Time for me to take you back to your mommy."

Olivia has texted me a few times over the past two hours, checking on us, even asking for photos. Part of me wonders if she's just checking Jess isn't with us.

Nova runs across the field with Butterscotch and me in hot pursuit. She stumbles and trips. I swoop in, picking her up, and carry her to my truck.

The drive to her house isn't long, but she's nodding off by the time I pull up in front of it.

I unfasten her from the car seat, gather up all the things that usually come with Nova—like the diaper bag and her bunny—and carry her to the porch.

Olivia is standing on the other side of the door, waiting for us, when I open it. She grins at us both.

"Mommy!" Nova leans forward, reaching for her.

I pass her to her mother. "We played soccer, so I think she should be worn out now."

"Did you have fun with Uncle Troy?" Olivia asks her.

Nova bounces in her mother's arms. "Yes!" She then squirms to be put down. Clutching her bunny, she runs toward the living room.

Olivia hugs me. "Thanks for taking her out. It means so much to her."

That's an odd thing for Olivia to say. I've been doing this

regularly ever since Colton's body was lowered into the grave over a year ago. "You know I love spending time with her."

"I know. But that doesn't mean I'm not thankful for you doing it." Olivia tucks her hair behind her ear, her bottom lip caught between her teeth. "Those reporters...do they know?"

"Know what?"

"That you're dating her. Jessica." The unwarranted harshness nipping at her vowels has me frowning.

"Probably. Not that it's any of their business. But you know how the gossip is around here." Plus, it's not like it's a secret. Butterscotch and I have been staying overnight at Jess's house off and on for several months—and vice versa.

Olivia nods, knowing firsthand how bad the gossiping can get in Maple Ridge. Six months after Colton's death, rumors spread that I was dating his widow. Everyone knew the three of us had been best friends since we were kids, but that didn't matter. Of course I was going to be there for her after he died. What did people expect?

"Just be careful. For"—Olivia nods toward the living room—"for her sake. I don't want Nova exposed to any of that."

"She won't be. Her safety's my number one priority." I doubt it will get to the point, though, where I have to worry about reporters following me to get a different angle to Jess's story.

We say goodbye, and I'm driving to Jess's house when my phone rings. *Mom*. I click it through to the truck's speaker. "Hey, Mom."

"So, I bumped into a friend of mine at the grocery store today," she tells me without even bothering to say "Hi" first like she usually does. "She...she mentioned your girlfriend isn't who she seems to be. That she's not even called Jessica

Smithson." Mom's tone is one I remember hearing growing up. Her you've-got-some-explaining-to-do-young-man tone. Her I'm-about-to-ground-your-butt tone.

Shit. I should've given my parents a heads-up after I saw Cora's article. That would have been better than them being blindsided by the news. I just didn't think her past would be a problem for them.

Clearly, I was wrong—or Mom's mad because she thinks I've been keeping secrets.

I inwardly groan. "What are you trying to ask, Mom?"

"How long have you known she's Savannah Townsend?" Her tone hasn't changed, but I can't tell if she's pissed at me or something else.

"Almost two months."

A yawning silence stretches between us. I can't be bothered to fill it or ask her what her real concern is.

"Two months?" she repeats, the pitch of her voice scaling two stories. "And how long did you know her before you found out the truth about her identity and past?"

"About three months," I reply calmly, my eyes on the road ahead of me.

"You were with her all that time, and you had no idea she used to be in a prison?" Mom doesn't say it, but the serrated edge of "maximum security" cuts through her voice. "When were you planning to tell your father and me?"

"I wasn't. It isn't yours or anyone else's business. Jess has been trying to start her life over after everything she's been through. She deserves that much."

"I get it. But I don't like it when people lie and keep secrets." The harshness in Mom's tone has faded, replaced with distrust and the uncertain shake of her head I can't see but I know is there.

"I know, but sometimes people have a good reason for

their secrets. All you can do is respect their decision. I've gotta go. I'll talk to you later, Mom." I end the call before she can say anything else, and I turn onto Jess's street.

Shit. I hadn't expected Mom to react that way. The woman I just talked to is not the same one I grew up with. The woman I grew up with believed in giving people a chance to prove the kind of person they were. That woman didn't judge someone based on gossip.

What happened to her? Where did *she* go?

The number of protesters outside of Jess's house hasn't diminished since I dropped her off after work. If anything, the number has grown. *Dammit.*

I slowly drive down her street, inching along while I wait for people to move off the road. There aren't as many protesters as yesterday, but enough sign-carrying individuals swarm the sidewalks and the street to be a pain. Don't these people have better things to do than harass an innocent person?

I pull into the driveway and park closer to the garage than I normally do—and far enough from the road that I can't make out the reporters' questions as I carry Butterscotch to Jess's back door. The protesters' chants drown out the questions yelled at me.

I knock on the door and wait and wait and wait. No one answers it and Bailey doesn't bark. I knock again.

Jess still doesn't answer. I try the door in case she left it unlocked for me. It doesn't open. I rap once more, louder this time. Still nothing. Jess didn't say anything about her leaving the house while I was gone.

I text her.

Me: Jess, I'm at the back door.

No little dots appear indicating she's typing a reply.

A bad feeling twists in my gut. Something's wrong. I

have a spare key to the house for emergencies. Jess gave it to me a few weeks ago. With everything going on, this—her disappearance—counts as an emergency.

I unlock the door, step into the house, and enter the reactivation code on the alarm. "Jess?" I call out. Butterscotch wanders into the kitchen.

I kick off my sneakers and walk farther into the house. Other than a bunch of books lying haphazardly on the living room floor, nothing seems out of place.

Frowning, I pick the books up and put them on the coffee table. Jess is the kind of person who respects books. She doesn't mistreat them and she doesn't bend the pages.

I pick up the last one from the floor. A nonfiction book about Allied spies who armed the French Resistance and helped the Allies win the Second World War. Jess's phone is on the floor where the book was a moment ago.

I grab her phone and press the home button. My text is the only notification that pops up on the screen. There's nothing to indicate where Jess could have gone.

I stride into the foyer. Bailey's leash is on the hallway table, which means Jess hasn't taken her for a walk. I check the front door. It's locked.

Where the hell is she?

Butterscotch gives a small bark and bounds up the stairs.

I follow him. "Do you know where Jess is?"

The guest bedroom door is open. Kellan, Lance, Noah, and I have been working on the room. Jess promised she wouldn't peek inside until we finished it.

I push the door open wider. The room is how we left it when we were working on the renovations. There's no sign of Jess.

I turn to leave.

A faint sound comes from the closet. The door was

closed the last time I was in the room. Now, it's partially opened.

I widen the gap in the doorway. Heartbroken sobbing spills from the closet, the sound still muffled.

A dim light pours into the space from the bedroom window, enough for me to see the bookcase along the back wall. A bookcase that I don't remember opening away from the wall like a door. But that's exactly how it is now.

The sobbing is coming from the other side of the bookcase. Butterscotch barks and scrambles through the narrow opening.

I turn on my phone flashlight and crouch by the entrance to what appears to be a small space. The beam of light falls on Jess and a pile of blankets and pillows on the floor. She's shaking from her sobbing and is curled up on her side, her hand resting on Bailey. Bailey gazes at me with sad eyes.

"Jess?"

She doesn't respond. She keeps sobbing.

The opening between the wall and the bookcase is too narrow for me to slip through. I pull on the bookcase, creating a gap wide enough for me to squeeze past. *Holy shit.* I had no idea this room was here. It's the perfect hiding space—especially if you're a kid. How long has Jess known about it?

I crawl into the space. "Jess?"

Her sobbing doesn't slow. I have no idea if she even realizes I'm in here.

I put my hand on her arm. Jess doesn't react or say anything. Bailey pushes to her feet and watches me intently. She whimpers.

At a loss at what to do, I lie behind Jess and spoon her, my arm draped over her waist. I don't tell her everything's going to be okay. I can't predict that when I have no idea what's going on. *Fuck.* Did one of the protesters threaten her?

I lean over her and kiss her forehead. "How can I help?"

She shakes her head, inhales a deep, jagged breath, and shifts to face me. I lie back down, putting my head on the pillows. She rests her head on my chest.

I stroke the dip of her spine. Bailey lets out another whimper and lowers herself to the floor. Butterscotch settles himself next to her.

We lie on the blankets, not saying anything. Jess is no longer sobbing, but I sense her need to cry again hovering under the surface. I feel so helpless but at the same time relieved to have found her. I hold her a little tighter.

My phone is on the floor next to me, the beam of light hitting the ceiling. The doorway to the space might be short, but the ceiling looks to be the same height as it is in the bedroom. The walls are covered with drywalling and have been painted white.

"Ten-year-old me would've loved this place," I murmur into Jess's hair.

She laughs, the choked sound wet and amused. "Ten-year-old me would've loved it too. I once removed all of my grandmother's books from her bookshelves, positive one of them would open a secret door."

"To Narnia?"

"Definitely not. I had no interest in stumbling across evil winter witches."

I chuckle, my fingers continuing to stroke the curve of Jess's spine. "Good idea. They tend to make life more challenging." I glance around the space. "When did you find this place? I had no idea it even existed."

"While I was clearing out the magazines in the closet. The bookshelf hadn't been pushed in all the way. Otherwise, I would never have found this room."

"Ten-year-old-pirate me wants to know if there is any buried treasure in here. Or hidden maps leading us to a giant pot of gold."

Jess laughs harder this time. "I think that would be a leprechaun." She says it with a badly faked Irish accent, and I laugh with her. Christ, I love this woman.

She looks up at me, and a grin curves her lips. Her damp lashes sparkle in the glow from the flashlight. "Sorry, no buried treasure or maps." The smile fades away. "I put the blankets and pillows in here after Violet left her husband."

"Violet and Sophie stayed in here?" I glance around the space once more, seeing it with new eyes. It's the perfect place for kids to hide in when they're playing, but it's small for an adult to have to stay in for long.

"A few times. Whenever the cops came to the door. The day her husband beat me, I was praying Violet would hear him and she and Sophie would hide in here so he couldn't find them."

Shit. "He might've killed you if she had done that and not tried to stop him."

"It was a risk I was willing to take." She lays her head back on my chest. "For Violet's and Sophie's sake." Her voice cracks on Sophie's name.

I hold her a little tighter, thankful things hadn't gone the way she'd planned. "Is there any particular reason you're in here crying?" I know she misses Violet, but I doubt that's why she's hidden away.

Jess draws in a long breath and releases it. "Craig, my brother-in-law, phoned."

Her muscles tighten under my fingers, and I silently curse him. Whatever he told her couldn't have been good.

"He and Grace decided it's not a good idea for me to be part of Amelia's life. Because...because of his dark past with his brothers." An intense tremor takes Jess's body hostage. Dampness seeps through my T-shirt, the spot growing larger and wetter.

Dammit. How could they do that to her?

"What kind of dark past?"

"He never went into the details, but it was enough for him to leave his family and never look back. I know his brothers bullied him, which is why he believed me when I told the police my husband was abusive. They had a hard time believing it—because of his stellar record as a cop— but Craig believed me."

I don't know how to respond. The Marines prepared me for many things, but not this. Not for dealing with a woman whose heart has been broken so many times. I'm not sure how to permanently weld it together again.

Or if that's even possible.

Everything she's been working toward was based on her having that happily ever after with her daughter in her life. But now what? How can she move on from this?

"I came in here," Jess says, "because I needed a place to go where the protesters and media couldn't hear me scream."

"Maybe we can find a family lawyer and see what they can do for you?"

"I can't do that. I gave up my daughter so she could have a better life. What kind of better life will it be if I get lawyers involved? And what good will that do? Grace and Craig don't owe me anything."

"Sure they do." I stroke the curve of her hip. "They owe you for giving them the daughter they love. They owe you for giving up the daughter *you* love because you put her first. Even now, you're putting your daughter's happiness over your own."

"It doesn't matter. Amelia's happiness and safety will

always come first for me, no matter how much it breaks my heart to lose her."

I close my eyes against the pain of knowing what all of this means. Jess had already said she didn't want kids because she was worried she might lose them. This—what happened tonight—will only make things worse. She put herself out there. She reached out—only to have her heart crushed to pieces. Now, I know for sure that Jess will be so scared of going through this again, of losing her daughter, she won't want to risk any more heartbreak.

Thousands of parents each year lose their children to accidents, stillbirths, diseases, and violence outside of the home. Their grief is real, yet many of them go on to have more kids—whether naturally or through adoption.

Lucas and Simone have been seeing a grief counselor to help them deal with the loss of their baby from ten years ago. But what about Jess? Will she ever be able to move on and open her heart to anyone else, knowing her daughter is out there somewhere, but she can never see her or hold her?

Or maybe that's just the excuse I'm clinging to, an easy explanation. There's still the possibility she fears she will end up in the same situation she found herself in with her late husband. She doesn't trust me enough to know I'll never be that asshole. Maybe she'll never be able to trust in the way she needs to for her to love me the way I love her.

Perhaps Robyn will know what to do, but she's away on summer vacation for a few more weeks.

I hate this. I hate how the callousness of one man has wrecked her so I'll never fully have her the way I want her.

All I can do is be the shoulder to cry on, her friend, the man who loves her and will do whatever it takes to keep her safe, to make her feel loved and protected...knowing she might never love me in return.

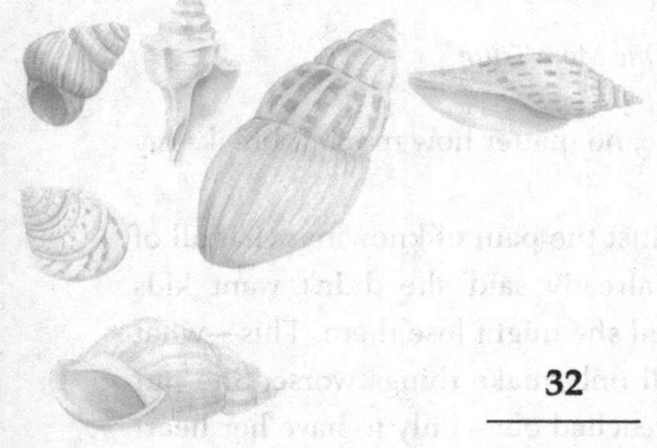

32

JESSICA

August, Present Day
Maple Ridge

T roy eventually coaxes me out of my safe place in the guest bedroom closet. I don't sneak a peek at the renovations in the room. It's too painful knowing Amelia will never see it.

I clutch Angelique's journal as I walk downstairs, Troy's hand on the small of my back. I didn't want to leave the journal behind in case Troy returned to the hiding space and found it. Anne needs to see it before anyone else does. I owe that to Iris.

The books I'd shoved onto the floor are back on the coffee table. I slip the journal into the bottom of the pile and sit on the couch.

Troy hands me a glass of water. I drink it, soothing my scream-scratched throat.

"So, what's your book about?" He nods at Garrett's

writing craft books on the table. "Or are you still figuring it out?"

"A little of both."

"What do you mean?" Troy sits next to me, and I pull my feet onto the couch, curling into him, touching as much of him as possible. My body physically aches to hold even more of him, to wrap around him, to sink into him.

He is my happy place.

My safe zone.

Even though it's early evening, the chanting beyond the closed living-room curtains is louder than it was this afternoon. The protesters have brought back their greatest hits, along with a few new ones:

"Protect our children."

"Convicts not welcome."

"Make our street safe again."

"Go back where you belong."

I put the empty glass on the table. "I was playing around with the first chapter. I wrote it to see if I enjoy writing historical fiction."

"Do you?"

I nod. "Very much so. Or at least so far I do." It's surprising just how much I enjoyed pouring myself into the story. It wasn't easy—but that didn't matter. Maybe it was the challenge of being someone else, of being in their head-space and exploring how they feel...maybe that's what I loved.

"I still think it's really cool you're doing this," Troy says, and my heart swells. He has been nothing but supportive of the idea ever since I told him about it. "Can I read it?"

"It's just a short scene. I haven't finished writing it." What I wrote was enough to make me even more excited to keep going.

He brushes his thumb along my jaw. "I would still love to see it. Unless you think it will jinx you or something."

"Is that the excuse Garrett gives you when you ask to read a scene from his books?"

Troy smirks, his hand dropping away from my face. "You really think my brother lets any of us see his stuff before it's published? He sends the manuscript to his editor after he's finished it, but that's about all. Unless there's a scene he wants one of his experts to check over first."

"What kind of experts?"

"FBI agents. Criminologists. Things like that."

"Wow, he is thorough." I'm not sure who I could contact to make sure my details are accurate. Iris is dead. Most people who were part of the French Resistance or the SOE or who knew Angelique during that time would also be deceased.

Johann would most definitely be dead by now. Or over a hundred years old.

"That's why his books are so popular, even with people who work in the field. His attention to detail makes his stories feel so real." Troy leans back on the couch. "So are you going to give me a hint what your story's about? Or are you gonna drive me crazy wondering about it?" His gravelly-rough voice drops low, as if he's seducing me into telling him.

But do I really want to open myself up by letting him in on this secret?

The answer comes easily. Yes. I know he won't mock me or make me feel foolish like my late husband would have. Troy is the kind of man who supports people's dreams. Who cheers them on. Who does what he can to make their lives easier, fuller, richer. That's why he's part of the Wilderness Warriors group, why he specializes in modifying homes for people with special requirements.

My late husband wouldn't have even believed women were capable of doing what the female SOE agents did during the war—the same sexist attitude shared by most men in Germany and the UK at the time. The Germans underestimated what women could do, which ended up being the best thing for the war.

If not for the ingenuity and courageousness of the female SOE agents and female resistance fighters in occupied countries, the war would have lasted a lot longer and thousands more lives would have been lost.

"It's about a female spy during the Second World War who works for the SOE. The British Special Operations Executive."

He nods at my laptop. "Can I read the scene?" The heated, seductive tone is back in his voice, and my insides go fluttery.

Warmth rushes to my cheeks. "Are you sure you want to do that? It might suck."

The question is, am *I* certain I want him reading it? Sure, he's read my PTSD articles based on the interviews I've done, but this is different. Somehow, it's more personal.

"I bet it won't suck," Troy says. "And I would love to read it. But only if you're okay with that."

The hope in his voice embraces me. Solidifies my decision. Tells me I have nothing to fear from sharing this part of me with him. "As long as you remember I'm still working on it." I grab my laptop from the coffee table and power it on.

A few minutes later, Troy is reading the scene about when Angelique met with Allaire in Paris to discuss getting a wireless operator for her region.

Fear and panic and eagerness clutch and claw at my stomach. I want to know what he thinks about it and I don't want to know. I'm curious and I'm twitchy...more so than I ever was when handing in a journalism assignment.

I redirect my attention to the chanting outside the living room window. It does nothing to calm the emotions storming inside me. If anything, it makes them worse, but in a different way.

I itch to get up and pace, but if I can't handle Troy reading the scene, how will I survive Anne reading the book?

"Wow," he says after a long moment. "I knew your writing was good, but this is something else. Everything felt so real. You've gotta keep writing this. I want to know what happens next."

A wave of dizziness surges in me. Not a bad dizziness, like the kind before a dead faint. This is more like...relief. Joy. Doing cartwheels in the street. "Are you sure? You're not just saying that because I'm your girlfriend?"

"I'm saying it because it's true."

My grandmother and my professors always told me I was a talented writer. But it's one thing to write nonfiction articles; it's another to write a novel.

It's one scene. That's all Troy has read. All that I've written so far. But the honesty in his words ignites something in me I haven't felt in a long time. Passion and excitement. Desire. A desire to exercise my voice. To challenge my own thoughts and convictions and prejudices.

Prior to reading Angelique's words, I thought all Germans and their allies had supported Hitler. Had supported his hatred for Jews and his ugly, twisted beliefs. The more research I've done on World War II, the more I realize how wrong I was. There were those who didn't agree with the war or his politics. There were those who tried to make a difference, who tried to bring down the regime, who were brave when they had no reason to be.

Okay, maybe I could be exercising my voice when it comes to prejudices abused women and inmates face. Specifically, inmates who have been wrongfully convicted or made a mistake they regret. For some—like the one friend in Beckley I'd had for a short time—their situation left them feeling like they didn't have a choice and they took the wrong path.

Yes, I could exercise my voice for those causes, but those traumas are too fresh for me. I'm not looking to be an advocate for anything I've been forced to deal with. Not yet, anyway. Besides, first things first. I need to write Angelique's story.

I brush my lips along Troy's mouth. "Thank you. I appreciate your vote of confidence."

He cups the back of my head, keeping me close, and kisses me deeply. His other hand guides my body so I'm straddling him.

"The story..." His warm breath mists over my mouth. "Angelique's story. It's important to you, isn't it?"

I nod.

"I can tell. I can't explain it, but there's something different about the way you are with this writing compared to when you were doing the photos for Theresa's wedding. You seemed happy to be doing that, but nothing like this." He trails kisses along my jaw. "I get it now."

"Would you still be supportive if I spent a little less time with you so I could work on the book?" I hold my breath, waiting for his answer. Waiting to see if he really does understand how important this is to me.

"I just want you to be happy, Jess. If writing the book makes you happy, even if it means you're spending less time with me, that makes me happy." The corner of his mouth tilts up. "But you're mine whenever you can fit me in. And I'm gonna make the most of that time." He slowly kisses my neck, drawing a moan from me. "And if you should get stuck like Garrett does sometimes, instead of you pacing or working on your garden, I'll be happy to give you multiple orgasms to get the words flowing again." Troy's eyebrows dance, and I giggle.

God, I love him.

I still, the words swirling in my head. I gaze into his eyes, his love for me gleaming in them unrestrained.

I open my mouth to say the three simple words to him, but I can't. The chanting outside the window halts them, yanks them back into my throat.

I love him, but I'm not ready to admit that. Not yet. Not when there are so many uncertainties we're dealing with. The protesters who are trying to drive me away. My feelings of not being good enough for him. My history of losing the people I love. My decision not to have children, even though he wants a family.

So, I just kiss him, letting him know without words how I feel. Pouring my love for him into the kiss.

I only hope it's enough for him.

For now.

33

ANGELIQUE

February 1944
France

"**A**re you sure you are up to doing this, Éve?" Lise's astute blue eyes drop to my swollen belly, visible under the brown cotton of my dress. I close my valise, which only has a few items of clothing in it, and lift it from the bed.

In the two months since I left Dr. Hubert and Rosita's home, the baby has grown considerably. But due to the constraints of the occupation, the bump is smaller than it should be for a woman in her early third trimester. Françoise, the midwife who is monitoring my pregnancy, has reassured me my baby is fine.

"I'm positive," I tell my flatmate. "The Germans are less likely to pay attention to a pregnant woman."

A fair number of pregnant women are walking around Poitiers these days. A good proportion of the pregnant bellies are the result of liaisons between German soldiers and French women or are the product of rape. I embrace for a moment the memory of the man my heart still beats for. I can guarantee none of those soldiers abandoned their unit to join the maquis because of the new life they had created.

"Delivering propaganda is about the only thing I can do these days." I lovingly caress my belly, letting my baby know I do not resent her for that. She is my precious world. One of the few people I live for.

Lise knows the truth about my relationship with a German officer and how he helped me escape after the Gestapo arrested me. She hasn't asked me many questions about my time in the *Cashmere* network. She only knows that one of our own turned on us.

After I left Dr. Hubert and Rosita's home, I headed south to where Lise had been assigned. It took me two weeks once I arrived in the city, but I was fortunately able to track her down. We have tried to find news about Johann, but so far there hasn't been any.

I keep busy so I don't have to think about how much I miss him. Some days it's hard to breathe, wondering what happened to him and where he is. I try not to think beyond that. Try not to think beyond surviving each moment. But at night, when my mind refuses to sleep, memories of our time together, the way he made me feel when he made love to me, slip in.

And that only makes me miss him more.

"Alright, if you insist," Lise says. "But you really shouldn't press your luck for much longer. The baby is due in just over two months. You need to take things easy."

"What my daughter and I need is for the war to be over." And for me to locate her father. "That won't happen if I'm dillydallying in your flat and not doing my job."

"What will happen if a German officer inquires to see inside your valise?"

I walk to the hall mirror and check my brown wig is secure and my stage makeup makes me appear five years older than my true age. Well, more like five years in addition to the five years this war has added to my age of twenty-nine. I celebrated a birthday last month. "It hasn't happened yet. Most seem relieved it wasn't their seed responsible for the baby in my belly. They treat me as though I am an incubator for a deadly disease and they don't want to risk touching anything I've come in contact with."

Lise shrugs on her coat. "When are you planning to tell Baker Street you're pregnant?"

"Maybe they already know. I told Allaire." What we don't know is if he communicated it to London before the Gestapo captured him or if he never had a chance to relay the information. "I haven't confirmed with them exactly what they know about it. I'll do that soon."

"Soon?" She shriek-whispers. "Your baby will be born here if you're not careful."

"Just a few more weeks. I promise. It's probably too late for them to get me out of France now. And I certainly won't be able to waddle over the Pyrénées."

Lise chuckles, though the worry doesn't leave her eyes. "That would be a sight."

"I'm just lucky Françoise is a midwife." Who also works with the local resistance circuit. I can only hope she is not out blowing up railway tracks when I go into labour. "I should get moving."

"I'll help you with the valise."

We leave the flat and walk downstairs. Nosy Madame Blanchet peers out her front door. I'm positive she is a Nazi collaborator. She has asked me more questions than I would like, including ones about the father of my baby. My new cover has me as a widow again, only this time my husband was ineligible to fight in the war and recently died due to his declining health, but not before he got me with child. Lise is my cousin.

Outside, I walk one way, carrying my valise. Lise heads in the opposite direction for her meeting with the leader of the *Pirouette* network. I haven't met him and likely won't. They don't want to take that risk after what happened to the *Cashmere* network. I have no idea if he's aware of my impending motherhood or if he'd even care if he did know.

Despite my winter coat, the cold February wind bites at my skin. The coat was far from new when I got it, the fabric worn in places, but it's better than nothing. Even prior to the war, it would have been big on me. Now, it drowns my slight frame, but it has the additional benefit of hiding my pregnant state, if I wish.

I keep walking along the cobbled street, ever vigilant of my surroundings. I have always been that way since coming to this country, but after my arrest, I've become even more so. It is one of the few times when I don't let my thoughts drift to Johann and how much I miss him.

I disappear down a side street that sees little foot traffic and continue until I get to the third door on the left—the back door to a business that was abandoned a year ago due to the war. I glance around the area. Reassured I haven't been followed or watched, I unlock the door and slip inside the building.

I descend the dingy stairs to the basement where the printing press is set up. The room is dimly lit and cold, and no less depressing than the world outside the brick walls.

"*Bonjour*," I say to Armand as he looks up from the machine. As always, Conrad is standing guard in the doorway. The tall, imposing man doesn't talk much. He gives me the standard nod in greeting.

"I have a new leaflet to be printed." Leaflet writing is one of my tasks in the *Pirouette* network, along with distribution. I slip a sheet of paper from the secret compartment in my handbag and hand it to Armand.

He reads it. "Alright. I'll do that now." He gets to work setting up the printing press that creates the propaganda leaflets.

"How are you doing?" he asks after a few minutes. His gaze lands briefly on my belly hidden under my coat. He is one of the few people in the network who knows about my pregnant status—that I know of.

"I'm fine, thank you."

"Why don't you sit down? Rest while you can. You won't have the opportunity once the baby is born." He knows what he's talking about. He has a toddler.

"Thank you." I sit on the wooden chair a few feet from the press and wrap my coat tighter to myself. The basement isn't any warmer than it is outside. I can't imagine many buildings are much warmer, given the lack of heating these days. "Is there any news?"

He doesn't look at me, his attention on the metal letters he's placing on the press. "I'm sorry. Nothing substantial. There are whisperings about a man who could fit the description you gave me. And if it is him, then he's alive. But that's all I know. I sent a message to him that you are safe. I have no idea if he received it."

"Thank you. I appreciate everything you've done for me."

"You care about this man, *non*?"

I rest my hand on my belly. "Very much."

"Well, I hope you get to see him again soon."

All I can do is pray the man he's talking about is Johann

and my love is doing well. But that is the problem with rumours. They can fill you with hope and they can take it away, but at the end of the day, it's hard to know if there is any truth to them.

I've reread Johann's letter so many times in the past two months, I am surprised the ink is still readable and the paper doesn't disintegrate in my hands.

I glance at Conrad, but he doesn't seem to be paying attention to our conversation. The only thing I know about him is that he's a communist and barely escaped from being rounded up as a political prisoner. The fate of an English operative and a political prisoner is the same once caught by the Milice or the Nazis. Neither of us will get to live to see the end of the war if that should happen.

If I am caught again, I won't be as lucky as I was last time. I flex and extend the fingers of my damaged hand, reminding myself how fortunate I am. If not for Johann, the least of my problems would be how badly my hand aches in the cold weather and how much dexterity I have lost.

Armand prints the leaflets for me.

"Thank you. And this..." I remove another piece of paper from my handbag and pass it to him. "This is to be included in your next newspaper."

He reads the article, which contains an update about the war, and nods. "I should have room for that."

I place the leaflets in my valise and cover them with the few pieces of clothing in there. The clothing won't deceive the Germans should they stop me and search the valise's contents. But the clothing is enough to deceive the Germans should they only give the contents a cursory glance.

Armand gives me a copy of today's newspaper. This isn't the version he prints, with the truth about the war and the

Allies successes. This newspaper is filled with Nazi propaganda.

I put several leaflets inside it, placing them far enough in so they're secure, and slip the folded newspaper into my handbag.

I leave the basement room and head for the university library. Like earlier, no one appears to be following me. I slip into the building and go to the science section. A few people are in the area, sitting at the tables, but no one seems to pay attention to me or my valise. Had this been Paris, my bags would have been searched before I was permitted to enter the building.

I open the valise, grab a stack of leaflets, and slip them into random books throughout the bookshelf. All the leaflets I left here two weeks ago have been removed. Each was taken by a member of the resistance circuit in the area and contained information needed to execute the latest round of sabotage. Only members of the circuit understand the instructions. The leaflets are meaningless should they fall into enemy hands. The French Milice won't have any idea where the attack will occur. They won't be able to ambush the men and women executing the plans.

I repeat the same task in several other sections of the library. Afterwards, I walk towards my flat, stopping at a park on the way to sit and catch my breath. I find an empty bench overlooking a garden that currently lacks any sign of life. I unbutton my coat, revealing my rounded belly.

I don't have to pretend that I am tired. The lack of food, my pregnancy, and the constant moving around my job entails takes a lot out of me. The amount of sleep I get each night isn't ideal either. I no longer have nightmares about the Gestapo going after my sister. Now, I'm forced to relive my arrest, my nightmares twisting it into something more horrific.

A tiny hand or a foot pokes at my side. I rest my damaged hand over the spot and smile softly at my daughter, sending her all my love. Once she has settled again, I slip the newspaper from my purse and pretend to read a story on the front cover. Then I place the paper next to me on the bench and yawn.

"Beautiful day for a walk, isn't it?" a familiar female voice says.

I turn to find Lise approaching the bench with a tall, good-looking man who appears as exhausted as the majority of French inhabitants. His blond hair is a little on the long side and he's carrying a walking stick. From the way they smile at each other, I would think they were lovers. But I know Lise does not have anyone special in her life, neither here nor in England.

I push to my feet. It's harder to do that now than it was a month ago.

Lise and I air-kiss.

"Henri, this is my cousin, Éve," she explains, introducing me to him with my new alias.

I recognise his name. The man is the head of the *Pirouette* network. And now he knows I'm pregnant. It's unlikely he's missed that detail.

"*Enchanté*, Éve." His gaze drops to my bump, now hidden under my coat, and his eyebrow raises in question. "Lise never mentioned you're pregnant."

Lise giggles, but I cannot tell if it is real or faked. "Oh, heavens. I cannot imagine how I forgot that little detail. Silly me."

"Does Mother Goose know about it?" he asks, Mother Goose being our code name for Baker Street.

I shrug, the rise of my shoulders barely noticeable under my coat. "I did mention it to my friend prior to his disappearance. I don't know if he told Mother Goose."

"And the father?" Henri looks around as if expecting the man to magically appear. He shares a glance between Lise and me, waiting for an explanation.

"I don't know where he is. It's likely he has gone underground." The last part is spoken quietly.

"Is he aware that he's going to be a parent?"

"He is. He just doesn't know where to find me. We got separated after he helped me with my situation." I lift my bad hand, indicating what situation I'm talking about.

Henri was apprised of what happened to my hand when I first joined his network. I told Lise that Johann was the one who rescued me. She knows about our love story. I don't know how much of it she has recounted to Henri.

I suspect he knows a lot more about the situation than he is letting on.

"You do live a complicated life, Éve."

A small smile curves my lips and heat flushes my wind-kissed cheeks. "I certainly do."

"Lise and I should get moving. But you should know that Christian is no longer a problem. He was captured last week and executed."

"Thank you," I whisper, beaming broadly as if Henri just told us a great joke. I don't feel an ounce of remorse at how Christian's life ended.

"It was nice to meet you, Éve," Henri says, the signal we need to go our separate ways so not to draw the wrong kind of attention.

It's also the perfect cover for forgetting my newspaper on the park bench.

A cut-out will pick it up shortly. Her job is to pass it to one of the resistance circuit members responsible for propaganda, who will distribute the leaflets inside the newspaper to the appropriate parties. It's not blowing up railway tracks and tunnels or attending parachute drops like I was doing before, but it is still a necessary task in the fight for freedom.

34

JESSICA

August, Present Day
Maple Ridge

Late Tuesday afternoon, I power off my work computer and click Bailey's leash onto her collar. "You ready to go to the festival committee meeting?" I grab my purse from the bottom desk drawer.

Troy texted a few minutes ago that he was detained at the job site due to a water main problem on the street. He has to wait until the town's emergency work crew deals with the issue, but since the marketing committee meeting is at the library, Bailey and I can easily walk there. And because she's wearing her *Service Dog in Training* vest, she's allowed in the building. The members of the committee know that I'm training her and they know I've been diagnosed with complex PTSD—but until news about my past was recently leaked, they hadn't known what had led to the diagnosis.

I step through the main doors to the building, and my

stomach sinks. Several reporters and camera crew swarm around the entrance.

Fuckers. I'm surprised it's taken them this long to track down my place of employment.

"Savannah, what are your thoughts on the petition to have you removed from Maple Ridge?" a woman reporter yells out.

Someone actually created a petition to force me out of Maple Ridge?

This is my home. My new start. Why can't people accept I'm not the monster they think I am? Why can't they give me a chance to repair the life someone else tried to destroy?

I push past the reporters. The protesters didn't follow them here. Thank God for that small miracle.

Bailey and I walk to the library. The sky is cloudy, the rain shower from earlier having left the ground speckled with large puddles, but the threat of a late afternoon storm looms overhead.

The reporters trail us like a gaggle of geese hoping for a scrap of bread. I want to scream at them to leave me alone. Haven't they done enough damage? They stole everything from me—my privacy, my safety, my dignity. I wouldn't be surprised if they were another reason Craig didn't want me in my daughter's life—albeit a short-term reason.

Tears blur my vision. I blink them away before the reporters can notice them. I don't want to give the protesters any satisfaction when they watch the evening news.

Bailey and I go into the library and head straight to the small meeting room the committee booked for today.

The meeting is private, which means I get to have a short reprieve from the reporters. If I'm lucky, they'll grow bored and leave before the meeting ends.

Evie turns her head to me as I sit in the empty chair

next to her. Her black chin-length hair with purple streaks swings against her jaw. "Hey, Jess. I heard about the protesters and reporters. I can't believe anyone can accuse you of any of that stuff."

"That's because those idiots don't know Jess like we do," Amy, who used to be in my yoga class and who is the committee's secretary, declares from across the table. "The protesters would never say stupid things like that if they did."

Evie narrows her eyes at Amy. "Isn't your friend, Katelyn, one of those people who's been spreading mistruths?"

God, what lies is she telling about me now? I haven't noticed Katelyn with the protesters outside my house, but that doesn't mean she hasn't found other ways to make my life more difficult.

Amy cringes. "I'm sorry, Jess. I've been trying to convince her to stop. She knows you're nothing like what those protesters are claiming."

"It's not your fault." It's not like Amy can control what her friend does. Katelyn is probably still annoyed that Troy is with me and is pissed at her for trying to manipulate him to get what she wanted. Him.

The door opens and more committee members stream into the room, including Simone and Avery. While they get settled, I check my emails on my phone. I've received two new ones since leaving the office. Both from newspapers I'd queried to see if they would publish my articles about PTSD and the festival.

I click the first one open and read it.

To: Jessica Smithson

From: Colleen Faith

Subject: re The Forgotten Heroes

Dear Ms. Jessica Smithson,

Thank you for your pitch regarding the

article "The Forgotten Heroes." The
subject matter was interesting, but it's
not what we're currently looking for.
Please keep *Oregon Living* in mind for
future articles.

This isn't the first time I've received rejections, but this one smarts because it isn't for a class assignment or my career. The article highlights the purpose for the festival and how it will benefit families in the area.

I check the next email.

To: Jessica Smithson
From: Philip Tang
Subject: re The Forgotten Heroes
Dear Ms. Savannah Townsend,
Thank you for your press release. I
would love to talk to you about your own
personal experiences with PTSD and the
sequence of events that led to you
having it.

I groan. Couldn't he have tried to do a better job veiling that he's salivating for an exclusive interview with me? The community newspaper isn't interested in my personal experiences with PTSD. It's only interested in hearing about my late husband and my time while incarcerated. This isn't the first reply like this I've received.

I don't bother responding.

"How are things going with getting media coverage for the festival?" Susan Hodges's gaze shifts between Evie and me. The head of the committee's smile is bright, faint worry lines creasing the corners of her eyes. Her short blond hair is free of gray, but I can't tell if the color's natural.

"I've had a few smaller community newspapers offer to publish the articles I've been writing," I tell them. "That will help spread awareness of the festival's goals."

But let's be honest. Pushing Limits headlining the festival will be the thing that draws in the ticket sales.

My articles are just the checkmark in the PTSD-awareness box.

"And that will hopefully result in additional donations," Amy says. "The tickets are going on sale this weekend, but the finance committee is hoping to drum up additional funding through other means, such as donations and merchandise sales."

"Have you seen the T-shirts that Taylor designed?" Simone asks the group.

We all shake our heads, and she nods at Evie.

Evie pulls up a drawing on her iPad of a birdcage with the door open and four birds flying out. It's a simple silhouette, but the message is clear.

I examine the drawing. "Those are gorgeous. I didn't know Taylor's an artist." Evie's girlfriend is incredibly talented if this is a sample of her work.

"She used to be a tattoo artist in Eugene before moving to Maple Ridge."

Wow. I didn't know that. "How come she's not doing that anymore?"

"Lack of time since running a bar is a full-time job as it is. But she still occasionally does tattoos for family and friends." Evie pulls the neckline of her top to the side, exposing the skin below her clavicle and the three pink and purple dual-toned flowers tattooed there. Three single petals float around them. "She inked these for me a few months ago when we visited her friend in Eugene who has the tattoo studio. A nod to my South Korean roots."

The door opens, and a man enters. Jason Barnes. I don't know him all that well. He's part of the equipment committee.

But the cold glare he skewers me with warns me he

sides with the protesters' demands that I move away from Maple Ridge. "Shoulda realized you're here," he drawls. "What with all the reporters out front."

My body turns icier than his glare. *Fuckers. Please tell me he isn't planning to tell the protesters where to find me.*

35

—

TROY

August, Present Day
Maple Ridge

I glance at my phone. Jess's committee meeting is almost over, and I'm still waiting for the emergency street crew to finish work on the busted water main.

I make the most of the time and order a pair of noise-canceling headphones for Jess. At least with those she can work on her novel outside, and the protesters' racket won't bother her.

A red truck pulls up on the opposite side of the street as I finalize the online order. Lance climbs out and crosses to where I'm standing.

"Hey, Boss." His expression is the opposite to the happy one he had when he left work an hour ago, and his shoulder muscles are bunched up tight.

"You forget something inside?" I jerk my head toward the house we've been working on this week.

275

"No. I was just over at Olivia's."

I frown. He's not usually moody after spending time with Olivia and Nova. Hell, he's not usually moody period. He's one of the happiest guys I know.

My body tenses, and I'm one step away from jumping into my truck and driving to their house. "Is something wrong with Nova? Olivia?"

He shakes his head, and his breath releases on a hard hiss of air. "I can't help you anymore with Jess's renovations."

Shit. It doesn't take Einstein to figure out why. "She got to you, huh? Olivia?"

His expression flickers through a series of emotions. Frustration. Disbelief. Regret. Resignation. "She's angry that I was helping Jess."

I nod, not at all surprised by this, but no less frustrated than Lance. It helped having someone working with us who was skilled with renovations. "Losing Colton has made her paranoid."

"I'm not sure that's what I'd call it."

That's exactly what I would call it. "She used to be the kind of person who would give someone a second chance without question. Now, she believes the lies being spread about my girlfriend."

"I tried to get her to see otherwise, but it backfired. Olivia can be infuriatingly stubborn."

I snort a laugh and smack him on the back. "You're only realizing that now?"

"How is it you're allowed to date Jess, and Olivia doesn't have an issue with that? But I can't help renovate Jess's house without being the bad guy?"

I lean my ass against the side of my truck. "Oh, believe me, Olivia has an issue with me dating Jess. But there isn't anything she can do about that. I'm in love with Jess. Nothing Olivia says or does will change that."

But even as I utter the words, I wonder how true they are. How am I supposed to keep my promise to Colton about looking after Nova and Olivia if Olivia is making things difficult for me? There are no provisions in the best friend contract for situations like this.

My phone pings with a text.

Simone: Reporters and protesters are outside the library. They're waiting for Jess.

"Fuck!" I respond in a near growl.

"What's wrong?"

"Reporters and protesters have figured out Jess is at the library." I glance at the men working on the street. "Dammit. At the rate these guys are going…" I leave the weight of my words hanging.

"Go. I'll stay."

I don't argue with Lance, even though it's my responsibility to stay and not his. I climb into my truck and drive to the library faster than I normally would under different circumstances.

The number of protesters and reporters waiting outside the building isn't as bad as it is in front of Jess's house, but there are still too many for my liking.

I park my truck and sprint to the library entrance. The group of about a dozen or so people are standing to the side. They aren't exactly blocking the entrance, but they are causing a disturbance.

A mother and her two young children hurry past the group.

"*Convicts not welcome!*"

"Keep our children safe!"

The mother looks worried, her forehead puckered in a frown. The kids look as if they're expecting the group to turn into hungry monsters and chase after them. The protesters are accusing Jess of being a risk to children's safety, but it's the protesters who have these kids scared—and the idiots with their chants can't even see that.

The mother pulls open the glass door, and the three of them duck inside the building, leaving the protesters to yell at the closing door.

I stalk past the reporters and the protesters, doing my best to avoid getting into a verbal altercation with any of them. That's the last thing the With Hope Festival needs.

Jess and the other members of the marketing committee are coming out of one of the classrooms when I enter the building. Simone and Avery spot me approaching, and their worried expressions morph into relief. They give Jess a quick hug.

I join them, and Jess's face brightens with a wide smile.

She glances at the entrance and groans, her smile falling away. "The reporters followed me from work. I didn't know about the protesters." She sounds on the edge of fed-up and defeated. Can't say I blame her.

"Let's get you and Bailey out of here," I tell her, gentling my voice so she doesn't hear in it my murderous thoughts directed at the assholes outside.

"Before they stone me," she mutters, her words dialing up my less-than-pleasant thoughts.

I put my hand on the small of her back, keeping myself between Jess and the group outside. "They'll have to get through me first."

And they really won't like what I plan to do to anyone who tries to physically hurt Jess—festival be damned.

But it's their words—the way the protesters are trying to destroy her self-esteem—I can't protect her from, as much as I want to.

And that's killing me.

36

—

TROY

August, Present Day
Maple Ridge

I park my truck in the visitor's stall for Zara's apartment building. It's Friday night. Game Night.

I turn off the engine. Jess makes a move to open her door.

"Not yet." I reach behind my seat and pull out the sealed medium-sized shipping box. Hopefully the contents will cheer her up. She seems sad, which is hardly surprising with everything going on, especially after protesters showed up at the library on Tuesday. "This is for you." I hand it to her.

She takes it and stares at the brown box with my name and address on it, confusion wrinkling her forehead. "What is it?"

The beginnings of a smile twitch on my mouth. "If you open it, you'll find out."

She slowly opens the shipping box as if savoring the moment. As if getting a present is a foreign concept. It well may be, given how long it's probably been since she last had a Christmas or birthday gift. Who knows if her late husband gave her anything when they were married—or if the gifts fell far and few between?

Jess removes the box containing the headphones I ordered the other day.

"You wanted a magical dome over your garden so you can work outside and not hear the protesters," I explain. "I don't know anything about getting one of those, but these noise-canceling headphones should do the trick too."

Jess doesn't look at me. She just stares at the box in her hand. "You...you didn't have to do that." Her whispered voice comes out rough and small, as if trying to disappear on itself.

I study her beautiful face, attempting to see past the gentle curve of her lips that turns down instead of up. Attempting to understand what the problem is. It hurts seeing her this way. All I wanted was to make her smile and to make things easier for her.

Her eyes squeeze shut, and her breath quickens. Like she's having a panic attack.

I cover her hand with mine. Her hand jerks at the touch.

"Jess, what's wrong?" It's not as if I've given past girlfriends gifts like this one—this expensive—but when I did give them gifts, they didn't result in panic attacks. My mind scrambles for a way to fix whatever I did wrong.

Her breath comes in faster, her eyes still squeezed shut.

"Jess, you're hyperventilating. Cup your hands over your mouth and breathe in." I gentle my voice so not to worsen her panic attack, but I also keep my tone firm in hopes it will get through to her.

She lifts her hands to her mouth and does as I suggest, inhaling and exhaling into her cupped hands until her breathing slows. She lowers her hands to the package on her lap, her gaze unfocused and lost somewhere outside the windshield.

"Any idea why you started hyperventilating?" I ask, needing to understand what just happened. There are times when I feel like I'm not only walking on eggshells with Jess's past, I'm at risk of stepping on a land mine—and if that should happen, Jess and what we have between us will be the casualties.

Her gaze drops to the headphone box, and she traces over the picture on the front.

"I'm guessing it wasn't the headphones themselves that caused the panic attack. Am I right? Headphones don't scare you?"

She slowly nods but still doesn't look at me. "He used to give me presents. It was part of the cycle."

He, who? "What cycle?"

"According to Robyn, it's called trauma bond. During the good times with my husband, he would shower me with gifts and affection. That's why when he first hit me, I was surprised. He'd never done anything like that before. He'd been a great boyfriend and husband."

Jess swallows, and her gaze returns to the windshield and whatever she's staring at. "After he hit me, he apologized, said it had been a bad day at work. He promised it wouldn't happen again. You know how it goes. He showered me with gifts and affection to make up for it. Things were fine after that...until the abuse cycle started. The hitting, the mean comments that made me feel bad about myself, followed by the period of gifts and intimacy and affection."

Jess continues looking out the window as she traces

over the surface of the headphone box. "Robyn told me the gifts and the periods of affection and intimacy were positive reinforcement."

"Positive reinforcement for what?"

"The gifts and affection..." Jess turns her face to me. "According to Robyn, they caused my body to release dopamine. That's like a happy hormone."

The role of the hormone does sound familiar.

"Dopamine creates feelings of pleasure and can lead to addiction," Jess explains. "The gifts and physical affection diminished the emotional hurt from the abuse, and that made it harder for me to leave my husband. Everything I did to try to please him was because I was desperate for that dopamine rush. Only I didn't know it at the time."

Shit. And here I am giving her noise-canceling headphones. I want to make her life easier, and her asshole of a dead husband has made that impossible. She's scared of falling into that cycle of abuse again.

And now I have something new to worry about with Jess. It's not just inadvertently setting off a PTSD trigger I have to worry about. She's like a delicate flower poking through the pavement. Easily missed and stepped on. Easily damaged or destroyed, even though that's not what I had intended.

"How about we start over? Those are my headphones" —I point to the box on her lap—"but I'm lending them to you if you want, so you can work on your book outside and not be bothered by the protesters?"

She worries her bottom lip. "That might work." A small smile breaks through on her face. "It was a sweet gesture, Troy. And if I had been any other woman, you would have gotten a different response." She leans in and kisses me on the cheek.

I want more than the chaste kiss. I want to pull her onto

my lap and kiss her until her breaths come in fast but for a different reason this time. But I'm not sure if Jess also wants that, so I don't push it.

I just keep reminding myself that Jess is like no other woman in so many ways.

She's a woman who's worth taking the time to get to know and fall in love with. A woman who's still confronting so many challenges because of her past.

A woman who's dealing with so many losses—some of which she's unsure if she'll ever be able to move on from.

"I'LL BE BACK IN A MOMENT." JESS'S BREATH BRUSHES MY EAR. "I just need some air."

She gets up from Zara's couch and walks to the balcony door. Bailey goes with her.

I can't leave tomorrow morning. All week, I've been hoping the protesters will be gone before the next Warriors weekend, but it seems they're committed to the cause. And I won't be here to protect her.

Jess steps onto the balcony and closes the door behind her.

Zara is in the kitchen. Emily, Kellan, Lucas, and Garrett are sitting on the couch and armchairs discussing...I have no idea what. I haven't been paying attention.

Simone walks over from the kitchen island with a glass of white wine in her hand and sits next to me. Her gaze goes to Jess. "I'd ask you if she's okay," Simone says, her voice low, "but clearly she isn't."

"It's been a rough week for her. And it won't get any easier if things don't change with those idiots outside her house."

"Do they ever go home?"

I nod, the movement robotic. "Fortunately, they're not nocturnal. She gets a break from them at night, but they're waiting for her first thing in the morning when I pick her up."

"Why doesn't she sleep at your place?"

"She's worried they'll follow her there and nothing will change...except the protesters will irritate my neighbors instead of hers." I watch Jess for a beat looking out at the mountains; then I push to my feet. "I'm gonna check on her."

I step onto the balcony, but part of me wonders if I'm making a mistake in joining Jess. There are so many things I need to be aware of with her. So many booby traps I need to defuse without accidentally detonating them.

She glances over her shoulder and gives me a smile that makes me wish I didn't have to leave her tomorrow. The curve of her mouth and her expression are surprisingly blissful, content. I can't remember the last time she looked that way.

She turns back to the view. The setting sun has turned the mountain face golden, the deep shadows highlighting the rugged terrain. In a few months, those same mountains will be covered in snow.

I slide the balcony door shut behind me. "Okay if I join you?" I never want to take anything for granted with Jess.

"Of course." The smile in her voice doesn't completely obliterate the sadness clinging to her.

I pull her to me, my arms securing her to my body. She fits so perfectly, her back against my front. I kiss her cheek, wanting and needing to keep her safe and happy, hating that I'm failing.

"It's so peaceful," she whispers.

It's not really. Noises leak from the various apartments

on this side of the five-story building, including Zara's. Laughter and talking. Cheering for what sounds like a football game the apartment below us is watching.

But compared to the loud chanting from the sidewalk in front of Jess's house, it is quiet here.

We stay like this for a few minutes, not saying anything. Just enjoying the view.

I kiss the side of her head. "I'm canceling going with the guys tomorrow."

Jess turns in my arms. "Is your shoulder bothering you?" She tenderly touches the shoulder that's recovering from the recent injuries, including the dislocation from over two months ago.

"No, it's fine. I've been a good boy, following doctor's orders, doing PT with Lucas." I give her a Boy Scout salute. "Promise."

"So why are you canceling?"

"I don't like the idea of leaving you alone in that house."

"Nothing's going to happen to me while you're away. I won't even leave the house if that makes you happy." She mimics my Boy Scout salute. "Promise."

"It doesn't make me happy. I hate that they've turned your home into another form of prison." A helluva lot nicer prison than the one she'd spent a good portion of her incarceration in, but a prison no less.

"Don't worry about it. I'll be making the most of the time working on my book. And when you get back, I'll make the most of the time I'm with you." She plants a soft kiss on my lips. "I'll be thinking of you while you're gone."

"I'll be thinking about you too." I lean closer, my mouth caressing the shell of her ear. "I'll be thinking of all the dirty things I want to do to you."

A rough, sexy laugh tumbles from between her parted lips, and her beautiful golden-brown eyes turn dark. "And

I'll be thinking naughty thoughts about you, Mr. Carson. I'll be thinking of all the naughty things I want to do to you as a way of thanking you for lending me your noise-canceling headphones."

I groan playfully, my cock getting excited at the possibility. "You make me sound like your dirty boss."

"Well, you are my boss. And you do have a dirty mind at times." She leans to the side and looks past me. "Time to go back inside. I think everyone's ready to start the game."

Screw that.

All this talk about the naughty things Jess wants to do to me has me in no rush to join our friends. I cover her mouth with mine and kiss her thoroughly, giving her a taste of what I plan to do to her after we leave here. Giving her all of my heart. Trying to erase the sadness she's wrapped up in.

We're both panting for air by the time we pull apart.

"Let me know if you change your mind about me going away for the weekend," I say, my hand still on her neck, my thumb stroking her jaw.

She smiles, her eyes a little unfocused after the kiss, a reaction I'd usually feel smug about, but not this time. "Never. Those veterans need you. I'll be fine, Troy. I'm a big girl now. And I've survived worse than what those protesters can do to me."

"Doesn't matter. You shouldn't have to put up with them. You should never have been forced to survive worse than that."

"I know. But whoever said life is fair?" She pulls away from me and walks to the balcony door as if she doesn't have a care in the world.

More than anything, I wish that were true.

37

JESSICA

August, Present Day
Maple Ridge

I type away on my laptop, the words pouring from me like rain during a hurricane. A nature soundtrack, with birds chirping merrily in the background, plays through Troy's noise-canceling headphones.

One moment Bailey is snoozing beside my feet on the cobblestone patio, the next, she scrambles to a sit, her attention on the garden gate. I turn my head to see what has her excited.

Simone waves and opens the wooden gate. Jasper is with her, pulling on his leash to get to Bailey that much sooner. Bailey isn't wearing her *Service Dog in Training* vest and doesn't wait for my command. She rushes to her friend, her tail wagging like crazy.

I stop the soundtrack and put the headphones next to the laptop on the small round table. "Hi. I see you made it

288

past my prison guards." I flash a smile so Simone knows I'm kidding...kind of.

Who knows what the protesters will do if I leave my house without Troy by my side? They have the same effect on me that many of the prison guards at Beckley had. I fear them. I loathe them. They're the ones calling the shots.

Treating me like a caged animal.

Deeming me only worthy of manipulation and neglect.

"I thought you might want a lunch break." Simone lifts up the Picnic & Treats bag she's carrying. "And I figured someone wouldn't mind going for a you-know-what." She points at Bailey.

"Thank you! For both of those things." Bailey has hinted more than a few times this morning that she wants to go for a walk, but I don't feel safe doing that with the protesters in front of my house.

Fewer protesters are out there now compared to during the first couple of days. It's mostly the diehards who haven't given up yet. But it's also Saturday, so there are more of them than yesterday. The number of reporters has also declined. The rest, no doubt, left to report on something far more earth-shattering than me sitting in my house all day.

"I'll take the dogs for their walk first, and then we can have lunch," Simone tells me. "How much longer do you need?"

"Thirty minutes? Does that sound okay?" That should be enough time to finish the chapter.

"Sounds good."

I fetch Bailey's leash from the hook inside by the back door and fasten it onto her collar. "You be a good girl for your Auntie Simone?" I give Bailey a hug. Her tail wags in response or in excitement for the walk. "Thank you. You're the best." I plant a kiss on the top of her head.

Simone and the dogs go out the gate, and I sit back down on the chair.

The protesters' voices grow louder. "She and Lucas don't have kids," one woman yells, and my heart ceases to beat. "Of course she doesn't have an issue hanging out with a dangerous offender. She'd feel differently if she had children like the rest of us."

White-hot anger propels me to my feet. I fling open the gate and storm to the front of the house, not giving much thought to the risk I'm taking. Right now, I don't care if they hurl rotten tomatoes or whatever at me, I refuse to let them treat Simone that way. She's been nothing but sweet and kind toward me. She's made things more bearable when the protesters have been stripping away my freedom.

"You're angry at me," I yell. "Don't take your ignorance out on people who have done nothing to hurt you."

"It's okay, Jess," Simone urges, worry and sadness choking her voice. She lost her daughter years ago when she was pregnant and a drunk driver stole the precious life from her.

There's no way I'm letting that mean woman's comment slide.

"It's not okay. Simone did nothing to deserve this," I shout. "*I* did nothing to deserve this. You're no better than my husband who used to physically and verbally abuse me. Who used his strength and mind games to intimidate and manipulate. You're nothing but selfish bullies who believe in twisted lies and not the truth. I. Did. Nothing. To deserve this."

I throw Simone one more apologetic glance for what they put her through and stomp back into the safety of my backyard.

I grab the noise-canceling headphones, hit Play on the nature soundtrack, and resume writing. I pour my anger and frustration into the words and wrap them with sadness. The sadness that's been growing in my chest for the past few days and will only get worse tomorrow.

On Amelia's birthday.

By the time Simone returns from walking the dogs, I have not only finished the chapter, I've started writing a healthy chunk of the next one.

I remove the headphones. The chanting hasn't stopped, but the intensity is far less than it was earlier. Maybe some of the protesters have gone home for lunch or my words got through to them. I hope my words got through to them.

Bailey bounds over to me, and I stroke her, happy to see her again. Her tail wags, and she plonks her ass on the cobblestones by my feet.

I look up at Simone. "I'm sorry for what they said to you when you left."

She offers me a wide smile that's like a big warm hug, and it eases something in me. "What you said out there... you shocked a lot of them. They weren't expecting you to say any of that. They weren't expecting you to stand up for yourself."

A short, self-deprecating laugh huffs over my lips. "Maybe if I had stood up for myself a little more while in prison, I wouldn't have almost died."

"Do you really believe that?"

"No," I say on a sigh. "From day one, it was like some of the prisoners and guards were out to get me. I was afraid. *So afraid*. Not just of them hurting me, but of what would happen if I tried to protect myself."

Simone's eyes seem to delve inside me and search for what makes me tick. And for once, I don't try to refortify the wall around me. The wall Troy has been slowly destroying brick by brick. I let her see the raw, uncensored pain that's been hidden inside me for too long.

"How are you doing?" she asks. "I don't mean about what happened out there." She points to the gate. "It's like you're sad. Sadder than normal."

I'm not sure how to answer. Later in my marriage and during my incarceration, I made myself numb so I didn't have to feel much of anything. And now that the safe containing my emotions has been flung open—thanks to therapy—I'm dealing with a flood of emotions like never before. Therapy is helping, but there are days when the coping strategies I've learned are not enough, and I'm left trying to keep my head above the water.

"Let's go inside for lunch." I don't need anyone else hearing any part of this conversation.

The four of us go into the house, and I grab a couple of plates from the cabinet and pour lemonade into two glasses. The dogs settle down on Bailey's bed. It's barely large enough for them both, but they don't seem to mind.

I pile the samosas from the Picnic & Treats bag onto a serving plate and take a seat at the kitchen table.

"Sooo," Simone begins, removing a samosa from the plate, "why do I have the feeling it's not just the protesters that are responsible for making you sad? Does it have something to do with your daughter?"

I startle at how easily she's pinpointed part of the problem. But after what she went through with losing her own baby, her mother's instincts shouldn't surprise me.

I nod and tell her about the phone call from my brother-in-law. "Amelia's eighth birthday is tomorrow. I was hoping to get to spend it with her. Or at least see her sometime soon." I fiddle with my samosa, pulling tiny bits of deep-fried dough from it. "It was delusional thinking, but five years of living in prison can have that effect on you."

"There's nothing wrong with hoping to spend your daughter's birthday with her. After I lost my baby, I'd go to

Lily's grave on her birthday. And every year around that date, I would struggle with depression."

"I struggled the most in prison when it was Amelia's birthday. It was one more painful reminder of everything I had lost. Did visiting your daughter's grave help?"

Simone dips her samosa into her chutney container. "Yes. No. Until Lucas recently learned the truth that I had once been pregnant, Avery was the one who'd been there for me on Lily's birthday. But that didn't help me move on. Not in the way I needed. What do you usually do for your daughter's birthday? How do you celebrate it?"

"I threw parties for her first two birthdays. After I was arrested, I had to treat Amelia's birthday like it was any other day." I would dream about her birthday parties—the ones I wasn't part of—and of her blowing out her candles, but that was all I could do.

"You know, there's no law that states you can't commemorate your daughter's birthday if you can't be with her. Her birthday is still a reason to celebrate. You gave birth to a beautiful baby girl, and she's able to have a wonderful life because of the sacrifices you made for her."

I take a bite of my samosa and chew it, mulling over Simone's words. She might have a point. I swallow the spicy food. "You're right. I'd never thought of it that way before."

"You can get a small birthday cake to mark the day. Maybe include Troy in the celebration. I'm sure he would love to do that for you. Or you could celebrate it on your own. Do whatever will make the day special for *you*."

Evie mentioned the other day that Taylor used to be a tattoo artist. The memory of the gorgeous hibiscus design on Evie's shoulder sparks an idea. "I think I know what I want to do," I tell Simone.

I call Taylor. She answers on the third ring. "Hey, Jess."

"Hi. What is the name of the tattoo studio you used to work at? I'm thinking of getting a tattoo."

"What kind of design are you looking at?"

I explain my idea to her. "It's to symbolize someone who is special to me, but who can't be with me. I want a way to keep her close."

"The studio is usually closed on Sundays, but let me call Jeannie. I'd be happy to do your tattoo for you, Jess, if you want. I love what you're thinking of doing."

Gratitude swells in my chest. Gratitude and excitement. "Thank you. I would love that. Evie showed me the flower tattoo you inked on her shoulder. It's gorgeous."

A few minutes later, everything is set. Taylor will drive me to Eugene tomorrow morning and tattoo my forearm.

"I'll sketch a few designs based on what you've told me, and we can go from there," she tells me.

I can't stop grinning, excited at the idea.

"I didn't realize you've been thinking of getting a tattoo," Simone says after I end the call.

"I hadn't. Or maybe I had. I fell in love with Troy's tattoo the moment I saw it. Even more so when he told me it symbolizes his friendship with Colton." The sentiment behind it is beautiful. The maple leaf tattoo with the mountain scenery is beautiful. "Maybe deep down I wanted to get one but didn't realize it until now." I take another bite of my samosa.

"I think it's a great idea. I have a tattoo on my hip, symbolizing my daughter. That way she's always with me." She touches her left hip, and her fingers linger for a beat. Her hand drops away, and she picks up her glass. "You might also consider grief therapy. Lucas and I have been talking to a therapist to help us deal with the grief of losing our daughter."

"But Amelia is still alive."

"She's alive, but given your situation, it makes sense that you're grieving her. She's no longer part of your life, but she's very much with you." Simone places her hand over her heart. "Grief counseling might help you adjust to losing her."

"Even though I'm not ready yet to fully give her up?" I know I shouldn't hold out hope...but today—twenty-four hours from when she turns eight—it seems hard to fathom that Craig will truly keep her from me for the rest of her life.

"I hope your brother-in-law and his wife change their minds. But if they don't, grief counseling might help you come to terms with that."

My chest tightens at the thought of Grace and Craig not changing their minds—and a chunk of the hope crumples like a dry leaf. There's a strong possibility they won't change their minds, a reality I can't do anything about even if I wish it weren't true. I can't blame Craig for feeling the way he does. I'm not my late husband or his brother, Lincoln, but that doesn't mean Craig's feelings are any less real. "I'll bring it up with my therapist when I see her next," I tell Simone. I have an appointment to see Robyn in eleven days—on September second.

"It's helping me and Lucas. I lost my uterus due to the car accident. It means I can't get pregnant and carry Lucas's baby. That option was taken from me. Therapy is also helping me come to terms with that."

"I'm not looking to have any more kids." Our situations are so different. I hate how that option was stolen from Simone.

"And there's nothing wrong with that. Focus on grieving the loss of your daughter. Not every woman wants to have kids. And not every woman who wants kids can conceive them."

I used to dream of having more than one child, but that dream was from before I was married. Back when I dreamed of having a great career and three kids and a wonderful husband who adored us.

Now, I'm left with shattered fragments of that dream, unsure what to do with them.

Troy wants kids. Troy would be a great father.

The memory of Nova playing with him at the beach plows into my thoughts. It's the same thought I've had previously—only now it's more painful.

More painful because this time I'm in love with Troy.

In love with him, but unable to give him what he really wants...what he deserves.

38

ANGELIQUE

March 1944
France

Spring is a time of hope and new beginnings. This first day of the season is no exception. The French who oppose the German presence are hoping the war will end soon with the Allies the victors. The resistance and SOE agents are hoping D-Day will soon be upon us.

And I hope my baby is all right, and I'll soon get word from Johann that he is safe.

I gaze out of the flat window, the longing to be out there and doing resistance work strong. Henri recently decided I am not to participate in any more missions. For now, all I'm permitted to do is go for short walks, not get noticed by the Gestapo, and look like every other pregnant woman in France who prays her baby will be all right.

Henri has apprised Baker Street of the situation since he is down one agent. They agreed it's too dangerous to evacuate me out of France. I need to wait until the baby is born.

The one piece of news Baker Street hasn't been told about is that the baby's father is The Wolf—the German soldier Allaire told them about when I had questioned Johann's loyalty to Germany and Hitler. They also do not know—as far as I am aware—that The Wolf has deserted the German Army.

"Do you need anything?" Lise asks, wrapping her faded silk scarf around her neck. "I won't be long."

I grin, hiding my agitation at not getting to do something useful. The smile, though, is genuine. None of this is Lise's fault. "I don't think you can get most of the things on my list." *Including Johann or word of him.*

Discomfort twinges in my lower back. I shift on the settee in an attempt to get more comfortable.

"You're sure you will be all right while I'm gone?"

"I'll be fine. I'll be sitting here reading." It's about the only thing I can do. I have read *Voyage au bout de la nuit* so many times, I am close to having it memorised.

Lise leaves, and I pick up my book from the coffee table.

The discomfort in my lower back grows, and I shift position again. It doesn't make a difference. Lately, I'm uncomfortable most of time. Four more weeks. That's all I have left until my baby will be in my arms and the discomfort will be gone. Unless...unless the baby is coming early.

I shut that thought down and try to focus on the novel once more. I am not prepared yet. I really want Johann to be here before the baby arrives.

An hour later, the flat door clicks open with Lise's return, and the discomfort is no longer just in my lower back. As of fifteen minutes ago, it has shifted to include my belly. There's no doubt now that I am in labour.

Bloody hell, I'm not ready for this.

While I was engaged to Charles, I'd imagined us one day having children. But not once had I imagined I would be in a war-torn country occupied by the enemy when the baby came into the world, and the location of my baby's father would be unknown.

I push myself unsteadily to my swollen feet and waddle around the cramped space. One hand rests on my lower back, the other on the knot of muscles surrounding my belly. I focus on the cloudless sky outside the window and breathe through the discomfort.

"Are you okay?" Lise asks.

My attention remains on the sky, but I don't miss the concern in her tone.

"I think I might be in labour." My voice comes out casual and breezy—the opposite to how I feel.

"Oh. Do you want to sit?"

My gaze drops from the not-quite-so-calming blue of the sky to Lise. She's wringing her hands, deep lines stretched across her brow.

"I'd rather keep moving." I resume waddling.

"I'll get Françoise. I won't be long." Lise doesn't give me a chance to respond. She darts out the door to fetch the midwife.

Another contraction hits, more intense than the other ones. The pain I experienced when Dr. Hubert repaired my hand was worse than this, but knowing that doesn't bring me much comfort. I groan.

If feels like a lifetime and a half before Lise walks into the flat with Françoise. She was probably only gone for a quarter of an hour. They come into the drawing room the same moment I release a long moan. Fluid trickles down my leg and pools on the hardwood floor.

"It looks like your baby is eager to come into the world." The soft smile in Françoise's tone is no doubt meant to reassure me, and I allow myself to relax and catch my breath.

"Let's get you on the bed, Éve, and see how things are progressing." She lists off the items for Lise to round up for my baby's grand entrance into the world.

"She's beautiful," Lise says, peering at the small bundle in her arms, wrapped in the softest blanket I could find when I was pregnant. She sways on the spot, rocking my daughter. "She looks like her maman."

I laugh, the sound weak from exhaustion, strong with love and joy. "She looks like every blue-eyed, bald baby. But I agree. She is beautiful."

Neither of us points out the obvious. My daughter is small for a newborn. But she is also four weeks early. If it hadn't been for Lise and Henri, as well as Dr. Hubert and Rosita—all who made sure I had enough food while I was pregnant—my daughter would have been smaller and less likely to survive.

"Do you have a name for her?" Lise asks.

"I was thinking of calling her Anna, after her Austrian aunt. Her name is...or was...Anja."

Lise nods. She knows a bit about Johann's sister and how she was deaf and trying to escape the Nazis. "Do you think your daughter is...?" Her gaze drops to Anna.

"Do I think she's deaf too? I don't know. Time will tell." It was a worry that constantly visited me while I was pregnant.

"It's a good thing the Nazis are too busy to pay attention to whether she's deaf or not..." Lise doesn't have to finish her sentence for me to know what she's referring to. Hitler stopped publicly rounding up disabled adults and children years ago, but it doesn't mean he altogether ceased killing or sterilising them in secret. They don't fit his view of the perfect Aryan society.

If Anna is deaf, her life will be at risk if I don't get her out of France.

"Hopefully the war will be over before any of them concern themselves with that," I say, praying it's true. D-Day is coming soon. The SOE and resistance networks are preparing for it, even though we don't have a date yet. Sabotage has increased on the factories manufacturing supplies for the Germans.

I hate that I can't be part of it, but my daughter's well-being comes first. Right now, my plan is to do whatever I can to keep her safe.

Lise hands me the sleeping bundle. I eagerly take my daughter, desperate to keep her safe in my arms. Willing to fight Hitler himself just to protect her.

I peer down at her beautiful face, and more love and joy than I thought any person could possibly feel blooms in my chest. I kiss her brow, sending all my love to her in that tiny gesture. She's the most perfect thing to come out of this war.

"I'll let Henri know your baby is out in the world now," Lise tells me, a soft smile in her tone. "Until Baker Street can get you and her out, he wants you to stay hidden."

"Female members of the resistance have been pushing around prams with hidden explosives in them," I remind her, "and none of the Germans or Milice have suspected them of wrongdoing."

"That might be so, but the last thing you want is for them to become suspicious and hurt your daughter while they search her pram. The Germans sense something is coming. They won't take any chances. More people are resisting. It's making the Germans antsy."

She's right. As much as I want to help end this war, it is too dangerous. I'm all my daughter has. There are already so many orphans in France and Britain and everywhere else this war has impacted. I am not ready to add my daughter to the list, especially when I have no idea where Johann is.

"I need to leave for a few hours. Stay safe, you two, while I'm gone." Lise heads for the door with a quick stride and departs the flat.

And I'm left dwelling once again on my daughter's future and where her father might be.

I push my fears aside, not wanting our little angel to sense them. "How about I tell you about the brave and loving man who is your father? The man who will be so excited to finally meet you, *ma petite*."

39

JESSICA

August, Present Day
Maple Ridge

I examine the beautiful work of art on my forearm. The pink hydrangea and a couple of forget-me-nots poke up from the opening of the tulip shell. The shell was one of Amelia's favorites.

"It's gorgeous," I gush to Taylor, my mouth tilting into a wide grin. "Thank you! I can't get over just how incredible it looks. It's even better than I was hoping for."

Taylor smiles, her chair facing mine. "I'm glad you like it."

"I love it! Thank you so much. It means everything to me." The tattoo doesn't erase the pain of losing Amelia, but it does symbolize how much I love her.

Craig and Grace can keep me from my daughter, but they can't take away my love for her.

Taylor touches my arm, the gesture tender. "I'm so sorry

for your loss, Jess. I can't imagine what it's like to lose a child like you did."

My smile wavers, my hold on it loosening. "Thanks."

"Do the protesters know you have a daughter? Maybe they wouldn't act the way they are if they knew the truth."

"I doubt it would make a difference."

She releases a long huffed-out sigh. "I guess you're right. It's no different than social media. You post something positive or reveal your greatest hurts in hope it will help someone else, and the trolls find a way to tear you apart." She pushes to her feet and starts to clean up the area.

"Exactly. There are times when I feel sorry for them. Their lives must be so dark since they feel the need to poison anything good. It must be exhausting living with that much hate." I saw enough anger and hatred while in prison to last me several lifetimes.

Taylor pauses cleaning up and stares at me for a second. "You really are amazing, Jess. I wish those protesters had a chance to know the real you. Maybe then enough of them would stand up for you instead of hiding behind their cloak of ignorance."

"Me too. Maybe one day that will change." I hope it will, but I also can't see that happening any time soon. World War II ended more than seven decades ago and there's plenty of evidence of the Holocaust, yet anti-Semitic views still exist, and there are those who claim the Holocaust is a hoax.

All these years later and ignorance remains an issue.

"Maybe that's the problem." Taylor's gaze drops to the table top my forearm was resting on a short while ago. "Your friends, those of us who believe in you...why aren't we in front of your house, protesting the protesters?"

"Because you respect my neighborhood more than the

protesters do. You don't want to feed the trolls. And you shouldn't. I doubt staging a counter protest would solve the problem. It might make things worse." I sink back in the chair. "There are times when a counter protest is a good thing. This isn't one of them."

The counter protest might only encourage more protesters to come out, making the situation worse.

"You might be right about that." Taylor releases another frustrated sigh.

She drives us home to Maple Ridge. The number of protesters outside my house has diminished compared to before my little rant yesterday. I don't know if my words actually reached some of them or if they grew bored waiting for me after I left this morning with Taylor.

She pulls into my driveway, and I hug her. "Thank you again. For everything."

Her arms tighten around me. "You're welcome. And I hope once all the stupidity ends, I'll see you at Barside with Troy and everyone."

I promise her I'll eventually be there, and I get out of her car. I wave goodbye and hurry to the backyard gate.

Zara's sitting at the wrought-iron table on the patio, looking at something on her phone. Shadows from the oak tree dapple a pattern on the ground near her feet and paint the back half of a snoozing Bailey. A white box from Picnic & Treats rests on the table.

I push open the gate. At the sound of the creaking hinges, Zara's and Bailey's heads pop up. Zara smiles. "I have a special delivery for you." She taps the side of the white box.

Bailey waits with her limited puppy-patience for me to call her, her wide eyes pleading for me to say the magic words. "Bailey. Come." She bounds over to me and laps up my attention. I laugh. "Yes, I missed you too."

"Let's see your tattoo!" Zara strides toward us. Bailey and I join her at the edge of the patio. "Simone dropped Bailey off when I told her I was coming here since you were on your way home," Zara explains.

Simone had texted me a short time ago to also tell me that.

"Thank you." I lift my arm for Zara to see. The clear film clinging to my skin allows her to see the colorful design underneath.

"That's incredible...and so beautiful. I know Taylor is a talented artist. I just didn't realize the depths of her talents."

We walk to the table, and I open the white box. Inside is a small cake covered with white, rolled fondant and decorated with flowers and butterflies.

"Oh, that's perfect!" The words fly from me on a gasp. "Thank you for doing this on such short notice."

"Keshia was thrilled to make it for you."

"Does she know why I want it?" I'm trying to keep the number of people who know I have a daughter to a minimum.

"No. And she didn't ask any questions. Also, I've texted Garrett to send Troy here once they get to the cabins."

"Did you tell him why?"

"No. I told him it wasn't an emergency, so he doesn't give Troy a heart attack."

"Good thinking." Knowing Troy, he'd rush back, thinking I'm in great danger. His protective nature seems to kick into overdrive when he's been away for the weekend.

Zara leaves, and I let Bailey and myself into the house. I place the cake on the kitchen counter and collect my laptop from my bedroom.

I pause for a heartbeat inside my bedroom door, and then walk into the closet. I pull down from the top shelf the wooden box with the lotus carved in it. The box I bought at the festival in June. The box where I keep the few things of Amelia's I still have.

I sit on my bed, open the lid, and remove the items one by one. Amelia's baby shoe with tiny pink flowers painted on the white canvas. Her teeny-tiny sleeper with cute pink hearts all over it from Granny. Her birth announcement. And the only three print photos I have of her—when she was nine months, twenty months, and five years old.

I look at them for several minutes until tears make it impossible to see them anymore. I put them away in the box, return it to my closet shelf, and go downstairs.

A LOUD RAPPING ON THE BACK DOOR JERKS MY ATTENTION from the laptop. I'd been so absorbed in writing Angelique's story, I hadn't realized the time. I've been writing for almost an hour.

I turn off the laptop and let Troy in. It's obvious from the moment I open the door that Garrett didn't tell Troy it's not an emergency. He looks as if he's gone through hell to get here...or spent the weekend camping. Dirt and sweat are smudged on his handsome face.

"Did Garrett tell you it isn't an emergency?" I ask, wincing on the inside. "I'm fine. Nothing happened. I just wanted to see you."

"Yes, he did mention something like that." Troy pulls me into his arms, and his mouth catches mine.

I sink into his kiss, his arms, his love, and momentarily forget everything else. He smells of sweat and mountains and campfire. He smells of home.

My tongue swirls against his, letting myself feel his love with each stroke of his tongue. Sending him my unspoken love with each flick, each taste of mine. His fingers slip under the hem of my T-shirt, sending a burst of longing through me. *Damn*. I've missed this. Missed him.

After what could be a few minutes or a few hours, we finally come up for air.

"How long can you stay before you're due back at the cabins?" I don't want to take him away from his weekend responsibilities.

"About an hour. The men will be showering. Which reminds me." He grins that sexy one-sided smile that always leaves my body tingling. "I could use a shower. You wanna join me?"

He gives me a once-over as if he's imagining me naked in the shower, soapsuds sliding down my wet body. The tip of his tongue trails along his lush lower lip, and his gaze lands on my newly tattooed forearm.

He lifts my arm. "You got inked?" His husky voice sounds impressed, and a little surprised, and mostly turned-on.

"I did. For Amelia. It's her birthday today. I wanted something that symbolizes the day." And her.

And just like that, Troy's elated emotions from a moment ago flatline and his eyes narrow. "Is that a good idea? What with you dealing with your brother-in-law and his wife's decision about you not being part of her life?"

I jerk my arm away. "It's the perfect idea. I'm not her mother anymore." The words burn my throat, sear my soul. "But she'll always be part of me. This way I can make sure she's always with me."

I lift the lid on the Picnic & Treats box. "I also got a birthday cake to celebrate the day."

Troy opens his mouth to say something. I put my finger on his lips, stopping the words before they can form. "I can't just forget I gave birth to her, any more than Simone can forget she had a daughter. I know that's hard for you to understand, but that's the way it is."

He grunts out a sigh. "I don't expect you to forget. And you're right. I don't understand. But I'm trying to."

"Good. Then let me do this without you or anyone else judging me."

"I'm not judging you. I just don't want to see you get hurt more than you already are."

"I know, but you need to let me heal in whatever way I can and be there for me. That's all I'm asking. That, and to share this day with me. I'm not sure I can survive it without you."

He sweeps his thumb along my cheek, the frustration in his expression melting away. "I can do that. So, why the flowers and shell?"

"The tulip shell was one of Amelia's favorites. The hydrangea represents love and family. They're pink because that was her favorite color. And well, I don't think I need to explain the forget-me-nots."

Troy chuckles, the warm sound vibrating through me, wrapping my heart in love. "Yeah, that part is self-explanatory. It's beautiful. Just like Amelia's mother." He lightly presses his lips to mine, pulls away, and peers inside the box. "Are you putting birthday candles on the cake?"

"No. Amelia isn't here to blow them out and make a wish. So, I didn't see a point in putting candles on the cake. And we don't need to sing "Happy Birthday" either. But we do get to eat the cake."

"Shower first?" His eyes go dark, and his mouth curls in the way it always does when he's thinking about being buried inside me.

Heat burns low in my belly. I slide the tip of my tongue along my lower lip, already thinking about the taste of him, and nod. "Shower first."

Our hair is damp when we come downstairs forty minutes later, freshly showered and freshly fucked. And then freshly showered again.

I lift the cake from the box. Troy grabs two plates and a knife and places them on the granite countertop.

I take the knife from him and rest the blade on the smooth icing. "Happy Birthday, Amelia. I hope you had a wonderful day, and I hope all your birthday wishes come true." I cut into the cake and put two slices onto the plates.

I dig my fork into my slice and take a bite of the three-layered, raspberry-and-vanilla cake. It practically dissolves in my mouth, and I moan. "God, this has to be the best birthday cake I've ever had."

Troy eats a bite of his. "It is good. I'll have to get Nova one for her next birthday."

An image flashes in my mind of Troy celebrating Nova's birthday with her and Olivia. A happy family. With kids and a wife and their dog.

I stuff another piece of cake into my mouth, unable to look at Troy, my gaze on my tattoo.

I can't go through that heartbreak again.

I can't have another child at the risk of losing her.

I can't. I can't. I can't.

40

———

JESSICA

August, Present Day
Maple Ridge

Thursday, Bailey and I walk to the park where we usually spend our lunch hour. The reporters are no longer hanging out in Maple Ridge, hoping for an exclusive from me. I'm finally no longer newsworthy. I'm free to go wherever I want without them stalking me.

The day is warm and sunny, and the park is busy with families enjoying the last days of summer before school starts in less than two weeks.

Bailey and I sit on the grass, away from other people, my straw hat pulled down to hide my face. The protesters aren't bothering me so much now that the reporters have left town, but a dozen or so protesters haven't given up their fight. They show up at the house before Troy picks me up for work, and they're in front of the house in time for him to drive me home. According to Delores, they don't hang out during the day anymore.

I remove my laptop from my bag and place it on the blanket. A weird prickling at the back of my neck has me turning. No one is behind me, but that doesn't get rid of the feeling that someone's watching me.

I shrug it off as nothing more than paranoia and blame it on everything else that's been happening lately. Robyn is away on summer vacation for another week, so I can't even talk to her about it. I also have to wait to talk to her about my grief over losing my daughter.

I smile at the beautiful design on my forearm. The shell and flowers ease some of the pain that's been a part of me for so long.

I quickly eat my sandwich and power on my laptop. It whirs to life.

I turn on my phone timer and once again become lost in Angelique and Johann's story.

The timer goes off forty minutes later. Too soon as far as I'm concerned. I'd be more than happy to spend the afternoon here working on the story. Troy probably wouldn't care if I was a few minutes late to the office, but I can't do that. My job comes first.

I pack away my laptop.

The prickly feeling at the nape of my neck returns and has me glancing up from my bag. I scan the area. No one appears to be paying attention to me.

It's because of the chapter I just wrote. How could I not be paranoid after writing about the Gestapo and SS? The story has rewired my brain and my body, making me feel like I'm Angelique.

Bailey doesn't seem worried, so I push to my feet and gather up my stuff.

As Bailey and I walk back to work, I rhythmically

squeeze my arm muscle with my free hand, grounding myself like Robyn taught me to do. It's a trick to keep me from having a flashback.

The feeling of being followed is familiar. It's one I suffered through during the latter part of my marriage when my husband had been stalking me.

Bailey and I enter the building where Troy's company is located and walk along the corridor. A white envelope with my name scrawled on the front sits perched against the glass door to Carson Construction's reception area.

I pick up the envelope, unlock the door, and step into the office. I toss the envelope onto the desk. It lands next to the computer keyboard.

I stow my backpack and purse in the empty, bottom desk drawer. Bailey settles herself on her dog bed next to my chair.

I sit down, bring my computer to life, and open the envelope. I pull out a piece of paper and unfold it. The letter is written in the same scrawl as the name on the front of the envelope. But it's not addressed to Jessica. It's addressed to the woman from my past.

> *Savannah,*
> *We don't want your sort here. If you don't leave Maple Ridge, we will remove you ourselves. In a body bag. And we'll make sure no one finds your remains. You'll never get to be laid to rest. Die, bitch, die!*
> *Signed,*
> *A concerned citizen*

I reread the message, my hand shaking, my heart

pounding. What are the chances it's nothing more than a hoax, a way to scare me so I'll leave town?

And what are the chances it's not a hoax? That whoever wrote this is unbalanced enough to carry through with their threat?

I chuck the letter on the desk as if it's a venomous snake and stare at it, willing it to disappear. Praying it's nothing more than a bad dream.

The office phone rings. I startle, a high-pitched gasp squeezed from my lungs.

I pick up the receiver, my hand still shaking, my heart still pounding, my mouth dry. "Hello?"

"Hello, this is Roger Carmichael. I need to speak with Troy Carson, please?" The man's voice is stone cold, his tone sharp enough to draw blood.

I swallow my fear and try to rearrange my voice to that of a friendly office assistant who didn't just receive a death threat. "I'm sorry." My voice trembles and squeaks. I clear my throat. "He's not here right now. Can I take a message?"

"Tell him I don't appreciate him hiring a dangerous offender to work for him. Because of that, I'm canceling the kitchen renovation I booked with him."

Fuckers. "There seems to be a misunderstanding, Mr. Carmichael. Troy hasn't hired any dangerous offenders." I assume the man is referring to me.

"You're that ex-con I've heard about, isn't that right?"

My shoulders sag, the weight of all the false accusations crashing down on them. "Like I said, there's been a misunderstanding." I aim for a friendly voice. It comes out more like that of a terrified rabbit chased by a coyote. "I spent time in prison after being falsely accused of something I didn't do. But I'm nothing like what the"—*judges of the witch trial*—"what people who don't know me have claimed."

"Did you or did you not spend five years in a state prison with other murderers?"

I close my eyes, my throat tightening. "Yes." The word sounds more like a wheeze than an affirmation.

"That's all I need to know. Troy's services are no longer needed."

The line goes dead. And Roger Carmichael's sharp voice rings in my ears, accompanied by the rapid thrumming of my pulse.

41

TROY

August, Present Day
Maple Ridge

I sit on Garrett's garden bench, the sandwiches I picked up from Picnic & Treats on the table in front of me. The laptop he was working on when I arrived is perched next to his plate on the table.

"You sure you don't want a beer?" Garrett calls from the vine-covered archway that bisects the hedge separating this part of the garden from the house.

"No, I'm good."

"Are you and Jess still going to Mom and Dad's for dinner tonight?" He walks along the path, carrying two glasses of water.

"Yes...but I'm not sure if it's a good idea."

He hands me a glass. "Why not?"

"Mom wasn't thrilled to hear that Jess was Savannah Townsend. And I'd kept it from her." I shrug since it's too late to worry about that. "But she did invite us to come, so I guess we're all good...unless it's an ambush."

Garrett huffs out a chuckle. "Yeah, she's not a big fan of secrets and lies. As I learned the hard way quite a few times growing up. Don't worry about Mom. She liked Jess before she heard the news; I doubt that's changed any."

He sits next to me on the bench. Butterscotch wanders off to chase the butterflies hovering around the flowerbeds. "How's the protester situation going? Are they still a problem?"

"There're probably fifteen or so assholes who aren't letting up."

The rest of the protesters seem to have grown bored of harassing Jess now that the reporters have left Maple Ridge. Thank Christ for that.

Garrett's forehead scrunches into a frown. He takes a bite of his sandwich. "Must say I'm surprised you're here. Can't remember the last time you dropped in for lunch."

"Something's been bothering me about Jess's time in prison. Guess I just need a sounding board."

Garrett gives a single nod. "Fire away."

"I've been wondering why she was frequently attacked in there. Was it because she came off as weak and an easy target? Or was it an inside job that had something to do with her husband's murder?"

"What does Jess think about those two possibilities?"

"I haven't asked her. All I know is it wasn't always the same person who attacked or harassed her." My stomach clenches at how she went from living with an abusive husband to living in that hell, always having to watch her back. "She couldn't identify who almost killed her just prior to her release."

Garrett's frown deepens. I can imagine all kinds of plot scenarios are going through his mind. "The prison guards must know who it was. There had to be cameras where it happened."

"You would think there'd be cameras in the kitchen. Jess said it was dark when it happened. The lights were momentarily turned off and she was alone at the time."

"Alone? She was in a fucking prison. Why the hell would the guards leave her alone in the kitchen?"

"No idea. But now you see why I'm questioning things. Jess said if Beckley knows who did it, they're keeping silent." I take a bite of my turkey sandwich and chew on it as I recall everything Jess has told me.

A finch lands on the stone birdbath in the middle of the flowerbed in front of us. Butterscotch stops chasing the butterflies and barks at the small bird. The finch takes flight.

"Before her location became public knowledge," Garrett says, "did the Beckley administrators know where to find her?"

"Maybe. Possibly. Her brother-in-law knew. He was the one who arranged for her to move to Maple Ridge when she was released from prison. He and his wife share a mutual acquaintance with Anne Carstairs. I don't know. Maybe the prison admins knew to contact him to pass on any messages to Jess since she didn't have a phone when she moved here." I do know Jess hasn't reached out to Beckley or given them her information.

Her brother-in-law realized Jess needed a quiet place to recuperate from her ordeal. He might be keeping Jess from Amelia, but at least he did that much for her. Or was it his way of ensuring Jess kept away from his family? He is, after all, the brother of the asshole she married. Who's to say he isn't as manipulative as her late husband?

"As long as the San Diego police know where to find

her, they can contact her if they figure out who attempted to kill her." Garrett bites into his sandwich.

"That's *if* they decide to prosecute the guilty party."

"You don't sound like you believe they would," he replies around a mouthful of food.

"I don't know. I just wish I knew what the motive was for the attack."

"Why don't I see what my FBI contacts can come up with? I'm not promising anything, mind you. But maybe there's some intel they can drum up and share with us."

"While you're at it, see if you can get names of anyone else who's been released from Beckley since Jess got out."

Garrett's eyebrows lift over barely widened eyes. "Any reason why?"

"I just want to be prepared in case there's something we're missing."

"You think they might come after her 'cause they failed to kill her the first time?" He blows out a low whistle. "That would be pretty ballsy, especially when they won't be allowed to leave California for a while."

"It would be. But so is attempting murder while under maximum security." Whoever did that doesn't give a damn about the law and probation rules. "That's why I'm wondering what else they have at stake—and why murdering Jess was important to them."

A POLICE CRUISER IS PARKED OUTSIDE MY OFFICE BUILDING when I arrive there after lunch. It probably has nothing to do with Jess, but I still quicken my pace.

I yank open the door to Carson Construction and enter

the waiting area. A cop is standing in front of Jess's desk. Jess is also standing there, her face pale.

"Hey, what's going on?" My tone is stiff, my eyes narrowed. The last cop in here was Chief Wilson, and he'd been using intimidation tactics to get Jess to tell him where his wife and daughter were hiding.

The cop turns to me, suspicion shading his light-gray eyes. "Who are you?"

"Troy Carson. The company's owner. Is there something I can help you with"—I read the name on his badge—"Officer Hunt?"

"So-someone left a threatening note for me while I was away at lunch," Jess says, her voice shaky.

My gaze cuts to the cop. "What note?"

He holds up a plastic baggy with a handwritten message inside. "Do you recognize the handwriting?"

I read the message, and my blood sizzles and seethes. *Who the...what the fuck?* The muscles in my jaw tighten. "It doesn't look familiar."

"Have you noticed anything suspicious around the building over the past few days?" Officer Hunt inquires.

"Nothing that comes to mind. I'm usually only here first thing in the mornings and at the end of the day. Most of the time I'm on job sites. Or consulting with companies that hire me as a construction engineer."

"Anything suspicious at any of those locations that you can remember?"

"No. Nothing. I can ask the tradespeople I use if they remember anything." I read the threatening message again. "What about the protesters who've been harassing Jess? I wouldn't put it past any of them to be responsible for this." I hand the note back to him.

"Did any of the protesters threaten to harm you to your face?" He directs the question to Jess.

"Someone threw eggs at her when she was in my truck last Monday morning," I supply. "At approximately seven thirty. They hit the side passenger window."

"Did either of you see who did it?"

"No," I reply. Jess shakes her head, her face still pale.

"Anyone else you can think of who might have left this?" He holds up the plastic evidence bag.

"The first day of the protests," Jess says, "a woman told me to move away or else she would make my life miserable. There were other threats like that too."

"Do you know who she was?"

"Unfortunately not. I heard her yell at me, but there were so many people, I couldn't tell who said it."

"Any other suspicious activity over the past few days?"

A heavy puff of air breezes past her lips. "I don't know. Maybe. I had a weird feeling today while I was sitting in the local park that someone was watching me."

"When was this?"

"Around noon."

Fuck. Jess doesn't need that on top of everything else. She was struggling with hypervigilance when we first met. That hasn't decreased much since she started seeing Robyn. This—the feeling that someone is watching her and the letter—could set back her recovery.

"Did you see anyone who might have been watching you?" Officer Hunt asks her.

"No. I wasn't alone in the park. Other people were there enjoying the weather. But I didn't notice anyone actually watching me. It was just a feeling I got."

He asks a few more questions, gives us his card in case we think of anything else, and leaves.

"Why didn't you call me when you found the letter?" I gentle my tone even though what I really want is to rip whoever did this a new one.

"I was going to, but it didn't happen that long ago. I called nine-one-one. Officer Hunt was in the area and arrived before I could call you."

"Alright, but until the cops figure out who left the threat, Butterscotch and I will stay with you and Bailey at your house."

She nods, not bothering to argue my decision.

Relief floods in. Her ability to make her own decisions is important to her, but her safety is important to me. She has a security alarm, but that might not be enough if someone's determined to harm her. The hell if I'm taking that chance.

Still, my staying with her at her house might solve the problem of keeping her safe at night, but it doesn't do anything about her safety while in this office.

"Fuck, you need a huge terrifying rottweiler," I mutter and glance at the loyal but playful puppy sitting by Jess's feet. "No disrespect intended, Bailey." My gaze goes to the glass door to the reception area. "New rule. That door stays locked at all times." I point at it. "No one's allowed in here unless it's me or one of my brothers or Lance."

A small frown wrinkles Jess's forehead. "Why? You don't really think someone will be stupid enough to try anything while I'm here, do you? They still have to walk past the security cameras at the front of the building."

"I don't care how stupid or fucking intelligent whoever left you the threat is, I'm not taking any chances."

She releases a frustrated grunt, her shoulders deflating. "So, I'm back to being a prisoner."

"No, you're back to me trying to keep you safe. Something the prison guards fucked up doing too many times to count. I have no intention of making that mistake."

"Is this because you used to be a Marine? All this alpha protection mode you've got going." She waves her hand at my body, her expression not giving away what she's actually thinking.

"No. It's because I'm in love with you, Jess, and don't want anything bad to happen to you. The Marine training just means I'm a badass who knows a thing or two about protecting those I love. So get used to it."

I half expect her to cross her arms and scowl at me, and I wouldn't blame her if she did. If our places were reversed and I felt like my freedom was being taken from me, I'd be pissed too.

But she doesn't do any of that. She surprises me with a soft smile and kisses me on the cheek. "Thank you for caring so much about me. Other than my grandparents, I don't remember anyone else making sure I felt safe."

It blows my mind she's gone through life like that. My father and grandfather—both Marine vets—would've done everything in their power to keep my brothers and me safe when we were growing up. My brothers and I don't hesitate to do the same for those we care about. "You're welcome. I'm not letting anything happen to you, Jess. And I'll take you to the park during your lunch breaks so you can write."

Jess's eyes brighten, and I know I've said the right thing. There's been an unexplainable light to her ever since she began writing her World War II novel.

Her light extinguishes as quickly as it came. "I got a call just before I called nine-one-one. It was from Roger Carmichael about the renovations you were supposed to start next week. He canceled."

"He did?" That's weird. He and his wife were excited at the changes my crew and I were planning for their kitchen. Hell, I was excited about that project too.

"He didn't approve of you hiring an ex-con to work for your company. I tried to explain things, but he wouldn't listen."

"That's fine," I say, desperate to put the light back in her eyes. "If he's going to be ignorant, I'm not interested in doing the work for him." Or any other narrow-minded individual.

"You matter more to me than any of that," I tell her, and I mean it. I don't care how many demons I have to fight—I'll battle them all to free the woman I love from stalkers, prison guards, and the ghost of the man who stole her love.

42

***

TROY

August, Present Day
Maple Ridge

I open the gate to my parents' backyard. Butterscotch and Bailey trot past Jess and me, straining on their leashes. The smell of grilling burgers hangs in the air, and my stomach growls.

Jess laughs. "I take it you're hungry."

"I am now." My parents' barbecues have that effect on me. Everything always tastes great.

My brothers and Simone are already here. Simone's talking to Mom by the picnic table, the usual spread of food covering it. Lucas is helping Dad with the grill.

"Where's everyone else?" Jess scans the garden, the end of her ponytail brushing the back of her T-shirt as she turns her head.

"It's just family this time."

Jess stops walking and looks at me, her eyes wide and worried. "But I'm not family."

"You're my girlfriend, so that counts in Mom's book. If Garrett and Kellan had girlfriends, Mom would also expect them to join us."

Jess's honey-brown eyes go adorably wider. "Even if they've only been dating a few weeks?"

"Especially if they've only been dating a few weeks. How else would she get to check them out to make sure they were good enough for her sons?" I chuckle.

Except what was supposed to be a joke feels like less of one now. Mom's got to know Jess is nothing like the woman the protesters have been ranting about. Kellan spent three years in prison, and Mom didn't turn her back on him because he made a mistake. A bad mistake. He was guilty of his crime. Jess wasn't guilty of what she was accused of. Big. Difference.

Jess looks to where Simone and my mother are standing next to the table. It's obvious from the way Mom is smiling at Simone, she loves her like a daughter. But Mom has known Simone since Simone was six years old. She doesn't really know Jess. She has met her two other times, and one of them was only for a few minutes.

"It's gonna be okay," I tell Jess. "Mom likes you." I cross my fingers that hasn't changed from the last time Jess was here. Until my conversation with Mom a week and a half ago, I hadn't worried about it. Now, I'm hoping I'm not about to toss my girlfriend into an unexpected war zone.

I take the glass baking dish of dessert squares from Jess, transfer it to my hand holding Butterscotch's leash, and link my fingers with Jess's. The temperature outside is warm. Her fingers are cold.

I catch a glimpse of the flower-and-shell tattoo on her forearm. It's as gorgeous as the woman wearing it. While I question the wisdom of Jess getting it, given she's trying to move on after losing her daughter, I do understand her reasons. I got inked to keep Colton's memory alive.

We walk to the picnic table. I let go of Jess's hand and deposit the dessert with the rest of the food.

"Hey, Jess." Simone gives her friend a hug and whispers something in Jess's ear. Jess nods.

And I breathe a little easier. Simone's friendship with Jess will go a long way with Mom. She trusts Simone. She trusts Simone's judgment.

"It's nice to see you again, Joanne," Jess says to Mom.

Mom smiles at Jess, but it's the smile she reserves for people she's not fond of but doesn't want them to know that. "You too, Jessica."

Dammit. I hope I'm not making a mistake bringing Jess here, especially after she received the death threat earlier today.

I put my hand on the curve of her spine and tap with my finger the Morse code for ILU. I keep tapping, the message playing on an endless loop. Jess leans into me. I kiss the side of her head.

Mom's smile doesn't change. Simone is beaming.

"How was work today, Jess?" Simone's question comes out a little too brightly. It's possible I'm not the only one sensing the tension rolling off my mother.

Jess's muscles tense under my hand, and she shifts on her feet. "Um, it was..."

"Someone left a threatening note for her while she was away at lunch." I have no intention of sugarcoating the truth or keeping it a secret. Anger still roils inside me at what it said.

"What kind of threatening note?" Kellan's tone is hard, a thin edge of protectiveness beneath the surface. I didn't even notice him approach, his Marine-ninja moves deeply ingrained in him. That, or I'm losing my touch.

I turn to him. "It threatened her life if she doesn't leave town."

"Did you call Noah?" Simone asks. "Or the police?"

"The police." Jess wraps her arms around her chest, the fear in her voice twisting inside my heart. "They have the message and are investigating it." She lifts her shoulders with a small shrug, her trust in the police no less obliterated than before.

Creases form between Mom's eyebrows. "Any idea who might have left it?"

"It could be any of the protesters who were outside her house," I say. "Or it could be someone else we haven't considered." Like Katelyn. But would she really do something like that just because she wanted to date me when I'm not interested in her?

I have a hard time believing that. She's selfish enough to spread rumors. She's not selfish enough to threaten physical harm.

Dad comes over with a plate of grilled hamburger patties and puts it onto the table next to the buns. Melted blue cheese oozes across the top of each one. "Burgers are ready."

Mom passes a plate to Jess, her hand trembling. "Here you go, Jess."

Mom has the steadiest hands I know. But it's not only her hands that shake. She looks...twitchy. Nervous.

And that settles in me the wrong way. "You haven't heard anything about who might have left that message for Jess, have you?" Almost all emotion is stripped from my tone, other than a slither of anger that hits the last part like a hammer to nail.

Surprise or guilt or something else widens Mom's eyes. "Why would you think I know anything about it?"

I shrug as casually as can be even though suspicion pounds in my chest. "You seem nervous."

"Son, what exactly are you accusing your mother of?" Dad frowns, having no idea what I'm talking about. He was at the grill and too far away to hear the beginning of our conversation.

I raise my hands. "I'm not accusing her of anything. I was just wondering what she might know about it. She could have overheard someone talking about leaving a note at my office." I wouldn't put it past a couple of her friends who she's not super close with to be responsible for the message.

They're not the type to commit bodily harm, but they are the sort to leave the note to scare Jess away.

Mom lifts her shoulders and her chin. "I'm nervous because my son is dating a woman who was incarcerated with dangerous offenders."

"Mom!" The word explodes from Kellan, sharp and to the point. Garrett and Lucas appear dumbfounded—either because of what Mom said about the woman they consider a friend or because of Kellan's reaction.

Jess and Simone look like they'd rather be anywhere but here.

And Dad...Dad's expression is that of a man who has stepped into a parallel universe and has no idea what's going on. "Honey, Savannah Townsend wasn't guilty of her husband's murder. And Troy's a big boy. You don't have to worry about him. He can take care of himself."

She throws him a death glare. "He's still my baby!"

Dad wisely reverses a step. "He's a grown man."

"I'm also standing right here," I say. "Maybe Jess and I should leave till you come to your senses, Mom. I won't have you accusing my girlfriend of something she's not guilty of. She's already gone through enough without you hurting her."

Mom stiffens on the other side of the table, her spine straightening.

"N-no." The word stutters from Jess, unshed tears roughening her voice. "You stay, Troy. Bailey and I will leave. I don't want to come between you and your family." Her face is so pale and drawn. I want to hold her and take her away from here and punch a tree all at the same time.

"You don't have to leave. Either of you. I...I just need time to..." Mom's tone isn't unkind, but it's also not warm and friendly. She swallows. "I just need time to get used to this." She points to Jess and me, her finger lingering on Jess longer than necessary.

"No, we *do* have to leave," I tell Mom. The droop of Jess's shoulders and the shine to her eyes warn me she's barely keeping herself in one piece. I need to get her out of here.

My hand still holding Jess's, I lead her and the dogs to the side gate. No one tries to convince us to stay, and I'm grateful for that.

I get Jess and the dogs into the truck. Butterscotch jumps into the back. Bailey joins Jess in the front.

Jess looks at me from the front passenger seat, her eyelashes glittering with tears, her body shaking. "You should stay, Troy." One tear breaks loose and trails down her cheek. Followed by another. She hiccups a sob, her weary smile failing to mask her devastation.

I gather her in my arms, her head in the crook of my neck, and I hold her as she crumples into me under the weight of her sobs. "I've got you, Jess. I will always have you," I murmur against her temple, causing a wisp of hair behind her ear to flutter.

I have no idea if my parents' neighbors are wondering

what's going on as I stand beside my truck, a crying woman in my arms, outside Mom and Dad's house. I don't give a crap either way. The only thing I care about is the woman in my arms, in my heart, in my soul.

Butterscotch and Bailey whimper, ever sensitive to Jess's pain.

It takes a few minutes before Jess's sobbing is under control. I remain standing on the passenger side of the truck the entire time, holding her.

She sits upright and smiles at me, the curve of her lips a gentle up-kick. "I'm okay now. I'm ready to go home."

I wipe my thumbs under her eyes, drying away the tears. "I have somewhere else in mind first." I buckle her seat belt and jog to the driver's side of my truck.

I grab some burgers and fries at the local drive-thru, drive to Windermere Lake, and park near the entrance to the hiking trail.

We sit at an empty picnic table and eat the food, then walk along the trail, holding hands. Butterscotch and Bailey lead the way, sniffing the ground and tugging on their leashes. Jess and I don't talk. We let nature—the birds calling from the trees, the warm breeze, the pine scent—fill us with peace.

The trail widens at one point, forming a small clearing. The lake is on one side of us, the forest on the other. Dirt and dried needles and leaves make up the ground beneath our feet.

I stop walking and pull my phone from my pocket. I tie the dogs' leashes to the trunk of a tall skinny tree and select a Pushing Limits song from one of my playlists. I hit Play and put the phone on a large boulder close to the water.

I pull Jess to me and twirl her to the ballad, doing whatever it takes to put the smile back on her face.

She laughs as we move around the clearing. I dip her, and she giggles.

The song ends, and I pull Jess closer. The next one isn't a slow song, but I sway her on the spot as though it were. "I'm sorry about my mother. I'm not going to apologize for her behavior. Only she can do that. But I am sorry for the pain she caused you. I don't know what's gotten into her."

Jess's smile fades. "Like she said, you're still her baby."

I grunt, not exactly thrilled to have my grown-ass self referred to as a baby.

Jess laughs softly, the low sound vibrating through her chest and into mine. "You might not like that, but it's true. She might never accept me as your girlfriend. She might always think the worst of me." Jess looks down, hiding her face from me.

I lift her chin with my finger. "I have a hard time believing it. She's smarter than that. But no matter what she thinks, my brothers and our friends and I don't believe any of the lies about you. You'll always have us on your side."

"I know," she whispers, resting her head on my chest. "I know."

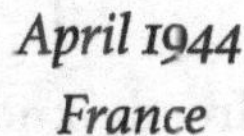

43

———

ANGELIQUE

April 1944
France

Exhaustion refuses to let go as I slowly open my eyelids. The afternoon sunlight streams through the window and brightens my bed with its sorrowful glow.

I roll over and push to a sitting position, blinking the room into focus. My gaze lands on a man in the rocking chair in the corner of my room, his golden hair glowing in the light.

Surprise widens my eyes. "Johann?" *Please tell me this is not a dream.*

My vision is a little blurry from my nap, but I'm positive it's him. Our two-week-old daughter is in his arms, cosy and asleep in her blanket. "Are you real? Or am I imagining you?"

He smiles the grin that always has my heart soaring,

and he laughs. That has to be one of my favourite sounds. He's as handsome as I remembered. He's also worn at the edges and thinner than the last time I saw him, but we all look like that after years of occupation and struggling to stay alive.

His clothes are frayed and soiled. It's obvious he has been in hiding for a while.

"I'm definitely real." The adoration in his eyes propels my heart into my throat, loosens a sob from my lungs.

"I can't believe you're here," I whisper and wipe away tears with my fingers, grinning at him in the same way he's smiling at me. "How did you get into the flat?"

"A rumour reached me that I now have a daughter. I was able to make arrangements to visit you. Your flatmate let me in before she left."

My heart splinters, already knowing the answer to my next question. "You won't be able to stay, will you?"

"Unfortunately, no. We still have so much to do to end this war." He pushes to his feet, walks over to the bed, and sits next to me. He leans down and kisses me softly. "God, I've missed you, Angelique."

I smile, hiding how my heart is cracking into several pieces. "I've missed you too."

His gaze slowly sweeps over my face as if to memorise it. His attention then shifts to our daughter in his arms. "She's beautiful. Like her mother." He tenderly strokes the fuzz on her head. "Your friend told me you named her Anna, after my sister."

"I did. Is that all right with you?"

He glances up, and his beaming smile is the only answer I need.

"I was afraid you were dead because the maquis didn't trust you," I tell him.

"That was one of their top choices when I first

approached them. It was only due to what I could provide —my language skills, my knowledge of some of the German plans, and my engineering background—that they let me join them. But that was not without a lot of arguing amongst themselves first. I've had to do things I never wanted to, but I don't regret it. Not much, anyway." His gaze returns to his daughter. "I've never been one for killing, whether it be animal or man."

Pain lies raw and naked in his voice. I want to hold him close, to banish it. This war is forcing us all to be something we aren't. It's a regret that will haunt us to our graves. At the end of the day, it does not matter if we're killing the enemy; we are still taking human lives. Not everyone is a monster in human clothing. The true monsters are the cruel and soulless ones getting other people to do their dirty work and the ones who relish killing. Everyone else...is just their puppet.

We've all lost so much due to greed and hate and ignorance.

"The maquis couldn't fully trust I was not a German spy," Johann says. "So guards were assigned to make sure I didn't do anything foolish that would benefit the Germans. But if it meant fighting a regime I don't believe in, it was a condition I was willing to accept."

"How long do we have together?"

"A few hours."

Nowhere near as long as I hoped for. "Is she asleep?" I smile at the precious bundle in his arms.

He nods. "She stirred when I came into the room and settled down when I picked her up."

My smile widens. I can't remember the last time I smiled this much. "She knows you're her papa."

He gently lowers Anna into her cradle. She whimpers and drifts back to sleep.

"She fed before I laid down for a nap," I tell him. "So, she'll probably sleep for another half an hour or so."

Johann yanks his jumper over his head and unbuttons his trousers. "That gives me half an hour to hold my fiancée."

A *thud* comes from the other room, followed by a muffled French curse.

"Someone is out there," I say, standing, panic infusing my tone. I know it's not Lise. She's not due back yet. I take a step towards the door.

Johann gently grabs my wrist. "It's okay. I told you the maquis group I'm with assigned guards to make sure I don't do anything that will put the group at risk. That would be one of them."

"You're a prisoner?" The question fires from me louder than expected.

"He's not a prisoner." The deep male voice comes from the other side of the thin wall. "Just ignore me."

"It's hard to ignore you when you're making all that racket." Humour lightens Johann's tone, softens some of the stress around his eyes.

The man on the other side of the wall laughs. "Don't let me stop you from being with your fiancée. I don't suppose her pretty friend is returning anytime soon, is she?"

Anna releases a small sigh but continues to sleep through the conversation.

Johann also releases a sigh, although his is nowhere near as small as his daughter's. "I might as well introduce you to Gaston; otherwise, we won't get any peace from him."

He pulls his jumper back on, takes my hand, and we walk into the drawing room.

The man standing by the side table looks to be about Johann's age but is a few inches shorter than my love. He rubs his hand against a jaw that appears recently shaved. I suspect that is not typically the case. Nothing states you're a member of the maquis more than when you are heavily bearded.

"Angelique, this is Gaston," Johann says.

I don't correct him and tell him my new alias. If he and Gaston found me, they must already know it. But to Johann, I will no doubt always be Angelique, even after he learns my real name.

"It's nice to finally meet you, *mademoiselle*. We've heard so much about you. Your fiancé doesn't stop yammering on about you." Gaston winks at me.

I grin, relieved Johann has found someone he can trust. That is a rare treat these days. These tiny pockets of humanity—of trust—are what give us hope and a reason to keep going during the darkest days. "I'm glad to hear he misses me."

"I'll let you two get back to being reacquainted. I'm here if you need me to look after your little princess. I haven't seen my own daughter in two years, but I do remember how to hold a baby."

Two years. That's what this war is doing to families. As it is, I probably won't get to see Johann again until the war is over and we are reunited. Soldiers are not the only ones separated from their families. Members of the maquis are not usually permitted to visit their loved ones. They remain hidden in the hills and woods, far away from their families.

"She's asleep now," Johann tells his friend. "But we will hold you to that if she wakes before we are ready."

"And your pretty friend?" The question is directed at me.

"Are you married?"

"I am. But that doesn't mean I cannot talk to another

woman. And talking to your friend is more exciting than staring at the cracked wall."

The corners of my mouth twitch. "She won't be back for another hour."

Johann settles his hand on the curve of my spine and guides me to my room.

After a quick peek at the sleeping form of our daughter, we remove our clothing and slip under the covers. I'm not healed enough to make love to Johann, so we hold each other, kiss, and whisper, "*I love you*," over and over. The words brush softly over our lips in a sweet caress, and we fall deeper in love.

His mouth moves on mine, languid, passionate, and I pretend this never has to end. But Anna has different plans. A small rustle from her cradle signals she's stirring awake. I climb out from under the covers, gather her up, and return to the bed where Johann is now sitting propped against the pillows.

I put her to my breast, and she hungrily nurses at what little milk my body is able to produce. Fortunately, it's been enough so far to keep her alive. Anna peers at me through alert eyes.

"Would you like your papa to hold you again?" I ask her once she's finished nursing. "I know he would like that very much." I pass her to Johann.

He strokes her cheek and sings a song I recognize—a French lullaby. He has a beautiful voice, but that hardly comes as a surprise. Everything about this man is beautiful.

We stay like this for an hour or so, relishing what little time we have together, telling Anna stories of magic and wonder. Of a world so different than the one we currently live in.

"I have something for you," Johann says as the door to the flat clicks open. Lise's voice comes from the other room.

She speaks quietly, and I cannot make out what she is saying to Gaston.

Johann climbs off the bed and pulls from his coat pocket a gold chain, the sunlight catching on the heart-shaped charm. "It belonged to my grandmother. I went to her sister's home after I got rid of the car like I promised I would. She used to live near where I was. She died a long time ago, but her daughter was living in the house, and I told her about you. Told her as much as I could without putting us all at risk. She gave me the necklace to give to the woman I love and whom I plan to marry as soon as the war is over."

He undoes the chain and fastens it around my neck. "Now you have a piece of me next to your heart." He slips the warm metal under the neck of my blouse, hiding it from those who would happily steal it.

I tenderly stroke our daughter's head and smile at him. "I already have something of yours close to my heart."

Time used to frustrate me when I was a child. When I wanted something to last forever, it would be over in the blink of an eye. When I wanted something to end quickly, time stretched endlessly.

I greedily soak in every second I have with Johann, as if it were my last, but eventually he and Gaston have to leave. He reluctantly hands his daughter to the man to hold and then kisses me. Every ounce of love he feels for me and our daughter is poured into that kiss. Every ounce is returned by me in equal measure.

He pulls away and rests his brow on mine. "I'll see you again one day soon, Angelique. But promise me, if an opportunity arises for you and Anna to return to your country, you won't refuse it. Just send word so I know you're both safe. I need you both to be safe."

"I promise," I say, even though I plan to break my word

and wait for him. I cannot leave France without him by my side.

"As soon as this war is over, you will be my wife." He kisses me one last time, and I do my best to bottle up my emotions. He needs to see me strong and not weeping.

Needs me to be brave and fierce like I was before our daughter came into the world.

"I love you." My breath mists his lips with an endless promise.

"I love you too."

44

TROY

August, Present Day
Maple Ridge

Monday evening, Jess's doorbell rings. I walk over to answer it.

Garrett is standing on the front stoop with Noah, Lucas, and Kellan. Each of them has either a toolbox or a can of paint or an electric hammer in their hand. The usual verses of *Convicts not welcome*, *Go back where you belong*, and *Protect our children* play in an endless loop in the background. The chants clash with each other since no one today has thought to coordinate things better. It's all an unruly noise with a few new protesters joining the dozen or so lingerers.

"God, where's their kill button?" Garrett grumbles.

Lucas glares at the group standing on the sidewalk. He's still pissed after hearing about the callous comment a woman shouted at Simone almost two weeks ago.

"Finally, a cop with common sense to lock that bitch away," a man yells, ignoring how Noah is wearing jeans and a T-shirt and not his uniform.

Kellan doesn't say anything. His murderous scowl says it all. He's barely holding himself back from decking the man. I can tell from the tightness of his exposed arm muscles. He met resistance when he returned to Maple Ridge after his three-year stint in prison, but it was never anything like what Jess has been forced to endure.

Plus, he had Mom's support. She hasn't apologized for what happened Thursday night, though from what my brothers told me, they did talk to her about Jess. She just hasn't seen the light yet.

"I heard back from my FBI connections. You want to talk somewhere else, first?" Nothing about Garrett's expression hints at what he has to tell me.

I pull the door shut behind me. Jess, Avery, Zara, Simone, and Emily are hanging out in Jess's kitchen. I haven't told Jess yet that Garrett was going to look into something for me. I wanted to hear what he found out first. But it seems like the kind of intel that might be useful for me to share with my brothers—the men who know me best. "You guys wanna join us?"

Kellan, Lucas, and Noah nod without a clue as to what this is about.

I lead them to the single-car garage. Some of the supplies we've been using are stored there, so our coming here won't raise any questions from the women.

The space inside the garage is filled with all kinds of tools and discarded cabinets Jess hasn't dealt with yet. Dust motes dance in the late afternoon sunlight streaming through the narrow windows in the garage door.

"I asked Garrett to check if Beckley had information about the individuals who attacked Jess while she was incarcerated there," I tell my brothers and Noah. "Especially the last time, which almost cost Jess her life."

We all look at Garrett.

"My contact couldn't find out anything," he explains. "He tried several channels. All were dead ends."

I frown. "He didn't find anything about any of the attacks?"

Garrett shakes his head. "Only a few incidents were listed in any of the logs, one being for the near fatal attack, but no motive was given for that one. The assault that caused the scar near Jess's mouth wasn't even listed. And there are no suspects identified for the near fatal attack. Nor was there an explanation for how Jess bled out for as long as she did before a prison guard found her. She wasn't expected to survive."

"Convenient," I mutter. "What I want to know is if there was a connection between the attack and why it took so long for Jess to be found. She was in the kitchen when it happened. A place where you'd expect there to be video cameras."

"Did the cameras record anything?" Kellan asks Garrett.

"I don't know. My contact couldn't tell me about that part of the investigation."

"Jess said the lights went out just before the attack." I pick up the full box of screws I'd been heading out to the garage to get when the doorbell rang. "How did the attacker find Jess in the dark?"

Lucas crosses his arms, his frown deepening. "Sounds like there could be a bigger cover-up involved."

"At the time, Jess was labeled a cop killer," I remind them. "If the guards caught wind of a plot to end her life, it's possible they looked the other way and did nothing to prevent it."

"Maybe. And maybe not," Noah says. "We don't know

how the guards felt toward her. There are those who do want to make a difference and see prisoners rehabilitated so they make better choices when they leave the system."

Garrett leans his hip on Iris's old workbench. "What has Jess told you about her time in Beckley?" He directs his question to me.

"Nothing much. She prefers not to talk about it, and I haven't pushed her for details."

Garrett turns to Kellan. "Has she said anything about it to you?"

Kellan grunts a low scoffing noise. "What? You think we reminisce about our favorite guards and our prison-stay highlights?"

"Fair enough."

Lucas uncrosses his arms and lets them fall to his side. "Let's assume for a second it was an inside job, and some of the guards were involved. That means someone paid an inmate to kill Jess...and we're assuming it was an inmate. Maybe it was a guard. We don't have evidence either way."

"But why would anyone want to have her killed?" Noah's gaze slides to each of us in turn. "Jess isn't the kind of person looking to make trouble. Just the opposite."

"Did your FBI contact say anything about Jess's record while she was serving time?" My question is for Garrett.

"I did ask about that, but they couldn't tell me much. As far as they could tell, she kept to herself."

She told me she had one friend in prison at the beginning, but the other woman quickly realized that wasn't a good idea. It was too dangerous. Jess had been isolated almost from the start.

"The San Diego police haven't made any arrests in her husband's murder," I tell them. "Sounds like they have no idea the motive behind it."

Fuck. All the time wasted that could have been spent searching for the real killer, but instead, the SDPD had focused on Jess being the one who pulled the trigger. Now they're left with a cold case no one has thought about in a long time.

If someone hadn't questioned the evidence six months ago and realized the expert witnesses had been wrong, Jess would still be in prison or possibly dead.

An urge to kick something—a cabinet by the wall, the old barbecue in the middle of the garage—explodes in me. It takes all my restraint to rein in the urge. Kicking or shouting or punching won't solve anything. It won't make me feel any better either. Why the hell would anyone want to target her? That's what I want to know. Why target Jess and why murder her husband?

Kellan looks at me and his eyes mirror the same fury burning inside me. "The big question is...if someone wanted to end Jess's life while she was in prison, do they still feel that way now that she's out?"

"If they do, the media conveniently told them where to find her," I grumble, eyeing the barbecue again. I rake my hand through my hair.

"No one else in Beckley has reached the end of their sentence or has been out on parole since Jess's release." Garrett pushes away from the workbench.

"What about the death threat she got last week?" Lucas asks. "You think it could be linked to what happened in prison?"

I get Noah up to speed on that. "I doubt it. The threat was for her to leave Maple Ridge or else she would be leaving in a body bag. Sounds like something one of the protesters could have written." Or someone who hasn't been protesting but is angry that Jess lives here.

"Fuck," Kellan says under his breath. "People are assholes."

Noah shoves his hands into his shorts pockets. "Did she report it?"

"To the police?" I nod. "Officer Hunt responded to the call."

"He's a good cop. He'll do what he can to figure out who left it."

Frown lines deepen on Garrett's forehead. "Christ. Between the death threat and Mom's behavior last Thursday, I can't imagine how Jess is doing."

"She's surviving," I tell him. "But I want her to be doing more than just surviving." She deserves to be living the life she's dreamed of for too damn long. "The protesters, the threat, the feeling someone is stalking her, her brother-in-law refusing to let her see her daughter—it's all taking a toll on Jess."

I feel so goddamn helpless. I'm not sure what I can do to help her, and it's killing me. I want to protect her, make her feel safe, take away all her heartbreak and pain.

But even though I feel helpless over the situation, that's got to be nothing compared to what she must be feeling. And how she has felt for so many damn years. "As it is, her freedom is forfeit for a while. When she's at work, the main door to the company office will remain locked." But even that precaution won't be enough. The glass isn't bullet-proof. She'll have to work in my office to keep safe. Or better yet, I should demand that she stays home and keeps the curtains closed.

But I can't do that. I can't force her to give up the job because of one individual who might not even be a physical threat to her. I can't take away what little control she has over her life right now. Too many people have already chipped away at it. Chipped away until there's barely anything left for her to hold on to.

We return to the house and get to work on the renovations. By the time we clean up three hours later, the renovations Jess and I had planned to do to the house are officially completed.

And it looks amazing, especially compared to how the place looked when we started the project four months ago.

Everyone has seen most of the renovations. It's the work done in the spare bedroom that the women haven't seen yet, and that includes Jess. The day she hid in the secret room, she'd been too distraught to check out the space.

The room won't have the same impact for Jess now that Amelia will never see it. But that's not what I'm concerned about.

Jess got a tattoo to symbolize her daughter and everything she lost. Will this room trigger the land mine I'm most worried about? "Are you sure you want to see the guest room decorated like we'd planned?" I ask as she and I stand in her bedroom, my voice quiet so only she hears me. "If not, I can redecorate it." *Will the room cause you too much pain to come back from?*

Her eyes widen for a fraction of a second. Determination then slips in, brightening the honey color in them. "I want to see it, Troy. Just like we planned it."

"Alright." I tie a silk scarf around those beautiful eyes and kiss Jess on her forehead. "Ready?"

"Ready," she whispers.

I take her hand and lead her out of her bedroom and across the hallway. Everyone else goes into her room and waits there. I want Jess to see the guest room without them witnessing her raw from the pain of knowing Amelia will never see it.

Jess and I step into the room, and I close the door

behind us. I turn her so she's facing the window and press a light kiss on her parted lips. A small smile lifts at the corners of her mouth.

I brush my lips against the shell of her ear. "Ready?" The word comes out low and husky, my voice not betraying the nervousness pumping through my veins at what her reaction will be—especially since a lot of the extras I bought for the room, like the cushions, I got before she told me about trauma bonding. Now, I'm hoping she won't take it the wrong way—that they won't scare her.

"Yes."

"Keep your eyes shut while I untie the scarf."

"Okay."

I make a quick job of untying the fabric. "Alright, open your eyes."

She does, and a soft gasp tumbles from her. "It's beautiful." She slowly turns, the light catching on the tears in her eyes, and for a second regret burns in me at the pain the renovations are causing her.

She walks to the window seat and runs her hand along the wainscoting panel of one of the built-in bookshelves. The two white bookshelves on either side of the seat, facing each other, create a cozy nook. Perfect for reading.

"I love it. I can't believe how amazing it looks." Tears forge a trail down her face. Thank Christ I kept everyone else out of the room, giving her space to process everything...including how her daughter will never see it.

I pull Jess to me and hug her. Her tears soak through my T-shirt, the only indication she's soundlessly crying. I don't say anything. I feel so out of my element. I wish I did know what to say. Sorry just doesn't seem enough.

After a few moments, she pulls away and releases a soft groan. "I've made a mess of your T-shirt." Faint streaks of mascara are smudged under her eyes.

"It's okay, Jess. It's no big deal." I gently wipe the smudges on her skin away with my thumb.

"God, I probably look a mess too."

"You look beautiful as always." I mean it.

She snorts, the noise thick with unshed tears. "You always know the right thing to say."

"Believe me, I don't. I'm sorry if the room makes you sad. I'm sorry things didn't turn out the way you had hoped." I'm not talking about the room, but her soft smile tells me she gets what I'm trying to say.

"The room doesn't make me sad. It really is beautiful. I'm sure I'll make good use of it, even if it's not for the reason I had hoped." She leans in and kisses me.

It's not a heated kiss. It's slow and passionate, sweet and intense. It says so much and not enough. And I wish it didn't have to end. Wish we didn't have to eventually leave this room and deal with the real world. Deal with the ignorance and prejudice and heartbreak waiting for us beyond the front door.

Jess turns and steps closer to the nearest wall. She traces her fingers over the surface. "I love the color." She'd opted in the end to go with a light sage instead of the pink when I'd asked her about the paint color a few weeks ago.

"It was a great choice." The color and white trim make the room appear more spacious and peaceful.

She sits on the window seat and looks out through the glass pane. "The view would be better without the protesters." She sighs. "Hopefully by the time it starts snowing, they'll decide that they prefer sitting in front of their fireplaces than standing in front of my house."

"I hope it doesn't take that long." The first snowfall usually hits in November. Sometimes sooner.

She gives me a sad smile that echoes her heartbreak. The smile then widens and her eyes brighten. "This is so comfortable. I can see myself writing here once it gets too cold to write in my garden."

"So you like it?"

"I love it. Thank you." She jumps to her feet and kisses me again. "Thank you for everything you've done for me since—"

A knock on the door interrupts whatever Jess was going to say.

"Do we get to see the room?" Emily's voice comes from the other side of the door, her tone singsongy. "We're dying out here waiting."

Jess laughs and she sounds genuinely happy, her tears already drying. "Come on in."

The door opens, and Emily, Zara, Simone, and Avery pour into the small space. My brothers and Noah wait on the other side of the door.

Zara turns on the spot, taking everything in. "Wow, this is incredible. I can't believe the difference."

Simone walks over to inspects the bookshelves built into the window seat. "I would've loved this when I was a little girl. Granny would never have been able to get me to leave my bedroom." Her gaze shifts to the walls and the ceiling. "The whole place looks so magical."

"That was the look I was aiming for." Jess's smile remains on her face, but I know her enough to see the cracks in her veneer.

When Jess and I initially discussed the renovations, I didn't know she had a daughter. I didn't know that Jess was hoping her little girl would one day soon see the room.

I rest my hand on the lower curve of her spine. If only I could fix everything for her the way I can fix a house.

Jess walks to the doorway where my brothers and Noah are watching us, a slight bounce to her step. "Thank you for helping Troy finish the room and the rest of the house."

She turns to her friends. "And thank you for helping me too. My life might be a big mess right now, and I'm still figuring out who I am and my role in this world, but you've all given me a beautiful home, so that part of my life is looking better."

I can almost hear the words she leaves unspoken: *if only I knew what to do about the rest of it.*

45

TROY

September, Present Day
Maple Ridge

"Troy," George Cromwell, the head of the entertainment committee, says from the other end of the phone line. The rhythmic *churr-churr-churr* from the nail guns punctures the air as my crew frames what will be the infill home. "We've got a problem."

"What kind of problem?" I walk toward the garden next door so I can hear him better. Hip-hop music booms from the open upstairs window of the neighbor's house.

The pin-drop silence from George's end of the phone drowns out all other noises. Whatever's going on, he's not excited about being the messenger.

"Spill it. What's the problem?" I nudge.

"There's no easy way for me to tell you this. Pushing Limits had to pull out of the festival."

Fuck. Fuck. Fuckity. Fuck. This isn't just a problem. This

352

is a major catastrophe. Pushing Limits is the reason most people are coming to the event. With the band canceling, ticket holders might want a refund instead of coming to see the other acts. We have a number of great up-and-coming bands, but they aren't Pushing Limits.

My stomach aches thinking about what this means for the people I was hoping to help with the money raised from the festival proceeds.

I reverse a step and collide with a bush. Branches jab into the back of my thigh. "Did they say why?" I glance briefly down and move away from the rose bush. My attention returns to the frame my crew's working on and the phone conversation.

"The drummer, Tomas York, was in a car accident," George explains. "He'll be okay, but he's out of commission for at least a month. Their management apologized for the inconvenience."

"Any suggestions what we can do to save the event?" Rescheduling isn't possible at this point. The festival is in three and a half weeks.

"Sorry, I'm fresh out of ideas. I'll set up an emergency meeting for 5:00 p.m. today and send out an SOS to get as many committee members to attend as possible. We can brainstorm possible solutions then."

"Alright. Do that. And then remind me never to do something like this again." I run my hand down my face, wishing that was all it would take to fix this.

George chuckles, the sound falling on the sympathetic side of things. "Will do."

I phone Jess. She answers right away. "Carson Construction. How may I help you?"

For a second, I push aside my conversation with George and focus on the sweet sound of the woman I love. It won't solve the situation with Pushing Limits pulling out, but her voice is what I need to hear right now.

"How're things going?" I allow a smile onto my face and into my voice. "Any trouble?"

A hard sigh comes through the phone, and I instantly brace for more bad news. I have a feeling Jess's news has nothing to do with Pushing Limits.

"Another client canceled," Jess says. "Jeremy Webb."

My smile shatters. *That* isn't what I needed to hear right now either. "Did he give a reason?"

"The same one Roger Carmichael gave. They don't like the idea of you hiring an ex-con. He's worried about his children and what having someone like me around means to their safety."

I tighten my grip on my phone. "Christ, that's such bullshit."

"I know. I'm sorry, Troy." She sounds so heartbroken, I'm torn between rushing to the office to pull her into my arms and giving Jeremy a piece of my mind for his ignorant comment. Why do people have to keep accusing her of these goddamn lies?

Shit, as if she doesn't have enough going on as it is, now the job is fucking with her mental health. "It's not your fault, Jess. Don't apologize. You've done nothing to deserve those attitudes."

"I know," she whispers, her words lacking any hint of conviction. "Other than that, everything else is going well."

Maybe at the office.

"I'm going to be late tonight," I tell her. "I have an emergency festival committee meeting at five."

"What's the emergency?"

I don't answer right away, wanting to shield her from more bad news, but she's going to find out about it soon enough. "Pushing Limits had to cancel."

"Oh, no! What happened?"

"Their drummer was injured in a car accident and is unable to play for at least a month, so we need to figure out what to do."

"Can I come? Maybe there's something I can do to help."

"Sure." I can use all the help I can get. "Sounds good."

We end the call, and I phone Lucas to rebook my PT appointment with him since I won't make it today.

"Sorry about the band having to pull out," he says after I tell him what happened. "Let me know if there's anything I can do to help."

"Why did you have to give up your drumming lessons when you were a kid?" My question comes out on a half-hearted grumble.

Lucas releases a sharp bark of a laugh. "Because I sucked at it. As you pointed out several times."

I laugh, a low rumble in my throat, despite the world falling apart around me. "Yeah, I do seem to remember that part."

AN HOUR LATER, LANCE AND I ARE STUDYING A BLUEPRINT stretched out on the hood of my truck when he releases a low wolf whistle.

I turn to where he's looking.

Olivia's walking up the sidewalk, carrying her picnic basket. She's wearing a yellow sundress and a wide grin. "Hey, Athos. I thought you and I could have lunch."

I return the smile, but mine is nowhere near as bright as hers. Too much crap is falling on my shoulders, especially today, for me to muster the energy to do better than that.

"You look pretty," Lance says, his expression soft. Damn, he has it bad for her. "The dress looks great on you."

"Thanks." She gives him a twirl, and I swear my foreman freaking swoons.

I bite back a laugh. I can't remember the last time he acted this way around a woman. Hell, I can't remember the last time he hooked up with one. "Where's Nova?" I ask.

"At my mom's. So, are you free for lunch?"

"Sure." I let Lance know he can tell everyone to break for lunch.

"On it, Boss." He pushes away from the hood of the truck.

"Actually, I was hoping just you and I could have a picnic together," Olivia tells me. "We need to talk. In private."

Never in the history of "we need to talk" has it ever ended well. Olivia has already banned me from letting Jess hang out with Nova and me. What more can there be?

Lance must be wondering the same. His eyebrows are raised as if silently asking me that very question.

"Okay. Where do you want to go? I can't be long, though. I have a festival committee meeting later, and I have lots to do before then."

Lance leaves to talk to the crew.

Olivia flashes me a smile, easing my fear that she's about to dump more bad news on me today. "Why don't we go to the park? We should be able to find a quiet spot there."

I walk with Olivia to the nearby neighborhood park. We sit on the empty bench in the shade of a maple tree overlooking the fountain. Several young kids are chasing each other around it, their giggles and shrieks heard over the splash of the water.

"What did you wanna talk about?" I ask as Olivia passes me a turkey club sandwich. Cranberry sauce peeks from between the bread.

"Savannah." There's a fine edge of distaste in Olivia's tone, and every muscle in my body tenses. I don't have the time for this. Or the stomach.

"Her name is Jess. What about her?" Irritation hammers my consonants flat, hardens my vowels.

Deep creases form between Olivia's eyes. It's her I've-got-something-to-say frown. Her you're-not-going-to-like-it frown. "You're making a big mistake dating her."

"C'mon." I scowl at Olivia, something I never used to do with her—not until recently, when she first disagreed with my choice of girlfriend. "Give her a chance before you condemn her like everyone else has."

Olivia's frown falls away, and she glances to where the kids are chasing each other. "I have a child to think of, Troy. You know Nova will always come first for me...and that includes her safety. Katelyn told me more about Savannah's past, and I'm just thinking about my daughter."

For Christ's sake. Why do so many of my problems lately seem to point back to Katelyn? "Don't believe everything Katelyn tells you. She let everyone believe I'd had sex with her when I hadn't."

Olivia's eyes widen for a quick beat, my revelation clearly surprising her. Guess she'd heard that rumor too. She's never asked me about it. But then, she's never asked me about any of the women I've hooked up with in the past. Given her opinion about my girlfriends? Yes. But never the hookups.

"You know me better than a lot of people," I remind her,

"so why are you acting like I'm incapable of seeing someone for who they are?"

"That's not what I'm doing—"

"That's exactly what you're doing. Remember, if it hadn't been for Cora, no one would have known about Jess's past beyond those she confided in. Why? Because Jess has never given anyone a reason to not trust her or believe she's a dangerous offender."

I don't want to throw Cora's self-absorbed behavior in her sister's face, but Olivia hasn't given me a choice. "Jess is the victim in this," I point out, my annoyance at the situation and this conversation being no less than it was a moment ago.

Olivia scoffs. "How the heck is she the victim?"

"All she wanted was to start a new life after all the terrible things that happened to her. She didn't ask to marry a man who manipulated and abused her. She didn't ask for someone to murder him." I'm not sorry that someone did, but I am sorry for what it cost Jess. "His death should have meant she was finally free. But instead, she was framed for his murder and lost her child. The child she loved like you love Nova."

I turn to watch the kids climb onto the side of the fountain and toss coins into it. "How would you feel if someone took Nova from you, and you were forced to give up your parental rights because you thought it was the right thing to do? All Jess is trying to do is live the life she deserves after everything she's been forced to endure. But thanks to your sister, she can't do that." I narrow my eyes at Olivia, still unable to believe we're having this conversation. Still unable to believe one of my best friends is acting as though Jess is a monster. "Ignorant people who think they have the right to harass Jess have bullied her. What gives you the right to do the same, Olivia?"

"Because I love you, Troy." The words are flung at me with the force of a missile, her tone soft and certain. "And I know you love me too. And you love Nova like a daughter. We're a family." She looks at the fountain and releases a wistful sigh. A young couple is sitting on the edge of it, away from the kids, and they're kissing.

"You're right. I do love you, Aramis." I try not to groan at her confession and the way she's gazing longingly at the couple. "I love you, but not in the same way I love Jess."

Olivia's body jerks as if I've slapped her, and something flashes in her eyes. Hurt? Frustration? Jealousy? "You're getting it all wrong."

I frown. "I'm getting it all wrong? What exactly am I getting wrong?"

"We're supposed to be together." Her voice is a choked whisper. "Isn't that what you promised Colton?"

I close my eyes for a second against the growing headache that's not just the result of this conversation. "Olivia, I didn't promise him you and I would become a family." Now, it's my words that are whispered, the pain of losing my other best friend too close to the surface. "I promised him I would be there for you and Nova if one day he couldn't. But I never promised to take his place."

Olivia's face crumples in genuine pain, the pain I witnessed on her so much during the first year following his death.

She leans forward on the bench and covers her face with her hands. "I miss him so much. Why did he have to die?"

My frustration and the tension in my muscles fade, her words tightening around my heart and my throat. I pull her to me and hug her like I did in the early days after he took his life. And as she did back then, she sobs against my chest. I can see now how much Olivia came to rely on me, how she might have taken my feelings for her to mean something else.

She's one of my best friends, but she'll never be more than that. I love her, but I'll never love her the way I love Jess.

I hold Olivia while she sobs. She's not crying because I told her the truth about how I'm in love with Jess. I know these tears are all for Colton. They're a reminder of how I failed him.

They're a reminder of how I'm going to fail so many other widows like her if I can't fix the latest issue with the festival.

"I might not love you like you want me to," I say. "But I know someone who does love you like you deserve to be loved." Someone who I have no doubt will love her like Colton did.

Her eyes widen, teardrops sparkling on her lashes. "Who?"

I smile and wipe away her stray tears. "Are you really that oblivious?"

She lifts her shoulders. "Apparently."

Christ, I hope Lance doesn't hate me for what I'm about to tell her. If she were anyone else, I wouldn't say anything and would let them muddle through things themselves. But this is Lance and Olivia.

"Lance. Does the name ring a bell?"

Olivia smacks me in the chest, and a light laugh escapes her. "Smart-ass."

"You talking about me or Lance?" I rub the spot where she hit me, pretending to be wounded.

"Why would you think Lance is in love with me?"

I make a noise that is part laugh, part groan. "I know it's been quite a few years since you were last single, but you can't be that oblivious, Aramis."

She rolls her eyes. "Clearly, I am, Athos. So, you might as well spell it out."

I wait a beat, drawing out the suspense, and stand. "You know what?"

She glances up at me, her expression hopeful, her smile relieved. "What?"

"I'm gonna let you figure that out yourself." I tap her on the nose like I used to do when we were kids. "I might as well have some fun out of this."

She laughs, and the spark I remember from before we lost Colton flares to life in her eyes. "Fine. You have your fun at my expense."

"I'm sure I will." All humor fades from my expression. "Are you going to be okay?" I'm not talking about Lance or about how I'm determined to stay with Jess. I'm referring to how Olivia misses the man she has loved for a good part of her life.

"I think so." She looks like she's going to say something else but then changes her mind. She glances at her phone. "I should get back to my parents and pick up Nova."

"I should get back to work before Lance sends a search party. But I really wish you would give Jess a chance. I know you'd like her if you got to know her."

Olivia picks up her picnic basket next to her on the bench. "Just promise me you'll be careful, Troy."

"I'm always careful." Except being careful is the least of my concerns right now.

46

JESSICA

September, Present Day
Maple Ridge

M y phone pings next to me on Troy's desk.

Emily: I'm outside the door.

Me: Be right there.

I grab Bailey's leash from on top of a small pile of archi-
tect journals, click it onto her collar, and retrieve my purse
from the bottom desk drawer. The sky outside the window
is blue with a few wispy clouds streaked across it.

I walk through the reception area where I normally
would be working and unlock the door. Emily is waiting for
us in the brightly lit hallway.

She's not the only one there.

"Hey, Kellan. I wasn't expecting to see you." I smile at him. He nods back.

"Mr. Talkative insisted on joining us on our grocery shopping trip." Amusement and the equivalent of a hearty eye roll wraps around Emily's tone.

He grunts. "Needed to stretch my legs."

"Of course you did," she deadpans.

I bite back a laugh, enjoying the show. "Don't blame him. I'm sure Troy's responsible for him being here."

Kellan grunts again, which I take to be an affirmative.

We leave the building and walk toward the grocery store. The sidewalk and streets are busy with people checking out the shops or searching for a place to park. It's early afternoon. Prime tourist time.

"Kellan, Emily!" an older woman's voice calls out behind us. The pair stop and turn next to a giant concrete planter on the sidewalk. It's filled with a collection of fuchsia, purple, and white flowers that still look great even though we're in the final days of August.

I also turn and instruct Bailey to sit.

A woman shuffles in our direction, appearing a little out of breath. She's wearing a bright Hawaiian-print sundress that hugs her generous curves. Wisps of white hair have fallen loose from her low bun.

"Hi, Mrs. Davies," Emily says, smiling as if she's talking to a favorite grandmother.

Kellan nods at the woman. His expression holds a softness most people normally don't see on him and an almost-there smile.

"How are my two prize students doing?" Without waiting for them to reply, she breaks into a story about her granddaughter's trip to the Portland Zoo. "Suzi was so excited to see the elephants, it was impossible to pry her away from the exhibit." Mrs. Davies barely pauses to take a breath the entire time.

"Excuse me." A faded accent—Aussie, maybe?—loops around the vowels of a male voice.

At hearing it, the flash of a memory assaults me from the night everything changed for me. Of an argument. My husband saying something about an insurance policy. An accent. British? Australian? Something close to them? I have no idea what the memory means—and it's gone as quickly as it came.

I turn my head and find a man standing slightly behind me in jeans, sneakers, and a plain hunter green T-shirt. A dark five o'clock shadow covers his jaw, enhancing his rugged good looks. His kind eyes don't hurt either. Something about him seems familiar. Like he's one of those male models on the cover of a romance novel or an underwear ad. He probably isn't. He just has that appearance to him.

"Yes?" I ask, turning fully to him. Behind me, Mrs. Davies is still chatting about her trip to the zoo with her granddaughter.

"Have you seen a little girl in the past few minutes? She's eight years old with two blond braids and is with her mother. I stepped into that store for a moment." He points at the clothing store that caters to outdoor adventurers and tourists. "They were gone when I got out. Which probably means they went into one of the other stores."

"I haven't. Sorry." I glance down the sidewalk in case I can spot her—never mind that his height puts him at a greater advantage to see them. He must be at least six feet.

"Thanks. Guess I'll just have to check inside all the shops." Amusement crinkles the corners of his laughing brown eyes. "Just thought I could save time." He turns to leave. "Oh, there they are. Thank you!" He strides off after a young girl with braids and a woman in a sundress. They're heading in the opposite direction to us.

"And that's why I will always be a big fan of support dogs," Mrs. Davies says, and I swivel to her. Seems like we have something in common.

"This is Kellan's and my friend, Jessica," Emily tells her. "And her dog, Bailey."

Mrs. Davies's eyes widen, but her surprised expression doesn't morph into the one I dread every time I see a protester outside my house. There's no condemnation—just an open curiosity. Not the sort of curiosity you have for a caged animal in the zoo, with a small amount of fear for the damage its fangs could do if sunk into flesh. It's a gentle curiosity fueled by understanding and hope.

It's an expression I wish I witnessed on more people when they see me and realize who I am.

"Don't believe the lies you hear about her." Kellan's tone is respectfully fierce, and more than ever, I'm glad to have him on my side. I would hug him, but he's not the kind of man who's into being hugged.

She flashes him a soft smile full of affection. "You would know about that more than anyone." The smile she directs at me is friendly and bright. The kind of smile given to a stranger you hope to befriend. "It's nice to meet you, Jessica. I hope all the fuss about you dies away soon so you can finally find peace."

"Thank you." *Thank you for not treating me like a leper.* "I'm hoping that too."

"Oh, there's Edward. I'm sure I'll see you three again soon. Bye!" She waves at the white car pulling up to the sidewalk and shuffles toward it.

Kellan goes with her and helps her into the car.

"She was Kellan's and my fifth-grade teacher," Emily says. "She taught at the elementary school for forty years."

Em chuckles. "She had been there so long, I was beginning to think she'd one day be my kids' teacher." Her low laugh turns into a hard breath. "But alas, I'm still single and childless and she's retired." She winces. "Sorry. I shouldn't whine about that."

"What happened to me isn't your fault, Em. You have the right to be disappointed or happy or whatever. Don't let my past make you feel bad about that." I feel bad enough about it for everyone.

"Hey, Em. Jess." Katelyn approaches us, all smiles, and my stomach drops like a boulder thrown off a cliff. There's something a little too bright and cheery about her expression. "I just saw Theresa's wedding photos. They look great. The photos of her flower girl were super adorable."

Her compliment takes me by surprise, but my stomach stays where it landed. "Thank you."

"You should do children's photography. You're really talented, and it's in such big demand from what I've heard."

I doubt anyone in Maple Ridge wants me to take photos of their kids. Not when protesters are chanting for my removal to protect their children.

"You could start with Olivia and Nova," Katelyn goes on, digging a rusty nail into my sore spot. "And of course Troy too. Nova and Troy are so adorable together. They're like the perfect family."

"Katelyn…" The name comes from Kellan on a warning growl as he stalks back to my side.

"I'm just saying that Jess is such a talented photographer. Nothing wrong with that. See y'all around." She grins like a cat who's devoured a family of canaries and is picking her teeth with their bones.

She walks off, and I can imagine she's happily humming a tune. Her mission accomplished. My blood, drawn.

Emily touches my arm, pulling my attention away from Katelyn. "Don't listen to her, Jess. She doesn't know what she's talking about."

Emily's right. I should ignore Katelyn. She has caused Troy and me enough trouble. But she also didn't point out anything I haven't already thought myself.

I think back to what I overheard Troy's mother say two months ago, before she decided I wasn't good enough for her son. *"I can't understand how a mother could ever leave their daughter behind."*

She doesn't know about Amelia, but I bet she wouldn't want me in Troy's life if she did know about my daughter.

Olivia on the other hand...

Joanne has known Olivia forever. She adores Olivia's little girl. She loves Nova like a granddaughter, no doubt.

Troy wants to one day have children.

I can't be the woman to give him that. I really wish I could. Olivia could give him all the kids he wants, and I bet Nova would love to have him as her daddy. She would be the luckiest girl alive if that happened.

After my lunch break, Kellan and Emily escort me and Bailey to the office. A standard white envelope is propped against the door, waiting for me. Same style of envelope as the other day. Same handwriting spelling out my name.

I pick it up and open it, my hands shaking. I'm vaguely aware of Kellan saying something, but it's like the words are trying to make their way through water. They sound distorted to my ears.

I read the letter:

Savannah,

You murdered your husband and didn't serve the time like you deserved. Cop killer!

Unfaithful bitch!

Die, bitch, die!

Signed,

A concerned citizen

"Fuck." Kellan snatches the letter from me, touching only the edges of the paper. "Unlock the door, Em."

She takes the key from me, probably because my hands are too shaky to be of much use. She opens it, and we follow Kellan into the office.

He places the letter on my desk and takes a photo of it and the envelope with his phone. He taps at the screen and lifts the phone to his ear.

"Noah," he says after a moment. "It's Kellan. We have a problem. Are you on shift?"

There's a pause while Noah speaks. Kellan then tells him about the letter and reads it to him. "Okay. I'll stay here with Jess until you arrive." He ends the call. "Noah's on the way. We're not to touch anything until he and Officer Hunt get here."

"Don't call Troy," I tell Kellan.

Dark eyebrows draw together above bright-blue eyes. "Why not? He's gonna want to know about this, Jess."

"He will. But right now, he's got enough stress without me adding to it. Pushing Limits had to pull from the festival." I know Troy. I know he'll take the loss of the rock band hard because he's made the festival too personal. He doesn't have enough room in all that worry to pile this—the threat on my life—on top of it.

Something will eventually give—leaving him to crumple under the weight of it all.

And I'm scared. Scared at what cost it will be to Troy's mental health.

Em gives an imploring shake of her head. "Jess, we've got to tell him. He'll want to know about this."

"I *will* tell him. But not now when he's got so much on his plate."

It's bad enough clients are canceling their bookings with him because of my past. I can't add more to his stress level than I already have.

Olivia wouldn't be a burden to him.

My stomach twists and burns at the reminder.

"Please promise you won't mention this to him. For his mental health," I infuse a heavy dose of pleading in my tone, praying it's enough for them to see reason.

Troy has too much going on with the festival, his company, volunteering at the Veterans Center, and the Warrior weekends. He doesn't need me dumping my problems on him too.

"This is a matter for the police to handle," I remind Emily and Kellan. Not that I have much faith in the Maple Ridge police department...or any police department.

Olivia isn't risking Troy's mental health. Her past isn't harming his company.

"Okay, for now," Kellan says, a slight stiffness to his voice. "You're right. There's nothing he can do about it, and he's already trying to balance way too much."

Noah and Officer Hunt arrive and ask the same questions as last time. Did I notice anything suspicious when we left the building or when we returned? Do any of us recognize the handwriting?

The building cameras didn't give the police any clues as to who left the message last time. The man wore a hat that hid his hair and he made sure to keep his head down the entire time.

"Can you do me a favor?" I ask Noah once they're finished and have bagged the evidence.

"What kind of favor?"

"Don't mention this to Troy."

The expression on Noah's face warns me it's too late. Troy knows.

Fuckers. For once, couldn't the universe be on my side?

47

ANGELIQUE

April 1944
France

The storm clouds outside the flat window loom over Poitiers in a thick blanket. Anna is asleep in her cradle, her tummy full. Her tiny fist is pressed to her mouth. She looks so sweet and content.

I smile at the sleeping four-week-old, but inside I'm far from joyful. She's not growing as she should. Soon, she will wake up hungry again, and my body won't be able to meet her demands.

My stomach tightens into a knot, demanding to be fed. Lise has gone to find food, but I can't imagine she'll have much luck.

A persistent cough comes from the flat below ours. It belongs to the elderly woman who lost her husband to an illness last year. I've gone down a few times to check on her, but I'm at a loss as to how to help her. Without food and medicine, there is little I can do.

It doesn't help the Germans are making things worse with their retaliation for what the resistance and the Allies are doing in preparation for the upcoming attack. More prisoners are being murdered as part of Hitler's revenge. Morale could easily flicker out under these conditions.

But it hasn't.

An increasing number of French citizens are resisting the Germans. They sense freedom from the occupation is coming, and they're doing their part to defy the enemy. To bring this war to an end.

I only hope it ends soon enough for the elderly woman in the apartment beneath this one and for my baby.

The flat door opens, and Lise hurries into our residence like a gale force wind. Her breath is coming in fast as though she sprinted to our building from several streets away, and there is a sadness about her that grips my heart in an icy fist.

Alarms blare through my body, and my muscles tense, ready to react, ready to fight. Did she get word the Milice or Gestapo are looking for me? For us?

"Is something wrong?" My words come out in a rush.

"There was an explosion on a railway track about one hundred miles south of here. It was the work of a group of maquis, but some of the raiding party weren't able to get away in time. The Nazis gunned them down." She closes her eyes for a second. "I'm sorry, Éve. Johann is dead."

It takes two rapid heartbeats for her words to soak in, and then it's as if the floor crumples away and I'm falling, falling, falling down a cold, black pit. I shake my head, scrambling to make purchase on the slippery walls.

Lise is wrong.

He cannot be dead.

After everything we've been through, my love cannot be dead.

"No." My voice is nothing more than a croaked whisper, the air in my lungs failing me. "It wasn't him. Whoever told you that was wrong. It was someone else. Johann is farther south. It wasn't him." *It's not him. It's not him. It's not him.*

Cracks inside me begin to form, splintering through my body and carving out my flesh.

Lise sniffs. "It was him. Gaston was with him. They were both shot. They both died."

A harsh sob rips through me, tearing me to pieces. I'm vaguely aware of Lise embracing me in her arms, of me crying on her shoulder.

"He cannot be dead. Please, God. Please let them be wrong. Please let them be wrong." The words aren't for her. They're a prayer to a God I don't believe in—not after everything that has happened. I pray the man I love was nowhere near the explosion. That he escaped. Defied the Nazis.

Lise guides me to the settee and sits me down. She doesn't say anything. No false words of comfort. No promises that Anna and I will be all right. That we will get through this.

She holds me until I have no more tears to spare. Holds me until I slip into a void filled with nothing but nightmares and an aching loss.

I don't know how long I've been sleeping when a small cry breaks through my new round of bad dreams. I slowly pry my swollen eyelids open, and my new reality rushes in with a tidal wave. I'm drowning again in a grief so strong, I don't have the strength in me to swim to the surface no matter how hard I try.

Lise cradles a crying Anna in her arms, rocking her, doing everything in her power to soothe the hungry baby.

She sings softly to her, the lullaby an English song, and for that I am grateful. I wouldn't be able to handle it if she sang one in French. Her words are quiet so no one outside the flat door can hear them.

Fatigue drains every part of me—every emotion, every cell. But I still find a tiny reservoir of strength deep inside and reach out and take my daughter. Anna and my sister are all I have left in this world.

Memories of Hazel during our childhood trickle in. She used to tell me stories about fairies when we were younger and I was feeling sad. They had a way of making me feel better.

They gave me hope.

I attempt to come up with one to tell Anna, but nothing jumps to mind. I wordlessly nurse her and stare at her sweet infant features. Features that will one day morph into a combination of mine and the man I love.

As I always do while feeding her, I fiddle with the heart pendant Johann gave me, rubbing it between my fingers. Silent tears trickle down my face and land on Anna's soft skin.

I don't know how to go on without him, but at the same time I know I have to be strong for myself and for Anna. His death doesn't change the world we're living in. It doesn't end the war and the sense of loss everyone is feeling. Anna isn't the only child who lost a father after the maquis set off that explosion. She is not the only child who has been made fatherless because of the war.

She might have lost her father and I've lost the man I love, but we have each other.

"It will be alright, *ma petite*," I coo to her, trying to desperately patch up those cracks inside me with whatever hope I can find. "We will be okay."

I keep repeating the words over and over and over until

they're ingrained in my thoughts, ingrained in my soul. I will always feel that burning loss for the man I love, but I cannot let it drown me. Not now. Not when Anna's life and my life are constantly at risk.

Once Anna has finished nursing, I push to my feet. My legs tremble as does the rest of my body, but it has nothing to do with the lack of food. *We'll be okay. I just need to keep breathing. That is all.* I swallow the pain and emptiness that threatens to consume me again.

Just one breath at a time, and one day I won't have to keep reminding myself of that.

Two weeks after the news that still leaves me gasping for air when I least expect it, I push Anna in her pram along the street to the park. The day is sunny, the weather warm, and she's gazing up at the cloudless blue sky.

She makes a sweet cooing sound. I smile at her, my heart squeezing in my chest. I focus on Anna, my beautiful, beautiful daughter. The only bright star in this world of darkness. The reason I'm outside and not curled in a ball of grief in the flat.

Under the mattress of her pram, near her feet, a stash of leaflets lies hidden. A week after I received the news about Johann, I begged Henri through Lise to let me do something again to help the resistance movement. My heart isn't in it like it once was. There is only so much passion I can drum up when the man who inspired me is dead. But helping the network is the right thing to do to help bring an end to this war. To make the world a better place for Johann's and my daughter.

Besides, it gives me something to occupy my mind, to distract me while I wait for news of my return to England.

Now that Anna is more active—as active as she can be given her less than ideal body weight and energy levels—it's obvious I have a real baby in the pram and not something the Nazis would frown over.

That's not entirely true. They wouldn't be impressed that the sweet baby in the carriage is a mix of Austrian and English blood.

"Should we visit the blossoms at the park, *ma petite*?" My voice is cheerful even though my body is on high alert. I might have the perfect cover for what I'm about to do, but that doesn't mean vigilance is no longer my top priority. Our safety and the success of the mission depend on it.

I steer the pram onto the path leading into the park. Everything around us—the trees, the shrubs, the flowers—are fresh with dew and hope. Hope that the upcoming Allied attack is the beginning of the end of the war. Hope that someday soon, this long nightmare will finally come to an end.

I casually survey the area, doing my best to not draw attention. The place is free of German soldiers and anyone else in uniform. I release a long breath, ever conscious that not all danger is obvious.

A woman not much older than me walks past. She's holding the hands of two small girls, their blond plaits gleaming in the bright afternoon sun. They walk to a nearby flowerbed, the colourful petals an assortment of pink, yellow, and violet.

I push the pram to an empty bench several yards from where they're standing, gently pick up Anna, and sit. Smiling at her, I kiss her tiny fist. "Who's my precious sweetheart?" She watches me with her beautiful blue eyes.

So far, I have not recognized any signs of her aunt's deafness in her.

I chew on my lower lip, the skin cracked and dry. Anna will probably never get to meet her Austrian aunt or grandmother. Even if they survived, it will be challenging for a while to find them once the war is over. Their home might have been destroyed by then, and I have no idea where they went. The world will be in chaos as everyone tries to find their loved ones. Anna may never have the opportunity to know any of her grandparents. But perhaps she will eventually get to meet her Aunt Hazel, Uncle Charles, and all her cousins. She won't be completely without family.

A young man approaches the park bench, his noticeable limp slowing his pace. But if the Gestapo were to descend on the area and he felt the need to run, I have no doubt the limp would be miraculously healed.

"What an adorable baby," he says. "Does she enjoy monkeys swinging from the lampposts?"

"Only when crocodiles sing a lullaby."

"I'm happy to hear that. I have something for *you*." From his pocket, he pulls out a wooden clown with a white face, black painted hair, and a red hat. "Henri sends his regards." He lowers the toy rattle into the carriage, stealthily removes the bundle of leaflets from under the mattress, and slips them inside his jacket. "I hope you and your little angel have a pleasant day." He nods at me and quickly moves on.

I nonchalantly scan the area, as if looking to see what other interests the park holds for me and my infant daughter, but no one seems to have paid attention to the cut-out's and my interaction.

Anna and I stay in the park a little longer. I'm not ready to be hidden away in the flat just yet. I scan the area once more, searching for signs of something other than heartbreak and pain. An unexpected wave of grief washes over me again, and a small sob escapes.

I push aside the need to touch the heart pendant Johann gave me. Caressing the delicate leaves etched in the gold sometimes helps with the never-ending ache, but I don't dare to do that here in case someone sees the pendant and tries to steal it.

I tighten my hold on Anna. She doesn't cry. She just watches me with that calm expression of hers. I tell myself the same thing I do every day when I first open my eyes each morning: one breath at a time, and one day I won't have to keep reminding myself of that.

"Are you okay, Madame?" The strong German accent kicks my body into fight-or-flight mode.

I look up.

A blond Wehrmacht soldier is standing next to Anna's pram. The tension in my muscles lessen slightly; he isn't SS or Gestapo. A gaping hole spreads in my chest, formed from too many memories of Johann once wearing the same uniform.

The soldier eyes me with a mix of concern and curiosity, a small frown crinkling his brow. "Is there something I can help you with?" he asks.

I want to scream at him, tell him to go back to Germany. End this war. Fall in love with a sweet woman and never leave her. I want to tell him to stop risking his life for Hitler and the cold-hearted bastards who have stolen so much from all of us.

But as much as I want to say all those things and more, I cannot. I cannot risk being arrested. Cannot risk Anna being taken from me. Cannot risk her losing both of her parents.

"Not unless you can bring the man I love back to life." There's a sharp edge to my words, the slap of heartbreak and pain in my tone that I regret the moment the words are out. Now is not the time to provoke the enemy.

His gaze drops to Anna in my arms, and I can see my pain mirrored in his expression. He has also lost someone he cares about.

He shakes his head, the movement slow, rusty with remorse and sadness. "I wish I knew how to do that."

I nod, not knowing how to respond.

"She's a beautiful baby."

"Thank you," I whisper, the sound choked with a new round of tears.

He responds like most men do when they see a woman cry. He grows uncomfortable, shifting on his feet, clearly uncertain what else to say or do. He wishes me a good day and hurries off.

And I am left at the crossroad, not knowing if I should giggle at his reaction or cry some more.

"We should return home," I tell Anna, "before anyone else is silly enough to approach a grieving woman."

I lower her into her pram and cover her with the blanket. The rattle rolls off the blanket and bangs lightly against the inside of the pram.

I pick up the rattle, shake it for Anna to see, and slip it into my handbag. Then I wheel the pram out of the park and along the street.

I don't go directly to the flat. I take a few detours until I am positive no one is following me, appearing fully the part of a young mother taking her baby out for some fresh air.

At the apartment building, I push the pram through the front doors. It's awkward at best.

"Collaborating whore," a woman says, descending the staircase, making no attempt to assist me. Her words sting but they lack enough venom to maim.

I ignore her. She's been calling me that from the

moment she first learned I was pregnant. I scoop Anna out of the pram, retrieve my handbag, and walk up the steps to the flat. I unlock the door and step inside.

Lise is sitting on the settee, reading a book. She looks up. "How did it go?"

"It went well." I don't bother to tell her about my breakdown in the park and how it drew the attention of a German soldier. Ever since she brought me news of Johann's death, Lise has carefully watched me, as though expecting me to shatter at the drop of a hat pin. I cannot say I blame her. There are still days when I feel that way too.

She takes Anna from my arms. "Is your maman training you to do our job?"

"I'm hoping the war will be over before it comes to that."

She rocks Anna from side to side. "I could not agree with you more."

I remove the rattle from my handbag and examine it. "What's that?"

"A rattle. The cut-out gave it to me from Henri." I inspect the figure closer. A piece of paper sticks out from the hole through one of the beads that makes up the clown's leg. I use my fingernail to draw it out and unroll the tiny piece of paper, revealing a coded message. "I think I understand now why he said the rattle was for *me*."

I decipher it and write down the date and time and location, followed by:

Plane will be landing to drop off two agents.
You and Anna will be on it when it leaves.
That is an order.

The world stops spinning for a fraction of a second as the words sink in, and I suck in a sharp breath. *We're going home.*

I crumple to the floor, relief, grief, and an endless exhaustion pulsating within me. A sob wracks my body, tears wetting my face, falling to the ground. As much as I want to stay and help the cause, my heart hurts too much from being in the country where Johann no longer exists. And I have a baby to take care of.

"What does it say?" Lise asks.

"Anna and I are going home. I'm being recalled." I hand her the message, a whirlwind of emotions clashing and tumbling inside me. *We're going home. We're really going home.*

Prior to Johann's death, I would have come up with any excuse for why I had to stay in France. But my reason for remaining is dead and buried, and the network doesn't need me as much as my daughter does.

I am finally ready to go home. Ready to start the lengthy healing process, to create a new life for Anna and me.

Assuming the weather cooperates.

Assuming nothing goes wrong.

# 48

JESSICA

September, Present Day
Maple Ridge

Kellan pulls his SUV to the curb. Troy's waiting for me at the library's front entrance, a new weariness lining his handsome features. The latest death threat and everything he's got going on are clearly weighing heavily on him.

It's my fault. It's my fault. It's my fault.

I'm the one who's damaging Troy's mental health. I'm the one who dumped more weight on the teeter-totter than he can balance.

"It's better he knows about the note," Kellan says from the driver's seat, his gaze on his brother. "He's a Marine. Our father and grandfather were Marines. Protecting people, especially those he loves, is in his blood."

"I know, but I still wish he hadn't heard about the newest threat." I open the door and slide out of the passenger seat. "Thanks for the ride, Kellan...and for everything." I shut the door.

Troy walks to the driver's side of the SUV. Kellan puts the vehicle in park and gets out. The brothers exchange words. I can't hear what they're saying, but I can guess what it's about. Death threat number two.

I scan the area surrounding the library entrance and the nearby parking lot, my hypervigilance on high alert. I can't shake the feeling I'm under surveillance, but there's no sign of anyone paying attention to me. No protesters. No reporters. Nobody. Only a family is on the sidewalk, and neither of the kids nor the mother is looking my way.

Sunlight peeks through the breaks in the clouds that promise an early evening storm. The wind has picked up since Kellan and I dropped Bailey off at home. My hair blows into my face. I smooth it behind my ear.

Kellan gets back into his SUV, and Troy comes over to where I'm standing on the sidewalk. He hugs me, and I sink into his arms, enjoying his warmth and strength. I hadn't realized how much I needed his hug, his touch, until now.

"Are you okay?" His breath brushes the side of my head.

"I'm fine." *Just don't stop hugging me.*

"New plan. You're taking a sabbatical."

I pull away. "Sabbatical?" I stare at him, trying to process what he's getting at.

"Yes." Troy smiles as if inordinately pleased with the idea. "You're gonna take a sabbatical, during which time you'll work on your novel. By the time you've finished it, people will have gotten over this ridiculous crap about you being a dangerous offender, and life can return to normal."

"I can't take a sabbatical."

"Why not?"

"I haven't been working for you all that long." I bet a

moment ago taking a sabbatical wasn't even an option available to his employees.

"Well, given that I'm the employer, I decide the rules. For the sake of your mental well-being and your safety, you're on paid sabbatical. As of now."

Paid sabbatical? Is that even a thing?

"I'll think about it," I say, not really meaning it. I don't want Troy put in the position of not having an assistant. He can't do that role on top of everything else.

"There's nothing to think about, Jess."

The reason he's so insistent hits me like a truck not stopping at a red light. It's not only my mental health and safety at stake. His company will eventually be in trouble if his clients keep canceling because I'm his employee.

I'm a bigger burden than I'm worth.

"Maybe it would be better if I quit." The words are softly spoken, each one slashing me from the inside.

"You're not quitting, Jess. If you're on sabbatical, my insurance will still cover your therapy. It's the only solution."

"How is you not having an assistant a solution?" My voice isn't soft this time. It's hard with determination. Determination to get him to see how he's burying himself under too much weight of responsibility.

"I'll figure something out, but your safety comes first." He's using that tone I recognize with him. He's already made up his mind, no matter my opinion on the subject. "So, it's agreed. You're on sabbatical."

"Fine." The word sticks to the roof of my mouth, reluctant to be released despite the fact that he's probably right —me being there isn't good for anyone's career. Not his, and not mine. "I'm on sabbatical. But it's not paid. I have money I can live on in the meantime." *As long as the sabbat-*

ical is short term. I try to enthuse my response with the appropriate amount of excitement, but it's hard to do that when the life I've been rebuilding is being yanked from under me.

And I'm worried. Worried Troy will do the job himself, along with everything else. Worried it will be the thing that finally breaks him.

"PUSHING LIMITS HAD TO PULL OUT OF THE FESTIVAL LINEUP," George Cromwell tells the twelve festival committee members who are at the emergency meeting.

A few muttered curses fly around the library conference room.

"Their drummer was in a car accident and is out of commission for the next month. They made a donation to the festival to make up for the inconvenience."

"But we still stand to lose a lot of money if some or all of the ticket holders demand a refund," Troy adds, appearing stoic to everyone but me. The strain is there in his features, recognizable if the others know what they're looking for. It's murky beneath the surface, but it's still there.

"Shit!" The word shoots from Jason Barnes's terse lips, his volume low but the intensity no less powerful. His cold gray eyes dart to me, and my stomach twists at the distrust in them. I shift in my seat and fiddle with my pen.

"You've got to admit that having Savannah Townsend participating in the festival planning isn't ideal." Stephanie Ross's tone holds a lot less venom than Jason served up, but it still has a biting edge to it. Both are looking pointedly at me, leaving me itchy, raw, defeated, like I'm waiting for my turn in a witch trial, my death sentence already decided, the noose knotted around my neck.

"Savannah Townsend isn't participating in the festival planning." Troy levels his turbulent gaze at Stephanie and then Jason. His voice is stiff like the wind swaying the trees outside the window. The trees they want to hang me from. "Savannah Townsend doesn't live in Maple Ridge."

Stephanie's brow wrinkles into a confused frown. "Sure she does. She's right there." She nods at me.

"That is Jessica Smithson." Troy's tone is firm, a silent warning for them not to venture into the territory they're headed for.

"That's the name I go by now," I tell them, shame turning my body hot and cold.

"And Jessica didn't cause the drummer to have the car accident," he reminds them.

"The good news," George says a little too brightly, his voice loud in an attempt to gain control of the meeting. "The good news is, all the costs are covered by the sponsorships. We won't fall into the red. But we also won't make as much money as we might have otherwise made when Pushing Limits was part of the lineup."

All eyes turn back to me.

"Why didn't you leave your husband if he was abusing you?" Stephanie asks, the bite of accusation in her tone masking any sympathy she might have otherwise felt for me.

The shame deepens, its icy fingers clawing inside me.

I touch the tattoo on my arm, the reminder of the most beautiful thing that came from my marriage. My beautiful little girl wouldn't exist if not for it.

"We're not here so you can judge Jessica." Troy's voice is calm, but the twitch in his jaw muscle betrays his anger at how the situation is spinning out of control, how I am now the target for their frustration.

The original reason for this meeting seems to have been quickly forgotten.

"We're not judgin' her," Jason Barnes grumbles, his voice prickly, ignoring how he showed up at the marketing-committee meeting two weeks ago and blamed me for the reporters that were outside the library. "But you have to realize the risk she poses to the festival. The media will be coming to it. And we all remember how it was two weeks ago with the reporters in town 'cause of *Savannah*. Havin' her involved in and at the festival will take away from what we've been workin' hard to achieve."

"And who's to say Pushing Limits canceled because their drummer is injured?" Stephanie adds. "Maybe it was a convenient excuse after they heard Savannah Townsend is involved with the festival. They don't want the bad press associated with that."

Jason nods, his expression darkening. "Stephanie's right. Savannah will steal the media's attention away from the purpose of the event." His gaze shifts to each person here, except for Troy and me. "It will end up being all about her"—he points at me—"and how she was wrongfully convicted of killin' her husband."

I look at Troy. Really look at him. He once pointed out the dark circles under my eyes due to my lack of sleep and the nightmares. Those same dark circles now plague Troy's face.

He's been working so hard on this festival—all the people here have been working hard on it—so no one else loses a friend the way he lost Colton, the way Olivia lost her husband, the way Nova lost her father.

My presence in Troy's life is hurting his business and

the festival. It's even causing a rift in his family because his mother doesn't trust me.

There's nothing left for me to say, pain and frustration spreading through me like a deadly mold, other than...

"I respectfully resign from my volunteer position." Emptiness leaks in with each word, but it must be done. I turn to Troy. "They're right. If I'm involved in any way with the festival, my past might overshadow what you're trying to achieve."

Troy opens his mouth as if to argue my decision but then closes it and nods, his expression more worn than before. He knows Stephanie and Jason are right.

"With that decided"—Jason sits straighter, a smug smile on his tanned face—"Savannah, you should leave now since you are no longer part of the festival."

The emptiness leaking in doesn't waste time. It consumes me, takes away another piece of control I was fighting hard to reclaim. Takes away the feeling of making a difference I so desperately wanted. To feel needed. Worthy. Whole.

And I'm left with a lonely stretch of nothingness inside me.

AN HOUR LATER, TROY FINDS ME TYPING AWAY IN THE CORNER of the library, my back to everyone.

"You ready to go home?"

"Yes." I close my laptop and gather up my things. "How was the meeting?"

"The committee has a list of what we need to do to keep the damage from Pushing Limits pulling out to a minimum."

He might not say it, but I can tell what he's thinking. He's not sure the suggestions will be enough.

He pulls me to my feet. "Your home or mine?" He kisses me, a barely-there pressure on my lips.

"Mine. All my research and craft books are there and there's a plot point I need to sort out. Assuming you're still serious about the sabbatical." Which hopefully won't last long—for both our sakes.

"Very serious. Until the cops figure out who's been threatening you, I don't want you alone at the office. We don't know what kind of person we're dealing with. They're leaving notes now, but what's next? Phone calls? Hiding in the parking lot, waiting for you to leave?"

Oh, God. The phone call. From a few weeks ago. I gasp, recalling it.

"What?" he ask quietly, so as not to draw any unwanted attention our way.

"It might be nothing, but a few weeks ago I answered the office phone. No one replied but there was a breathing noise on the other end, so I know someone was there."

"There was?" Troy frowns. "Why am I only hearing about it now?"

"It didn't seem like a big deal at the time. I thought maybe it was a prank call. Bored teens."

"Did you mention it to Noah or Officer Hunt?"

"No. I'd forgotten it until you mentioned phone calls." I grab my purse from the chair next to where I was sitting.

"Okay, I'll let Noah know about it. Do you remember when it was?"

I think back to that day. "Two days before the protesters showed up and someone defaced my front door."

So, almost three weeks ago.

Troy picks up my laptop. "Let's get out of here and swing by my place so I can get Butterscotch and my stuff.

And anything else you might need while you're working from home."

He doesn't say it, but the implied, *while you're practically locked away so no one can hurt you* settles in the air between us.

49

JESSICA

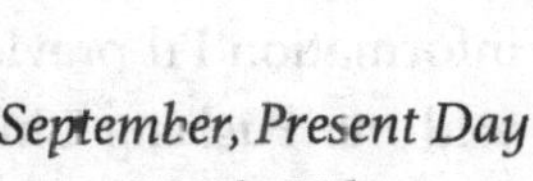

September, Present Day
Maple Ridge

On Wednesday, the weather decides to work against me. Bad news for the tourists who want to go to the mountains and enjoy a sunny day. Bad news for me since I love to write in my garden.

I'm sitting in the window seat in what was once to be Amelia's room...I mean the guest room. I have to start thinking of it as the guest room. Raindrops dribble down the fogged-up glass pane. My computer rests on my lap and Bailey is asleep by my feet.

The world outside the window is quiet, other than the wind playing in the trees and the splash of tires from the occasional vehicle driving past the house.

I turn my attention back to writing Angelique's story, but my thoughts refuse to focus on the words. They drift to

Pushing Limits and the festival, and a nagging thought keeps pestering me that I'm forgetting something.

I pull up my web browser. I'm usually good at staying off the Internet while I'm writing, but I allow myself this one exception and do a Google search on the band.

Article after article talks about their latest singles and the individual band members. There's nothing yet about how they've canceled their appearance in the festival. I read a couple of short news stories about the freak car accident involving a stray dog that put Tomas York temporarily out of commission. The dog is okay. She found a forever home as a happy result of the accident.

It's not until I dive deeper into the older online articles that I discover the information I'd previously read. I saw it shortly after Troy told me Pushing Limits had offered to headline for the festival.

Tomas York wasn't the band's original drummer. That would be Mason Dell. He left the band five years ago and has become successful doing other projects—including composing movie soundtracks. He won an Academy Award for best original song and a Grammy nomination for his work. He has a wife and two young children. None of the articles explain why he left the band.

I keep searching for more information about him. It doesn't sound as though he split on bad terms. I locate a more recent photo of him with the other members. They were at the same charity event, and a photographer snapped a photo of them together.

I stare at their smiling faces for a few moments. Would Mason be interested in possibly reuniting with the band for the festival?

Or maybe they've already asked him and he said no. The thought floats there on a slow sigh.

I close the browser and return to my story. But the

words don't flow like they normally do. Not when there's a tiny chance this information about Mason might save the festival.

I dial Troy's number.

He answers immediately. "I'm on my way." The words rush from him so hard and fast that my body jerks in surprise.

He thinks something bad has happened to me. "No, no," I hurry to say, "nothing's wrong, Troy. I'm sorry. I didn't mean to worry you."

"No more messages? No one's trying to get into your house?" The question comes out on a slow breath, as though he's calming himself after an adrenaline rush. I wince at how wound up he is from all the stress he's dealing with. Stress I inadvertently keep adding to.

"No, but I found out something about Pushing Limits that might change things with the festival. It's a long shot, but there might be a way they can still participate. If they want to..." As long as Stephanie wasn't right and the real reason they canceled was because I was linked to the event.

"I'll take whatever I can get. A long shot is better than no shot."

My feelings exactly. I tell Troy what I found. "Mason hasn't performed with the band for about five years, which means he wasn't involved with their newer albums." The words tumble out; I'm too excited to slow them down. "But maybe he'll be happy to help this one time. Or not. I don't know, but it's worth a try."

Stunned silence echoes through the line for a long beat. Troy's probably attempting to make sense of my landslide of words. Or he thinks I'm losing my mind and is searching for a polite way to tell me that.

"You don't think the band might have already asked him?" His tone doesn't come out like he believes I'm an idiot for not thinking of that possibility. It's more like he's wondering the same. Wondering if it's possible the band hasn't asked Mason if he would perform with them at the festival.

"I really don't know," I say, drawing a heart in the condensation on the window. "But you won't know for sure unless you ask them."

"Okay, I'll see what I can do." A warm smile fills his voice and sets off unexpected goose bumps along my arms. "Thanks, Jess. I love you." He ends the call, not waiting to see if I'll say it back to him.

"I love you too," I whisper to the dead phone line.

My mind flashes a sweet picture of Troy and Olivia and Nova together on the beach as a happy family. And I wipe my fingers over the heart on the window.

Distorting it.

50

TROY

September, Present Day
Maple Ridge

I end the call with Jess and stare through the truck window at the framing my crew is working on despite the rain. There are no walls or ceiling or roof. Just a wooden outline of where those things will eventually be.

Mason Dell. He must have left Pushing Limits for a reason. A reason that kept him from performing for the past several years.

Which means he might not be interested in performing with his old band again...or they might not want him to join them onstage.

Still, it's worth a try. I phone George and ask him for their manager's number.

"I hadn't expected the band to agree to help out when I originally called David," George explains. "And I only did that because my teenage daughter wouldn't stop

395

bugging me to try. She's in love with their lead singer. And their guitarist. And keyboardist. And bassist. And drummer."

I chuckle. "So basically, the whole band." Christ, will Nova be like that once she's a teen?

"Yep. You sure you don't want me to contact David?"

"I'm sure. It needs to be me this time who talks to him." Since the festival is my baby. "Hopefully, Colton is looking down from wherever he is and can help pull some strings for us."

"That certainly would be helpful. Well, good luck. I'm rooting for you, Troy."

I end the call, step out of my truck, and walk over to where Lance is busy nailing a two-by-four into place. "I'm heading back to the office," I tell him. "Call me if you need anything."

"Will do, Boss."

The company office is dark when Butterscotch and I step inside it twenty minutes later. I flip on the overhead lighting. The space feels empty without Jess. Even after she dumped me last month so she could help Violet and Sophie, and I came in early and late to avoid seeing her, the space didn't feel void of Jess's presence. It was the little things, like Bailey's spare chew toy Jess kept at the office, that made it feel like Jess was with me. All those things are now gone.

I go to my desk and listen to the voice messages. There are a few more booking cancelations using the same ignorant reason the others gave. "Fuck," I mutter.

I pinch the bridge of my nose, attempting to chase away the headache that's building, and dial the number George gave me.

A woman answers. I explain who I am and that I'm hoping to talk to David Dixon. I'm sent through to his line.

"Hello, Troy," David says, his voice upbeat. "How can I help you?"

"It's about Pushing Limits needing to pull out of the With Hope Festival. First, I want to say I'm sorry about what happened to Tomas. I hope he feels better soon."

"Thank you. I'll be sure to pass that on to him."

"Is he the only reason the band had to cancel from the festival?" I close my eyes, praying the answer is yes. That Stephanie hadn't been right and Jess's involvement with the festival had nothing to do with the band's decision.

"That's right. They were looking forward to participating. They support what you plan to do with the money raised. Especially Nolan."

"So their pulling out of the festival had nothing to do with Savannah Townsend living in Maple Ridge and the media circus that has caused?" I hate saying that name since it's not who Jess is anymore. That was her past. It's not her present or future.

"No, it had nothing to do with Savannah. It seems like she's already been through enough. But if there's anything the guys can relate to, it would be bad press. They've all had their share of it."

"That's good to hear. About it having nothing to do with Savannah...who now goes by the name of Jessica." I pause, not sure how to pose the next question. "Does the band's old drummer, Mason Dell, still talk with the guys?"

"Absolutely. They're all still friends. But Mason and his family don't live in LA. They come up to visit, but it's not their hometown."

Damn. It'd be one thing if they all lived in the same place, but if Mason doesn't live near his old bandmates, it would be difficult for them to rehearse together.

"Why are you asking?" David doesn't appear particularly put off by my question.

"I was wondering if Mason could fill in for Tomas so the band could perform at the festival. But that doesn't sound logistically possible now that you've told me he doesn't live in LA."

"Sorry about that." David attempts to make his voice sound cheery again, but sympathy dangles from his tone. "I wish I had better news."

I thank him for his time, end the call, and dive into my paperwork.

An hour later my phone pings with a text.

> Olivia: Are you still coming over to visit with Nova today?
>
> Olivia: She's dying to see you.
>
> Olivia: She wants to go to the beach if that's okay with you.

Relief spreads through my chest, its warmth a welcome touch against the cold frustration that's been settling there lately.

Nova always makes my day brighter. More manageable. She makes it easier to smile, especially when my days have been hell like they've been this week.

> Me: Happy to do that. See you after dinner.

Smiling, I hit Send.

51

————

ANGELIQUE

May 1944
France

A week after I received the message from Henri to let me know that Anna and I would be leaving France, I bundle her in a blanket and prepare for one of the most difficult journeys of my life.

I glance at the bed where Johann last held me. If he were still alive, I doubt I would have left France. But he's gone, and Anna and I cannot remain in this country any longer.

I leave everything I own in Lise's flat. At the earliest opportunity, she will rid the place of all signs I lived here.

We head downstairs, and I load into the pram the baby supplies that will last us until Anna and I leave the country. Hopefully that will be tonight, in about thirteen hours. The weather is clear and there are no storms in the forecast. From our perspective, everything is a go.

399

I lower Anna into the pram and push it through the front entrance of the building that has been my home for the past five months. Lise and I walk in the direction opposite to where we want to end up. Once we're at the park and positive no one is following us, we begin our long trek to the safe house near the landing zone. The journey there is more than five hours by foot.

The buildings become sparser as we reach the outskirts of Poitiers. Farmland surrounds us, but none of these properties are designated parachute drop sites. They are too close to the town.

The road we walk along is free of vehicles. These days the only vehicles capable of driving in the area are those commandeered by the Germans, as well as their Jeeps, trucks, and tanks. Other than public transportation, bicycles and horse-drawn carriages are the sole mode of transport now used by the French. We see none of them as we make our way to the safe house.

Anna sleeps for much of the journey. When she isn't sleeping in the pram or when she grows bored of it bumping along the uneven road, I carry her, and Lise pushes the pram. Our progress is slower than we would prefer.

As we walk, I rehearse in my head the story I will tell my sister about what I've been doing since I last saw her. A story that involves me temporarily working in Leeds as a secretary. A believable story—perhaps even more so than the truth.

"It isn't much farther," I tell Anna. "Say goodbye to France, *ma petite*. I don't know when and if we will ever return." My voice wobbles. The ache that has filled my chest since news of Johann's death grows, a breath-stealing sadness filling the space.

Lise squeezes my shoulder. I turn my head to her, and

catch the understanding in her expression. She knows it's not easy for me to leave the place where I found my true love. But she also knows there is nothing for me here anymore.

By the time we arrive at the safe house, the sun is low in the sky. The brick building looks much like Jacques's farmhouse, but the front window on the upper floor is cracked and ivy covers one wall.

My feet and legs and arms ache so much, I can barely plod another step. Lise parks the pram at the side of the house, hiding it from casual view, and we walk to the front door. She knocks.

A moment passes and the door opens an inch, revealing a woman possibly in her late fifties. Madeleine. She nods at Lise in acknowledgment and then turns to me and waits expectantly for me to say the password.

"It's a beautiful day for flying a kite," I tell her.

Anna coos in my arms as if she too is saying a secret password. Madeleine's mouth shifts into a grin, which is missing a few teeth. There are none of the accusations on her face that I have witnessed so many times from other people. No muttered words calling me a French whore.

She opens the door wider and steps aside to let us in. "You must all be tired. Perhaps not you, little one." She grins again at Anna. "And I bet you're all hungry. I have some food prepared. I was able to buy rabbit on the black market this morning."

She leads us to the bathroom so we can wash up, after which she serves us a rabbit stew that tastes heavenly. I eat slowly, savouring each bite.

"Hopefully things will go as scheduled," Madeleine says as I take another bite of stew. "The plane failed to show during the last two full moons, even though the weather conditions were ideal for parachute drops."

That is not the news I want to hear, but it's also not surprising. That happened on more than several occasions when I was the leader of the various reception parties in the Bourgogne region. Or the Lysander would come but then fly past without dropping a single parachute.

"Why don't you and your little one go have a nap," Madeleine tells me once the meal is finished. "You two have a long night ahead of you."

"Thank you." I carry Anna to the bedroom and settle her in the drawer on the floor that Madeleine has transformed into a cot.

After a few minutes, I begin to drift off to sleep, but part of me is ever conscious of the dangers that still exist. If the Nazis have pieced together the role Madeleine plays in the resistance, they could descend on the farm at any moment. Or the plane could fly past without landing. Or it could crash with Anna and me in it. So many things could go wrong.

I GASP AWAKE FROM A NIGHTMARE. MY HEART POUNDS IN MY chest and my body is damp with sweat. The remnants of the dream slip between my fingers, the ghost of an image I cannot fully grasp. But it's enough for me to remember the dream was about Johann. It takes several seconds before I recall where I am and why I am here.

I am safe. For now.

I breathe through the grief like I've been doing since Johann's death four weeks ago. It's only then I realize my face is wet with tears.

I unfasten the pendant from my neck and clasp it in my hand. I conjure up the memory of when he gave it to me, bringing with it a fresh bout of tears. But I would rather cry than try to forget the man I love, the man whom I know without a doubt was my soul mate.

Anna stirs from her nap. I refasten the chain around my neck and pick her up from the drawer.

The next few hours are spent waiting and praying the plane will not only show up, but it will also land. This could be Anna's and my last opportunity to escape France until after the war ends. We have no idea when that might be.

D-Day is coming. The day Baker Street has been gearing up for all this time. It's supposed to be enough to turn the tides of the war, but we don't know how long it will take before the Germans and Hitler admit defeat. A week? A month? Six months? A year?

Anna falls asleep again. I wake her shortly after midnight, and she drowsily nurses. I change her nappy and bundle her in her blanket. She drifts back to sleep, dry and with a full tummy. If I'm lucky, she will remain asleep for the rest of the night.

Lise gathers the supplies she needs for the reception party. I thank Madeleine for her kindness.

"Good luck to you both." She kisses me on the cheek and plants a soft kiss on Anna's brow. "I pray the next time I see you and your daughter, it will be under happier circumstances."

I smile. "I pray that will be the case too."

Lise and I step outside and slip into the night, guided by the light of the full moon.

The other members of the reception party are waiting for us when we arrive. They seem slightly taken aback by the sleeping baby in my arms but don't say anything or flash me disparaging looks. Everyone gets into position and the next waiting game begins.

Our ears are tuned to the sky, listening for the familiar drone of an approaching plane.

Please come. Please come. Please come.

As if God is granting my silent prayer, the faint drone of the Lysander reaches us from above the tree line. The reception party lights their beacons, signalling to the pilot it's safe to land and lighting up the landing strip. My rapid heartbeat is so loud in my ears, it's a miracle I can make out the steady vibration of the plane's engines.

I'm practically holding my breath as the pilot lands the silver plane on the stretch of field. I glance towards the road. No sign of the enemy.

As soon as the plane comes to a standstill, its propellers spinning, I lurch forward with Anna in my arms. My body is trembling, but I get it to move in the direction I need to go without too much effort.

Two female SOE agents are climbing out of the plane as I approach.

I kiss Lise goodbye on the cheeks. "Thank you for everything you have done for me and Anna."

"You're welcome." She hugs me tightly. "I'm going to miss you both. I'll see you on the other side of the war. Stay safe." She kisses Anna on her brow.

"You too," I say, reining back a torrent of emotions at leaving this place and the woman who has become a dear friend.

Then, without another word, I haul Anna and myself into the plane.

"Is that really a baby in her arms?" one agent asks Lise in French as I climb the steps. The shock in her tone almost has me smiling.

I sit on the seat behind the pilot, buckle the seat belt, and hold Anna close to my heart. "Alright, my love," I tell her in English. "Let's go home."

The time between the Lysander landing and taking off is barely more than a few minutes.

The airplane taxis the length of the field, and it feels like a lifetime ago when I was last on a plane. So much has changed since I parachuted into France almost two years ago and prayed nothing would go wrong with my landing. When I prayed I would survive my mission and not fall into the hands of the Nazis.

During those early days, I hadn't given any thought to anything beyond surviving and doing my job. I hadn't thought about my sister and everything I'd left behind in England.

In time, I came to forgive her for falling in love with my fiancé and marrying him. Talking to Johann about her had helped, and risking my life for my country put things in perspective.

Johann never got to see Anja after she and their mother escaped their home in Austria. I won't waste the second chance I have been given with my sister.

"Are you ready to meet your Auntie Hazel and Uncle Charles?" I whisper to the sleeping bundle in my arms, the loud hum of the engine obscuring my voice.

52

JESSICA

September, Present Day
Maple Ridge

As soon as Bailey and I step outside my back door, the question I've been dying to ask Troy since I called him earlier tumbles out. "How did it go with Pushing Limits?"

He smiles, but even before he can tell me, I already have my answer. That's not the smile of someone who recently received great news. "It was a good idea...but, unfortunately, the logistics weren't feasible. Mason and his family don't live in the same city as the band, so they can't practice together for the festival."

I hug Troy, pouring all the love I feel for him into it, my head on his shoulder. "I'm sorry. I was hoping they would be able to make it work."

He tightens his arms around me. It feels so right, so

good. His strong muscles pressed against my body feel so good, like a taste of heaven.

"Me too." Troy's warm breath kisses my cheek. "George and Susan are figuring out how best to go about it, but we'll have to make the announcement soon about the band canceling. We're not looking forward to that. It's gonna cause us all kinds of problems."

I lock the back door. Troy links his fingers with mine, and the three of us walk to his truck, where Butterscotch is waiting in the front passenger seat.

Troy drives me to the Veterans Center and walks me to Robyn's office for my first appointment since she returned from her vacation. He gives me a quick kiss good-bye. "I'll see you soon."

He leaves, and I take a seat in the waiting area. I'm a few minutes early.

"Hi, Jess," Robyn says from the doorway of her office as I skim through my *feel-good* photos on my phone. She's wearing her standard green Army uniform.

I rise to my feet and join her in her office. I take my usual place on the couch.

Robyn sits in her desk chair, which is swiveled to face me. "How have you been doing? A lot has happened since I last saw you."

I assume she means the protesters and reporters. She doesn't know yet about my last conversation with Craig. "Do you mean how's it going beyond me being frustrated and angry at what's been happening because my previous name was leaked?"

"All of it. The frustration and anger and any other emotions you've been feeling." Robyn wears her usual compassionate expression, her smile a slight tilt of encouragement.

I don't say anything for a moment, rallying up all my thoughts and feelings. "I'm tired. Tired of being judged by people who don't know me. I'm tired of the wrongful and hurtful assumptions." I could write a novel about those alone.

"What assumptions are people making?" She leans forward in her chair, her legs crossed.

"That I'm dangerous. That their children need protecting from me. That if my husband really abused me, I could have walked away."

Robyn makes a soft sound of acknowledgment. "The last point is one many survivors of abuse hear from people who don't know better. This is where awareness of the misconceptions surrounding abuse is critical. I'm sorry you're having to deal with all of that, Jess."

She straightens in her seat. "Do you believe there's any truth to the words people are saying to you?"

"I know I'm not dangerous. I'm scarred because I didn't defend myself in prison." Even back then, I'd tried to disappear into my surroundings like a chameleon. I hadn't wanted to get into trouble and risk my sentence being extended. Troy told me Garrett had his FBI contact look into what happened to me while I was in Beckley. And I still have no answers as to why I was targeted during my stay there. No clues. No confessions. No convictions of the guilty parties.

"How do you view yourself after everything you've been through?" Robyn asks. "And that includes what happened with Violet and her daughter."

I rub my palms on my shorts to give my hands something to do. "I'm stronger. Braver. But also scared. Alone. And...and ashamed."

"I would definitely use the first two to describe you. What you've accomplished has made you stronger. And that's good." She leans forward again. "Tell me more about being ashamed."

"I let down my daughter. If I hadn't fallen for my husband's charms...if I had left when the abuse started, I wouldn't be in this mess."

"*Hmm.* It sounds like you believe what those other people have been saying, despite it not being true. You have no reason to blame yourself or be ashamed. The only person at fault was your late husband."

I give a small nod, knowing she's right. But it's hard to remember that at times even when I know better.

"I want you to try a new exercise," Robyn says. "Each time you say or think something negative about yourself that comes from the place your late husband built, I want you to reshape it."

"Reshape it?" I toy with the hem of my shorts, my gaze still on Robyn.

"For example. Instead of saying you're ashamed you didn't stand up against the people who wanted to harm you in prison, reshape it to you're proud you took the high road and didn't retaliate. You stayed strong in your convictions. It will feel awkward at first, but with practice, it will go a long way to diminishing your feelings of shame."

"Okay. I can do that." I think.

"Give it a go."

I bite my lower lip, contemplating what to say. There are so many things I'm ashamed about. I'm not sure where to begin. "Instead of thinking I'm ashamed I let my daughter down...I'm...um...I'm proud...I'm proud I produced such a sweet and wonderful little girl."

Robyn nods, her smile widening, and I feel like the little girl who got a gold star on her first spelling test. But like with spelling tests, it doesn't mean next time I do the exercise it will be any easier.

"That's really good, Jess. That's your assignment for the next few weeks. I want you to practice turning the negative statements into positive ones."

"Okay."

"I see you have a new tattoo." Robyn points at my arm. I'm wearing a short-sleeved top that leaves the shell-and-flower ink visible. "It's gorgeous. Is there a reason you picked the shell and flowers?"

I roll my lips together, working up to telling her the truth. Taylor and Simone thought the tattoo was a great idea. Troy was less sure.

Robyn won't judge me for it, but vulnerability still nips at me. "Amelia loved searching for shells with me when she was a toddler. The times we did that are some of my most precious memories." And the ones I tend to revisit when I go to my happy place.

"What about the flowers? Why hydrangeas and..." Robyn shifts forward to get a better look at my arm. "Are those forget-me-nots?"

I nod.

"So why the hydrangeas?"

"Because they symbolize love and family."

"You got it to symbolize Amelia?" As expected, there is no judgment in Robyn's tone, but that doesn't stop me from wondering what she's thinking. Does she think it was a mistake? That it won't help me heal but will do the opposite?

"Yes. It was her birthday the weekend before last. I couldn't be with her"—will never be with her again—"and I wanted to celebrate the day."

Robyn tilts her head slightly to the side, her eyes taking in my face. God knows what she sees there. I haven't exactly tried to keep my emotions hidden from view.

"So you celebrated it with the tattoo?"

"Yes. And a small birthday cake. Troy's sister-in-law suggested it might help with my grief. Celebrating Amelia's birthday. My friend lost her baby due to a car accident she was in while pregnant. Since then, she has celebrated her baby's birthday every year."

"You're grieving the loss of Amelia?" Once more, no sign of judgment from Robyn.

I glance at my hands on my lap and discover I'm wringing them. I place them flat on my thighs and stare at them so I don't have to look at Robyn's reaction to my reply. "I contacted my sister-in-law again about being in Amelia's life. Her husband phoned a few days later to tell me it wasn't going to happen. I was too much of a reminder of the abuse he went through at the hands of his brothers growing up. They bullied him as a kid. He didn't go into much detail beyond that."

My shoulders curl in on themselves, grief slicing through me from just talking about it. "I can't blame him for his decision."

"What do his reaction and the birthday cake and the tattoo mean to you, Jess?"

"They mean never getting to see Amelia." The name comes out as a choked whisper, the word scorching a path in my throat. "It means I've lost the most precious thing to me."

The air has been sucked out of the room, and I can't find enough oxygen to fill my lungs. I'm suffocating, and I don't know what to do about it anymore.

"I'm sorry for your loss, Jess. I truly am. You've lost so much over the past ten or so years, and I'm not sure you've had a chance to fully mourn any of it. It's going to take time and work, but you'll eventually get there. I promise."

I nod, hoping she's right but also glad she accepted what I told her instead of trying to find the silver lining.

"Have you talked to your physician about seeing if an antidepressant or a medication to help with anxiety could benefit you? Not just for the grief but for your general mental well-being."

I shake my head.

"Talk to them. See what they say. The right medication might help you better manage everything you're dealing with. Sometimes therapy alone isn't enough. And there's no shame in needing medication that can help you get back on track." Robyn smiles, reassurance infused into the curve of her mouth.

I nod again, unsure how I feel about what she's saying. "Okay."

"And you might want to try using a weighted blanket when you sleep, especially if you're still having nightmares. Research has shown it can benefit those with PTSD and complex PTSD. The blankets aren't for everyone, but it might be worth a try."

I have read about the benefit of weighted blankets. I just wasn't sure if they were for me. But I guess I'll never know unless I try one out and see what happens. Maybe I'll be surprised. "I'll look into it. Thanks."

She shifts her notepad on her lap, her reassuring smile not wavering. "Alright. Let's talk about things you can do to help you process your grief..."

I'M EMOTIONALLY DRAINED BY THE TIME BAILEY AND I LEAVE Robyn's office. Zara is sitting on a waiting room seat, her attention on her phone.

"Hi?" I say, glancing around for Troy.

"Troy had to get back to the office due to some emergency and asked me to drive you home." She rises to her feet.

I glance at my phone. There's nothing from him. No text. No missed call. "Thanks." I smile even though Troy's absence sits heavy in my chest. I could really use one of his hugs right now.

Zara drives me to my house and pulls into the driveway. "The protesters finally decided to get a life?" She scans the area as if expecting one to lunge from the trees.

She's right. No one is on the street or the sidewalk, other than a woman walking her dog. You wouldn't know that only a few weeks ago almost a hundred people were here chanting and waving signs and trying to get me to leave Maple Ridge.

"Maybe they finally realized they were wrong about me."

Or chose to stick with just harassing me on social media. That's fine with me. I avoid those sites. I don't see their hateful and misguided rhetoric.

I thank Zara for the ride, and Bailey and I go into the house through the front door. The damaging words that were once there are completely invisible under several coats of blue-gray paint.

I have a few hours until Troy is due to come over, so I go upstairs to Amelia's—I mean, the guest room. I get comfy on the window seat and power up the laptop.

I resume typing where I left off, but instead of Angelique's story, restlessness hijacks my thoughts. The same restlessness that's been building for the past few hours.

Robyn reminded me in our session today that I need to focus more on my recovery and doing things I enjoy. I haven't been able to go hiking or canoeing or practice yoga lately. I haven't even taken any new photos. My life has been at a standstill since the protesters and media intruded on it. But they're gone now. I'm no longer a prisoner in my home—I'm only caged by death threats.

"You want to go to the lake?" I ask Bailey. She perks her head up, which I take to be a yes.

The street is empty of parked cars that don't belong there. No one I need to worry about is standing on the sidewalk. The rain from this morning finished hours ago, and the warmth of the day has dried up the puddles. It's gorgeous now. Perfect for hanging out at the lake.

Several minutes later, I'm pedaling toward it with Bailey in the trailer. My senses are on high alert, but no one seems to be paying attention as I zoom down the quiet streets.

At the lake, I steer Iris's rusty old bike past the beach to the start of the trail that circles the water. I lock the bike to the metal rack.

The tangy scent of pine wraps me in a comforting hug, and the chirping of birds from the trees cheers me onward. Robyn was right. I need to get back to doing the things I enjoy.

I pull on my straw hat so my face is less recognizable and shuck on my backpack, my laptop tucked safely inside.

Bailey and I walk along the quiet dirt path, pausing every so often so I can shoot photos with my phone. A chattering squirrel. A lonely wild blossom at the side of the path. The stretch of water reflecting the faded blue sky.

Two women, a decade older than me, approach from the opposite direction. I don't have time to duck my head. The gaze of the bleach-blond woman wearing *short* shorts falls to the prominent scar by my mouth. Her eyes narrow into a scowl, and she elbows her friend.

Her friend glances my way, and her expression twists into horror and fear, as if I'm stumbling about in a hockey mask and carrying a blood-soaked ax.

I drop my head, heat rushing to my face, and struggle to remember what Robyn told me a short time ago. *They think I'm a murderer. They don't think I'm harmless or safe to be around children.* I try but can't think of a way to reframe the negative into something positive.

I stop and study the photos I've just taken. None are worthy of any photography awards—even with editing.

Each one is a disappointment.

Like I've become.

Bailey and I continue walking a short distance and stop at a group of large boulders on the edge of the water—my favorite spot to sit. I position myself so I'm looking out at the lake. No one can see my face from the path.

I pull out my laptop and type, but the words I need still won't come. Instead, my head fills with the words I heard so often from my late husband and while in prison.

Failure. Useless. Worthless. Pathetic. Lazy. Stupid. Stupid. Stupid. The words pulsate and grow. Transform into hideous colors. Take shape into something prickly and barbed. No matter how much I try to twist them into something positive, the more they resist, the louder they become. They scream in my head, *Ugly, dumb, dumb bitch.*

I cover my ears with my hands, but that does nothing to quiet the voices, so lifelike, so real.

Maybe my late husband was right. Look at the mess I made of the festival.

Stephanie's words from last night stomp through my head. *"And who's to say Pushing Limits canceled because their drummer is injured? Maybe it was a convenient excuse after they heard Savannah Townsend is involved with the festival. They don't want the bad press associated with that."*

If more people don't want to support the event because I'd originally been helping with it, it might have dire consequences. More performers might pull out. Ticket holders might demand a refund. All the hard work Troy and everyone else has been doing will be for nothing.

I remain on the rock for who knows how long before I pack up the laptop and get up to leave.

Bailey and I hike along the trail, but this time my steps feel heavy, like gravity is pulling me down. It's a struggle to keep moving. Luckily, I don't bump into any more people. I just need to get past the beach without anyone noticing me and then I can hide away in my home again.

As I approach the beach, a sweet, girlish giggle has me looking up. My heart clenches and my stomach free-falls to the ground. I drop with it and crouch behind the long wild grass, hiding from the three individuals several yards away.

Troy and Olivia and Nova.

Olivia squeals and leaps to her feet. She hugs Troy, and he swings her around. They both laugh, her head thrown back, and he continues swinging her in a circle.

I press my suddenly cold fingers against my mouth, trapping the building sob. I guess Troy didn't have to work late after all.

Nova jumps up and down on her cute chubby legs, giggling and cheering.

They really do look like the perfect, happy family. The family Troy wants. The family he deserves.

My heart shatters, knowing what I must do. Knowing what's best for him, for them, for everyone concerned.

And maybe way down, down, down the line, what's best for me too.

53

TROY

August, Present Day
Maple Ridge

Nova stops walking on the sand near the water and squats. She turns her small yellow bucket upside down and bangs the bottom of it with her shovel. A couple of ducks quack, their bodies bobbing on the water a short distance from us.

Olivia kneels beside Nova. "That would work a lot better if you actually had sand in there, sweetheart."

"Maybe she's practicing to be a drummer." I chuckle, despite being frustrated as hell after the day I've had. I had to ask Zara to drive Jess home after therapy this afternoon. Another client canceled his booking with my company, and I had to go deal with the fallout.

"I don't suppose you could cover for Pushing Limits' injured drummer so they can play at the festival after all?" I ask Nova.

She bangs the bottom of her bucket again. "I drummer."

I laugh. "You're a very good one."

She beams and continues banging the bucket.

"I'm sorry about what happened with the band, Troy," Olivia says, shoveling sand into her red bucket.

"I'm not sorry I started organizing the festival, but with everything going on, their canceling is too much. I'll be glad once it's over." I crouch on the other side of Nova and begin scooping sand into my green bucket.

"I don't know how you're managing to stay sane with everything you've dumped on your shoulders."

"I haven't been organizing the festival on my own. I've had help."

Olivia looks up from her bucket, sympathy softening her expression. "I know, but you've made it more personal than anyone else has. You believe if the festival fails, it means you also failed Colton. But that's not true."

"I failed Colton way before the festival was even a spark of an idea." The words taste bitter on my tongue, regret and a sense of powerlessness coating them. "The festival has nothing to do with him."

Olivia huffs a warning I'm about to be lectured. I know the sound all too well. "There are two things infinitely wrong with all of that. First. You didn't fail Colton. He failed himself. And that wasn't his fault. It wasn't anyone's fault. You have to stop beating yourself up over that, Troy."

I grunt because she's wrong, but I do appreciate what she's trying to do.

She gives another huff, but this one is more like a strangled groan. "You're as pigheaded as he was. Remember how he would get all these crazy ideas when we were kids, and he refused to back down from the challenge? Always having to prove himself invincible..."

Her shoulders droop. "And then he wasn't invincible anymore." Her voice is a whisper, barely heard over the giggled shrieks farther along the beach from a group of little kids running in and out of the water. She shoves her plastic shovel into the sand.

My phone rings in my pocket, and for a fleeting second I'm tempted to not check who's calling. I don't feel like talking to another client who's canceling because I hired Jess.

But not answering won't change anything either. I accept the call, deciding to get it over with. Only then does it dawn on me that the area code isn't from around here.

"Hi, Troy Carson?" a man asks from the other end. There's something vaguely familiar about the deep cheery voice.

"Speaking." I push to my feet.

"Hello, this is David Dixon. I spoke with Nolan about your idea, and he talked to Jared, Kirk, and Aaron. They would be happy to perform at the festival with Mason...if you can convince him to join them. He's in LA tomorrow. The odds of convincing him might be better if you come here and talk to him in person."

"But how will that work when they live in different cities?"

"Convince him to join them, and they'll figure out the technicalities. If worse comes to worse, there's always Zoom."

"Okay, I can do that," I say, mentally rearranging my plans for the next few days. "Thank you!" I get some more details from David and end the call.

Olivia is peering up at me, her eyebrows lifted, silently asking what that was all about.

"That was the manager for Pushing Limits." I haven't convinced Mason of anything yet, but that doesn't keep me from grinning. There's still a chance the festival won't be a disappointing disaster.

A huge-ass smile curves across Olivia's face. "They changed their mind about canceling?"

"Not quite. Their old drummer will be in LA tomorrow. If I can convince him to join the band for the one day, Pushing Limits will perform in the festival."

Olivia shrieks, jumping to her feet, and hugs me. I spin her like I used to when we were younger, both of us laughing.

"That's amazing news, Troy," she replies as I continue swinging her in a circle.

Nova jumps to her feet and bounces like a bunny, giggling and cheering. She has no idea what the excitement is about.

"It was Jess who reminded me that Mason used to be the band's drummer. Otherwise, I would've never thought to ask if he could fill in for Tomas." I put Olivia down and pick Nova up. Laughing, I swing her around too.

"Good thing she thought of it." The equivalent of a wide smile wraps itself around Olivia's words.

I lower Nova to the sand. "I have so much to do before I can go," I tell Olivia. "Like check if I can even get a flight to LA. If not, I'll need to drive there." If that's the case, I'll have to leave ASAP if I hope to make it in time. David is arranging for me to meet up with Mason late afternoon.

Nova lifts her arms up to me. "Up."

I hoist her into the air again. She giggles some more.

"Sorry, sweetheart," Olivia says to her daughter. "Uncle Troy has to go do something very important. We'll have to hang out with him another day." She gathers up Nova's beach toys, putting them in the net bag.

"I promise you as soon as I come back from LA," I tell Nova, "we'll fill this beach with sandcastles."

Olivia laughs. "Be careful what you promise her. She'll have you doing exactly that."

"Hey, it will be worth it if I can get Mason to join the band for the festival." Shit, how difficult is this going to be? If it were easy, the band would ask him themselves.

We return to the truck, excitement and worry wrestling in my gut. I drop Olivia and Nova off at their house and drive home. Then I spend the next hour trying to arrange a flight to LA, but everything is either booked or arrives too late for me to meet with Mason.

The only chance I have is to drive to LA, which will take thirteen hours, depending on traffic. I pack an overnight bag and call Lance.

"I need you to keep an eye on things while I'm gone for the next day or two," I tell him after getting him up to speed. "But call me if you have any issues. I don't expect you will since we're framing the house."

"Don't worry, Boss. I have it under control. You think you can convince the old drummer to reunite with the band for the one show?"

"Hell if I know. Would help if I knew why he left the band in the first place."

"He had an issue with alcohol and had a gambling addiction. I don't know the full details, but it was enough for him to pull out of the band. Touring wasn't healthy for him."

Well, shit. My excitement deflates like a leaky balloon. No wonder the rest of the band hasn't bothered to ask him about the festival. They already know the probable answer. "Thanks," I tell Lance. "That's good to know." Damn, will this put an addict back on the path of something dangerous to him? It's something Mason, the band, and I will need to discuss if he agrees to help out. I can't let him play with the band if it could end up harming him and his family.

I end the call with Lance. "C'mon, Butterscotch. I have to leave for a few days, but I need to talk to Jess. You wanna stay with her while I'm away?"

I grab a quick bite and gather his supplies. The sky is still light as I pull up to Jess's house. I'll have a few hours of driving time before night falls, and then I'll have to stay in a motel somewhere to rest up for the next leg of the journey.

Jess's street is quiet, the opposite to what it was a few days ago. The protesters have clearly moved on with their lives. Thank God for that. One less thing to worry about.

I park in her driveway and kill the engine. I grab Butterscotch's supplies from the back seat, and he follows me to the front door. I ring the doorbell.

The door opens a moment later. Jess is standing on the other side, her face pale, eyes red. Her hair is in a messy ponytail, revealing dark roots she hasn't bleached since news of her identity was leaked. She's wearing a navy hoodie and black yoga pants.

She steps onto the front stoop, swings the door partially closed behind her.

My phone rings. I send it to voicemail.

"What's wrong?" If my arms weren't so full, I'd pull Jess into them and kiss away her pain.

Her gaze drops to the dog supplies in my arms. "What's that for?"

"I have to go to LA for a few days. I was hoping Butterscotch could stay with you while I'm gone."

Butterscotch plonks his ass down next to me.

"LA?" Jess's tone drips with curiosity...and something else. The something else has my heart stammering. "Why LA?"

"To see if I can convince Mason to reunite with Pushing Limits for the festival." I have to leave soon, so I don't have time to go into the nitty-gritty about everything their manager and Lance told me. "I couldn't get a flight, so I have to drive there."

She nods but doesn't crack so much as a smile. Bailey whimpers as if reading Jess's mood.

"What's wrong?" I repeat, searching her expression for a clue as to what's going on. She hasn't even let us in yet, which isn't like her. Usually that's the first thing she does when I show up.

Something flickers in her expression. It's gone before I can figure out what it was. I don't know why, but her reaction causes my muscles to tense.

My phone rings again. I send whomever it is also to voicemail.

She draws in a breath. "I know the timing isn't great... but...but I think we need to end things, Troy. Between us."

Huh? I stare at her for a beat. Have I fucking gone back in time to when we had the same conversation while she was hiding Violet and Sophie here?

"What the hell are you talking about?" I ask, still stunned by her comment.

"I saw you and Olivia and Nova at the beach." Every muscle in her body seems taut, like they're on the verge of snapping.

I frown. "So? You know I hang out with Nova." Does she think I lied about the work emergency? "Is this about me not being able to pick you up after therapy?"

"Not at all. And I know you hang out with Nova. But it made me realize...you guys are the perfect family. I'm mourning the loss of my daughter...and you...you've got such a great family waiting for you. Olivia. Nova."

I try to make sense of Jess's words. "Olivia is my friend. She's been my best friend since she and Colton and I were kids. You know that."

"Best friends often go on to make the best lovers," Jess

says, as if reading the quote from a goddamn romance novel.

"Olivia and I have never been lovers and never will be. It's not that way between us."

"Maybe it should be that way. You're perfect together."

Zara had warned me a few months ago that Olivia was falling in love with me. I had brushed it off as nonsense. Apparently, Zara wasn't the only person who saw things I'd missed with my best friend.

My phone rings a third time. What the hell? I go to turn off my ringer but this time it's Olivia who's calling.

I answer in case it's important. "Hey, what's up?" I ask, keeping my frustration at the situation between Jess and me out of my tone.

"Nova wanted to say good night to you. Here you go, sweetie." The last part was clearly for her daughter.

"Hi." Nova's small voice has the equivalent of a big grin in it.

"Hey, princess. Have sweet dreams." I can tell from Jess's crestfallen expression she knows exactly who I'm talking to, and I've just handed her more ammunition for why we can't be together—in her mind.

No matter what I do, I'm the bad guy.

"I'll see you in a few days," I tell Nova, still managing to keep the frustration in my tone at bay.

"Night-night!" She giggles and the phone goes dead.

I lower the phone to my side, my gaze not leaving Jess's face. All that she's thinking of is written on it. Every hurt. Every mistrust. Every lost hope.

She's breaking up with me. Jess is actually breaking up with me. Again. The realization is a slash to the heart. Pain pumps through my body, turning everything inside me to fire, like a lit fuse.

The protesters, the death threats, clients canceling, Pushing Limits pulling out, the stress of organizing a festival, running Wilderness Warriors and a construction company, the lack of sleep lately—everything I'm dealing with comes to a full boil. Hot lava pushes through the cracked surface, erupting like Mount St. Helens and taking me down with it.

Fuck. This.

I don't have time for this if I'm planning to save the festival. Save all those people I'm on the verge of letting down. The individuals with PTSD. Their families.

I slowly shake my head, but it's not enough to calm me. My fists clench at my sides, and I force out a hard breath. "Fine, Jess! We're done! I'm not doing this with you again and again. I'm tired of you constantly getting scared of what we have between us and pushing me away. You push away people who love you—"

"I don't push away people I love. They. Leave. Me." A wildfire of emotions flares in her eyes.

"For God's sake. Your parents left you. Your grandparents didn't leave you. They died. They weren't immortal. People die. That's fucking life."

Butterscotch and Bailey whimper.

I'm on a roll. My anger from when she dumped me last time never fully burned away after we got back together. "And as for your daughter, *you* gave her away to her uncle and aunt."

A small gasp escapes Jess, sharp and pained, but the fire in her eyes doesn't diminish. "She deserved to have a life filled with love and the advantages I couldn't give her. Especially not when I was locked away."

"I'm not blaming you for that," I say, the heat in my tone not cooling any. "That was the right call at the time. But the guilt you're feeling from that...the hurt you're feeling because you've been pushed out of her life is making you scared of ever loving anyone again."

"That's not true!" But even as Jess says it, I can tell from the slight widening of her eyes that's exactly what she thinks. It's why she keeps pushing me away...even last time, when she used Violet and Sophie as her excuse.

"It is true, and you know it. Tell me, Jess. Before, you said you weren't sure if you could ever have kids—is that really true? Do you plan to ever have a family? If I wanted to marry you one day, would you want to have another daughter or a son?"

She flinches and looks away.

"That's what I thought. It's not that you don't want a family. It's that you're too scared to take a chance again with one." I slap my hand on the front doorjamb. Jess startles.

Pain radiates through my palm. *Dammit*. I can't do this anymore. "I'm done, Jess. I love you. I've told you that so many times, and I've shown you how much I love you. But I've had enough...had enough of trying to prove my feelings to you when it's clearly not something you want to hear."

And with the reality of trauma bond and her relationship with her ex, I have no idea how to navigate that land mine. I'm not even sure it's possible.

I reverse a step. "Butterscotch, come. I'll drop you off with Lucas and Simone."

Jess steps forward. "Troy—" Her voice is soft.

"Forget it, Jess."

"I was just going to say I'm sorry. I really am." She isn't saying she's having second thoughts about pushing me away. She's just sorry she's dumping this on me at the worst possible time. "And I'll go back to work tomorrow...at the office. You'll need someone to keep an eye on things while you're away...unless...unless you want to fire me."

Her voice splinters, but it doesn't take a genius to figure

out why. It's not the loss of her job she's worried about. It's how connected all the parts of her new life are to me. Like it was with her marriage. The only difference is that asshole didn't want her to have a job. He wanted her to be completely dependent on him.

"You can't go back to the office," I tell her. "We don't know who left those threatening notes."

"A note can't hurt me."

"Even if that's true, you can't go back to work."

The frown lines on her face deepen, and icy-hot emotions spark in her eyes. "Why not? Are you saying you don't want me back 'cause I'm no longer sleeping with you?"

"No. I can't afford to lose any more clients due to people accusing me of hiring an ex-con."

The moment the words are out of my mouth, I regret them. I haven't told her more clients have been canceling. I'd kept that a secret, not wanting to hurt her.

She stares at me, her mouth slack in stunned shock. "Okay, then." Her words are spoken so softly, I barely hear them over the *thrum-thrum-thrumming* pulse in my ears. "Consider this my resignation."

She withdraws into the house and shuts the door quietly in my face, but it feels like my insides have imploded.

Even if I wanted to, I don't have time to deal with the fallout from our fight.

I need to drop Butterscotch off at Lucas's house and drive to LA.

54

JESSICA

September, Present Day
Maple Ridge

I shut the front door and close my eyes against the pain clamped around my heart.

"I can't afford to lose any more clients due to people accusing me of hiring an ex-con."

By the time Troy gets to Eugene, maybe even before that, he'll see I was right in ending things with him. He deserves the happily ever after I can't give him. My life—all that I touch—is a mess, and I can't risk it tangling anyone else in my web of devastation.

Bailey whimpers. I crouch next to her, hug her, and let my silent tears soak into her fur. I've screwed up everything for the man I love. I wish I hadn't moved to Maple Ridge. Then his business wouldn't be in trouble because he'd hired me, and the festival wouldn't be dealing with the possible fallout from me being involved with it.

I heave my ass off the floor and retreat upstairs to the guest room. If I'm going to drown in sorrow and grief, I might as well pour my feelings into Angelique's own pain and keep writing.

I sit in the window seat with my laptop and get lost in the words. Tears wet my cheeks, but I can't tell if they're for Angelique's pain or for my own or both.

The sky is dark by the time I finally glance at the clock. 1:50 a.m. *Oh. Wow.* I hadn't realized it was so late. I'd stopped to eat dinner several hours ago but went back to writing afterward. Guess whatever had kept my words from flowing is gone.

Careful not to accidentally kick Bailey, I put the laptop to the side and move off the window seat, my muscles stiff. She fell asleep a couple of hours ago, her body squeezed between my legs and the ledge.

I take a moment to stretch my muscles. I should feel tired, but I'm not. I'm not sure I could even fall asleep. I'm too wound up. About the festival. About Angelique's story. About what happened with Troy.

I don't know what I'm going to do now. I'm unemployed again, which for now isn't too big of a worry since I have the money the State of California paid me for the wrongful imprisonment. But that won't last forever. I'll need to begin planning for the long term now that I'm no longer working for Troy.

I go into the bathroom and flick on the light. Troy performed miracles with the small space, like he did with the rest of the house. It's beautiful and functional. Not an inch of space goes to waste.

He knows how to fix up things that are falling apart and need a fresh start. Too bad his talent wasn't enough to put me back together. Put me back together so I'm a new and improved model.

I pull the elastic from my hair and let the long strands fall past my shoulders. The dark roots are a stark contrast to the blond. Until the fallout of Cora's article hit Maple Ridge, I'd been meticulous with my roots. Now, they're one more reminder of how messed up my life has become. How my dream of starting over has met roadblock after roadblock.

I go to the toilet, wash my hands, and return to the guest bedroom. Bailey is no longer sleeping. She's standing on the window seat and looking outside at the night sky. The street is quiet. No one is walking or driving past.

"You want to go for a walk?" I ask her. She barks and jumps down.

In the foyer, I attach Bailey's leash to her *Service Dog in Training* vest and peek through the gap in the living-room curtains to make sure no one is watching the house. No one is, and we step outside.

I inhale the fresh scent of freedom and pine and walk along my path to the sidewalk.

Bailey sniffs the ground and pulls me toward the small patch of neatly mowed grass that makes up my front lawn. She does her business and I survey the front yard. I have a plan for what I want to do to it over the next few years, but now I might not be able to see it come to fruition. If I can't find a job in Maple Ridge or a way to make a steady income from home, I might have to eventually sell my beloved house and move elsewhere.

I'll have to start my life over once again.

How many times will I have to move because people think I'm a bad person due to my unfortunate past? Will pitchforks be the welcoming committee no matter where I end up?

Living in a city might be my sole option for starting over. I'm not the only former inmate who's released and needs a job. There are places that will hire me regardless of where I lived prior to Maple Ridge. Jobs that are no one's idea of a dream occupation, but I might not have a choice.

The person who killed my husband took so many of my choices away from me—choices that would have given me the happily ever after I so desperately want.

If it weren't for the restitution payment, I would have to face the reality of moving sooner rather than later. Hopefully by the time I have to move—if it comes to that—my past will be less of an issue than it is now. People will have moved on and no longer think the worst of me.

Bailey and I wander along the sidewalk, and I think about my options of where I could move to. Hawaii? Caribbean? Iceland? I snicker, exhaustion beginning to wiggle its way through my body. While they sound like marvelous places to move to, they're probably not feasible choices.

Realistically, I'll have to pick someplace in the U.S. The only place I won't move to is Seattle, where Amelia lives. Knowing she's so close but I'm not allowed to see her would be too painful.

My thoughts drift back to Troy, and a throbbing pain grows in my chest. Angelique's words come to mind from when she lost Johann: *Just one breath at a time, and one day I won't have to keep reminding myself of that.*

I try to do as she suggested, but it's not easy. The memory of those final minutes between Troy and me—the argument, Olivia phoning him so he could say good night to Nova, of he and I severing what we had between us—suffocates me. I can barely draw in a lungful of air.

THE NEXT MORNING, I HELP BAILEY INTO HER TRAILER AND cycle to the grocery store. After I finally went to bed around three, I tossed and turned most of the night. My legs feel like I'm cycling through quicksand. It's a miracle I'm actually moving. My body's sluggish as hell.

I arrive as the store is opening. A teenage employee near the shopping carts gives me a once-over. His gaze lands on the scar by my mouth, and he grimaces, his disgust unmistakable.

I ignore it. It's not like I care what he thinks of my appearance. Or maybe it's my past he's shaming me for.

Bailey and I walk through the store, picking up the items I'll need for the next couple of days. My last destination is the haircare aisle. I reach for a box of the blond color I've been using.

My hand pauses midair, hovering like a moth in the light. It drops several rows, and I grab a different box than the one I had intended to get. Chestnut brown. My natural hair color.

I locate a pair of scissors for cutting hair, put them in the shopping basket, and make a beeline for the till, not allowing myself the chance to change my mind.

The self-serve checkout isn't open yet, so I'm forced to go to the cashier. I don't bother to make eye contact with her. I don't need to see the condemnation on her face or how she fears for her children's safety. I keep my eyes on my purchases, my head hanging forward.

"That will be thirty-nine-eighty," she says.

I open my wallet and remove two twenties. I pass them to her, my hand trembling, and brace for her mean words.

A warm beige hand lightly squeezes mine. The unexpected compassion seeps into my blood and leaves me not feeling so alone.

My gaze darts to the cashier's. Her young brown eyes

are filled with understanding—perhaps the understanding of someone only too familiar of what it's like to be in an abusive relationship?

I'd offer her a safe place to stay if she needs one, but I don't know how safe my home is. I'm living day to day, waiting for something else to happen. More protesters to arrive. A new wave of reporters knocking on my door.

I reciprocate the gesture, letting her know I'm here for her if she needs someone on her side.

She hands me my change.

I don't bike my usual way home. I take a route that doesn't see much tourist traffic. A route that's longer, with steeper hills. A punishing route.

My ribs are supposed to take about twelve weeks to fully heal. The car accident occurred two months ago. Good enough.

When I first moved to town, my legs and lungs would burn cycling up the steep inclines. A lifetime of living at sea level and then moving to the mountains will do that. Five months ago, there were so many things I didn't think I would be capable of.

And now, there are still so many things I can't do. I glance at the tattoo on my forearm—moving on from losing my daughter is one of the things I struggle with most.

Maybe Robyn is right. I would benefit from medication. Too bad I didn't talk to a physician about it while I had medical insurance.

Eventually, I pedal down my street and onto my driveway. I put the bike and trailer in the garage, and Bailey and I go into the house through the back door.

I deactivate the alarm and carry the bags toward the kitchen. "I have to finish a few things first," I tell Bailey as I enter the kitchen and put the bags on the island. "Then we can hang out in the garden while I write."

The day promises to be pleasant, the cool morning air hinting at the coming fall, and Bailey loves being outside as much as I do. Now that the protesters are gone, I don't have to use Troy's noise-canceling headphones. I get to listen to the real sounds of nature while I write.

I put away the groceries and phone the medical clinic to book an appointment with a physician.

As soon as I end the call, I turn on my laptop and google a YouTube video on cutting my own hair. "Okay, you ready for this?" I ask Bailey, the question more for me than for her.

I head upstairs, carrying the laptop, the new scissors, the box of hair color, and walk into the bathroom.

I put the laptop on the counter and rewatch the video two more times. I take a long breath through my nose and let it out slowly. *I can do this.*

I'm a cliché...cutting my hair after breaking up with my boyfriend. But this, what I'm about to do, goes deeper than that.

I follow the video step by step, snipping away at the long strands until the ends fall above my shoulders. The woman in the video makes it appear easier than it is, but she's a trained hairstylist and I'm not.

I add layers throughout my thick hair, freeing loose waves the long length had weighed down. Next, I give myself bangs. It's the first time I've ever had them.

Once I'm finished, I clean up the hair from the floor, apply the hair color, and blow-dry my hair, styling it into something casual and carefree. Then I study the outcome in the mirror.

I look...different but still like me—the old me. The before-I-got-married me—especially with the brown hair color.

A smile tilts the corners of my mouth. The movement

resembles more of a smirk than a full grin. I'll always be scarred, both inside and out. Nothing I can do about that.

I nod at the reflection in the mirror, happy with how my hair turned out.

New haircut. New hair color. New start.

THERE MUST BE SOMETHING TO DRAMATICALLY CHANGING your hair after a breakup. As soon as I sit in my garden and open my laptop, the words begin to flow.

Just not the words I had originally intended.

No, instead of working on Angelique's story, I write an article. "Confessions of an Abused Wife."

My experience as an abused wife and the things Robyn and I discussed during some of our sessions are stirred into the words. The trauma bond, the repeated cycle of abuse, the feelings of unworthiness, the positive reinforcement, the fixation on the "good" days, and the role dopamine plays in trauma bonding—it's all added.

All the things I've never said to the people who've questioned why I didn't walk away like they think they would have been able to, all those words are liberally mixed into the article.

And then I type all the other ideas I have for articles based on the past ten or so years. Articles that give voice to all the hurts I've been forced to endure. The pain, the prejudices, the hate.

Articles that unfortunately too many people can relate to. Articles that are raw and eye-opening.

I have no clue what I'll do with them. For now, they're only for me. Part of my therapy. Like journaling. But now that I've gotten those words down, I'm ready to return to Angelique's story.

I hit Save on the article and pick up the last of Angelique's journals I still need to read and transcribe. I flip through the pages to see how much farther I have left to go. My page-flipping takes me to the empty pages about a quarter way through, an envelope I didn't know was there marking the spot. A bookmark?

The name Elizabeth is written on the front in faded blue ink, the handwriting the same as in the journals.

I turn the envelope over. It's sealed.

I put it to the side on the table and get to work transcribing the last journal. It could be that whatever is in the envelope is meant to be read after reading the journals.

"Wow!"

I startle at Avery's voice. She's standing at the wooden garden gate, her eyes wide, lips parted in surprise.

The angle of the sun tells me it's already late afternoon. I've been writing nonstop since I came out here several hours ago.

"I love the new hairstyle and color." Avery unlatches the gate and enters the garden. "It looks amazing on you."

"Thanks. It's my fresh start." I play with the ends near my face. I'm still getting used to the length being considerably shorter than it's been in over a decade. "Can I ask you a question about your mother?"

Not seeming at all shocked at my question, Avery sits on the wrought-iron chair opposite me, her loose red curls gleaming softly in the sunlight. "Sure. Ask away." She bends down and pets Bailey, who is currently not wearing her *Service Dog in Training* vest.

"How long did it take until she felt like she'd reclaimed her life after leaving your father?"

"A while. But everyone's journey is different. You can't measure your progress compared to anyone but yourself." She straightens, her gaze studying me for a heartbeat. "Is there any reason you're asking me this?"

I dig my teeth into my lower lip. Might as well tell her the truth now. Everyone will hear about it soon enough. "I broke up with Troy."

If I thought her eyes went wide when she saw my haircut, that's nothing compared to now. "You did?"

I nod, shame washing over me at how it all went down. I didn't mean to hurt him, but I also didn't mean for my past to hurt his company either. He deserves better than me, better than the disruption my life has caused him.

"I couldn't give him what he wanted."

"And what's that?"

"Troy will make a wonderful father one day," I reply, not directly answering her question. "And Nova deserves a father like that."

Like Amelia deserved a wonderful father and eventually got one.

A spark of understanding shifts in Avery's eyes. "From what Simone told me, Troy and Olivia have been best friends since they were kids."

"Olivia is in love with him." I shrug as if that says it all.

"Does he love her?"

I'm sure Troy's brothers, Zara, Simone, and Emily can answer the question better than I can, but I nod anyway. If he can fall in love with me, the woman who is so messed up she doesn't know which way is up, I have no doubt he'll fall in love with Olivia. They deserve that love after they lost Colton, the person they both cared deeply for. "He does."

"But is he in love with her?"

"Doesn't matter. That will come. Isn't that what happens? Two people who've lost someone important to them lean on each other to get through the bad days and fall in love?"

Avery stares at me for a beat and bursts out laughing, head flung back. "Are you sure you're not writing a romance?"

I snort a laugh, even though she won't understand why. Angelique and Johann's story wasn't a romance. A love story with a heartbreaking ending? Most definitely. But a romance with a happily ever after wasn't in the stars for them. Unfortunately.

Tears prick my eyes at how Iris lost the one man she loved, and she never loved again. Is that my future too?

The only difference is, unlike Johann, the man I love is alive and will likely have a long and happy life.

I just won't be in it.

I look up at my home—the home with echoes of Troy in every inch of it. The place brings me joy, but it also brings me great pain due to those memories.

If I stay in the house, will I eventually be able to move past that pain? Or would I be better off selling my home and moving far away?

55

ANGELIQUE

May 1944
England

My good hand tightly grips the Lysander seat while the other arm cradles Anna. *Please let us survive this.*

The plane's body rotates in the air, turning the Lysander north, the direction we need to fly to return to England. Nausea churns in my belly.

Strong vibrations travel from under my feet and up my legs and arms. Everything about me is vibrating—either due to the plane's engine or from fear.

Holding Anna a little more snuggly to my body, I peer out the window to the moon-lit road beneath us. There's no sign of the enemy driving along it, but that doesn't mean we have not been noticed.

"Please, nobody spot us," I whisper to myself, the fast

cadence of my heartbeat accompanying the words. "Please, nobody spot us. Please, nobody spot us."

My gaze shifts to the cloudless night sky, and I search for signs of the Luftwaffe. If they should happen to spot us, they would not hesitate to shoot us down. And Anna and I would be with Johann that much sooner.

But while I know he would have loved to spend more time with our daughter, to watch her grow up, he wouldn't want her life to end now just so he could be with her. He would prefer she grows old and lives the life he never got to appreciate. My love, he died too young.

As far as I can tell, the enemy is not in our vicinity, but there's still a risk they will be before we reach English airspace.

Please let us survive this.

I let out a shaky breath. I won't be able to breathe properly until we have landed safely on English soil. I don't remember being this nervous while flying to France at the start of my mission, even though I had to parachute from the plane.

We fly over fields and wooded areas that eventually give way to the French coast and English Channel. Only then do I allow myself to relax a little.

I glance at my sweet, sleeping baby. This will probably be one of the biggest moments of her life—a moment she will never remember. And because of the Official Secrets Act I signed prior to leaving England for France, I'm not sure I will ever be able to tell Anna about it. Perhaps that is just as well.

After what feels like several hours of clutching the Lysander seat, my hand cramping something fierce, the most beautiful sight comes into view...the white cliffs of the English coastline.

"We're almost home, poppet," I tell Anna. Not much

longer and I can finally take a deep breath. Not much longer and I can finally make amends with my sister.

WHEN ANNA AND I ESCAPED FRANCE LESS THAN TWO WEEKS ago, I foolishly thought I would travel to Bristol the following day to see my sister. But things were not as simple as that.

First, I was required to debrief. And because I'd spent over two years in France, there was a lot to debrief on, especially regarding what happened with Christian.

Second, Anna and I had not been in the best health, so we were forced to stay in the hospital.

"I heard that bastard baby is a Jerry." The curt woman's voice comes from the other side of the door to my private room.

I don't need to see her face to know which nurse the voice belongs to. This is not the first time I have witnessed the nurse's scathing attitude towards Anna and me.

No one in the hospital knows why I was in France, but they somehow found out I was there. And they understand the odds of Anna's father being a German soldier is greater than of him being French.

I cuddle Anna closer, protecting her from the hatred. It was the same hatred I witnessed directed at the Jews by those who clung to anti-Semitic views.

The doctor walks into the room, followed by the nurse who made the hateful comment.

"How are we doing today, Miss Bromfield?" His focus is on the patient chart in his hand. He doesn't give me even a cursory glance.

"We are ready to leave." It's the same reply I have given

him during the past week every time he's asked me that question.

He continues to study the chart. "You and your daughter seem to be doing better. You have both gained some weight, which I like to see. There is no reason you can't be discharged today."

Thank God.

The hospital is an improvement over where I've been living for the past few months, but I am tired of the scorn I have been forced to endure. The same scorn I faced in France. I'm a single mother with no job and my baby has been branded as a Nazi.

The SOE has agreed I am not a threat to the country and I am not a double agent. I could tell the commander who interrogated me was not impressed a German soldier had fathered my baby, even if Johann had helped me on more than one occasion. Even if he had joined the maquis. In their view, I seduced information from him, the act of which the SOE frowns upon. They cannot fathom that I fell in love with him—and everything he told me was done of his own free will.

I fiddle with the heart pendant Johann gave me. Because of the British Official Secrets Act I signed, I cannot tell Hazel where I've been all this time. I cannot tell her about Johann. I cannot tell her any of the truth. I can only tell her lies.

The same lies I will have to tell Anna about her father.

And I hate that. Hate that she will never get to hear about Johann's bravery. How he sacrificed his life to protect his sister and his mother and his daughter. But I will tell her stories about him. The stories that I'll be able to share. I'll make sure she knows what a wonderful man her father was.

The doctor signs our discharge papers, and I gather up Anna's and my few possessions.

We take a taxi to Paddington station. I almost tell the driver to take us to a different location, only for Anna and me to then take another taxi to the station. But we're back in London. The enemy isn't following me. I don't need to continue practicing the anti-surveillance skills I used in France.

I buy a train ticket for Bristol and walk to the platform. My gaze constantly scans the area for danger, for anyone who isn't what he or she appears to be. A woman watches me with curiosity, and I have the urge to blend into the crowds, trying to escape the person my mind tells me is Gestapo.

A man brushes past me. I tighten my hold on Anna, her head cradled in the crook of my elbow. My good hand clutches the handle of my valise.

She fusses in my arm.

"Sorry, poppet." I kiss the top of her head and walk to the nearby wall. It's only once the wall is behind me, I can breathe a little easier.

I have spent the past two weeks dwelling on what to tell Hazel about Anna. I have to make up a fictitious boyfriend, who left to serve our country and never returned. I have to disgrace Johann's memory with a lie I don't wish to tell. Will Hazel believe me? If I tell her my mysterious boyfriend was RAF, will Charles ask questions I cannot answer?

I board the train and locate an empty seat next to the window.

A man approaches me in the aisle, a fedora on his head, a kind smile on his face. "Can I help you with your bag, ma'am?"

"Yes, thank you." I smile at him in gratitude and take my seat.

I position Anna in my other arm so she can see the sky as the train moves.

The man takes the seat opposite mine. "Hello, I'm Mark."

"Iris," I say, sounding out the name that still feels foreign on my tongue. It's been a while since I've been Iris and not Angelique or Carmen or Éve. I'm not even sure if I am Iris anymore. In truth, I don't know who I am...beyond Anna's mother.

Mark pulls out a newspaper, and my brain goes into agent mode as I automatically catalogue his features: dark-brown hair slicked back, straight nose, lips that are slightly thinner than Johann's were, an old scar bisecting his right eyebrow.

I stare out the window, my body tense as if expecting the Gestapo or SS to board the train and demand my papers.

I am safe. I am safe. I am safe. The Germans cannot hurt me anymore.

I repeat my new mantra the entire train ride to Bristol as Anna and I watch fields pass us. The war has impacted England with the bombings and rations, but the hope that burns in this country is brighter than the embers that smoulder in France. The English haven't faced occupation. Their food hasn't been stolen to feed German troops and the German populace. They haven't witnessed friends and family dragged away to labour camps or concentration camps or to be executed.

But even so, the death and damage the Luftwaffe has levelled on London and the rest of the country is devastating. My heart breaks for the thousandth time, after returning to this side of the English Channel, at what the war has cost everyone.

An hour into the journey, Anna's eyelids grow heavy, and she falls asleep in my arms. I tenderly kiss her brow and let my thoughts drift to the war I left behind in France, drift to my memories of Johann. Of when he and Dieter first arrived at Jacques's farmhouse with the notice that Johann would be billeting there. Of when he told me about his sister. Of all those times he was kind to me. Of Oskar and Margrit and Sonja. Of the first time he and I kissed. Of the first time we made love. I then replay in my head all the other times we made love, which was by far not enough of them. And I replay the memory of the first time he saw and held his daughter.

His memory keeps me company for the remainder of the trip as I continue staring out the window at the fields scarred with signs of the war.

"Do you live in Bristol?" Mark asks me as the train approaches the city. This is the first time he has spoken to me since the train left Paddington station. He was busy reading his newspaper the entire way.

"My sister and her husband do," I say as we pass the rows of brick houses near the tracks, and I try not to think about how many homeowners' lives have been changed since the beginning of the war.

"You and your daughter are here for a visit, then?" Mark's tone is casual, friendly. It's nothing like the tone I faced during my debriefing or when Captain Krüger and Christian interrogated me.

I turn my head to catch him gazing at my sleeping daughter. "I'm not sure yet." It depends if Hazel wants to see me again. "What about you? Do you live in Bristol or are you visiting family?" I don't really care. I am only asking to be polite.

He looks out of the window, but not before I catch the grief in his expression. "I'm just here to tie up my family's affairs."

I nod and pray he doesn't ask me any more questions. He doesn't. He also doesn't enquire over Anna's father, and for that I am grateful. I am not ready to begin lying yet about Johann.

I never answered that question at the hospital about who her father was. Lieutenant Vera Atkins and Coronel Maurice Buckmaster knew. The captain who debriefed me knew. As for everyone else, even if I hadn't signed the Official Secrets Act, they haven't earned the right or my trust to hear the truth.

Maybe when the war is nothing more than a chapter in a schoolbook and the act that I signed is a distant memory, no longer needing to be abided by, I will be more open about who Anna's father is—as long as it doesn't hurt her. But until then, it's a secret I have to bear alone.

The train pulls into the station. Mark tugs my bag down from the luggage compartment above my head and helps me off the train. I thank him.

"Are you taking a taxi somewhere?" he asks. "I can carry your bag to the taxi stand if you would like."

A polite smile curves my mouth. "Thank you. That's nice of you to offer."

He helps me to the taxi stand and into the next available car. I thank him and tell the driver Hazel and Charles's address.

The driver's brow creases into a frown. "Are you sure that's the address you want, ma'am?"

I nod. "Yes, thank you."

"All right?" The word is drawn out in what sounds more like a question than a note of agreement.

He travels through the city that has changed so much since I was last here. Mounds of rubble replace buildings that were once homes and businesses. An icy chill invades my body the closer we get to Hazel and Charles's neighbourhood.

We drive down a street to find a row of semi-detached houses in various degrees of wholeness. Some are still standing, others half destroyed. Dread fills my belly.

The taxi steers left onto Hazel's street, and I gasp.

"Oh, God." The words might have been whispered. I don't know. My pulse is pounding loudly in my ears, and I can barely breathe.

He drives around a small crater and parks in front of the address I gave him. The building remains standing, but it has also taken a hit.

"Are you sure you want to get out here?" the taxi driver asks, sounding rather doubtful.

What a daft question. Of course I want to get out and find where my sister went. Someone in the neighbourhood is bound to know. She might be staying with a friend or a neighbour.

I block from my mind the other option—the one I cannot face.

"Yes." I pay him without voicing any of this to him and climb out, holding Anna close to my chest.

I walk to the path leading to where the front door once stood and stop. I put my valise down next to me, my gaze not shifting from the house. I'm vaguely aware of the taxi driving away, but other than that, the world stands motionless.

Hazel and Charles weren't in the house when it was bombed. The air-raid sirens would have gone off, and they escaped to the nearest shelter. They're alive. I know it. I just have to discover where they went. Perhaps one of their neighbours could tell me.

Shuffled footsteps warn me someone is approaching on my left. My muscles turn to concrete, but I don't have it in me to turn to see who it is.

"Bloody Jerrys." The crackly voice is that of an elderly man. "I hope once this war is over, Churchill kills the lot of 'em." The venom in his voice is enough to take out a troop of armed men.

My gaze remains on the house. "Did they escape?" My voice is not much more than a raspy murmur.

"Who? Hazel and her young'un?"

It's only then that I look at the man. "Hazel has a child?"

"A baby. She was about this one's age." He nods to Anna in my arms.

My insides shift, no longer stable, ready to crumple like one of the shell-hit homes. "Was?"

He nods again. "Both Hazel and the baby died in the bombin'."

My legs give out from under me as if they've turned to smoke. If not for the man steadying me with his arm around my waist, I would have gone down.

A sob is yanked from my lungs. *Too late. Too late. Too late.*

The only thing that barely got me through losing the man I loved was knowing one day soon I would have a chance to repair things with my sister.

But I am too late.

Anna fusses in my arm, responding to my distress.

"What about Charles? Did he get out of the house in time?"

"Charles has been dead for seven months now. From what I heard, his plane went down over France. No survivors."

I close my eyes against his words. So many questions and possibilities twist in my head. Charles's plane could have landed, but he hasn't yet found his way to one of the escape routes. Or he was recovering from an injury and is on his way over the Pyrénées mountains at this very moment.

Hope flickers, but it extinguishes as quickly as it flared up. The odds of him surviving this long is low, especially if he was injured. If the Germans captured him, he might be as good as dead.

"How do they know there were no survivors?" Unshed tears turn the man blurry.

He hitches his shoulders. "I wasn't there when his body was recovered, so I can't answer the question. I just know what Hazel told me."

Oh, God. And I wasn't here for her when she needed me the most. I was in France, recovering from my wounds, waiting for Johann to return to Dr. Hubert and Rosita's home.

I look at the house and my legs propel me towards it.

"You can't go in there," the man calls after me. "It ain't safe."

I sniff, tears dripping onto Anna's blanket—the soft pink blanket Vera had given me when Anna and I landed on English soil. "That was my sister's house. I need to go in there." I need to find something that will keep her forever close to me.

"Like I said," the man grumbles, "bloody Jerrys. The lot of them." He spits at the ground.

"Could you watch my bag please? I won't be long." I don't wait for his reply.

I'm taking a lot of risks entering the house. I know that. A wall could collapse. But if they were going to fall, they already would have. Besides, for the past year, I have done nothing but take risks. I have lost so much. I just...

I just...

I just...

The entire time Anna and I were getting ready to escape France, I feared the Nazis would capture us before we got away. I never considered the possibility my sister was dead.

I walk around to the side of the house and go in through the huge gap in the wall. I step into what was once the drawing room, a pile of rubble in the centre burying what might have been the settee. Blue sky peers down at me from the hole in the second-floor roof.

In the corner of the room is a playpen. I cautiously walk over to it, careful not to trip on the debris or step on it wrong. A stuffed rabbit lies in the corner, forgotten, dusty. I lean over the railing and retrieve the toy.

I scan the area and spot two framed photos on the bookshelf against the other wall. My progress to it is slow as I navigate several obstacles that could have once been the roof or ceiling or furniture.

I pick up one of the photos and remember the day it was taken, several months prior to Charles proposing to me. Hazel, Charles, and I were grinning at the camera, genuinely happy. Carefree. We hadn't known at the time that three weeks later, Hitler would invade Poland, and Britain and France would go on to declare war on Germany.

On the shelf beneath the one with the photos is a carved wooden box I recognize. It used to belong to my grandmother. If not for my damaged hand and Anna nestled in my arm, I would take the box with me.

I struggle for a moment to open the lid, my fingers clumsy and uncooperative. I finally manage to lift the catch, and I pry the lid open.

I search through the contents. Letters. Old photos. Several legal documents. I pull the documents out one by one and read them. Hazel and Charles's marriage certificate. Their will. I put them aside, not caring to whom Hazel and Charles bequeathed their worldly goods. There are a few other documents that are also of little interest to me.

I unfold the last piece of paper. A birth certificate with Hazel's and Charles's names listed. The date of birth is April 22, 1944. Their daughter, Elizabeth, was only a month younger than Anna.

All those times I dreamt about Hazel and I having daughters the same age had been more real than I realized. If Hazel and Elizabeth had survived, Anna and Elizabeth would have grown up to be more like sisters than cousins.

The document shakes in my hand and a new round of tears sting my eyes.

I close them, and memories of the last time I saw Johann seep in. The pride on his face when he looked at his daughter. He and I had envisioned a life together one day. A family filled with love and joy. But that life was stolen from us. It was stolen from Hazel and Charles.

The cruel words I've heard over the past four months about Anna's father being a Nazi repeat in my head. The ignorance and the hatred. Johann wasn't German. He was an Austrian who hated Hitler and the Nazis and everything they stood for. He was only a German officer because he hoped it would be enough to protect his mother and deaf sister.

He risked everything to protect his daughter and me—like I'll do everything to protect the person most precious to us. To protect her from the ignorance she will face because her mother is unwed...and the hatred that would follow if anyone were to discover her father was a German soldier.

"From now on," I whisper on a sob, "you are no longer

Anna. You're Elizabeth Ashley Wright. And I am not your mother. I'm your aunt who loves you so very, very, *very* much." I kiss her on the top of her head as if that makes my declaration official.

With the documents and photo in hand, we leave the house. The house littered with broken dreams and broken hearts.

56

JESSICA

September, Present Day
Maple Ridge

I check my phone for what must be the twentieth time in the past ten hours. Still no text from Troy. A cloud drifts over the sun, throwing me into shadow, cooling the temperature on my patio.

Why would he want to text you? You. Dumped. Him.

He left two days ago to convince Mason Dell to play in the festival with his old band. I haven't heard if Troy was successful. I only know he hasn't returned to Maple Ridge.

The festival is in twenty-two days. The organizers haven't yet posted on the website that Pushing Limits had to cancel.

Bailey grows restless, a sign I need to take a break from my writing.

I'm still reeling from the news Iris wasn't Anne's great-aunt. She was her grandmother—and Anne wouldn't have existed if Iris and Johann hadn't fallen in love and if Iris hadn't gotten pregnant. If she had survived the war without knowing and loving Johann, she might have eventually married someone else and had his child, but Anne wouldn't have existed.

And this new life of mine that Anne and Troy helped make possible...it wouldn't have happened. Who knows where I would've ended up after I was released from prison? It wouldn't have been Maple Ridge. I didn't know the town existed until Anne offered Iris's home for me to stay in while I recovered.

I would still be the same broken woman I was when I left prison. I wouldn't be the woman who is seeing a therapist and pursuing a new purpose in life.

Heck, if Johann hadn't risked his life to rescue Angelique after she was arrested, the Gestapo or whatever prison camp she was shipped to would've more than likely killed her. Lizzie wouldn't have existed—and neither would Anne. Johann gave up his plan to save his mother and sister in order to protect the woman he loved and their unborn child.

And indirectly, Johann also saved me.

I wipe at the new tears that are falling because of everything Iris lost. Hazel. Johann. Getting to hear Lizzie call her Mummy instead of Auntie. "How about we go for a walk and work on your training?" I ask Bailey, needing to clear my mind.

She scrambles to her feet, indicating she's all for the idea. The walk part of it, anyway.

I take my laptop and reference books inside the house and make a move to leave them on the kitchen table, but the edge of my computer catches on a chair, jarring the pile in my arms. One of the books slips off and falls to the floor. A piece of paper flutters down next to it.

I put the pile on the table and pick up the fallen book and scrap of paper. I turn the paper over and discover a Morse-coded message. Troy must have hidden the note in the book, but I hadn't seen it until now.

I should just toss it away and pretend I never found the message. I should. But instead, I straighten and spend the next few moments decoding the dots and dashes.

You are the sexiest writer I know.

I bite my lower lip, keeping back a giggle, but I'm unable to stop the unexpected grin from stretching across my face.

And then I remember my new reality, and my heart crumples. I release a rough sigh.

I still don't throw the paper away. I return it to the book, unwilling to get rid of the message just yet.

I grab Bailey's leash and pop the straw hat on my head. Between that and the new hairstyle and color, I don't, at first glance, resemble the woman who moved to town five months ago. But there's not much I can do about the prominent scar on my face—the one thing that gives away my identity.

Bailey and I walk to the off-leash park. The neighborhood street is busy with kids playing hopscotch, chasing each other, biking, and enjoying the last days of freedom before school starts next week.

The weird prickling on the nape of my neck from the other day returns. I look over my shoulder, but nothing seems out of place. No one appears to be paying attention to me.

I pick up my pace and walk the several blocks to the park. The off-leash area is busier than I would like, with a dozen or so dog owners playing with their four-legged friends.

I find a quiet area where Bailey is less likely to get distracted and reverse away from her, her training leash slack with the length I've unwound. "Stay." I keep moving backward.

A dog from somewhere on the other side of the field barks. Bailey's head twitches to the side but she stays put. Her full attention returns to me.

"Good girl!"

We spend twenty minutes training and head home, walking across the grass where dogs need to be on a leash. Bailey trots by my side, not pulling or lunging—just being the perfect service dog in training.

A woman sitting on a picnic blanket watches her three young children kicking a soccer ball on the grass in front of her. She laughs and her gaze falls in my direction. Her eyes narrow, but I'm not sure why. Because she recognizes me and is another member of the *I hate Savannah* club?

I glance down at the grass, hoping it's enough to keep her from noticing the scar—if she hasn't already seen it.

She rises to her feet and stalks toward me. I jerk my head up in time to catch her face pinch into a frown.

She stops a few feet in front of me, blocking my path. "How dare you come here, Savannah!" The growl in her tone, like that of a high-strung Chihuahua whose bone has been swiped, startles me. My heart clambers into my throat.

Bailey presses her body against my leg, sensing like she always does the growing tension in my muscles. Sensing my fear of mean words chosen to destroy what I've been repairing and rebuilding.

"We don't want your sort here," the woman blusters on. The soccer ball rolls to the side of the picnic blanket, forgotten as her kids watch on with interest. Listening. Learning that bullying is okay. "I can't believe the mayor even let you into this town. I won't be voting for her during the next election." The woman's chest puffs with each poison-filled word.

"That's enough, Meg," Lance says, jogging over to us. His tone is firm, his frown unyielding. "The school teaches children it's not okay to bully others. You're setting a bad example for your kids."

"I'm not bullying!"

Bailey whimpers from the heat in the woman's voice. Or maybe it was me who whimpered.

Lance stops in front of me, a bulwark against her hatred. "You and I clearly have different definitions for bullying."

"He's right," another woman's voice calls out.

I turn my head to see who else has witnessed the latest round of *Let's Stone the Ex-Con*, adding fuel to the flames of shame that consume me every day.

The voice belongs to Olivia. *Of course.* The universe hates me that much. She's carrying Nova in her arms. I look away, wishing I'd worn sunglasses so Olivia couldn't see the pain in my eyes.

"Jessica wasn't guilty of the crime she served time for, and she's not the person you've made her out to be. You never even took the time to get to know her." Olivia's tone is that of an elementary school teacher gently reprimanding a student for talking during class.

Speechless, I stare at her, but not because she's defending me. She didn't bother to get to know me before she threatened to keep Nova from Troy if I joined him and her daughter for their together time.

Thinking about Troy is a laceration across the heart. I put my hand over it as if that will ease the pain.

Walk away and keep your head up. Don't let them see how much you hurt.

I hurry toward the street, my gaze on the grass under my feet. The weight of condemning glares from people who heard Meg yell my name presses down on me.

Olivia only defended me because I gave her the one thing she really wanted—other than Colton returning. I gave her Troy as something more than just a best friend. Once he comes home, she can start moving forward with her goal of Nova, Troy, and her being a family.

"Wait!" Olivia's voice comes after me.

I move faster. *Just let me get home before the waterworks start.*

"Wait! Jess!"

I stop walking since I don't need anyone else paying attention to me. Her yelling my name will only make things worse.

I turn to Olivia, my mouth incapable of curving into a smile. I don't have it in me to even fake one.

"Did you hear the great news?" Her eyes are glowing.

I shake my head, having no idea what she's talking about.

"About Pushing Limits? Troy managed to pull it off. Mason is joining the band for a reunion performance. The *only* reunion performance he's planning to do with them."

Despite the pain from my lacerated heart, I allow a small smile on my face. *He did it!* Troy will kick ass after all with what he set out to do with the festival. "That's great. Thanks for telling me." I turn to leave, my smile wilting.

"I'm sorry about what happened. With Meg," Olivia rushes to say.

I nod and walk away, not bothering to hand her false platitudes about it being okay. It isn't okay. I have feelings. The people who end up in prison for a crime they didn't commit, the people forced to stay in jail because they don't have bail money or who are given longer sentences than they deserve because of systemic racism...we all have feelings.

Our pasts might play a hand in shaping the people we become, but they aren't the only factors.

Fortunately, Olivia gets the hint and doesn't follow me. I really don't want to talk to her right now.

Or ever.

Delores is working in her garden as I approach my house. "Hi, do you need a hand?" I ask one of the few people on the street who never turned on me when the truth came out.

She smiles at me, her white hair tied back under her own straw hat, and awkwardly pushes to her feet. I help her up, my arm supporting her.

She takes in my hair, and her smile widens. "It looks great. I almost didn't recognize you. The color suits you." Her smile fades. "I saw that article today in the newspaper..." She pauses as if unsure how to finish what she began to say.

"What article?"

"With your brother-in-law. Well, the article wasn't all about your brother-in-law. It quoted him saying he still believes you were guilty of his brother's murder."

"Craig thinks I'm guilty?" Is that the real reason he and Grace don't want me to see Amelia? They helped me start my life over but never truly believed I was innocent?

Delores's eyes widen. "Craig? No, it was some man named Lincoln. Did the reporter get it wrong?"

Oh, *that* brother-in-law. "No, that was my late husband's younger brother." The one who wasn't estranged from the family. He was at my trial and sat on the opposite side of the court room from where Craig was sitting.

"Sometimes it's hard for those who've lost a loved one to move on and see the truth for what it is. But hopefully in time he will, and you'll no longer be a news story he can capitalize on." Delores pulls me in for a hug, one I've been so desperate for during the past few days. I return her hug, not wanting the moment to end.

I'm so tired—a tired that has nothing to do with me writing late into the night. I'm tired and I'm trying so hard not to break down in tears.

"It's going to be okay, Jess," Delores says, her voice a low lullaby. "I promise you, things will eventually get brighter again. But do let me know if you need anything."

I release her and step away. "I will. Thank you. And thank you for everything you've done for me."

She touches my cheek. "Of course, dear. You've become like a granddaughter to me."

Her words crack the dam holding back my tears, and I almost choke on a sob.

I excuse myself before she can see them, and I rush to my house.

57

JESSICA

September, Present Day
Maple Ridge

I step into the backyard, a stack of paper and a pen in my hand. The blue September sky is free from clouds that might have otherwise been a nightmare for the festival today. Troy couldn't have asked for better weather.

I shove down the pang of pain that has sat in my chest since the day I pushed him away. The antidepressants I've been taking for the past three weeks can take up to six weeks to fully kick in.

But even then, expecting them to heal my heart is probably asking too much.

Troy hasn't texted or called me. He hasn't made any attempt to reach out, not even as a friend. I lost him as that too.

His brothers—especially Garrett and Kellan—have regularly come by to check on me during the past three

461

weeks. Garrett mostly talks about writing novels and gardening. Kellan just sits and doesn't say much, which I appreciate more and more with each visit. I gave him the noise-canceling headphones Troy lent me and asked him to return them to Troy.

Simone, Zara, Emily, and Avery have also come over to make sure I don't bury myself too deep in the novel I'm writing...and too deep in my grief.

I sit on the wrought-iron chair where I've spent the past six weeks writing about Angelique's time in occupied France. Anne is due to drop by in a few hours. I told her I have something important for her.

Bailey picks up her toy fire hydrant from the grass. The loud *squeeeeeeeak* startles a small bird in the tree. The bird flies away.

I draw in a long breath, filling my lungs with the soothing scent of pine and the early days of fall. Autumn began three days ago, and the colors of the leaves are already starting to change.

I open the article "Confessions of an Abused Wife" and read through it for the final time. I do the same for three other articles I've written since I poured my heart out on that one. The articles have become part of my therapy. Like journaling.

As expected, each one is raw and hopefully eye-opening and compelling. They don't include quotes from experts I've interviewed—because I haven't—or from other people going through the same things that I have.

The articles are completely based on my experiences, with quotes from credible sources to solidify my points. Points about discrimination against those who have spent time in prison for minor crimes or who have been wrongfully imprisoned. About the misguided beliefs some people have toward the victims and survivors of domestic abuse.

They are a voice for those who don't feel like they have one. Fuckers, maybe I still don't have a voice. For me to have a voice, people have to hear it.

I reread the carefully crafted pitches and press releases I wrote over the past week. Each one is for a different article and for a different media outlet. None of the places are the ones that had requested an exclusive interview with me when I had pitched the PTSD articles.

Once I'm satisfied with everything, I email the query letters and articles to the appropriate individuals. It might be that in the end no one will be interested, but if I don't take this baby step, I'll never be able to move forward. I'll always be stuck in the past, buried under a shitload of shame and regret.

With that done, I pull out my phone and click on the photo Grace sent me of Amelia playing with her dog. She's so beautiful. So happy. *I can do this.* It's time I move on, as much as it hurts.

I put the phone on the table, pick up the pen and paper, and get to work on writing the letter I've been thinking about for the past four days. A letter I'm not sure I could write if not for the medication that is beginning to help with my anxiety and depression.

> Dear Craig and Grace,
> I promise this is the last time I plan to reach out to you about your daughter Lia.

I fill my lungs again with the soothing pine scent and push past the pain of using the name that isn't the one I gave my baby.

I understand your fear of letting me into her life. I would feel the same way if our places were reversed. You never had the opportunity to get to know me. To see me as someone not linked to your brother. You made your decision based on your painful past, and maybe due to what you heard from other people. People who don't necessarily know me. People who don't care to know me.

Craig told me his decision to exclude me from Amelia's life was because I was a reminder of the bullying he'd endured as a kid, but I know it's more than just that. How can the decision not be impacted by everything that has been going on lately with regard to my past?

You believed I was a victim in my marriage with Wayne, and I thank you for acknowledging that. And thank you for taking Lia in when there was nowhere else for her to go, other than the foster care system or with your brother Lincoln. You have given her a wonderful life and a chance for a wonderful future. You gave her something I couldn't. You have given her a home filled with love and happiness. I never want to take that away from you or Lia.

All I wanted was to be part of her life, as a family friend or her aunt. I guess in a way that's what I am—Lia's aunt. I would have loved to be that aunt I never had but dreamed of growing up. I would have been the best aunt ever to your daughter.

Thank you for all you have given me. Without your kindness, I would never have had the chance to start my life over. Granted, I'm still looking for that new start after the truth about my past was laid naked for all to dissect. I hope one day I'll get to experience the love and happiness you two have found together.

I wish you all the best for the future.
Sincerely,
Jessica

I put the letter in an envelope and write their address on the front. This is my first step in moving on and letting go of my daughter. I seal the envelope and stare at it for a moment through the tears that wet my face.

I let the tears steal some of the pain in my chest. It's not enough to help me breathe again. Only one person can do that, and I pushed him away.

I put a stamp on the envelope and walk Bailey to the nearest mailbox before I can change my mind about the letter and rip it up. I push the envelope through the slot.

It drops to the bottom with a soft *thud*.

THE DOORBELL RINGS, AND MY HEARTBEAT STUTTERS. I STOP flipping through the photos on my phone of Troy and of Troy and Nova together—something I've done a lot of during the past three weeks—and answer the door, already knowing who's on the other side.

Anne and her husband, Dan, step into the house. "I almost don't recognize the place," he says, smiling approvingly.

Dan hasn't been here since I moved to Maple Ridge. The house has come a long way from the time it was over-filled with magazines and everything looked dated. The magazines with articles about World War II and D-Day had been an important part of my research for Angelique's story, but they didn't help me as much as the journals that now sit on the coffee table. The rest of the things I found in the secret room are in the box next to the journals.

Anne hugs me, her arms warm and welcoming and just what I need today. The day of the festival that I can't attend. "I love the new look," she tells me. "Your hair looks so pretty like that."

I grin for the first time since acknowledging to myself this morning just how hard the day will be for me. I don't even have Angelique's story to get lost in. The finished manuscript is sitting on the coffee table with everything else. "Thank you. Did you want a tour of the house first?" I ask.

Anne's eyebrows disappear under her bangs. "First? There's something else you want to talk about?"

I nod. It's time she finally learns the truth about Iris's relationship to her, and what a truly amazing woman she was.

I show them around the house. There are lots of "Oohs" and "I love this" and "Auntie Iris would have adored that."

We walk into the room that has given me so much

solace, in part due to the secrets I discovered behind the wall.

"I bet Mom would've loved the window seat." Anne runs her hand over the cushions and the bookshelves, and her gaze roams over the newly decorated room with sage-colored walls. "It's so beautiful."

"There's something else I want to show you." I lead them into the closet, turn on the light, and kneel in front of the bookshelf.

I pull it away from the wall, revealing the hiding place and turn to them. "Did you know about this?" Based on her wide-eyed expression, that would be a no.

She drops to her knees next to me and peers into the space. "Holy, shit!"

I press my lips together to smother a laugh. "I take it you didn't know."

"I didn't. I don't think Mom knew about it either. If she did, she never let on."

I'm pretty sure her mother didn't know; otherwise, Anne would already know what I'm about to soon show her. "I found the space while I was clearing out the magazines that were in here. That wasn't the only thing I found behind the bookshelf. And that's the real reason I asked you to come over today."

I rise to my feet and take Anne and Dan downstairs to the living room. I point to the couch, gesturing for them to take a seat. I remain standing. "I found a box in the secret room. And these journals." I pick up the first journal. "Inside them, Iris talks about a time in her life that changed everything for her. I started reading them while you were away, not realizing at first they were about Iris, and got sucked into the story. Your—" I bite back the word I was going to say.

Anne needs to read the journals to learn the truth. I won't ruin the surprise.

"Iris was an incredible woman," I tell Anne. "Incredible in ways you didn't realize. The room behind the bookshelf wasn't the only secret she'd kept all those years. She once led a life that you, and I'm guessing your mother, didn't know about." I hand her the journal. "The journals are difficult to read because of her arthritic hand and because the ink has faded with age."

I pick up the thick binder from the coffee table. "I took the liberty of typing them out so the content would be easier to read. That's why I didn't tell you about them once you returned from Europe. I was still typing them out and hadn't gotten to the end of her story." My face heats at how I hadn't been totally honest with Anne back then.

I open the flap on the box. "The journals aren't the only things Iris left in the secret room." I lay out on the table the French Croix de Guerre medal, the unopened letter to Anne's mother, and the heart pendant—the one Johann had given to Angelique.

A confused frown scrunches on Dan's brow. "Is that...?" His gaze jumps up from the medal.

"It's the French Croix de Guerre from the Second World War. Well, after it, actually. The medal was Iris's. The journals explain why she had it. The same with the heart pendant. It's all in there." I flash Anne a smile that I hope comes off as the apology I mean for it to be.

"I'm sorry I didn't tell you sooner and I kept reading them without your permission. I couldn't stop at that point. I had to know what happened." I pick up the blue binder from the coffee table. It's narrower than the other one but still a considerable thickness.

I hand it to Anne. "And this...I wrote a historical novel based on Iris's journals. To bring to life the great acts of heroism she performed during the war. It's yours. You can decide what you want done with it. She was your relative. It's your choice if you want her story made public."

I really hope Anne does. More people should learn what Iris did to earn the medal. How she was part of the plot to bring down the Nazis and end the war.

And Anne deserves to know more about the Austrian family she's never heard of.

The family I never even had a chance to tell Troy about. And now, I likely never will.

58

TROY

September, Present Day
Maple Ridge

"I still can't believe you convinced the band to perform after all," Simone says as she and I watch Pushing Limits onstage playing one of their big hits.

We're standing on the grass with our friends and my brothers, enjoying the warm day and the entertainment. The five men onstage are currently performing to a sold-out audience, their fans jumping and dancing and screaming to the rock song. The loud rhythmic beat pulsates through my body.

It's been three weeks since I drove to LA, but it still hasn't sunk in that I convinced Mason Dell to play with the band for the sake of the festival.

If I didn't know better, I would never have guessed they haven't played together as a band in more than five years.

470

They've played a mix of their older hits from when Mason was part of the band and their newer songs.

For the past two weeks, Mason and his family stayed in LA, partly so the band could rehearse together. And for that, I'm truly thankful. Today will go a long way in assisting individuals with PTSD and their families. The festival has also helped to build more awareness and understanding about the mental illness.

"I can't believe you managed to pull off the festival," Lucas says, hugging Simone from behind. "I bet you never expected it to be this successful."

"You're right. I didn't. But thank Christ it's almost over. And then I can return to having a normal, relatively stress-free life." Stress free and lonely.

Fuck, I miss Jess. If it weren't for her, Pushing Limits wouldn't be here. She was the one who told me Mason had originally been the band's drummer. I'd forgotten that.

The festival might be a huge success, but it doesn't feel that way without Jess being part of the day. She didn't want to risk showing up and bringing the wrong kind of media attention to the event. As it is, I've been fielding several interviews today and over the last few days about the festival and where the proceeds will be going.

By the time I'm finished here, I'm going to sleep for the next ten years. Or longer.

Nova is dancing to the music. I smile at the antics of the little girl...and at the sight of Lance's arms secure around my best friend's waist. Olivia is leaning back into him, looking happy and content. This relationship between them is new—only two weeks old—but I can tell it's going to last.

But as thrilled as I am to see them together, it does nothing for the ache in my chest that only Jess can fill. I won't go there again, though. I can't keep surviving the pull and push between us. Can't keep surviving the uncertainty and distrust that grows every time we're together and she decides to sever our connection.

"THANK YOU FOR JOINING US!" NOLAN TELLS THE CHEERING audience through the microphone.

The guys from Pushing Limits wave to the audience. They've just finished their second encore and the audience doesn't seem to be in a rush to see them go. Can't say I blame them.

The festival will be shutting down in another hour. I can already taste the beer and stiff drink I plan to have tonight at Barside Brewery.

The band strides off stage, heading to where I'm standing beside the sound tech. I came backstage a few songs ago, waiting to talk to the band before they head out for LA.

They gather around me, their T-shirts soaked with sweat from their performance.

"That was great," I tell them, fist-bumping each guy, my grin curved with gratitude and relief. "I can't thank you enough for doing this."

Mason nods, his smile friendly and bright against his brown skin. "You're welcome."

Nolan, the band's lead singer, surveys the lit backstage where the roadies are busy doing their jobs. Large black-and-silver cases are stacked in piles in the middle of the open outdoor space. "I don't suppose you know Savannah Townsend, do you?" he asks, sweat dripping from the messy light-brown strands of his hair.

Her name on his lips surprises me for so many reasons,

and I'm not sure how to answer him without asking a million questions first. So I opt for the simplest reply. "I do. Why?"

"I'd like to talk to her." There's nothing nefarious about his tone, yet his request still puts me on edge.

"Any particular reason you want to talk to her?" I do my best not to yank up my alpha-male superhero underwear. He and the band did me a solid by performing today. They didn't have to do that.

"She and I have something in common," he explains. "And I can imagine she's having a rough time with the fallout from all the media attention. I get that."

I guess he would understand. The media has been unrelenting at times for the band. "I can take you to her house." And stay to make sure she's okay...with Nolan being there. But not because I want to see her. And not so I can make sure she's okay—my brothers and our friends have insisted she's fine.

The guys return to their tour bus to quickly shower first.

The need to see Jess clenches my heart in a tight fist. I might have driven past her house once or twice over the last three weeks, but I haven't caught sight of her. And shit, if I don't want to catch sight of her, if only for a moment.

Looks like now's my chance.

Christ, I hope I'm not making a mistake seeing her again.

I drive Nolan, Mason, and Jared to Jess's house and park in the driveway. There's only enough room for four passengers, so Kirk and Aaron, the other band members, opted to stay with the bus.

I can do this. I can survive seeing her.

I walk with them to the front door and ring the door-bell. Just being here is a kick to the gut, and I'm ready to break out in a cold sweat. But my heart is also beating faster, the way it always does when I first see her.

The door opens, and all I can do is gape at Jess. Shit, she was gorgeous before, but this Jess, with golden-brown hair curling loosely above my favorite spot on her shoulder to kiss, is breath-stealingly gorgeous. She looks strong and unbreakable.

But I know that's not true. She might have begun to heal, but she's still shatterable. Amelia is the only thing that truly matters to her. The only thing she loves, other than Bailey.

Her beautiful brown eyes with flakes of gold lock on me, and for a second everything else vanishes. It's just her and me and my aching heart.

A polite *Have-you-forgotten-about-us?* cough jerks me back to my reality. The reality without Jess.

"Sorry," I say to the guys, to Jess, to whatever god is watching from above and cackling at me. "Jessica, this is Nolan, Mason, and Jared from Pushing Limits." I point to each man in turn. "Nolan wanted to meet you. Guys, this is Savannah Townsend. But she goes by Jessica Smithson now."

Jess stares at the guys as though she doesn't know what to make of the three men gathered on her front stoop.

Bailey barks and pushes past Jess's legs. Jess seems to snap out of her momentary shock, but not before Bailey looks up at me, her eyes round with excitement.

I kneel next to her. "Hey, girl. Haven't seen you in a while. You're getting so big." Butterscotch has been miser-able without his friend around.

Jess smiles sheepishly at the three men. "I'm sorry,

c'mon in. Bailey, I didn't give you the command to go outside." Her tone is gentle as she reprimands her dog. Hearing her voice loosens something inside of me. Like a vital screw that keeps everything together.

Bailey looks at Jess and grins as if to bemoan, "But it's Troy. Can't I say hi to your ex-boyfriend?"

"My family has two golden retrievers," Noah tells Jess. "I always miss the dogs when I go on tour."

"You can't bring them with you?" she asks.

"They're not the most practical-sized dog to bring on the road, and I prefer they stay home to watch after Hailey and our kids."

"That's so sweet." Jess smiles, and I really wish she hadn't.

I have to glance down at Bailey because it hurts seeing that smile. A smile not directed at me. A smile that will never be meant for me again.

Jess steps aside, letting the guys into the house. "Do you mind if we sit outside in the backyard? It's so nice out there with the sunset."

Mason, Nolan, and Jared tell her they're good with that, and she leads the way. I follow in the rear, enjoying the way her sexy ass moves as she walks. Luckily for me, she doesn't turn and notice me appreciating the view, which I shouldn't be doing. It only results in more heartache.

Bailey comes with us and makes the rounds to each man to officially greet them as we walk.

The garden hasn't changed much since I last saw it, other than the early signs of fall. The flowers have faded and drooped and the leaves in the oak tree are turning reddish-brown—the color enhanced in the soft glow of the setting sun.

Jess offers them a drink. The guys thank her and tell her they're fine. Everyone takes a seat.

Nolan sits next to her and leans forward, directing his words to her. "We're heading back to LA soon. But I wanted to meet you and tell you I'm sorry for everything you've been through. My father was abusive. My mother and I were his favorite punching bags." The pitch of his voice drops, his tone unfaltering. "He murdered her and my sister when I was nineteen, and I struggled for years from the guilt of not being able to protect them."

Jess's face pales and sympathy widens her eyes. If her husband hadn't been murdered, that could have ended up being Jess's and Amelia's fate.

The thought of that almost brings me to my knees and hurling in a bush.

"I moved to LA," Nolan goes on. "Changed my name. Pretended to be someone I wasn't. It left a hole in me. I did eventually find the help I needed to heal, but that was after the media made my past everyone's business. It was brutal."

"I can imagine." Jess's voice is barely louder than a whisper.

"I recommend talking to a professional," Nolan says. "A therapist. That helped me a lot."

Jess smiles, the gracious curve of her lips soft. The scar at the corner of her mouth tries to prevent the smile but fails. "Thank you. I am seeing a therapist. And you're right. It is helping."

I look at Jess long and hard, but I can't tell if she's telling the truth and is still seeing Robyn. Robyn hasn't told me anything, and I haven't inquired this time. I just hope Jess hasn't given up on therapy because she's no longer on my company health insurance. She can afford to see Robyn because of the restitution payment, but who knows if she's willing to use it for therapy? She was saving that money for her future.

I shouldn't have let her quit her job. I should have

fought harder to keep her on my payroll. It shouldn't have made a difference that she wanted to break up with me. Pride can be such an asshole.

Of course, part of my stupidity had to do with my company. Now that she's no longer my employee, clients have quit canceling their bookings. I haven't had a cancelation in three weeks, so at least there's that benefit.

The guys chat with Jess for a short time. I don't say anything. I just watch her, keeping my feelings for her off my face. I need to get away from Jess soon before I do something I'll regret. Like kiss her. And beg her to take me back.

"It was nice meeting you, Jessica." Nolan gives her a hug, which she happily returns.

"Thank you so much for performing in the festival. What you did will help so many families." She gifts the men one of her brightest smiles. "And especially thank you, Mason, for joining them so today was even possible."

"Glad I could help." He also hugs her and tells her something that I can't hear.

She smiles and nods at him and gives Jared a quick thank-you hug.

The guys and I leave via the backyard gate. Jess walks with us to the front of the house, holding on to Bailey's collar, no doubt so Bailey doesn't go chasing after one of the neighborhood squirrels.

The men get into my truck. I nod bye to Jess but still don't say anything to her. I can't. It hurts too much.

I'm afraid if I speak, all my feelings will spill out.

"So, what's the story with you and Jessica?" Nolan asks from the front passenger seat as I drive to the festival grounds.

"Damn, with the sparks flying between you two, I thought you both were gonna combust." Mason, who's in the back seat, mimes an explosion with his hands.

"It's nothing," I reply. "Ancient history."

"Can't be too ancient," Nolan says, "given that she hasn't lived here long. You two obviously aren't over each other. Not that I'm one to give relationship advice"—a snort comes from the back seat, but I can't tell if it was from Mason or Jared—"due to how much I screwed things up with Hailey before she forgave my sorry ass and eventually agreed to marry me. The emotional scars my father left me with after years of abuse really messed me up. Luckily, Hailey never gave up on me."

"Duly noted," I respond, even though it isn't.

His wife is clearly stronger than me. Or she didn't have to deal with Nolan constantly pushing her away out of fear of moving on. Pushing her away like Jess kept doing to me.

My skin prickles with the need to turn the truck around and go back to her.

I white-knuckle the steering wheel and keep my gaze on the road ahead of me.

59

ANGELIQUE

June 1965
New York City

Lizzie and I walk along Madison Avenue. The New York City sidewalk is busy with people bustling to their jobs or the next tourist site they want to visit. The honking of car horns adds to the backdrop of the city noise, so different from the quiet in Maple Ridge, Oregon.

Unlike everyone else, we're not in the same rush. We're here to absorb the atmosphere, to mark off another city we wanted to visit.

Lizzie stops and looks up at the tall skyscrapers. New York City. The city of dreams. At one point, she aspired to be an actress and work on Broadway. But in the end, she decided an American history degree was more practical.

"It's so different here compared to being in a small town," she observes. Not a single vowel or consonant mark her English beginnings. "New York City is groovy. Maple Ridge is dull."

Four years after the war, we immigrated to America—California, specifically—where I used my French and German skills as a translator in my secretarial job. Eventually, we moved to Maple Ridge. It was the town Johann had dreamed of moving to one day. The place is as beautiful as he imagined it would be. It's the only place where my heart has felt settled.

"It is different." I smile at Lizzie—the name having more meaning than she could ever imagine. Lizzie was the nickname RAF pilots gave the Lysander during the war. I thought it was only fitting to shorten her name—Elizabeth—to that because a Lysander had rescued us from occupied France so we could begin our life anew. My daughter has grown from being a scrawny, malnourished baby into a beautiful, spirited twenty-one-year-old.

"But I've lived in a number of cities and small towns," I tell her, "and I still think Maple Ridge is the best place of all."

We start walking again.

Lizzie tosses her long blond hair over her shoulder. "I can't figure out why you would think that. There are places full of history and incredible architecture..."

She didn't major in architecture, but I know what she means. Maple Ridge is a new town by most standards. It lacks the historical architecture of the northeastern states that she's drawn to. It lacks the historical architecture found in Britain and Europe—her heritage, even if she doesn't know the truth behind that.

"What can I say? Maple Ridge has a special place in my heart," I tell her.

She makes a sound that has me smiling on the inside. I

recognize it. I'm about to be lectured by my headstrong, romantic daughter.

"Auntie, how can you say that? You haven't even found a man there to fall in love with."

My breath draws in slightly at the word *Auntie*, but not enough for Lizzie to notice. Twenty-one years and it still hurts—has done so from the first time she called me that.

I never got to experience the joy of her calling me *Mummy*. Instead, I got to witness her use the word in reference to Hazel's photo. Sometimes, I would pretend Lizzie was saying it to the other woman in the picture. Me. The woman who fell in love with her soul mate, only to lose him to the senselessness of war.

Lizzie has never commented on how she looks more like me than the other two people in the photo I took from Hazel and Charles's bombed house.

"There's more to life than falling in love with a handsome stranger," I remind her. The gold pendant Johann gave me presses warmly on the skin over my heart.

My love for him hasn't dimmed since I fell for the man who was supposed to be the enemy. Not a day goes by that I don't think about him.

"Have you ever been in love?" Lizzie gives me a questioning side glance.

"Once. A very long time ago."

Her eyes widen. My love life has never been up for discussion. That's not to say she hasn't tried to push me to find someone. When she was younger and realized she was the only girl in her class without parents, she wanted me to find her a daddy like all her friends had.

"Who?" she asks.

"You didn't know him. It was during the war."

Lizzie is familiar with the war that cost her the love of a father she never got to know. I've talked about him. But she believes Charles was her father—only he's not the man I describe. The man she knows in her heart to be her father is all Johann.

She makes an exasperated sound. "Auntie, that ended almost twenty years ago. You don't get only one love in your lifetime." She walks around a young couple who stopped to take a photo of the New York Life Building.

I smile at her. "You do when he's your soul mate."

"There's no such thing as soul mates. Gosh, do you realize what a bummer that would be if there was only one love for you out there, and he died, and you could never experience love again?"

I chuckle, the volume barely noticeable against the New York City hustle. A cab drives past, honking. "I thought you were the romantic. I'm the practical one."

"I am. But that's just sad to believe you can't love again if your so-called *The One* is dead."

I hitch my shoulders. "I guess you're right."

"Glad you think so. Does that mean you'll give love another try?"

"We'll see. It's not as if I have found anyone who has captured my heart."

"That's because you live in a small town with no possibilities." She makes a funny face, her eyes—Johann's eyes—going cross-eyed.

This time I laugh, the sound hearty, carefree, full of life. "You might be right about that."

It's not as though I haven't met men over the past twenty years who have shown interest in me. But I am also not the same woman who went off to war, ready to serve her king and country. That woman went through so much while living in France during the Nazi occupation. She still struggles with frequent nightmares that have her waking in the middle of the night, gasping for air. She keeps expecting the Gestapo to show up at the house and drag her away to interrogate her.

I wiggle my fingers—the ones Christian damaged. Even after all these years, my hand is not the same as it once was. The war might have ended for most people almost twenty years ago, but for those of us who lived in the heart of it, the memory never goes away. It lurks in the dark corners.

But I was lucky. I am alive. So many SOE agents perished at the hands of the Nazis. So many lives were changed due to the sacrifices we made. Changed for the worse and changed for the better. We helped pave the way so D-Day could happen. We helped pave the way so the war could end with the Allies the victors.

"Oh, look at that dress." Lizzie grabs my hand and pulls me to the shop window that shows off a simple pink sheath dress hanging on the mannequin.

"It's pretty." I scan my surroundings, my body tense for no reason. The reaction is another souvenir from my time in occupied France. While it's not as bad as it once was, every so often I feel like I'm back in Paris, watching out for the Milice and collaborators. The sensation is worse in big cities. Another reason I prefer Maple Ridge. The memories of the Gestapo don't taunt me as often there.

A man and two women are strolling towards us. The younger woman, who looks to be five or six years older than Lizzie, glances at the window with the dress.

My daughter turns to me, her expression bright with excitement. I recognize it. Lizzie is a talented seamstress, a gift she inherited from her Austrian aunt. Johann once told me Anja had a special knack for designing and sewing beautiful dresses. That expression means Lizzie is thinking of how she can replicate the dress for herself.

A small sound from the direction of the man and the

two women has me turning my head. The man stares at Lizzie as if he's seeing an apparition.

He says something to the older of the two women. Her eyes shift to my daughter and go wide. Her mouth forms a perfect "O."

Something about the man and woman tug at a recollection buried deep in my mind, but I don't know why. They're about my age, but they aren't anyone I've recently met.

Their gazes move from Lizzie to me and recognition flares in their eyes. The pair closes the distance between us, and the younger woman, who appears oblivious to their conversation, continues walking to the window where Lizzie is standing.

"I'm so sorry," the man tells me, a slight accent staining his words. It's weak, but there's a quality about it that makes me think he once lived in Austria or possibly Germany. "I don't mean to be rude, but your daughter...well, she looks so much like someone we once knew."

"She's not her, though," the woman says before I can correct him and tell him Lizzie is my niece. "Anja died during the Second World War. And she was a few years older at the time than your daughter."

At the name, it's as if the world has leapt back in time, and I'm standing outside of Jacques's barn, watching Johann talking to the young family. I look between the pair. "Oskar? Margrit?" Their names are whispered, the feel of them rough against my throat.

And now I'm not the only one back in occupied France. I can see it in Oskar's shocked expression. "Angelique?" My cover name stumbles past his lips.

Lizzie hasn't notice what is happening behind her. She and the other woman—who, if I am right, is Sonja—are busy chatting about the dresses in the window.

I step away from them, not wanting Lizzie to overhear

our conversation. "My real name is Iris," I tell Oskar and Margrit, keeping my voice low. "Angelique was the name I used while I was with the resistance." I'm not allowed to talk about the real reason I was in France, but they knew me from that time, and they know my role in helping them escape to England. There's no reason to pretend I don't know who they're talking about. "That is my daughter—but she has grown up believing I'm her aunt and not her mother, even though I am the one who has loved and raised her. It was simpler that way."

This is the first time I have spoken the truth to anyone. Even the SOE was more than happy to pretend I hadn't given birth in France. The truth tastes both bitter and sweet on my tongue.

I keep telling myself one day I'll be honest with Lizzie, but when is a good time for that? I lied to her to protect her. I'm still protecting her by not revealing the one person she has trusted all this time has lied to her about her parentage. But the fact is, the British Official Secrets Act I signed still prohibits me from telling her the truth I want her to hear. The truth about her father. The truth about my time in France.

A timeless silence stretches around us as they digest my words. It's Oskar who is the first to state what they both have pieced together. "She's Johann's daughter, isn't she?"

I nod, my heart aching at the sound of his name on someone else's lips.

It must show on my face because Margrit's expression turns to one of sadness and grief. "You loved him."

It's not a question, but I nod again all the same. "Very much. He died while fighting with the French maquis. He lived long enough to meet his daughter, Anna, whom he loved very much. She and I escaped to England soon after."

I check that Lizzie is still preoccupied with the dress.

"My sister, like me, was English. She and her baby were killed when the Germans bombed their home a short time before Anna and I returned to England. And since my brother-in-law was also dead...I took my niece's birth certificate and let the world believe that Anna is my niece..."

The sorrow in Oskar's and Margrit's eyes tells me they understand my reason for doing what I did, although they don't know the full extent of why I had to lie about Lizzie's parentage. They escaped Austria and France and Hitler's assault on the Jewish population, but the anti-Semitic attitudes didn't stop on the southern side of the English Channel. Even now, it's rampant in America. The negative stigmas that disabled people face and the racism against people of color both remain strong in this country.

Hitler and his National Socialist Party might be dead, but the hatred and ignorance he fanned the flames for are very much alive twenty years later.

Perhaps Lizzie wouldn't face the same level of condemnation now about her father being a German soldier as she would have when the post-war wounds were still fresh, but I'm not sorry for the choice I made. If I hadn't signed the Official Secrets Act, my decision to pretend she was my niece would still have been the right choice at the time. She was an innocent child, the one thing right with the world.

She was proof that out of so much anger and hate, something beautiful could bloom.

"We always wondered what happened to Johann." Pain, sadness, and relief play tug-of-war on Oskar's face. "We tried to locate him after the war, but we found no records of what happened to him. We were able to learn that his sister and mother died, but nothing beyond that." He looks at Lizzie. Hope blossoms alongside the pain. "Are you living in New York City?"

"No, we live in Maple Ridge, Oregon."

Oskar's mouth shifts into a wide smile, and an unmistakable amusement gleams in his eyes. "Is it as beautiful as he dreamed it would be?"

"Very much so. He would have loved it."

"There is so much about America he would have loved." Oskar's smile falters. "We owe you so much, Iris. If not for you, we probably would never have survived. I hope we can stay in touch this time. I would love to get to know my best friend's daughter. She might never find out about my true link to her, but I would still love to be there for her. Just like you and Johann were there for my family and me."

"I would love that," I say, fighting back the tears I haven't shed in so many years. "I would love that so much. Thank you."

Oskar and I hug. And then I hug Margrit. Hug the remaining links to the man I loved, the links to the world we have since left behind.

60

JESSICA

October, Present Day
Maple Ridge

A cop car is sitting in front of my house when I turn onto my street. My chest tightens, and my breath comes in fast and shallow. No one is sitting in the cruiser. There's no cop on my front porch. Where the heck did they go?

A moment later, I have my answer. My wooden gate creaks open. Noah and Officer Hunt, both in uniform, step out of my yard with another man, his arms pulled back behind him. His short dark hair is peppered with gray, and his skin is tanned. There's something familiar about him, with his thin lips and well-shaped nose.

"What's going on?" I ask Noah.

"Your neighbor phoned in that they saw a man they didn't recognize snooping around the outside of your garage and go into your backyard. They knew you weren't home and became suspicious. Do you know him?"

"No." I might have seen him before but I can't be sure.

"It looks like he tried to break into the garage. The side door is damaged. He also had this on him." Noah holds out a plastic evidence bag with a white envelope inside. My name is written on the front in the same handwriting that was on the two envelopes left outside Troy's office.

"He's the one who's been leaving me death threats?"

The man they arrested glares at me, hatred foaming from his pores. "You murderous bitch!" He spits out the words, spittle flying. "They don't see you for what you are, but I do."

I shudder, taking a step back out of his range.

"They don't see you for what you are, but I know better," the man said, an Aussie accent shaping his harsh tone. "You stole the information. Didn't you?"

"Let's just say it's an insurance policy," my husband replied, sounding equally pissed.

"Against whom?"

The memory flickers out as the man who tried to break into my garage continues screaming his tirade.

"That's what we plan to find out," Officer Hunt says, ignoring the man's rant. "We'll be in touch with you soon." He and Noah escort the man to their cruiser, leaving me standing in my driveway, stunned at the memory, stunned they've possibly caught the man who's been leaving the death threats.

If that's the man who threatened me, it means my life is no longer at risk. If something happens to me while he's out on bail, he would be the cops' first suspect. He wouldn't get away with it. Which hopefully means he now won't try to end my life. That nightmare is over.

Relief bubbles inside me, and I feel a little lighter.

The emotion is quickly snuffed out. He ignited the fuse that brought everything crumpling down for Troy and me, but he wasn't the detonator that destroyed my relationship with the man I love.

That was me.

But I did it for a good reason. Nova deserves to be part of a loving family, with Troy as the adoring father.

I check the damage to my garage door. Noah was right. The man tried to pry the door open with some sort of tool. The door is splintered near the doorknob. I unlock it and put away my bike.

I open the back door to the house to find Bailey waiting for me in the mudroom. The alarm isn't going off, so whoever that man was, he hadn't tried to get into the house...just the garage.

Restlessness churns inside me. At the memory? At the man trying to break in? At losing Troy? Or from it all combined?

I need to get out of here.

As Bailey and I walk along a residential street on our way home from the dog park, the prickly sensation at the nape of my neck from the other day is back. Stronger. More insistent.

The street we're on is busier than most, with the elementary school nearby. But the school isn't close enough for me to worry about a mob of angry mothers stoning me, because they believe I'm a danger to their children. My nervous system is just working overtime again. My medication hasn't diminished my hypervigilance.

A man is standing on the street corner. There's something familiar about him. Tall. Good-looking. Wearing jeans and a T-shirt. Then it hits me why he seems familiar. He's the guy who was searching for his wife and daughter last month on Main Street. The man who I thought could be on the cover of a romance novel.

Our gazes connect for a beat, long enough to tell me he recognizes me. He looks away, and I wouldn't be surprised if he has since learned I'm someone to condemn and not treat like a human being. He must be here to pick up his daughter from school.

Bailey and I continue past him and eventually turn onto our street.

Anne's car is parked on my driveway. She never mentioned anything about coming over. I haven't heard from her after I gave her all the items I found in the secret room and the novel I wrote based on the journals. That was five days ago.

I'd be lying if I said I haven't been wondering about her reaction to finding out Iris was her grandmother. And learning her grandfather was a German soldier during World War II.

Anne isn't in her car. Maybe she went for a walk while waiting for me to come home. She probably thought I was at work. I never mentioned when I saw her on Saturday that I no longer work for Troy. I avoided all topics involving the man I'm in love with.

Seeing him the other day was murder—but I'm glad he came.

If I do get a job that enables me to stay in town, maybe one day he can be my friend again.

Maybe one day, it won't ache like this.

On the off chance Anne is in the backyard, I walk up the driveway and open the gate. The hinge squeaks, letting the woman sitting at the patio table know I've returned.

Anne looks up from her phone and rises to her feet, smiling. She gives me an exuberant hug, an uncontained excitement buzzing in her. It leaks inside me, feeding the excitement that grew in me from the moment I started reading her grandmother's journals.

"Thank you, Jess." She releases me. "Thank you so much for the journals and the book you wrote and the medal and the pendant. Thank you for bringing my grandmother's story to life."

"You're welcome." I search her eyes for signs she's mad at me because I withheld the secret for so long, but all I find is pure gratitude. I let out a soft sigh of relief.

Anne's only wearing a lightweight cardigan, and the temperature is a little chilly for sitting outside in it.

"Let's go inside," I suggest. "I can make some hot chocolate."

We go into the kitchen. I remove Bailey's *Service Dog in Training* vest so she can take a break from her training. Anne sits at the table and visits with her while I make the hot chocolate. I place the steamy mugs of hazelnut hot chocolate on the table and take a seat across from her.

"I have to say I was shocked when I read the journals. I knew nothing about her life during the war—other than she lived in England at the time." Anne wraps her hands around her mug. "I wish I had known all of that. It explains so much about her hand and about her growing paranoia near the end of her life. But it also explains her love for life and her intense love for my mother and me. Did I tell you how I'd catch her sitting by the lake, talking to it in German, especially as she got older?"

I shake my head.

"I would ask her what she was saying. She would smile

and tell me she was talking to the Nixie. Now I understand why. It was her way of keeping her memories of my grandfather alive. I'm sorry she never got to tell me about him herself. I have so many questions about him and my European roots. Questions I might never get answers to." She pushes a folded piece of paper toward me.

I pick it up. "What is this?"

"It's the letter she wrote to my mother. Read it."

I unfold the page and read the shaky yet familiar handwriting.

To my dear sweet Elizabeth,

If you're reading this, it means I've moved on to a better place, and I'm hopefully with my one true love. I promise you if that is the case, I am very, very happy.

I started writing the journals years ago once I'd fully come to terms with what happened during the Second World War. You and I were living in the United States at that point. It was a country that had lived through the war but hadn't experienced it the way they had in England and the rest of Europe. Even England hadn't experienced the war the way the countries occupied by the Nazis and Fascists had. It was a very different time back then, but also a time that hasn't changed as much as it should have in the years that have passed.

I'm assuming you have read the journals and have so many questions. I'm sure many of them I can't answer because I was unable to find the answers myself after the war. Maybe in the future, you will have better success than I did. Maybe information will be made available to future generations, or maybe those answers will remain buried for all time. I fervently hope the latter is not true.

The latter point is part of the reason I wrote the journals. I could not give them to you while I was alive at risk of violating the British Official Secrets Act. But once I am dead, I will no longer have to keep the secret about what I survived through, and you will finally know the truth about your father.

Here are the answers I can give you. Jacques Gauthier, the man who was like a second father to me—he risked so much for me, for the downed RAF pilots making their way to the escape lines, for his country, and for his son. I took you to France shortly before we departed for the United States to start a new life here. I wanted to know what had happened to Jacques after the Gestapo took me away.

I am delighted to tell you Jacques survived the war, as did his son. Jacques was one of the few survivors of the war who knew the truth about your father and me. He was the only one who witnessed the love Johann and I shared for each other. The moment Jacques saw you, he knew the truth that no one else did—that you are Johann's daughter. He died fifteen years later from a stroke, but he wanted you to know your father was a great man who was thrown into circumstances none of us wanted to be in.

It's easy to say in hindsight that if more people who hadn't supported Hitler's politics had stood their ground, the war would not have happened. The murder of the disabled and mentally ill would not have happened. The Holocaust would not have happened. So many people would not have been killed, so many children would not have been left with only one parent or as orphans. But the world doesn't work that way when you're dealing with someone who is that hungry for power. They'll do anything to get it and keep it, no matter the cost to others. Maybe one day a world without dictators will be possible. I wish I had lived long enough to see it.

Your father never wanted to fight in the war. He only wanted to love and protect his family, and that includes you. Please never forget he loved you so very, very much. I love you so very, very much. It hurt to not be able to tell you I was your mother. You can't begin to understand how proud I am of you and of your beautiful little daughter. Perhaps now you will understand why I suggested the name Anne after you gave birth to the precious sweet angel. It was to honor your father's sister, Anja. If I couldn't call you Anna like I had originally planned, I wanted to make sure I was able to honor Anja through your daughter. Thank you so much for allowing me to do that.

I've never regretted any of my decisions from during the war and afterwards, and that includes my decision to never settle down with another man. I knew no other man could fill the hole left by my love, the man who would have been my husband if we had lived in another time and place.

Thank you, my sweet love, for everything. Just know that I am with the only man I ever loved, and I am truly happy.

Love,

Mum

Through welling tears, I reread the letter several times, feeling once again Iris's love for Johann. The letter has given me the closure I needed, but I'm sure it's only the beginning for Anne as she tries to find out more about the relatives she never knew she had.

"Sonja—the daughter of Oskar and Margrit," Anne says

with a soft smile. "She was my godmother. That summer when my mother and grandmother were in New York City, Mom and Sonja quickly became friends and stayed friends, even though they didn't live in the same part of the country."

"Do you know if Sonja is still alive?" Maybe she remembers her uncle Johann—remembers enough to share with Anne.

"She died a few years ago. But she and I kept in contact after my mother died. She never said anything about living in France during the war. She never mentioned anything about what was in the journals." Anne's smile returns, wider this time. "My grandmother...wow, it still feels strange thinking of Auntie Iris that way. She told me my grandparents had loved each other very much, and they fell in love with my mother the moment they saw her. I had no idea all those times she told me that she was referring to herself...and my real grandfather instead of the man I thought was my grandfather."

"I can imagine it will take time to get used to the idea that nothing was what you had thought." Her family members weren't who she had thought they were.

"You're right. Anyway, you said on Saturday that it's my choice if I want my grandmother's story made public."

I nod, mentally crossing my fingers Anne will want to share the story with the world.

"I want everyone to know about my grandmother's contribution to the war and about the man she fell in love with. I understand why she kept it a secret after the war, but there's no reason why no one can learn about it now." Anne's face and eyes light up with an all-consuming smile.

She's correct in thinking that. The British Official Secrets Act that Iris had been tied to has long since died.

More and more information about the SOE and the role it played during the war is now public knowledge.

"I read the story you wrote, Jess. You're extremely talented. I don't know anything about the publishing industry, but I would love for you to see if you can get the book published. I want you to get credit for your hard work."

The excitement I felt while writing the book rushes in and embraces me. "You do?"

"I do." She reaches across the table and rests her hand on mine, her palm warm from holding her mug. "You have a lot to say, Jess. It's about time the world listens."

Now it's me who's wearing the all-consuming smile. I can't believe how Johann ending up at Jacques's farmhouse and falling in love with Iris was the ripple that has ultimately changed my life around. It has resulted in me having a beautiful home, friends, and a new passion and purpose in life. "Thank you! So much!" I mean that both ways: for her allowing me to see where I can take the book when it comes to being published, and for telling me it's time the world listens to what I have to say.

My late husband might have stolen my voice, made silence my preferred language while we were married, but over the past few months, I've become less of the woman I once was. I've become more of the woman I want to be. And I have my friends and Robyn and Troy to thank for that. I have people on my side who have never shamed me for what I have to say. They have never shamed me for using my voice, and for that, I am grateful.

"Let me know how things go with the book," Anne tells me. "I look forward to seeing what happens with it."

"Definitely."

Garrett has offered to read the story. Maybe he'll have suggestions on aspects I can improve before I query agents.

For a heartbeat, I want to text Troy and tell him I've

finished writing the book. Tell him about the real contents of the hidden room and about Iris's secret life during the war.

But I can't.

Because Troy has moved on, and I'm no longer part of his life.

So...I text Garrett instead, the hollow sensation in my chest, from missing Troy, heavy.

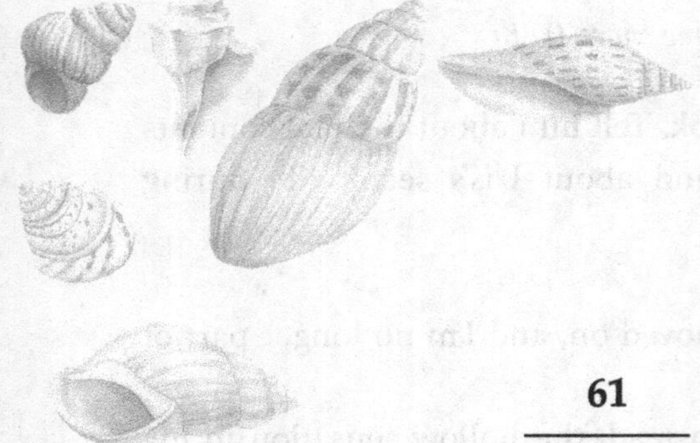

61

______

JESSICA

October, Present Day
Maple Ridge

"How are things going with your relationship with Troy?" Robyn asks during our next therapy session. Until a moment ago, I was still buzzing with excitement over Anne's and my conversation from yesterday. Robyn's question is the swinging arc of a butcher knife, cleaving my excitement in two, letting my joy bleed out.

I wince, scrambling too late to keep the pain from showing on my face. "I ended it a month ago." Right after my last appointment with Robyn. I hadn't planned to bring it up, and he clearly hasn't mentioned it to her, but we're only a few minutes into our appointment and I've already revealed that knife-to-my-heart truth.

A flicker of surprise barely registers in Robyn's expression, the otherwise calm mask of professional curiosity. She leans forward in her chair. "Do you want to discuss what happened between you two?"

No. Not really.

"Well, first, he had so much going on at the time." The words rush out before I can stop them. And then I just let them continue to spill, my fear for him fueling them on. "I was afraid all my problems were just adding to his load. It wasn't good for his mental health. I didn't want him to break because of me."

"He has been dealing with a lot lately. And so have you. That can definitely put a strain on a relationship, as well as on you both individually. You said first. Was there another reason for ending things with Troy?"

"He wants a family one day," I blurt, my runaway mouth clearly on a roll.

Robyn doesn't say anything, possibly waiting for me to elaborate.

My breath fans over my lips as I consider how much to divulge. But Robyn has a way of getting me to reveal my darkest secrets, so I might as well jump straight to this next truth. "I'm not sure I can give him that."

"What do you mean?"

Her question is so straightforward. The answer isn't. It's convoluted and messy. It requires stripping away the layers of myself, spreading myself out bare. "I-I've lost Amelia..." My throat tightens with all the emotions battling to have their say. I can barely rein them in. "I-I can't go through that again."

"When you say you can't go through that again, do you mean giving your child to another family because the situation at the time forced you to make that choice? Or do you mean in a more general sense?"

"In general. Life is fragile. Anything could happen to the child." I'd known this was a possibility before I became pregnant with Amelia, and it hadn't bothered me then. It's a risk all parents face whether a child is biologically theirs or adopted. But the truth to it hits harder after giving up the rights to my daughter.

"That's true. Having children is scary when you think about it in those terms. And there's nothing wrong with not wanting more children. But I'm wondering if there's more to it than just you ending things with Troy."

I lift my shoulders in an easy shrug, not allowing myself to squirm on the couch in response to her knowing gaze. "He lost his best friend to PTSD last year."

I see in the brief glimpse of emotion that slips onto her face that Colton had been part of her life too. That makes sense. She went to school with Troy, which means she would have also known Colton and Olivia.

"I just figure Troy and Olivia would be better together than Troy and me. He adores Olivia's daughter," I explain. "They're already a family."

Robyn leans back in her chair. "Did Troy tell you that he would rather be with Olivia than you?"

"No. But why wouldn't he? They've been best friends since they were kids."

A small smile appears on Robyn's face, a flash of nostalgia creasing the corners of her eyes. "In school, we always called them The Three Musketeers. You rarely saw one without the other two. Or at least it was that way until Olivia and Colton became a couple." Robyn's smile eases away. "So you think Troy and Olivia should be a couple because they've been best friends for forever?"

"Not just because they're best friends, but because they're perfect for each other." Saying it aloud sounds less convincing than it did in my head.

"And does Troy agree with this?"

"He didn't when I broke up with him, but maybe he's

changed his mind." Now that I've practically pushed Olivia and him together.

"And what if he hasn't?"

I shrug again, giving my shoulders quite the workout. "It doesn't matter. Troy got tired of me always breaking things off with him. According to him, I push away people I love."

Robyn's head tilts to the side, her eyes diving deep into my soul, searching for the answers I'm not sure I even know. "Is he right? Do you keep pushing the people you love away?"

I open my mouth to say they leave me, but Troy is right. Granny didn't intentionally leave me. Amelia didn't leave me; I gave her away for her own good. Only my parents gave up on me.

When it comes to pushing away people I love, only Troy fits in that category. I didn't push my late husband away. I'd tried to escape him for my daughter's sake and mine. "No. I only pushed Troy away," I tell Robyn.

"Do you love Troy?"

I hang my head, the sound of his name an arrow shot through my heart.

I lift my eyes to Robyn's. "I do." No point denying it. It's not as if she's going to tell him. They aren't in middle school anymore. She's a therapist. A professional.

"Did you tell him you love him?"

I shake my head.

"Why didn't you?" There's no judgment in Robyn's tone, but I do wonder how much of her interest in the answer has to do with her personally knowing Troy.

Why didn't I tell him? I close my eyes for a moment, exploring the question and answer from several different angles. "Because...because I'm not good enough for him. I'm damaged." There. I've said it.

"Are you damaged?" Robyn asks. She has that professional challenge in her eyes I've seen numerous times during our sessions. A challenge that has me questioning my own assumptions about myself. "The woman I see sitting in front of me isn't damaged. She's growing stronger and is dealing with some of her past issues so she can be a strong and healthy and happier woman. She has worked hard to be where she is today. You've worked hard, Jess."

I bend down and stroke Bailey. Robyn's right. I might still have dents that haven't yet been removed from my previously damaged shell, but I'm not the same woman who left Beckley more than six months ago.

I'll probably always have dented armor, but it doesn't mean I'm the mangled wreck I once was.

"My late husband enjoyed making me feel unworthy." A fact I've shared with Robyn during one of our earlier sessions. "He did a great job at it, and I guess I learned his lesson too well. I..." *I...what?* I left prison feeling unworthy of love. My late husband did that to me. He made me doubt myself. Made me feel weak and helpless.

I'd clung to that lie even when Troy told and showed me countless times that he loved me. I'd clung to that lie even when Troy showed me again and again and again he is nothing like my late husband.

Instead of telling Troy I loved him, I kept the truth from him. I tried to protect myself from him eventually believing I wasn't good enough for him. I let the protesters feed that lie until it consumed me. And I let myself cling to those self-destructive feelings Wayne ingrained in me.

I haven't been honest with Troy, and I haven't been honest with myself. I was too busy pushing Olivia toward him to see it. Olivia. Nova. Amelia. I've been constantly hiding behind them. Constantly using them as a shield.

"Do you think...do you think I've been using Amelia

and Nova and my fear of having a family as an excuse for not letting Troy fully into my heart? Because I feel unworthy of his love? And that's why I couldn't tell him I love him?"

"I think you might be on to something." A pleased smile quirks her mouth. "You seem to be constantly focused on making sure everyone else has a better life—like Violet and Sophie, Amelia and Troy—you tend to ignore your own needs.

"Do you remember what we discussed about Maslow's Hierarchy of Needs? To reach the higher levels of esteem, recognition, and self-actualization, your lower-level needs must be met first. And that includes love and belonging."

I nod. I do remember that. For now, my physical and safety needs are met, and I have friends, but I haven't allowed myself to fully love...because I let Wayne and the protesters and anyone else who thought I wasn't good enough...I allowed them to manipulate me into believing deep down they were right.

Maybe that hadn't been everyone's goal, but I still let them have that power over me.

I had let my late husband's mind games win.

I release a slow breath through my nose. "Too bad I hadn't figured this all out sooner." Before I broke up with Troy. It would have saved me a lot of heartache.

"It could be now that you're on the antidepressant, you're able to see things clearer. Your depression and anxiety fed into your misguided view of yourself. It became an endless cycle that was hard to break from."

That makes sense. "Alright," I say, feeling somewhat better, but no less brokenhearted. "I'll do better in opening my heart to another man. In the future. But it's too late with Troy. He's now with Olivia and Nova."

Robyn's eyebrows lift in surprise. "I'm usually not in the

business of reporting on gossip, but I saw them at the festival last weekend, and it looked like Olivia is with Lance Reid."

She is? I mean, I know Lance is really into her. That much was obvious the day I interviewed her for the PTSD article and he came over to her house. But I had no idea they were seeing each other.

"It's still too late," I point out. "Troy doesn't want to take a risk with me again. I have a bad habit of breaking his heart." I grimace at how often I've done that, believing each time I was doing the right thing. For Violet and Sophie. For Troy and Olivia and Nova.

"Only you can decide what you want to do, Jess. But it wouldn't hurt to be honest with him and tell him what you've told me. That would be a start."

Be honest. I can do that. The question is, will Troy give a damn about what I have to say?

Or has my emotional breakthrough come far too late?

62

JESSICA

October, Present Day
Maple Ridge

I reread the email Garrett sent me yesterday, my butt sinking comfortably into my couch.

    Jess,
    I just read the first chapter of your story. I can't wait to read the rest of the book. If it's anything like what I've read so far, I'm sure my agent will want to see it. She also represents historical fiction. Looking forward to reading the rest of it once I return this weekend.
    Garrett

The Warriors group left this morning, which means I can't try to talk to Troy for a few more days. And now I have to survive however long it takes Garrett to read the book before I can breathe again. Anne loved it, but it's Garrett's feedback I'm most eager and anxious for.

His agent? *Oh, God.* I can't believe he thinks she might be interested in the book. That would be incredible.

Please let them both love the story like Anne did.

My gaze shifts to the floral box on the coffee table, with the Morse-coded messages inside. Do I dare reread them? Do I dare read how Troy once felt about me until I wrecked everything between us?

I trace over the flowers on the lid and pause when my finger touches a pink blossom. *You can do this.* I open the box and randomly pull out some of the pieces of paper.

I read through them, my aching heart pounding hard at his sweet and funny and sexy words. Yesterday was the one-month anniversary of the date I ended things with him.

A new email pings in my inbox. It's from someone I don't know, but the subject catches my attention: re Confessions of an Abused Wife.

My heart slams to a stop and stutters and stumbles. The email is probably a rejection. Or a request for an exclusive interview and not for the article I wrote.

I put Troy's messages back in the floral box.

The curser hovers over the email for a second. I click it open.

```
To: Jessica Smithson
From: Ruby Davis
Subject:    re    Confessions    of    an
Abused Wife
Dear Jessica,
Thank you for your submission. I enjoyed
your  article  "Confessions  of  an  Abused
Wife"  and  would  like  to  publish  it  in  an
upcoming   issue   of   Embrace   Life.   The
```

article was emotionally insightful, and I would love to read more of your work.

The rest of the email goes on to cover what the publication will pay me for the article. It's not a large amount, but it is a start. Every published article under my name adds to my credibility, especially if they're published in a major magazine like *Embrace Life*. Every article published is one more opportunity for my voice to be heard, one more chance for me to make a difference.

That's all I've ever wanted to do.

I close my laptop and fetch the vacuum from the laundry room. Bailey whimpers, not being a fan of the noise the vacuum makes. I open the back door to let her out into the garden.

I carry the vacuum upstairs and go into the second bedroom. I grab the headphones I recently ordered, which are nowhere near as good as the ones Troy lent me. I pull up *The Greatest Showman* soundtrack and hit Play.

I vacuum the bedrooms and head downstairs. The opening bars to "This is Me" plays, and I sing along to the lyrics. I direct them to all the people who've tried to cut me apart since they found out the ugly truth about my past.

I am bruised.

I am scarred.

But I'm also braver—like Robyn pointed out yesterday. I still have a long way to go. Healing from trauma like I've endured isn't a quick fix. PTSD doesn't go away overnight or after a few months of therapy—or even with the addition of a weighted blanket when I sleep. But maybe one day I'll be able to walk down the street without having to keep looking over my shoulder. Maybe one day my past won't have *any* control over me.

I park the vacuum by the coffee table in the living room,

put the headphones on the table, and walk toward the back door to check on Bailey.

A man is standing in front of the door, blocking the exit, thick arms folded across his wide chest.

Chills lunge through my body, robbing me of the air in my lungs. *Oh, fuckers.* "Lincoln?"

The last time I saw Wayne's brother was at my trial. The hatred he felt for me then hasn't diminished with time. His scowl is no softer than it was the day the jury found me guilty of all charges. He hadn't even seemed happy or relieved at the verdict. Just pissed he wasn't allowed to come near me. To kill me with his own hands.

Lincoln remains motionless, his deep-blue eyes locked on mine. And his gaze, filled with burning hatred, turns my body to iced-over stone. *Move. Scream. Run!* It doesn't matter how many times I say the words to myself, my fight-or-flight instinct continues to fail me.

"What are you doing here?" *And why didn't Bailey put up a fuss about you coming into the house?*

"Bailey?" I call out, my feet moving forward. *Has she eaten more poison?*

"Where is it, Savannah?" The edge to Lincoln's tone is more lethal than a rattlesnake's bite.

"Where's what?" I really have no clue what he's talking about. The restitution payment because I was wrongly imprisoned? Is that what he's after? He wants my money? Hell if that's happening.

"The information Wayne had. The insurance policy. He hid it. It wasn't in his house. Which means you took it. You know where it is."

Hid it? Why would he think Wayne hid his insurance policy? He kept them in a safe box in the laundry room. Lincoln should know that, given Wayne bequeathed our house to him. Even from his grave, my dead husband had a hand in manipulating my well-being.

He'd left very little to me and Amelia. Lincoln then went to court and made sure I received none of the money—because I'd supposedly killed my husband. The judge had sided with him...and Craig never contested the ruling on Amelia's behalf. He didn't want her to have anything that once belonged to her biological father.

"I have no idea what you're talking about, Lincoln. Which insurance policy?" I frown and take a step back.

"Information about the illegal activities he and I were involved in. He called it his insurance policy."

"They don't see you for what you are, but I know better," the man with the Aussie accent said. *"You stole the information. Didn't you?"*

"Let's just say it's an insurance policy," my husband replied.

"Against whom?"

Had Wayne been afraid his brother would double-cross him? Was that what all those arguments had been about several weeks prior to Wayne's murder? Something tells me I don't want to know what kind of illegal activity Lincoln's talking about.

But who was the man I've recently had the flashes of memories about regarding the missing insurance policy? The one with the accent?

I shake my head. "I have no idea what you're talking about. You honestly think Wayne would've told me where he put it? When I could have used it to secure my own freedom from him?"

That's exactly what I would have done—freed Amelia and myself from the abusive cycle I'd found ourselves in.

Lincoln might not have witnessed Wayne's abuse toward me, but I'm sure he knew about it. As Craig recently pointed out, Wayne and Lincoln were cut from the same asshole cloth.

"No," Lincoln says, his tone as lethal as before. "But I think you found it. Figured out what it was. Hid it."

God, does he really think I'm that dumb? "That doesn't even make sense. Why wouldn't I have given it to the DA when they prosecuted me?"

Lincoln nods—but his eyes aren't on me. His gaze is directed to something beyond my shoulder.

A meaty arm goes around my chest from behind, not giving me a chance to react or respond. It pins me to a solid body.

I let out a soundless scream, fear robbing me of my voice. I struggle and squirm, fighting for my life. *What the fuckers? Who the...where...where'd he come from?*

A sharp pressure pricks my neck, and a surge of adrenaline hits my blood. I kick and elbow whoever is holding me, searching for my voice. Searching for the ability to shout or scream.

My body turns numb, and I can't feel anything. No pain. No hope. Nothing.

The world goes black, the building scream in my lungs rapidly dying away.

I JERK AWAKE FROM A BAD DREAM. I THINK I'M AWAKE. MY brain is foggy, and everything is dark when I open my eyes.

My arms are tied in front of me, and I can't straighten my bent legs. I'm in some sort of enclosed space. My body is vibrating from whatever I'm lying on, and I can make out the low rumble of an engine. Car engine?

Shit. Shit. Shit.

My heart races and I can't get enough air into my lungs. I kick and wiggle and flounder like a fish tossed out of the water.

My body aches as if I've been cramped up for several hours, but that could be the effects of whatever I was injected with.

"Help me!" I scream, praying the car is on a residential street. Someone walking their dog could hear me and call 9-1-1.

My voice sounds sluggish to my ears, but I don't let that deter me. "Help me! Call nine-one-one!" I scream the plead again and again and again. My throat grows rawer with each cry for help, but I don't care. I'll keep screaming until I no longer have a voice if it means being rescued. "Please, someone. Help me!"

I strain to hear a sign someone heard my cries for help or a clue to where I am...beyond the trunk of an unknown car.

My chest tightens, an elephant-sized boulder pressing down on me, crushing the air from my lungs. They hurt— for all the good the screaming has done. There are no distant wails of sirens, no indication anyone heard me.

Why the hell did Lincoln stuff me in here? He's a goddamn cop. Like his brother was. Cops don't go around kidnapping people. It's against the law.

But so is trafficking assault weapons, and that didn't stop Chief Wilson and Officer Dunbar from being lured to the dark side.

Domestic abuse is also against the law. That didn't stop my husband from beating me.

And apparently it didn't stop him and Lincoln from getting involved in whatever illegal activity Lincoln was referring to.

Fuckers. Fuckers. Fuckers. I'm not going to get out of this alive. That much is obvious. Why confess all of that if he's planning to let me free? I'm a liability. A guaranteed prison sentence.

I kick my legs, lashing out at the inside of the trunk. *Thud. Thud. Thud.* Anything to gain a passerby's attention.

The car keeps going, giving no indication it's picking up speed, and my stomach sags to the floor. The driver either can't hear me or they aren't too concerned about anyone else hearing me because no one can.

I'm alone and no one knows where I am or that I've been kidnapped. I made plans with Simone, Zara, Emily, and Avery for tonight, but the car could be long gone from Maple Ridge before anyone realizes I'm missing. I'm screwed. I'm royally going-to-die screwed.

That realization sucks the fight from me.

I lie still, listening for something, anything, that will help me escape.

There's nothing but the quiet purr of the engine and the low vibration of metal against metal. I can't hear music and I can't hear talking. I don't know if whoever is driving is alone or if Lincoln and the man who drugged me are both in the car.

"What would Angelique do?" I ask myself out loud, so I don't feel so alone.

Unfortunately, I don't have an answer.

I feel around for a weapon or a way to escape, but between my hands being tied together and the small enclosed space, I'm limited with my movements.

The road switches from being relatively smooth to bumpy, like the car is driving over deep potholes. My body jostles about so much, I'm positive I'll be covered with bruises by the time the car stops. On top of that, the ache in my muscles from not being able to stretch out is getting worse.

My thoughts go to Troy. He won't be going to my house and wondering where I've gone. He won't be coming to my rescue, like Johann rescued Iris after the Gestapo arrested her. None of the Carson brothers will be.

Lincoln is a cop—or he was the last time I saw him—so I'm not expecting the Maple Ridge police department to come to my rescue either. The only person I can rely on to save me is *me*—and that's hardly reassuring.

The car stops. *Oh, God. Oh, God. Oh, God.* I still don't have an escape plan.

The crunching of gravel underfoot approaches the trunk from both sides of the car. Possibly two men. Or more. As far as I can tell, their strides are long, their footfalls rapid.

My muscles tense, bracing for the worst, bracing for my life to end in a round of bullets.

The trunk opens. Above me, bruised clouds obscure the sky—as do the broad shoulders of a man, his features dark in shadow.

The man reaches for my arm. All my shifting around while I was searching for a weapon achieved one thing: my legs are no longer where he left them when I was dumped in the trunk. I kick out.

My attempt to hit the man in the chest or face or anywhere else I can do damage is pathetic at best. He grabs my legs and yanks them hard. I'm pulled with such force, my top rides up, exposing my skin. Something rough on the edge of the trunk scrapes the length of my back, abrading my flesh.

A sharp pain rips through me. I shriek, but all the screaming I did earlier turned my throat raw. The sound comes out as a gasp.

The man releases me, letting me fall. The crown of my head hits the bumper. *Thud.* Pain ricochets through my brain, and I sag to the ground. Gravel digs into the exposed skin of my arms and lower back.

I lie there for several seconds, dazed and unmoving, too afraid to consider what's coming next. My breath is a ragged pant; my heartbeat the frightened flutter of a caged bird.

I look up at the man who hauled me from the trunk. His features are still obscured in shadow, and my vision is blurry.

He bends down, grabs my upper arm, and yanks me up. Gravel stabs the soles of my bare feet.

It's only then that I see him better. He's...it's...it's the man who looks like he could be a cover model. The man who was looking for his wife and daughter the first time I saw him.

Is that what this is about? He didn't want an ex-con living in Maple Ridge? He believed the lies I'm a risk to his child?

No, that doesn't make sense. Why would he be with Lincoln? How did these two men end up together if the stranger just wanted to get me out of town?

I shift my attention to the abandoned concrete building in front of us, with bars on the windows, as if it has the answers. The layout of the single-story structure is bigger than my house, but I can't tell what it was previously used for.

Trees surround us in all directions. Pine, spruce, and others I don't have names for. The ground is flat here, but I can't figure out if we're in the foothills or somewhere in the mountains.

A flash of metal in Lincoln's hand warns me he's armed and dangerous. He's going to kill me. No matter what happens, no matter what I tell them, my number of heartbeats is limited.

Fear and panic collide inside me, turning me cold.

I'm going to die.

I'm going to die.

I'm going to die.

I jerk my arm from Not-Lincoln's grip, the action fueled by the knowledge I won't survive, and I run.

I barely make it more than three steps when he grabs my arm and roughly shakes me. I lose my footing and stumble to regain it.

His grip tightens on my arm to the point where I'm positive my bone is about to snap in half. His other hand raises, and a hard slap stings my cheek. A stunned gasp falls from my lips.

Lincoln steps so close to me, his stale breath blows in my face. "Don't you fucking try that again," he growls, the mark the other man left on my cheek no doubt as red as his complexion. "Otherwise, the next time I'll shoot you."

My ears ringing, my cheek smarting, I'm half led, half pushed into the building and along a short corridor. Lincoln stops at an empty room that is not much more than four concrete walls and a concrete ceiling and a concrete floor. Thick metal bars cover the windows, and a decrepit toilet sits in the corner. And just like that, I'm back in prison, but I sense this one will be a new kind of hell.

My bound hands itch to grab the doorframe, to keep him from pushing me into the room, but common sense kicks in. It's not worth getting shot right now. I'll never have a chance to escape if I'm dead.

A laugh bubbles up inside me. It's not a happy laugh. It spills past my dry mouth and cracked lips.

Not-Lincoln shoves me into the room. I fall to the cold, hard floor. The door slams shut behind me, and a deadbolt on the other side slides into place.

The resounding boom of confinement echoes in the

room. It's accompanied by the rapid *thump-thump-thump-you're-dead* thumping of my heart.

63

___

TROY

October, Present Day
Maple Ridge

The late afternoon sun casts shadows on the leaf-covered ground as my brothers, the veterans, and I approach the rental vans, our backpacks loaded with camping and climbing gear. Various vibrant shades of gold, red, and orange color the surrounding trees.

The veterans, a group of men and women in their early forties who served together in the Iraq War, are laughing and teasing each other. They've been like this all weekend. The weekend and the group have been the perfect distraction now that the festival and the planning for it are over.

My life is now only filled with the Warrior weekends, volunteering at the Veterans Center, working out, and running my company. And that's giving me too much time to dwell on the one person I don't want to think about. We only have bookings for a few more weekends, and then

519

things will slow down in the offseason. Soon, I'll have way too much free time. Free time for my thoughts to easily stray to Jess.

Maybe instead of hiring a new office assistant, I'll do everything myself. Might as well. I've already been doing that since Jess quit. I haven't gotten around to finding her replacement yet.

I can tell the moment the van I'm driving enters cell-phone range on our way back to town. Everyone's phones ping with messages. The veterans laugh and joke as they post on social media about their weekend.

"Shit," Kellan mutters under his breath from the passenger seat next to me, the word a near quiet explosion.

"What?" I keep my voice low, in case he isn't interested in sharing the news with everyone in the van.

"Jess has gone missing."

"What do you mean she's gone missing?" My voice comes out louder this time but still low enough not to snare everyone's attention. I tighten my grip on the steering wheel.

"Exactly that." Kellan's phone rings. He answers it. "Yeah. Got the message. I haven't talked to her since Wednesday....No....No....Nothing....I'll ask him. Troy, when was the last time you talked to Jess?"

I keep my eyes on the road. "Last Saturday evening. I took the guys from Pushing Limits to meet her after the festival. The lead singer wanted to talk to her."

"Did she say anything about going out of town?"

"No." Not that we actually talked, just the two of us. The guys in the band and Jess did all the talking.

"He doesn't know anything about it either," Kellan tells whoever is on the other end of the phone. "Shit....What did Lucas and Garrett say?...Okay....I'll head to her place as soon as we get to town....Thirty minutes....Call me if you hear anything else before then."

I frown. "Are you going to tell me what the hell's going on?"

"Jess hasn't been seen or heard from since Friday—"

Kellan's phone rings again. He answers it.

I'm close to ripping it out of his hand so he can tell me what's happening. But his hand with the phone is too far from me to grab without getting us all killed.

"Yes, Zara just called..." Kellan tells whoever is on the other end of the line. "I'll go to Jess's as soon as we get back into town....Okay." He ends the call. "Delores spotted Bailey walking on the street late Friday afternoon, looking distressed. Jess wasn't with her."

"Where was she?" A bad feeling settles in my gut.

"That's the thing. No one knows. Her back door was unlocked and the alarm wasn't activated. Delores went inside, thinking Jess was hurt. No one was there. She left a note for Jess, saying she had Bailey."

My hands white-knuckle the wheel. "This was Friday afternoon?"

"Yes. When Jess didn't get back to Delores by early evening, she called the police."

"And?"

"Nothing. There was no sign of a struggle, and no one knows where she went."

"Dammit. The death threats..." I can't even say the next part.

"It wasn't him. The man was arrested early Friday afternoon. She hadn't gone missing yet. Noah saw her."

"Shit, this feels like *déjà vu*," I mutter. *Christ, please tell me she didn't get into another accident.* Except she doesn't have a vehicle and she didn't have my truck this time. "Is her bike in the garage?"

"Yes."

"Maybe she borrowed someone's car and drove somewhere? Or she took the bus to Eugene."

"Without her wallet? And without telling the girls she wasn't going to their movie night as she'd planned?"

Uncertainty and unease slice me open, turn me inside out. I don't know what to say. All the possible scenarios play out in my head—places she could've gone, reasons she would've left the alarm off and let Bailey run in the street.

And I don't like what they're adding up to.

She might be hiding in her secret room again, but without being there, I can't explain how to open the door if it's shut. I also don't think that's where she is if she's been missing for two days.

"What's wrong?" Jaxon asks from the seat behind Kellan's. I'd forgotten about the men. The laughter that filled the van a few minutes ago has gone silent. I'm only realizing it now.

Kellan and I exchange a long questioning glance. I nod for him to go ahead and tell them. They sense something's wrong, and I'm not going to bullshit them by telling them it's nothing.

Kellan fills them in. I focus on the road without pushing the speed limit. As much as I want to race to Jess's house, it's my responsibility to get everyone home in one piece.

Kellan tells them Jess is my girlfriend. I don't bother to correct him. He also gets them up to speed on Jess's past. My gut tightens. I've heard enough negative comments as it is about her on social media, from the regular media, from people in town, and from other Warriors we've taken to the mountains. I don't want to hear if the six men in the van also have asshole opinions to add to the list, especially since two of them are cops from California.

"I remember hearing her husband was murdered,"

Jaxon says, the disgust in his tone setting me on edge. "I was in prison at the time after being framed for stealing drug evidence. Before that, I'd worked for the SDPD."

This is news to me. "Did you know Jessica's husband?" I ask, not bothering to sound casual. There's a hardness to my voice that has to do with her disappearance and the fact Jaxon knew the monster.

"I did. He was a charismatic man. Most people liked him."

Christ, don't tell me Jaxon's another prick who believes Jess killed her husband.

Something about his tone slowly registers, sneaks past my protectiveness toward Jess. "But you didn't?" I glance in the rearview mirror and catch Jaxon and Nigel, the other cop, exchanging their own wary glances.

"My twin sister had been in an abusive relationship at one point," Jaxon explains. "It was while I was in the Army. I returned home during one leave and noticed the subtle changes in her. I brushed it off as my imagination—the result of serving in Iraq. But I was wrong. Her boyfriend turned out to be an abusive asshole."

"Did you ever meet Jessica?" My gaze flicks briefly back to the rearview mirror again.

Pain and regret cloud his features, the emotions so fleeting, I almost missed them. "I saw her several times over the span of about a year. I never talked to her, if that's what you're asking. But there was something about her that'd reminded me of my sister when she was with her abusive boyfriend. It was like Jessica was emotionally withdrawn. Nervous."

He shakes his head, as if disappointed about something. "The last time I saw her was at a barbecue Wayne was throwing. I knew then I needed to gain her trust, knowing she probably didn't trust men anymore if I was right about her relationship with him. I wanted to help her in the way I hadn't helped my sister while I'd been on leave. So I smiled at Jessica, letting her know I wanted to be her friend. I'd had a feeling she didn't have any, if I was right about Wayne."

"What happened after that?" I ask, appreciating him telling me this, but also knowing none of what he's saying will help me find Jess.

"I was arrested a few days later. Never had a chance to talk to her. That's one of the reasons I came on this trip. I heard Jessica was living in Maple Ridge, and I wanted to tell her how sorry I was that I didn't do something when I first suspected Wayne was hurting her. Maybe if I had done something, I could have gotten her and her daughter out of their situation. I could have protected her and saved them from what did happen."

"You can't blame yourself for that," I tell him, despite wishing he had stepped in. I likely wouldn't have met Jess if that had happened, but given that we're not together anymore, it wouldn't have mattered. She would at least still have Amelia in her life.

"So you weren't responsible for the drugs being stolen?" I ask, wondering why the hell someone would frame him.

"My husband took away a lot of things I loved. That was his way of controlling me. But my camera...my camera was different. That he smashed because he thought I was having an affair." Was Jaxon the man Wayne had accused her of having an affair with? He had seen Jaxon smile at Jess, became jealous, and framed the man?

"Definitely not," Jaxon explains. "But the evidence was too strong against me. A year ago, I was exonerated of the crime. I still wanted to be a police officer—to make a difference despite everything that happened—but I couldn't go back to San Diego. After everything, I only trusted a few people in the department."

Can't say I blame him. "So you think Wayne was responsible for you ending up in prison?"

"He was definitely a dirty cop, so that wouldn't surprise me," Nigel pipes in. He doesn't work for the SDPD. He's from San Francisco. "There was a woman officer who'd suspected he was a dirty cop, but she didn't have enough evidence to prove it. She was sexually assaulted by a different officer, but when she reported it to her captain, he turned a blind eye."

My gaze flicks to the rearview mirror again, my foot pushing slightly harder on the accelerator. I'm hoping some part of their story might help me figure out where Jess is. So far nothing they've said has given me a clue as to her whereabouts.

A scowl turns Nigel's expression stormy. "From what she told me, before she quit the force and moved to San Francisco, several of her colleagues made her feel uncomfortable. She started struggling with depression. She had survived hell in Iraq, but this proved to be worse than that."

"This all happened after I was arrested. I didn't even know she was going through this at the time," Jaxon continues. "She later told me there were several other cops in the department she suspected were involved in some sort of illegal operation with Wayne Townsend. She didn't know what it was, though."

"And this included his brother," Nigel adds. "She didn't know how far the corruption went in the department, but she did know he was involved."

Shit. "Is this the brother who adopted Jess's daughter?"

"Adopted?" Jaxon's eyebrows draw together into a dark line in the rear mirror. "I don't know anything about that.

The last I heard, Lincoln didn't have any kids or a wife or girlfriend."

"We're definitely not talking about the same man." Which is good. It's been hard enough for Jess to lose her daughter, never mind to find out that Amelia's adoptive father was a bad cop like her biological father. "Did any of this ever come up after Wayne Townsend's murder?"

Jaxon shrugs. "I wasn't involved in the investigation since I was in prison at the time, so I can't answer that. But my release did result in the opening of a new investigation. I don't know anything beyond that."

Kellan glances at his phone. "Does the brother still work for the SDPD?"

"Last I heard he was a vice detective," Nigel replies. "Also heard he was vocal about Jessica being released from prison. He was adamant she killed his brother."

"I wonder if he knows anything about Jess's disappearance," I say, voicing my thoughts out loud. Sure, there are other reasons she could be missing. For all I know, she's run away or has left to try to see Amelia. But she wouldn't have left Bailey on her own, and she certainly wouldn't have left her to roam on the street. In my gut, I know something is wrong. And this brother seems a likely suspect.

"I still have contacts in the SDPD," Jaxon informs us. "Let me call them and see if I can find out if anyone has seen him recently."

"Do it," I urge. My next words are directed to Kellan. "Call Lucas and Garrett and tell them we're going straight to Jess's house."

Kellan does that while Jaxon talks to someone on his phone.

"According to my contact," Jaxon tells us a few minutes later as I pull into town, "Lincoln is on vacation for the next nine days. He left Wednesday. My contact has no idea where he went, other than on some fishing trip."

"Shit. So we have no idea if he knows anything about Jess's disappearance, but he does have a reason for going after her. Revenge—if he believes she killed his brother."

"If he does have Jess"—anger tightens Kellan's tone, his usual ability to flatline his emotions gone—"we have no idea where he would've taken her. She could be anywhere."

"Call Noah!" The gravel-rough command fires from me. "He's working today. Tell him everything. And tell him to meet us at Jess's house. Now."

It feels like a lifetime before the van tires screech to a stop outside Jess's home. Police sirens scream in the evening air.

Flashing red-and-blue lights turn onto the street. The sirens cut off abruptly.

During the drive here, I compartmentalized everything Jaxon and Nigel told me, locking my fears away. But now that I'm in front of her house, those fears surge through me like a rogue wave. I might have pushed Jess away once and for all, but I haven't stopped loving her.

And now it might be too late to snatch back the words I hurled at her four weeks ago.

No. No. No. I'm going to find her. I'm not letting her down like so many other people have.

I sprint to the front door and turn the doorknob. It's locked. I use the spare key I never got around to returning to Jess and rush into the house.

"Jess!" I yell, even knowing that she's not here. I feel her absence in the cold air.

I race upstairs to the guest room and go into the closet. The bookcase is in place, and there's no sign Jess is hiding in the secret room. No heartbreaking sound of her crying like there was the day I learned about the space behind the shelves.

I pull the bookcase away from the wall. The blankets and pillows that were in the secret room are gone.

Noah enters the house as I jog down the stairs. I don't acknowledge him. I walk into the living room, searching for signs of where she could've gone.

A floral box I haven't seen before sits on the coffee table. I lift the lid, but the only things inside the box are the Morse-code messages I left around the house for her. I hadn't realized she'd kept them. I still have the ones she gave me. They're in my sock drawer.

An ache pulls in my chest at how she saved the messages I wrote for her—like they still meant something. I close the box lid and head for the kitchen.

The medicine container on the granite counter catches my eye. I pick it up and read the label. Sertraline. The prescription belongs to Jess. One of the physicians in town wrote it for her.

I google the drug. It's an antidepressant. According to the date on the container, she's been taking it for almost a month, starting after we broke up. *Shit.* I look up what could happen if she stops the drug cold turkey and read the list of withdrawal symptoms: headache, nausea, mood changes, sweating, tremors, seizures.

"Troy?"

I spin around to face Noah. "Her brother-in-law, Lincoln Townsend, might know where Jess is." The words come out in rapid fire, fear and anger pulling the trigger. "You should talk to the man you arrested. He could be linked to Lincoln."

"I don't think he is. Someone tried to break into Jess's garage. I thought the man I arrested was responsible for the damage. He claims the door was already like that when he was causing mischief, and I believe him. The evidence doesn't suggest he did it."

"Shit." My hand tightens on my phone. I would've been happier if the man Noah arrested was responsible. Now we have no idea where Jess might be.

"Before you do something rash and stupid," Noah says, a harsh command to his tone I've never heard from him until now, "let the police deal with this, Troy. We don't need a hotheaded civilian messing up the evidence and the case."

"I don't give a damn about that. I just want Jess back." Never have spoken words been any truer. I'll only rest once she's in my arms again.

64

JESSICA

October, Present Day
Maple Ridge

T he cold seeping through the concrete floor and walls chills me to the bone, but it's not enough to numb the pain wracking my body. Every single part of me hurts.

I shiver, which only intensifies the pain. My soaking wet clothes aren't helping. Dousing me with icy water was Lincoln's idea. To torture me into telling them what they want to know.

"Where is it, Savannah?"

I still don't know why he thinks I know where Wayne's insurance policy against him is hidden. And at some point, I stopped caring.

I also don't know what it has to do with the other man, who hasn't spoken to me since the kidnapping. Lincoln has done all the talking. Not a hint of remorse exists in the

530

other man's eyes to suggest I might be able to convince him to make it easier for me to escape.

I'm not getting out of here alive. I already know that. I'm cold and nausea is my constant companion. My head aches, one eye is swollen almost shut, and I have been beaten and tortured. I don't have the energy to give a damn anymore.

A shudder grips my body hard and sends a stabbing pain through me. I moan. I can't even curse the shivering; it means I'm still alive. It's when the shivering stops that I'll be in trouble.

Don't give up. Never give up.

It's not my voice I hear in my head. It's Angelique's.

A young woman crouches on the floor next to me—the woman from Anne's photo of Iris, Hazel, and Charles. I'm huddled on my side, doing what I can to retain what little body heat I have left.

I'm fairly positive the woman in the dark-green vintage dress isn't real. She's a hallucination. A dream. But I'm not complaining. A ghost from the journals is better than Lincoln and Not-Lincoln coming into the room.

Angelique strokes my arm. My eyelids fight to stay open.

"Be strong. Follow your heart." Her voice is the whisper of a breath through leaves. She gives me a sad smile and rises to her feet.

A blond man is standing near the wall. Johann. I'm pretty sure that's who my mind conjured up. He's also wearing clothes from the 1940s. Gray trousers, gray vest, blue shirt, beige tie. He's watching her, his face lit with love and adoration.

A tear slides to my hairline. Troy used to look at me that way.

Smiling, Johann holds out his hand to Angelique. She takes it, and they fade away.

"Thank you." The words are so quiet, I'm not sure if I said them or just moved my lips.

Another shudder goes through me, and I moan. I need to warm up. That might help me survive. But I don't have the strength to even get to my bruised knees.

My hands are still zip-tied in front of me, the skin around the plastic angry and raw. A day or two more like this, and I could be facing a nasty infection. My body won't have the energy to fight it.

I have no idea what day it is. I lost count after the third day. Maybe it's Monday. Or Tuesday. Or maybe I've been here for weeks. It feels like weeks.

For the first two days, whenever the two men left me alone in the room, I scoured every inch of the space. Searched for a way to escape or attack the men when they came in to torture me again. I found nothing.

Day three was spent plotting my escape. I came up with nothing.

Day four...I didn't have enough energy by then to do much more than breathe and dream.

Once again, I let my thoughts slip to my happy place. It's not the same place I used to disappear into myself while in prison. I'm not thinking about searching for shells on the beach with Amelia. I'm sitting in front of a fire with Troy, cuddled against his warm body. On the other side of him... is our two-year-old son.

What do I see?

Troy reading our son's favorite picture book to him. The mess of golden-brown hair on top of our son's head. The sexy grin Troy flashes me as he turns another page. His strong calloused hands that know how to make my body tingle. Bailey and Butterscotch snoozing on their bed by the fireplace.

What do I hear?

Troy's deep and melodically smooth voice as he reads the story. The funny, squeaky voices he uses for the animals' dialogue. Our son's giggles. The crackle of the fire. The dogs snoring.

What do I feel?

The rough denim under my fingertips as I tap out the Morse code for ILU on Troy's leg. *Tap-tap. Tap-taaap-tap-tap. Tap-tap-taaap.*

I smile at the image. My body is too cold to keep the tilt of my lips on my face for long. The smile fades away, but the image in my head doesn't.

The rough denim transforms into the chilled concrete beneath my body. *Tap-tap. Tap-taaap-tap-tap. Tap-tap-taaap.*

I think back to one of my favorite Hans Christian Anderson stories from my childhood. "The Little Match Girl." The orphaned girl was cold and homeless, hungry and alone. The small amount of money she earned came from the matches she sold. When she had only three left, she lit them one at a time. The first match brought to life the image of a warm home and a fireplace. But the flame quickly died away.

She struck the second match. The image that appeared was of a yummy Christmas dinner and a huge roasted turkey. But like with the first match, the image quickly faded away.

The third and final match brought the little girl a loving family. Before the flame flickered away, she died while imagining her mother's warm embrace. She died with a smile on her face.

If I'm going to die, that's how I plan to go. Thinking about Troy and the family we'll never have together, sitting in front of the roaring fire. It doesn't matter if Troy and I aren't together for real. In my mind, we will be.

Tap-tap. Tap-taaap-tap-tap. Tap-tap-taaap.

The door's deadbolt rattles as someone slides it to the side.

The door flings open and hits the wall behind it with a bang.

The first several times the door did that, I startled. Now, I can't find it in me to flinch.

Lincoln and Not-Lincoln enter the concrete room. I waste a tiny amount of energy hating them for how they're dry and warmly dressed. The hatred is enough to provide a flicker of heat inside me, but the heat dies away as swiftly as it came.

Not-Lincoln is carrying an old wooden chair. Fear slams into my body once more. I hate that chair almost as much as I hate the two men.

He sets it down next to me and yanks me to my feet. I sway unsteadily.

He tightens his grip on my arm. I doubt there's much skin left on me he hasn't already bruised. This abuse won't leave so much as a mark.

Not-Lincoln roughly shoves me into the chair. I'm barely able to sit upright. *Tap-tap. Tap-taaap-tap-tap. Tap-tap-taaap.* The denim of my jeans is rough against my fingertip.

I don't dare look at the tattoo on my arm. I don't want to give away how much it means to me. Though I'm sure if my body is ever found—and if my flesh is intact—there won't be a tattoo left with which to identify my remains.

I would shudder, but I don't seem to have it in me anymore to do that.

Lincoln leans in too close, his sour breath hot on my face. "Okay, Savannah. Enough of the games. Where's the information you took from my brother?"

"I-I di-didn't take any in-infor-mation," I reply through chattering teeth. *Fuckers.* I'm so tired of the same question again and again and again. It's his one-hit wonder he can't seem to break beyond.

I've long since given up explaining that if I'd had the information, I would have used it against my husband way before he was murdered.

Lincoln hadn't liked that answer.

Each time I told him that, it resulted in more torture. Torture that wasn't necessarily fueled by my answer, but I suspect by his need for revenge for his brother's murder. Murder that Lincoln believes I'm guilty of. Nothing that either the courts or I could say will convince him otherwise.

I don't bother to brace for what's coming next. I know from experience it won't make a difference.

He hits me across my swollen face, creating new splits in the weakened skin. My head lolls to the side, and I can make out at least five of him. My ears ring, the sound seemingly never ending.

I turn to Not-Lincoln. "Th-that day you asked me i-if I had se-seen your d-daugh-ter. On M-Main Street." The stuttered words come out on a murmured slur. I'm not sure if the men can even hear them. "Was that wo-woman and child re-really your wife and d-daugh-ter?"

"No. They were strangers I saw go into the store." The rough Aussie accent loops around his words, faded with time but stronger than when he spoke to me on Main Street.

A sense of *déjà vu* washes over me. It's like watching a TV show rerun I saw many years ago but can't remember how the episode went. And it's blurry, like it's behind a veil, with only parts of the picture wavering into clarity. It's not enough for me to understand what's going on.

I've heard that voice before. Not recently. Maybe it was

while I was married. I heard it on a TV show or in a movie. It's not like he's the only Aussie living in the U.S.

A memory shimmers in my mind, gone too quickly to take a snapshot of. It's a memory I've had recently. That much I recognize. But the torture and the cold and my weakened state are making it too difficult to find it again.

"You've b-been stalking me." I hadn't imagined it, and my PTSD hadn't been working overtime. Someone had been following me. "W-why?"

He doesn't respond.

"I didn't k-kill Wayne." My garbled words stumble out on a whisper. I can barely keep my eyes open. "Th-thirsty." So very thirsty. I can't remember the last time I had something to drink. After I didn't give them what they wanted during the first two days of captivity, they stopped giving me water to drink. They dumped buckets of freezing cold water on me, but the small amount that trickled into my mouth hadn't been enough.

Not-Lincoln removes his gun from his holster and points it at me.

"I didn't k-kill Wayne." It becomes a chant I repeat on an endless loop, but I don't know how much of it makes it past my dry, split lips.

"She's no use to us," Not-Lincoln says.

I frown. Or try to. My face is too numb to know for sure.

Snippets from the day Wayne died slip in again. The argument. Wayne and a man with an Aussie accent disagreeing about something. I told the SDPD about the argument, but there were no signs that someone else had been in the house. The cops thought I was lying. And I'd felt out of it from whatever drugs I'd been given—like I do now. Like I was gripping on to the edge of the world, knowing if I let go, I'd be forever lost.

Over time, I began to believe I imagined the argument.

I began to doubt the events of that night as I remembered them.

The only thing I was positive about was that I didn't kill my husband. Someone else pulled the trigger.

"You killed Wayne," I mutter incoherently even to my ears, my gaze locked on Not-Lincoln. "You killed Wayne. You killed Wayne." It's my new chant, one I fully embrace.

"What's she talking about?" Lincoln demands, his tone terrifyingly fierce.

I keep chanting, my eyelids giving up the attempt to stay open.

A loud bang assaults my ears. A heavy *thud* follows. With what little strength I have left, I open my eyes. Lincoln is lying in a pool of blood. His blood.

I'm vaguely aware of other sounds coming from somewhere inside the building.

I start to slouch sideways. Another loud bang fills the room.

Excruciating pain rips through my shoulder, but I barely make a noise. Dazed, I glance down. Red spreads across my pink top near my shoulder, swallowing smeared stains and dried dirt. After the lack of anything to drink for the past few days, I'm surprised to see the blood.

The room explodes with activity.

My body no longer feels like it belongs to me. I slump to the side, falling off the chair.

Someone catches me. I blink them into focus. Noah? The world is too fuzzy—he's too fuzzy—for me to know for sure. Maybe I'm already dead, and I'm imagining all of this. That last ray of hope before I finally slip away.

"We need a medic!" he yells through the fog in my brain. He's not looking at me. He's looking toward the door.

He gently lowers me to the ground.

"He k-killed Wayne. He killed Wayne." I have no idea if

Noah understands what I'm saying. He's talking to me, but I can't make out his words.

In the background, a man is telling Not-Lincoln he's under arrest for the murder of Wayne Townsend, obstruction of justice in the murder of my late husband, and for weapons trafficking. The rest of the words drift into a haze.

"T-tell Troy I l-love him," I whisper-croak, knowing I won't survive this to tell Troy myself. "T-tell him that I w-would have loved t-to have a f-family with him." *Tap-tap. Tap-taaap-tap-tap...*

My shivering stops and blackness welcomes me with warm open arms.

65

TROY

October, Present Day
Maple Ridge

Jess's face is so pale against the hospital pillow, if it weren't for the steady beeping of the ICU monitors, I would think she was dead.

I tighten my hold on her hand, as if that's all it will take to keep her from departing this world. I haven't left her side since I was finally allowed to see her this morning. Her eyes are closed, partly due to the swelling on one side of her face where the bastards repeatedly hit her.

Every part of her body is bruised or bandaged or both. Samuel told me she'd been beaten with what could have been a belt. She's got a long recovery ahead of her.

I can't believe I almost lost her.

Noah enters the room in uniform. He was the one who called me yesterday to tell me Jess had been found—two days after I learned she was missing.

539

"How is she doing?" Noah asks, his voice just above a whisper.

"It was touch and go for a bit." The words stick in my throat like burrs. "But she's been upgraded to stable."

I almost lost her twice yesterday. When she coded in the ambulance and during surgery when her body gave out on her. I haven't been this terrified since finding out Colton had tried to end his life and the hospital was attempting to resuscitate him.

"Has she woken up yet?"

"No. Not yet. Any news about why the two men kidnapped her?"

"I can't tell you much right now. The Feds have been investigating the case after new evidence came to light a few days before Jess went missing. But I did learn that Scott Moore—the man who shot Jess and killed her brother-in-law—had been part of the homicide unit investigating her husband's murder. New evidence revealed he'd tampered with the police evidence collected from the murder scene, with the goal to frame Jess."

"Jesus," I mutter.

The steady beeping of the medical equipment is the only sound in the room for a long moment. Exhaustion weighs down my shoulders, dulls my ability to talk.

"She told me to tell you she loves you," Noah says, looking at Jess. "I was also supposed to tell you she would have loved to have had a family with you."

I should be happy to hear this, but instead, sadness and bitterness twist together inside me. "When did she tell you that?" When she thought she was dying? When she thought she wouldn't have to say it to my face and finally admit her feelings? I shake my head, the movement barely registering.

"Shortly after we found her." Noah clasps my shoulder in a gesture of support. "Keep me updated on her condition, would you?"

I go back to watching the steady rise and fall of Jess's chest. "Will do." I know he's asking as a friend and not as a cop. As difficult as it has been for Jess to trust the police, she has let Noah in. They've become friends.

Who knows what it all means, though, for her opinion about cops in general. Two SDPD officers tortured her, but the Maple Ridge police department saved her life.

Noah's soles squeak on the hospital floor as he turns to leave.

"Thank you. Thank you for being there for her and finding her." It had killed me not to be the one who went looking for her, but Noah was right to tell me to stand down when all I wanted to do was tear Maple Ridge apart, searching for her. They only located her when a state trooper saw the car, which matched the description of a vehicle seen parked near her house, heading into the mountains. I want to make sure Scott Moore spends the rest of his life locked away for what he did to Jess. That might not have been possible if my brothers and I had tried to do Noah's job.

"You're welcome."

This time I do let Noah leave.

The day of the festival, as I drove Nolan, Jared, and Mason to their tour bus, Nolan told me the emotional scars his abusive father left him with had really screwed him up, but Nolan's girlfriend never gave up on him. And now they're happily married. Jess might have left me twice, and nearly broke me into pieces each time, but I can't walk away from her anymore. Being with her is worth the risk.

I stand and kiss the side of her face not covered in

bandages. "I love you, Jess. Keep fighting for me. I'm not going anywhere."

THE NEXT MORNING, JESS REMAINS UNCONSCIOUS. HER condition improved slightly overnight. The swelling on her face is starting to go down, but the bruises are still a stark contrast to her pale skin.

Shit, when I think of all the ways I failed her...like I failed Colton...

I rub my hand over my face. "I'm so sorry, Jess. I love you. I've never stopped loving you." I gently tap the back of her hand. *Tap-tap. Tap-taaap-tap-tap. Tap-tap-taaap.*

A movement in the doorway catches in my periphery. Mom is standing there, her lips pressed in a sad smile. Or a smile that barely hides her disappointment.

My finger stops tapping.

Mom and I haven't talked about Jess or my feelings for her since the day of the barbecue, when Mom made Jess feel unwelcome. I've seen her at least once a week, but we haven't talked about Jess or about Mom's behavior that day. I've tried not to hold what happened against her. There doesn't seem to be much point given that Jess and I are no longer together.

I know Mom loves me and was being overly protective. She's my mother. I love her and I won't turn my back on her. She put up with my sorry ass when I was a know-it-all teen.

I just want her to love Jess like I do.

Mom steps into the hospital room. "How's she doing?" Her voice is low, barely louder than the beeping machines.

"Stable but still unconscious."

"Is she going to be okay?"

I lift my shoulders in a slow, weighted shrug. "Hopefully. Eventually. She's been through a lot. It's gonna take time." My attention returns to Jess, but I can feel Mom's eyes remain on me, watching, evaluating, assessing.

"You look exhausted," she says after a beat. "Have you gotten any sleep since you found out she was missing?"

"I'll sleep soon enough." I went home last night after the ICU nurses shooed me out, but I didn't sleep much. I grabbed a quick bite and a shower before heading back here.

I push out of the chair, and Mom hugs me. I didn't realize how much I needed it until now.

Her gaze drops to Jess for a second and returns to me. "I'm worried about you, sweetheart. You've been spreading yourself too thin for a while now. Putting too many demands on yourself."

"I'm fine, Mom."

"You overloaded yourself with the festival, Wilderness Warriors, your company, volunteering at the Veterans Center, working out," she continues as if I hadn't just said I was fine.

"The festival is over, so you don't have to worry about that anymore."

"Until you pick up something else to bury yourself under." Mom crosses her arms in front of her, her tone implying she thinks I'm being stubborn. "You're running from something, Troy. Maybe it's time you stop running before it's too late and you break."

I huff out an exasperated breath. "I'm fine, Mom."

She shakes her head, a silent tutting accompanying the movement. "You haven't been fine since Colton ended his life. What happened wasn't your fault. Stop blaming yourself. I can guarantee this isn't how Colton would want you to live."

"You don't know that." As soon as the rashly-spoken words are out, I want to yank them back. She's right. This isn't how Colton would want me to live. He would want me to hike the toughest trail. Have fun. Enjoy life. It's what I would expect of him if our places were reversed.

But that's easier said than done. Guilt is ingrained in my bones and swims through my veins. I can't let it go like it's nothing more than a leaf floating on a wave.

"I do know that's not what he would want. And so do you." Mom looks at Jess, compassion in her eyes. "I can't believe everything she has survived through. She's a real fighter. And I don't mean that in a negative way."

"She is." I pick up Jess's hand again and resume gently tapping ILU.

"I'm sorry I misjudged her and listened to what other people were saying."

"It's not me you need to apologize to," I remind Mom.

"I know. And I plan to apologize to her once she's conscious." A tiny smile eases onto Mom's face. "I know you two broke up a month ago—Simone told me—and I hope I didn't have anything to do with that. Either way, I hope you're planning to fight for her."

"I am." That's assuming Jess lets me back in her life after I walked away because of my bruised and dented pride.

"And while you're fighting for her, make sure you're fighting for yourself." Mom's smile widens a small amount, sad like earlier but a little less so this time. "Why don't you take a break, and I'll sit with her for a bit."

"It's okay. I'm—"

"Don't even finish what you were going to say, young man." Her tone is unbending, but there's no missing the thread of amusement in it. "You're not fine. Now go! Take a shower. Eat a meal. Go for a walk outside, for crying out loud. I'll text you if there's any change in her condition." She gives me one of those mothering looks I learned as a kid to not brush off. It's her I'm-right-and-you-know-it expression, complete with a raised eyebrow.

A low laugh rumbles deep in my chest. "Alright. You win. I won't be long."

66

———————

JESSICA

October, Present Day
Maple Ridge

My mind and body are swimming through an ocean of thick, *thick* mud, my strokes slow and awkward. But with every few strokes I take, the mud becomes a little less dense, a little easier to move through.

My subconscious breaks the surface of whatever nightmare I've been trapped in. I'm buoyed into a dark place where a steady, rhythmic beeping surrounds me.

A dull pain radiates through my chest, starting below my right shoulder. I try to piece together the cause of the pain, to stitch the fragments of my memory into a simple quilt. But instead of a quilt of clear recognizable patterns, I'm looking at it through a steamed-up window, and nothing about the image makes sense.

I let my eyelids flutter open and slowly blink the world

546

into focus. The light in the room is dim, but it's bright enough for me to make out I'm in a hospital room.

I'm not alone.

Troy is sitting in a chair that doesn't seem all that comfortable for his tall muscular frame. But it must be comfortable enough for him to fall asleep in. One hand props his head up, his elbow on the armrest. The other hand, warm and strong, holds mine. I don't dare move and break this connection between us. I've missed it. I've missed having my hand safe in his.

"How are you doin', love?" a woman asks from the head of the bed, her volume a few notches above a murmur.

I turn my head in her direction. She's my age and wearing cartoon-cat scrubs. Her hair is pulled back in a braid.

"Tired," I whisper, unable to talk much louder than that, my mouth drought dry. "What happened?"

"You were shot in the chest. That's all I know." Something about the way she's looking at me—something beyond the sympathy etched on her face—tells me she knows a lot more than she's letting on.

Shot?

Why? When?

I reach across my body with my free hand. My fingertips brush my hospital gown and the bandages underneath it. Bandages that cover my shoulder and chest.

"How's the pain?"

"It's fine." It's no worse than the pain I've had to deal with in the past, though that's partly due to the meds they've no doubt given me. I'm sure the pain would be a lot worse without them.

She glances at Troy and smiles, revealing straight white teeth. "You've got yourself a really fine boyfriend in that one." She nods at him.

"He's not...he's just a friend." I'm not sure what to call Troy. Other than when he brought Nolan, Mason, and Jared to my house after the festival, I haven't seen or spoken to him in over a month.

"It wouldn't hurt to be honest with him and tell him what you've told me. That would be a start." Robyn's words from our last appointment echo in my head.

"Well, your friend is very sweet. He's been here practically the entire time. I wish my boyfriend was that attentive." She releases a dreamy sigh. "Is there anything you need? Water?"

"Water, please." There are lots of things I need, but other than water, there's not much she can do about them.

"Alright. I'll be right back. And then I'll let you rest, love." She pats my arm. "The physician will be around later to check on you."

"Thank you."

She quietly leaves the room. Troy keeps sleeping.

A few memories leak in of being in a concrete room. Of thinking I would never see him again. Of tapping on the cold floor, secretly telling him I love him.

I tap with my thumb the three Morse code letters on his hand, soft enough not to wake him, and keep tapping them.

Despite what the nurse might think, Troy isn't my boyfriend. But for a few minutes, while he sleeps, I pretend he is.

TROY

October, Present Day
Maple Ridge

I wake to a hospital room that is brighter than when I let my eyelids drift shut. I have no idea what time it is or how long I've been sleeping. The only thing I do know is that it's Friday. And Jess has been unconscious for the past four days.

Except...she isn't unconscious now.

She's watching me, but her eyelids are droopy as if she's groggy and dazed, and her beautiful face is still pale.

My hand hasn't stopped holding hers, even while I was sleeping. The only thing I did stop doing was tapping ILU. Or maybe I was doing that in my sleep.

Seeing her...alive. Here. Her heart pumping in her chest. It's all too much and not enough. My own heart stutters, weeps, rejoices, and for the first time in what feels like forever, my mouth curves into a smile. A real smile.

I sit up straight and tighten my hand around hers. "Hey, you're awake. How are you feeling?"

"I hurt, but...I'm happy to be alive." A drowsy smile flickers at the corners of her mouth, and her gaze roams over the room. *Get Well* floral arrangements fill every available surface. Their light scent cuts through the disinfectant-heavy air. "I'm assuming I'm alive and not in heaven."

I chuckle, more out of relief than anything. "You're definitely alive. Have you been awake long?"

"Only a few minutes. What about you? H-how long have you been here?"

"Since you came out of surgery." I'm not sure if now's a good time to tell her she's been unconscious for the past four days.

"Surgery." She sounds out the word as if trying to recall why she would need to go under the knife. "Because I was shot?" A whirlwind of emotions clouds her eyes.

"Do you remember what happened? How you got shot?"

"No. Not really. Only bits and pieces."

"I'm not sure what happened either. Noah told me one of the men, Scott Moore, was arrested for killing your late husband. He didn't tell me much more than that." I stand and kiss her forehead. "Rest, and we'll talk more once you're feeling up to it."

Talk about what happened while she was missing. Talk about us. Because I'm not going anywhere. And I'm not pushing her away like I did when she convinced herself that I belong to Olivia.

The only person I belong to is Jess.

I had accused her of running away from people who loved her, but she hadn't been the only one to run, as Mom pointed out. Only instead of running away, I was happy to fix other people's problems so long as I didn't have to face my own emotions.

Jess nods, her eyelids sliding shut. They open wide... and slide shut again. This time she loses her battle to stay awake and drifts back to sleep.

I check the phone number Robyn texted me an hour ago. The number for a therapist she recommended. For me.

ON JESS'S TENTH DAY IN THE HOSPITAL, I WALK INTO HER room to find Emily perched on the windowsill. That's nothing unusual. All of Jess's friends have been regular fixtures in her room since she regained consciousness a week ago.

The number of vases filled with flowers in her room has doubled in the past seven days. They now crowd the sill on either side of Em and are scattered about on every available surface. And in the spaces that aren't packed with flowers, *Get Well* cards are prominently featured—including the ones from Mom and Olivia. They each, individually, visited Jess briefly the other day and apologized for their behavior. It was the first step in healing what Cora had inadvertently damaged with her article. It was the first step in Jess and Olivia becoming the close friends I know they'll eventually be.

And Mom is already talking like Jess is part of the family.

Olivia gave her sister a piece of her mind about what she did and how she almost cost Jess her life by giving away her location to the men bent on ending her life. Unfortunately, beyond her sister telling her off, there were no repercussions for Cora. Legally, she did nothing wrong.

Zara is sitting in the chair where I spent much of those first few days when Jess was hospitalized. Jess is on the bed, dressed in jeans, a cardigan, and a sling. She's all smiles, probably because she finally gets to go home today. She's just waiting for her discharge papers.

She's possibly also all smiles because the media has thoroughly dissected news about who really killed her late husband as well as the charges Scott Moore faces. And people around Maple Ridge are realizing how wrong they've been about her. She's not a dangerous offender like they made her out to be.

She's a strong and beautiful woman who wanted a new start to her life, who wanted a chance to heal and move on.

The same thing any of us would want if we'd been in her situation.

A few of the people who'd canceled on me have phoned while Jess was recovering and apologized for being wrong about her. Not all of them have had the balls to do that, to admit their ignorance warped their perception of Jess, but I guess I'm not too surprised. Some people prefer to cling to their hatred and prejudice than to embrace the truth. Prefer hatred over love and acceptance.

Jess's face isn't swollen anymore. Only several faint bruises and some new scars remain on her forehead, chin, and cheek. Her body is a dense roadmap of cuts and scrapes, but they're starting to get better.

It's the scars I can't see that will take a lot longer to heal.

Jess and I haven't talked yet about what went wrong between us. We haven't had a chance to do that. Not unless we wanted to be interrupted by the constant flow of people coming and going from her room.

I've held her hand over the past few days, and she hasn't pulled away or given any indication she's uncomfortable with me doing that. Just the opposite.

I'm taking that as a good sign.

For now, I'm being her friend as I slowly navigate back to the road we were originally on together.

I also haven't mentioned what she told Noah to tell me —about loving me and wanting to have my children. When she said that, she thought she was dying and was barely conscious. She might not have actually meant any of it.

Jess is my family. Having children with her isn't what will make me happy. Being a major part of her life—that will bring me joy.

The argument between us the night she broke up with me was my fault too. I threw the question—the one about having children—in her face. I was angry and disappointed and hurt. I lashed out and I'm not proud of what I said.

"Are you sure you don't want me staying with you at your house?" Emily asks Jess. "So you won't be alone?"

"I won't be alone. I'll have Bailey." Jess is practically vibrating with excitement and relief. She hasn't seen Bailey in almost two weeks. And Bailey will be excited to finally see Jess again.

"But you also won't be able to reach the top shelves in your kitchen while your shoulder is healing," Emily points out.

"Don't worry, I'll be fine. I don't often use the wineglasses, anyway." Jess flashes her a quick grin, then looks toward the door, her eyes wide, her bottom lip caught between her teeth. "I just need to get those darn discharge papers and I'm out of here. Garrett's sending me feedback today on my novel, and I can't wait to get started on the edits."

"I still can't believe Iris used to be a spy in France during the Second World War," Zara says, reclining in the armchair. "I can't wait to read the book, Jess. Garrett hasn't stopped talking about it."

Emily kicks her legs up, her ass precariously parked on the edge of the windowsill. "But don't worry—he didn't tell us anything that happens. He said we have to wait until it's published."

Jess laughs a soft, sweet sound deep in her chest. She winces, pain flickering on her face—no doubt due to the gunshot wound she's healing from. "First, I need to finish those edits and see if an agent wants to represent the book. And then I have to wait to see if a publisher is interested in it."

"They will be." Zara looks at me, and then back at Jess. "You sure you don't want me to drive you home? Stick around, cook you some dinner?"

"I've got it," I tell Zara, my voice stern enough for her to get the hint. Jess and I are finally going to talk, the two of us, without any interruptions. Plus, Noah will be coming over to update us on the kidnapping case.

"Are you sure there's no media waiting outside of my home?" Jess asks me, clearly unsettled at the thought of going through all of that again—minus the protesters this time.

"None at all."

The media has requested numerous times to interview Jess. I told them she needs to heal from her ordeal and to please respect her wish for privacy. Anything they want to know will have to come from the various police departments involved in the case and the FBI.

A nurse comes into the room and goes through the patient care information on gunshot wounds with Jess. She leaves after answering Jess's questions.

"What about Robyn?" Jess has spoken with several social services support staff while in the hospital, but what she really needs is to see Robyn again.

"I called her earlier. I have an appointment tomorrow

with her. And just so you know, I was still seeing her after... um...after what happened." She lowers her eyes, and a light blush sweeps across her cheeks.

"Fortunately, the money Skye Backlund raised to cover your medical and therapy expenses will pay for it, so the cost won't have to come out of your nest egg."

Skye, the president of the high school PTA, decided her participation with the protesters outside of Jess's house tarnished her reputation in the community. She took it upon herself to start a fundraiser to help Jess out.

And made sure the media knew about it.

The reaching out to the media was partly self-serving on Skye's part, but I'm not complaining. Jess will need Robyn's support and guidance even more now as she processes everything that happened. The money that was raised will help, so she doesn't have to use the restitution money the State of California gave her. Both mean that I won't have to offer to help Jess out, which I know is important to her. She doesn't want to be reliant on anyone but herself.

"And your old job is still available," I tell her. "But only if you want to come back and work for me."

She nods, but her eyes lack enthusiasm at the suggestion. I let it slide, for now. The two of us will discuss it further once we get to her house.

There are a lot of things we need to discuss.

Jess stands from the bed. "I still can't believe Skye raised money after trying to get me to leave Maple Ridge."

Emily chuckles. "I'm not too surprised. Her youngest is in Olivia's class this year. Olivia spent a week at the beginning of the term talking about bullying and being mean to people. And she made sure to assign homework for the kids' parents to help with."

I pick up Jess's overnight bag. Em and Zara gather up

the *Get Well* cards and walk us to my truck. The nurses will be redistributing the flowers to other patients' rooms.

We're not even out of the parking lot when Jess's phone rings.

She answers it. "Hi....No, that's fine. I'm happy you called." She truly does sound happy, maybe a little nervous too, her words slightly hesitant. She mouths *Jaxon* to me, and her reaction makes sense. I'd told her about him a few days ago and about how he had come to town, hoping to talk to her. She remembered him and was sorry for everything he'd gone through. Things she could relate to only too well.

While they talk, I slip into my thoughts, my attention on the road. Thoughts about what she and I need to discuss once we get to her house.

Jess ends the call as I pull into her driveway. "Thank you for giving Jaxon my number."

"How's he doing?" I haven't spoken to him since he and Nigel returned to California, but I did keep him updated on Jess's condition.

"Good. We plan to keep in contact and talk some more soon."

Maybe that's what they both need to help them heal—someone who can relate to what the other person has gone through and be there as an additional support system.

Simone is waiting inside Jess's house with Bailey when we arrive. As soon as Jess walks through the front door, Bailey charges over to her and jumps her front paws onto Jess's stomach.

"Down, Bailey," I command.

Jess crouches next to her and puts her good arm around Bailey in a careful hug. "I've missed you."

She lets go of Bailey after a long moment and slowly pushes to her feet, struggling slightly with the effort.

My arm goes to her waist, and I help her up. She feels so right slotted against me. I can't imagine ever letting go of her. I don't *want* to let go of her.

But what I want and what Jess wants seem to be two different things. She steps away from me and gives Simone a one-armed hug. "Thank you for looking after Bailey." Her gaze turns to the kitchen. Her eyes widen. "Wow, who are the flowers from?"

A huge-ass vase of orange, yellow, and burgundy flowers is parked in the center of the kitchen table. All I know is, they aren't from me.

"I don't know," Simone says. "They arrived ten minutes ago."

Jess walks to the table and removes the small envelope tucked into the flowers. She opens it and reads the card inside. "They're from Anne. That's so sweet." Jess sniffs the flowers. "She messaged yesterday and asked me when I was getting sprung from the hospital."

Simone picks up her purse from the coffee table. "I'll leave you two alone." She flashes me a sly grin. "But let me know if you need anything else. I'll be over tomorrow to see how you're doing." The last part is directed to Jess.

Simone leaves, and I finally have Jess all to myself. I've been waiting for this day since I found out she was missing. Waiting for this day since she regained consciousness.

"Do you need anything?" I ask, my fingers, my lips, my soul craving to touch her again.

"No, I'm good." She strokes an orange rose petal. "You can...er...leave now if you want. I'll be fine."

Hell if that's going to happen. This talk has been a long time coming.

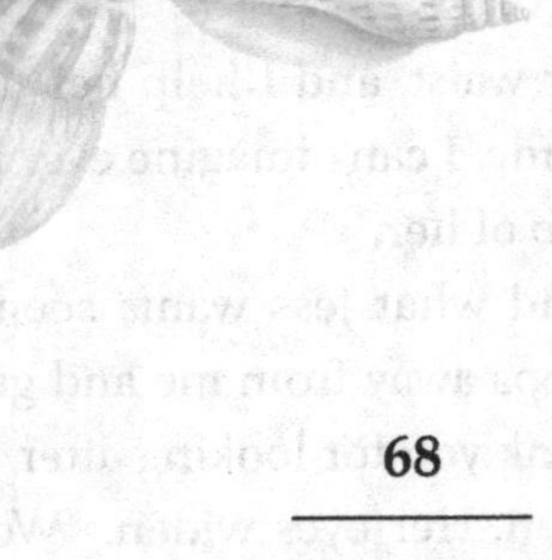

68

JESSICA

October, Present Day
Maple Ridge

ervousness has been churning inside me since Troy told me in the hospital that we need to talk, but he wanted to wait until I was better... that nervousness bubbles over now that we're alone in my house. I have no clue what he wants to talk to me about.

"It wouldn't hurt to be honest with him and tell him what you've told me. That would be a start." Robyn's words repeat in my head like rings on the lake from a thrown stone.

I sit on my couch and stare at the nasty red lines encircling my wrists from the zip ties. They're healing but will always be one of many scars reminding me of what I've survived through. And that's who I am—a survivor. I am strong. They didn't break me.

Troy sits next to me and takes my hand. He traces over

the red mark on one wrist as if reading my mind. My skin sizzles at his touch, the heat kissing my soul.

"I swear, between you swerving to miss a deer and ending up down an embankment, almost getting yourself killed when you rushed into Violet's house to save her, and then getting kid—" His deep voice falters and cracks, and he clears his throat. "Then getting kidnapped. And all of that in the first seven months of me knowing you. How about from now on, no more near-death situations?"

A small humorless laugh escapes me. My gaze remains on the red mark Troy's still tracing over. "Sounds heavenly to me. I'm ready for a normal life...a life free of danger... with...with the man I love and our family."

Troy's finger pauses, his contact with my skin unbroken. "Do you mean that?"

My eyes meet his, and for a heartbeat my words are lost, vaporized. "Do you know what I was thinking about during those last moments before I was shot and the police found me?" I block from my mind, for now, the rest of the time I was locked away in the concrete room, and I focus on the dream I clung to for those final minutes, when I thought I was going to die.

Troy shakes his head, his eyes fixed on mine. An emotion I can't grasp hold of—its essence both rugged and delicate—shines back at me.

"I was thinking about us sitting in front of a fireplace. I was cuddled into your side. And you were reading a story to our two-year-old son. The same thought is what got me through much of my ordeal."

A hesitant smile tilts the corners of his lips, and then eases into a generous curve of his mouth. "Our son?"

"Yes. Our son." Shyness heats my cheeks, and I glance down. "He looked like a much younger and adorable version of his daddy."

"With brown hair like his mommy and daddy?" Troy tugs on a strand of my hair. "I love the new look, by the way."

Warmth swirls in my belly, and I smile, my gaze returning to his. "Yes, with brown hair like his mommy and daddy."

"And big beautiful brown eyes?"

"Most definitely beautiful brown eyes." I couldn't look away from Troy's smiling eyes, even if I wanted to. They have me mesmerized, spellbound.

Our heads drift closer. So close that if I lean in a fraction of an inch more, my mouth will press against his. "I love you, Troy. I've been in love with you for several months now, but I was too afraid to say anything. Too afraid of what would happen if I did. Instead, I hid behind my feelings and used Amelia, Olivia, and Nova as an excuse as to why I couldn't be with you. I let my past rule over my feelings for you. I gave it the power it didn't deserve. But I do want more kids. More kids and you. I very much want you."

Neither of us moves, the words now out there, ready to heal or destroy, nourish or ruin.

"Jess, you do realize that I love Olivia, right?" His voice is gravel-rough, the kind of voice a woman wants to wake up to, but his words are a kick in the solar plexus, the water dousing the fire.

I jerk away. *Oh.* I didn't see that coming. Did Olivia change her mind about Lance? Had Simone and Robyn been wrong about him and Olivia?

Troy gently grabs my arm, preventing me from further widening the gap between us. "I love Olivia, but I'm not in love with her. Never have been and never will be. You're the one I'm in love with, Jess. Only you." His lips brush my mouth, testing this new truth between us. "I'm in love with you, Jess, and I have no intention of letting you go again.

And if we never have kids, that's okay with me. As long as I'm with you, that's all that matters. But...if you pull away again..."

He swallows. "Even knowing you might pull away again when you get scared, love is worth that risk. And if that does happen, I won't be an asshole and throw it in your face like I did last time. I'm so sorry for how I acted. I was hurt, but that didn't give me the right to say those things to you." His eyes—so honest, so raw—search mine, and the truth to his words tugs at my heart.

The memory of his words and my fears, of my assumptions and his accusations is like a slap to my face. Shame and guilt flicker inside me at how much I hurt him. But I don't give them the chance to burn and obliterate. If we could rewind time, we could stop the hurtful words before they spilled. But maybe they needed to be said. Then our fears could be addressed, allowing us to move on. Together. "I won't pull away. I promise. I'm done being scared."

"Promise me if you do ever feel scared and overwhelmed—about us or anything—you'll talk to me about it." He skims his thumb along my jaw, my skin tingling in its wake. "You're not in this alone."

I nod. "I will. But I'm done running. I'm done giving in to my fears. I love you, Troy. That won't change."

He smiles, and it's the most beautiful thing I've ever seen. More beautiful than a sunset after years of going without them. His grin warms every part of me.

"If you don't want to return to your job with my company..." He leaves the rest of the sentence dangling, but I can see in his eyes what he's trying to say.

"I do want to return, but I also think it would be better if I find another job. It would be healthier for us to have our own space, and part of that means me not working for you. I want to be independent and not reliant on a man again."

Troy's quiet for a beat, and I can tell he's thinking through everything I've just told him. "That makes sense. If you want, you can work for me until you find a new job. It's completely up to you."

Thanks to the restitution money, I have that option. A lot of women who are trying to start their lives over after escaping a life of abuse don't have that luxury. They lose everything at the hands of their manipulative partner—their car, their bank cards, their clothes, their home.

Granny had given me an out when she left me her house in her will, but even then, my husband was still in control of me—until he died.

"You aren't worried you'll lose clients?" I ask Troy.

"People have realized how wrong they were about you. And those who haven't...well, I don't want to work for someone who's that ignorant. The job is yours for as long as you want it, Jess. And I'll even be a reference, if you need one, while you're job hunting."

"Thank you. And thank you for understanding why I have to do this."

"I know how important that freedom is to you. And I never want you to feel like you have to give up on what's important to you." His lips taste mine once more. The tender touch leaves my heart stuttering for joy. "I've decided to start seeing a therapist."

"You have?" That was the last thing I expected him to say.

"I have. I was so adamant about you seeing Robyn, I ignored the part where I needed to talk to someone about what happened to Colton. Hell, I tried to get him to talk to a therapist when I knew he was struggling, yet I couldn't see I wasn't doing much better after he died."

"And then I came along and added to your load." I

cringe at how much of a weight that must have been on his shoulders.

"No, you were the one thing helping to keep my head above water. But I'm not just seeing a therapist to help me deal with what happened to Colton. I need help knowing how to support you in a way that's best for both of us." His thumb caresses my healing cheek. "Especially after what you've just gone through. I can't pretend to have the answers when I don't. I don't want to flail about, trying to make things better for you but only making them worse."

We were both flailing for a long time, both without a life jacket, both trying to cling to driftwood but losing our grip every time. "I think that's a good idea. All of it."

"And I think we should go to couples counseling. We're dealing with a lot of challenges due to your previous marriage. Counseling might help us to better navigate things between us, and make sure I don't screw anything up."

His words yank the breath from me and return it in sweet lungfuls, fresh like the crisp mountain air. "I think that's a great idea." I run my fingers through the silky strands of his hair. I'm so buoyed by this new future for us, I don't need therapy to navigate my way through this moment.

But I do it anyway.

What do I see?

This beautiful, kind man in front of me.

What do I hear?

The beating of our hearts, their rhythm united as one.

What do I feel?

Happy. So very, *very* happy.

Our mouths join, and we deepen the kiss, making up for the six weeks we've been apart. Silently promising each other we'll never be that way again. His kiss makes me feel more alive than I have felt in a long time. *He* makes me feel more alive.

Troy pulls away ever so slightly, his breath soft on my lips. "I know you told Emily you were fine on your own and don't need her staying with you while you recover, but I want to be here for you. I want to wake up in the morning and be able to pull you into my arms. I want to be the one to help you while you're healing." He lightly brushes his fingers over the bullet wound, barely grazing it.

And my heart jumps at how much I also want everything he described.

The doorbell rings, and I swallow a silent groan at the interruption. Noah's timing when he rescued me was good—although it would have been better if the cops had arrived several days before I was shot.

His timing now...sucks.

69

TROY

October, Present Day
Maple Ridge

Jess's doorbell rings.

"That'll be Noah." I inwardly groan at his crappy timing. I finally get to kiss Jess after being apart from her for more than six weeks, and he picks *now* to show up.

I go answer the door. The sooner Noah updates us on the investigation, the sooner Jess and I can go back to making up.

Noah isn't alone. A woman in a white blouse, navy pants, and suit jacket is with him.

"Hey, Troy," he says with a casual nod. "This is agent Deidre Knight with the FBI. And this is Troy Carson. Jessica Smithson's..." He looks to me to fill in the blank.

"I'm her boyfriend." I open the door wider and let them into the house.

565

Noah flashes me a quick glance that's easy to read. He's both surprised and delighted to hear the news about Jess's and my new relationship status.

They kick off their shoes, and we go into the living room. Jess is sitting on the couch with Bailey by her feet.

I introduce her to the FBI agent. Noah and Agent Knight take seats on the armchairs. I sit next to Jess and link my fingers with hers for moral support. And because I can.

"How are you doing, Jessica?" Agent Knight asks.

"I've been better. But I've also been a lot worse. I guess it's all relative." Jess gives the woman a fragile smile.

"I'm sorry about what happened to you. The abuse, the wrongful conviction, the kidnapping, and the events with the former Maple Ridge chief of police. If there's anything you need, please let me know."

Jess nods but doesn't say anything. I have no idea what her stance is regarding the FBI and how much she trusts them. From the sounds of it, she's never had to deal with them, other than two months ago when she tried to save Violet from Cole Dunbar.

"I've been working on the case surrounding your late husband's death," Agent Knight continues.

Jess's hand tenses in mine. I caress the side of her hand with my thumb, reminding her she's not alone. Whatever this is about, I'm here for her.

"I've also been working on the case surrounding Alex Wilson, since the two are connected," Agent Knight explains.

"You mean because I was involved with both of them?" Jess asks.

"No. That was just an unfortunate coincidence. I've been working for the past few years on cracking one of the largest crime rings in the U.S. I'll spare you the details, but suffice it to say, your late husband, Lincoln Townsend, Scott Moore, Cole Dunbar, and Alex Wilson were working for the same crime organization—as were numerous other officers from different police jurisdictions all over the country."

Agent Knight leans forward in the armchair. "Unfortunately, when the news story leaked information about your new name and location, Lincoln Townsend and Scott Moore were able to track you down. We had been preparing to arrest the two men after incriminating documentation was recently found in your grandmother's old house, Jessica."

Shock rounds Jess's eyes. "It was? You mean like the insurance policy Lincoln had been going on about?"

"That's right. I can't give you details about what was in it, other than it was enough to incriminate a lot of individuals. One being Wayne's former supervisor. It also incriminated Lincoln and Scott."

"They never mentioned that part while they held me captive. Lincoln made it sound like it would've kept them out of trouble if anyone planned to double-cross them."

"They might not have known about that part," Agent Knight explains. "It looks like your late husband kept it as an insurance policy against anyone he thought might turn on him."

None of this surprises me given what lengths he went through to get Jaxon out of the picture, after the man tried to reach out to Jess and help her. Wayne probably wasn't the only one responsible for Jaxon's arrest. Were Lincoln and Scott Moore also involved?

"Why is it you only recently found the documents?" I ask instead of the question in my head. "Hasn't someone been living in Jess's grandmother's house for several years now?"

"We wouldn't have known about them if the new homeowners hadn't decided to do renovations. They pulled down a wall and found the memory stick behind the floorboards."

Jess's forehead crinkles into a shocked frown. "Wayne hid it in my grandmother's house? He must have stolen the key from me after she died and then hid the documents. Maybe that's why he never insisted I put the house on the market after I inherited it. It was another way to keep me from disappearing on him. He knew I would never just abandon the place. And as long as I didn't sell the house, the documents were safe."

Shit. If the FBI had figured out Wayne Townsend had been part of the crime ring sooner, they could have spared Jess from going to prison. They could have spared her from the nightmares that still affect her physically and emotionally.

"Why did Scott kill Wayne?" Jess asks Agent Knight. "Because he was worried Wayne would double-cross him?"

"We're still figuring out all his motives, but yes, that's a strong possibility. We believe he framed you because you were a convenient scapegoat. If you were found guilty of your husband's death, the case would be closed and he would get away with it."

"Please tell me the asshole will never get out of prison." The snarl in my tone is aimed at the asshole in question and not at Noah or the FBI agent.

"That is our goal." Determination tightens the agent's jaw, steadies her voice.

"Lincoln was so sure I was the one who murdered his brother." Jess shudders and the ghost of an emotion flickers on her face.

I take her hand and tap ILU on her palm. The reason for kidnapping and torturing Jess might've been because Lincoln and Scott thought she knew where the information was located, but I suspect revenge also fueled Lincoln's motive.

"We've also been investigating the allegations of misconduct that took place while you were in Beckley State Correctional Institution," Agent Knight goes on to add. "It looks like Lincoln had connections with several of the prison guards. We believe he might have been indirectly linked to the attacks on you, which explains why some of the ones you told Noah about were never entered into the incident logs."

My fingers pause their tapping. "Because he thought Jess killed his brother?"

"That looks to be the case," Noah says.

Agent Knight and Noah ask Jess more questions and fill her in on the investigation as much as possible. Once they're finished, I walk them to the door.

I return to Jess on the couch. "How are you surviving? You wanna go upstairs to rest? Or I can make you lunch." At some point, I'll need to fetch Butterscotch and my stuff from my house, but they can wait a little longer.

"I was thinking more along the lines of making out." The spark that was missing in her eyes while Noah and Agent Knight were here shines bright with lust...and love. "We have about six weeks' worth of kissing to make up for."

I drop down next to her on the couch, my smile taking up much of my face. "Sounds like a plan. I've missed kissing you here." I lift her hair and kiss the back of her neck. Her breath quickens. "And here." My lips graze the shell of her ear. "I love you, Jess." My voice is a low rumble, heat and adoration seeping into the words. My mouth traces along her jaw. "And I've missed kissing you here."

A tiny whimper escapes Jess, and I grin at the effect my kisses are having on her. "Enjoying that are you?"

"Absolutely." She cups my face and strokes her thumb

along my bottom lip. "I love you, Troy." She leans in and brushes her mouth against mine, teasing me.

The doorbell rings, and we both groan.

"I'll get that." I push to my feet. "Don't go anywhere."

She laughs softly. "I'll be waiting right here for you."

I hurry to the front door, eager to get rid of whomever it is. Maybe I should put a *Do Not Disturb* sign on the door so Jess and I can have some alone time for a few hours.

I open the front door. A man and woman I don't recognize are standing on the stoop. The woman's shoulder-length hair is dark blond, and she's wearing a navy sweater dress and heeled boots. The man's hair is light brown, and he's wearing brown slacks and a gray blazer.

But it's the girl standing in front of them, with long golden-brown hair and familiar honey-brown eyes, who halts my breath. She's eight years old and holding a small bouquet of flowers.

She smiles at me, her face lighting up. "Hi! Is this where my Auntie Jessica lives?"

EPILOGUE

JESSICA

Two Years Later
Maple Ridge

"Hi, Auntie Jess," ten-year-old Lia says, racing into the living room and over to where I'm standing next to the light-gray couch. Troy decided to update the house's interior when I permanently moved in a year ago. The place went from being completely masculine, to a soothing blend of neutral with splashes of country cottage. It's our dream home—one we designed together.

Lia throws her arms around me, gifting me with one of my favorite hugs. The I've-missed-you hug, even though we just talked a few days ago on Zoom. "Congratulations!"

"Thank you, sweetheart." I return the hug, squeezing her even tighter. Troy and I drove to Seattle last month and

I saw her in person. Other than that, we talk on Zoom at least once a week. I can't believe how quickly she's growing.

She glances down at Bailey standing beside me in her PSD jacket. My need for Bailey as a PSD isn't as great these days as it was when Troy arranged for me to be her puppy trainer, but I do appreciate the support she gives me every time the past traumas sneak into my subconscious. Fortunately, those times have grown to be few and far between, thanks to Robyn.

Troy walks in with Grace and Craig. They're all smiles and laughter.

Grace, the woman who has become like a sister to me, hugs me. "Congratulations! How does it feel to be a *New York Times* bestselling author?"

"Surreal. And weird, given that I'm working on the next novel my editor and I discussed." It's also historical fiction, but it takes place in the 1960s. While writing Iris's story, I discovered I love writing historical fiction and learning about other eras. And about everyday women who fought to make a difference.

"I can't wait to read it. I loved your book. It was soooooo good. I couldn't put it down."

Craig chuckles. "She's not kidding. I swear, she stayed up all night reading it." He hugs me like the brother he's become. "I can't believe you lived in Angelique's house. I wouldn't be surprised if fans of the book drive to Maple Ridge to take photos of the place."

"Hopefully they don't." The thought of fans of the story doing that pinches my stomach.

I still own the house, but after I moved in with Troy—my husband of three months—I offered the place to a young mother who recently left her abusive husband. Lydia and her two kids are living there rent free while she gets her life back on track. It was the least I could do after everything Anne did for me. I wouldn't be where I am today if not for Anne. If not for Anne and my friends and Troy.

The doorbell rings again, and Troy goes to answer it.

His parents enter the room a moment later, followed by Garrett and Zara. Garrett's carrying a large white box with the Picnic & Treats logo on the side.

Joanne hurries over to me, wearing the same proud smile I've seen directed at her sons and me plenty of times over the past two years. "Congratulations, Jess!" My mother-in-law gives me a big embrace. She's the mother I never had. The mother I dreamed of growing up. Granny would have loved her.

Garrett puts the box on the dining table and opens the lid.

I peer inside, and a surprised laugh bursts from my lungs. "This is incredible. Is there any reason the cake looks like it came out of a fairy tale?"

The cake resembles the cut off base of a tree trunk, with red-and-white-spotted mushrooms scattered around it. The window and door on the side of the trunk complete the look. The cake is adorable.

"Keshia had a conversation with Lia over Zoom, and they decided this was the way to go," Zara explains, trying to hide the grin twitching on her mouth. "They decided it was the only way to celebrate both you and Garrett hitting the *New York Times* list in the same week."

"That would explain it." Lia loves fairy tales as much as I still do. "Tell Keshia I love it. It's perfect."

Troy's by the kitchen island, talking to his brothers. I take the moment to appreciate the man who I love more with each passing day. If not for him, I'm not sure where I would be right now. His love and kindness and determination saved me when I was struggling to breathe and save myself. That same determination was the driving force behind us becoming emotionally healthy. As individuals. As a couple.

And nineteen months after I was released from the hospital, after my life was finally back on track, I agreed to be his wife.

We had been hiking, just the two of us—and Bailey. It was something we'd been doing regularly during hiking season. A recommendation made by our couples counselor.

We'd stopped at the top of the hiking trail and looked out over the forested valley. Troy hugged me from behind and kissed my neck. Nothing new there. Hiking is an aphrodisiac for Troy. The man gets horny as hell every time we hike together. Just the two of us.

"Do you know what I want to do?" he murmured in my ear.

I laughed, the sound carrying on the light wind. "I know exactly what you want to do." I turned in his arms and rubbed against him.

He dropped to his knee, which wasn't what I was expecting. "Jess, from the first day I saw you on the beach, you had my heart. Through all the ups and downs and challenges and joys, you've had my heart."

He shoved his hand into his pocket and pulled out a diamond ring. The diamond sparkled in the sun, much like I imagined the tears that sprung to my eyes did.

"Now I'm hoping you'll be my wife." He'd grinned at me, the hope in his expression more breathtaking than the view.

I glance at the rings on my finger. It wasn't hard to say yes to that. We were married two months later.

I walk over to join him and his brothers by the kitchen island. He pulls me to him, his body warm and strong against mine. My bulwark from the storms that still try to bring me down from time to time.

He captures my mouth in a sweet kiss that doesn't leave his brothers groaning. They do, though, walk off, giving us a moment on our own. As *on our own* as we can be when in the middle of a party with friends and family.

Olivia, Lance, and Nova enter the living room. Four-year-old Nova rushes to Troy. He scoops her up in his arms and gives her a big hug.

Lance is holding his wife's hand and looking blissfully happy. Olivia is glowing, but that might have something to do with her being six months pregnant.

"Hi, Nova," I say to the little girl who I adore as much as Troy does. "Love the braids."

"Daddy did them," she explains, seemingly proud of that fact.

"Your daddy's very talented." Apparently, Lance has some impressive hair-styling skills I didn't know about. I thought Olivia was the one who was always braiding Nova's hair.

I hug the two people who've also become my close friends.

Troy lowers Nova to her feet. She gives me one of her extra-special hugs and runs off to visit with Butterscotch.

"I just heard from the realtor," Troy tells Lance. "The couple agreed to our price. They're buying the house."

"That's great!" The two men fist-bump, huge smiles on their faces.

Troy eventually got to do as he'd hoped when he originally wanted to buy Iris's house. He and Lance bought a house last year that needed major work and renovated it, showcasing their talents. But instead of the money going to Olivia like Troy had planned, they decided to donate the proceeds to an organization in Oregon that supports widows of first responders.

Olivia and I congratulate and hug our husbands. We know how important the project was for them.

"Before I forget," Olivia says to me, "Mom asked if you can come to her book club meeting next month. She's excited that she knows a famous author."

"I would love to be there. But I'm definitely not famous."

Troy wraps his arms around me from behind, my favorite place for his arms to be. "You're famous. People are talking about your novel and about your nonfiction articles. You've touched a lot of people and opened a lot of eyes. In my book that makes you famous." He leans down and whispers in my ear, "Plus, you're smart and gorgeous and a brilliant author. And you're still the sexiest writer I know."

I turn my head to him and flash him a grin. "And you're biased."

"And let's not forget, you're a great photographer too." He nods at the collection of photojournalistic style pictures on the wall.

My photography is just for me. It's my stress reliever. My passion.

Between working part-time at Picnic & Treats—something I started doing a few months after leaving the hospital, because Zara needed the extra help—and writing my next novel and the articles, I don't have time for my photography to be more than a hobby. And I'm fine with that.

Troy taps on my hip. *ILU.*

I tap it on his arm.

And then I tap something else. Something I've never

tapped until now. Something I need to tap several times before Troy understands what I'm spelling out.

You are going to be a daddy.

I can tell the moment it clicks. The sudden press of his chest against my back gives it away.

"Oh, I forgot something in the bedroom," he tells Olivia and Lance a little too fast and a little too loudly. "I'll be right back."

He links his fingers with mine and quickly pulls me through the living room, weaving past Simone and Lucas, past Anne and Dan, past Avery and Noah. I barely get out a squeaked "Hi" to our guests before he has me in the hall-way. Bailey walks alongside me.

Troy tugs me upstairs to our bedroom and shuts the door. "Tell me again." Excitement lights his face, his smile.

"You're going to be a daddy." An amazing one at that.

He cups my still flat stomach. "How far along are you?"

"Eight weeks. I only found out this morning."

We were planning to start trying soon. I'd stopped taking the pill a few months ago, but we'd been using condoms until we were ready.

Except for the one time.

Troy grins. "So, it happened when you jumped me in the mountains?"

And now I'm grinning. "It was a very good hiking trip."

He pulls me to him and kisses me deeply. Kisses me because he is my past, my present, my future. The man who loves me unconditionally. The man who is my anchor, my support.

The man who shows me every minute of every day how much he loves me. The man who has shown me what love is about. Who has shown me how real and honest and affirming it can be with the right person.

The man I trust with my heart.

Get your free copy of the bonus short story with Jess and Troy at https://BookHip.com/HMGNWAA

THE NEXT CARSON BROTHERS BOOK IS COMING FALL 2025...

One More Heartbeat will be a standalone romance. Sign up for my monthly newsletter to receive updates about the book.

https://stinalindenblattauthor.com/newsletter

YOUR BOOK CLUB READING GUIDE

AUTHOR'S NOTE

I hope you have enjoyed reading the Hidden Secrets Trilogy. Angelique's story and the *Cashmere* and *Pirouette* networks were fictional, but real-life people and events inspired several characters and events in the World War II story.

Mary Herbert was the inspiration for Angelique. She was multilingual and a courier for the *Scientist* network in France, and specifically, for fellow SOE agent Claude de Baissac. Several months after her arrival in the country, the two became lovers, and Mary subsequently became pregnant with Claude's child.

In time, the Gestapo became suspicious of Mary's clandestine activities, and they arrested her. Her baby, Claudine, was given away to a group of nuns. Mary convinced the Gestapo that she was not part of the *Scientist* network and that her husband had abandoned her and her baby. After she was released from prison, she searched for Claudine and eventually found her being cared for in a local orphanage.

Miraculously, both mother and daughter survived the war. Mary and Claude married for the sake of their daughter but never lived together. Sixteen years later, they filed for divorce. Claude remarried; Mary never did. Their daughter would later emigrate to California.

France awarded Mary with a Croix de Guerre. Britain never acknowledged her work with the SOE, which was also the case for many former SOE agents.

Anton Schmid of the Wehrmacht was the inspiration for Johann. During the war, the Austrian sergeant was assigned to Vilnius, Lithuania, where he smuggled food to help starving Jewish families. Anton acted as a courier between the thousands of Jews hiding in Vilnius and their friends locked in the ghetto. He also brought in whatever drugs he could locate and the German weapons that he stole for the resistance fighters. And he did all of this without payment for his clandestine aid.

This is only a sampling of what he did to save the lives of over 350 Jews. Unfortunately, his superiors became suspicious of his activities, and after a speedy trial, he was executed on April 13, 1942.

He has since been awarded numerous medals. In 2000, a German Army base was renamed Feldwebel Anton Schmid Kaserne. At the dedication ceremony, Defense Minister Rudolf Scharping stated that[1], "Too many bowed to the threats and temptations of the dictator, and too few found the strength to resist. But Sergeant Anton Schmid did resist..."

I took some creative license when it came to the time-frame for when Hazel and her daughter died. Bristol did get bombed, but the Bristol Blitz occurred between 1940 and 1941, and not shortly before D-Day as was the case in the story.

If you would like to learn more about the female British SOE and American OSS agents who helped the Allies win World War II, I recommend reading:

D-Day Girls by Sarah Rose
The Heroines of SOE by Beryl E Escott
Spymistress by William Stevenson
Sisters and Spies by Susan Ottaway
A Woman of No Importance by Sonia Purnell
Game of Spies: The Secret Agent, The Traitor, and The Nazi by Paddy Ashdown

My research also included the British SOE training syllabus *How to Become a Spy: The World War II SOE Training Manual.*

Recommended novels:
The Alice Network by Kate Quinn
The Lost Girls of Paris by Pam Jenoff
The Paris Agent by Kelly Rimmer

YOU DID NOT BEAR THE SHAME
YOU RESISTED
SACRIFICING YOUR LIFE
FOR FREEDOM, JUSTICE AND HONOR

—From The German Resistance Memorial, Berlin

1. Hull, Michael D. "Sergeant Anton Schmid: Saint in a Feldwebels Uniform." *Warfare History Network*, January

2009, warfarehistorynetwork.com/article/sergeant-anton-schmid-saint-in-a-feldwebels-uniform.

BOOK CLUB QUESTIONS

Please note discussion questions contain some spoilers. I recommend not reading ahead if you want to be surprised.

1. How do you feel about Craig's initial decision for Jessica to not be part of Amelia's life?

2. What are your thoughts on Jessica's decision to refer to Amelia as Lia near the end of the book, when she wrote to Craig and Grace?

3. Jessica has faced several losses over the years. How do you feel that has shaped the person she is at the end of the book? How does that compare to who she was at the beginning of *One More Secret*?

4. At the beginning of *One More Secret*, Jessica was reluctant to talk because of her late husband's past belittlement of her. How has she changed when it comes to reclaiming her voice over the course of the trilogy?

5. What were your thoughts when Jessica broke up with Troy for the sake of Nova and the family he wanted to have one day (and that Jessica felt she couldn't give him)?

6. Jessica has a stable job working for Troy. At one point, she and Simone talk about spouses/romantic partners working together. What are your thoughts about working with a romantic partner when it comes to a career?

7. After Troy reads the first few pages of Angelique's story, Jess thinks, "It's one scene. That's all Troy has read. All that I've written so far. But the honesty in his words ignites something in me I haven't felt in a long time. Passion and excitement. Desire. A desire to exercise my voice. To challenge my own thoughts and convictions and prejudices." Has there been a time when you have found your voice about something that's important to you? What was it and how did you get to the place where you were able to exercise your voice on the topic?

8. Once Jessica was released from prison, she needed to pivot the direction she had originally planned for her life to take prior to her marriage and find a new passion and path. Have you had to make a major life change of direction? How did you handle coming up with new skills or charting your new path?

9. Do you have a favorite or least favorite character in the story, or one whom you most identify with? Why did you feel this way toward them?

10. Has your opinion of Johann, a German officer, changed from the time he moved into the farmhouse in *One More*

Secret to the end of *One More Truth*? How and why has it changed (or not changed)?

11. *One More Truth* is at the forefront a romance, but it is also historical fiction, women's fiction, and a story of empowerment. What parallels are there between the modern-day story and the World War II story?

12. What emotions did you feel when Iris/Angelique learned of what happened to her sister and made the decision to refer to her daughter as her niece? What emotions did you feel when Jessica chose to do the same when it came to Amelia?

13. Did you have a scene that you enjoyed the most? If so, what did you enjoy about it? Was there a scene that made you feel uncomfortable? If so, what about the scene made you feel that way?

14. Successful romantic relationships require trust. In what ways was trust explored in the *One More Truth*? In what ways was the trust between Angelique and Johann reflected between Jessica and Troy?

ACKNOWLEDGMENTS

First of all, I would like to thank you, the reader, for giving Hidden Secrets Trilogy a chance. The story has been a passion project of mine for the past few years. One that required a lot of research for the two timeline stories, and one that required I plot the equivalent of four books (even though Hidden Secrets is a trilogy). I have loved every moment of it. But a passion project is even more meaningful when an author's words touch a reader's heart, and when readers fall in love with the characters as much as the author fell in love with them.

As always, I want to thank my wonderful editor, Lauren Clarke, for her insight, wisdom, and sheer brilliance when it came to *One More Truth*. Her suggestions for the three books in the trilogy helped me make the story even better than I had first imagined. Her comments always left me smiling.

It was my daughter's therapist who first told me about trauma bond in domestic abuse. That led me to do additional research on the topic, so I could make the story as authentic as possible. One of my goals for the trilogy is to help bring awareness to the long-term ramifications of domestic violence. I hope that I achieved that. I would also like to thank Fear is Not Love. Their resources and a conversation I had with someone at the local organization also helped me with my research.

And lastly, I would like to thank my husband and kids

for their support and understanding of why I love disappearing into my story worlds. I especially would like to thank my daughter, Anja, whose name I borrowed for Johann's sister. She has been my biggest supporter from the very beginning. Naturally, she wasn't too thrilled when she found out what happened to her namesake and comically complained to her friends.

ABOUT THE AUTHOR

Born in Brighton England, Stina Lindenblatt has lived in a number of countries, including England, the U.S., Finland, and Canada. This would explain her mixed up accent. She has a kinesiology degree and a MSc in sports biological sciences.

In addition to writing fiction, she loves photography, and currently lives in Calgary, Canada, with her husband and three kids.

For news about her books and to sign up for her newsletter, check out her website at stinalindenblattauthor.com.